SYMBIOSIS

TONY BATTON

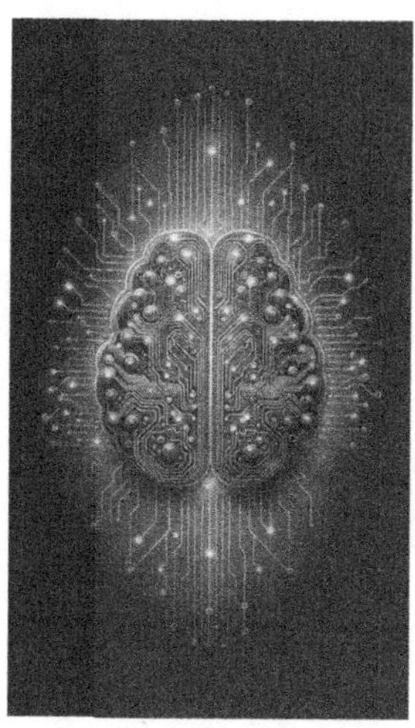

Two years ago, CERUS Biotech's illegal neural interface experiment had only one success. And one survivor: Tom Faraday.

CERUS has changed its ways, but much of its most dangerous technology was lost or stolen - speculative research projects with dangerous potential. Tom plans to use his abilities to hunt down and destroy CERUS Biotech's dark legacy. But he is not the only one searching.

And if he doesn't get there first, human and machine might be about to get too close.

ALSO BY TONY BATTON

The Interface Series

Interface

Resurface

Symbiosis

Standalone Novels

Unstolen

Prediction

Short Stories

Artificial Inheritance

Resurgence

For Alex & Nathan

"As we embed technology into our very being, we must ask: are we elevating humanity, or are we merely machines in gestation?"

Dr. Rajesh Singh, "The Singularity Dilemma"

~

"Nanotechnology could be humanity's greatest triumph or its final folly; the scales are still in balance."

Dr. Anika B. Rutherford, "The Nexus Point"

ONE

ELI GIBBS LEANED against the cold steel wall of the Rig's cramped waiting room, the rhythmic groan of hydraulic stabilisers echoing in his ears. The air in the windowless chamber was thick with oil and saltwater, and devoid of any touch of human comfort. Each vibration underfoot whispered of a world far removed, a place that choked out the hum of normal life. He folded the well-worn photo of his nearly four-year-old daughter and tucked it away in his wallet. "I know why I'm here," he muttered to himself, "but no amount of money is worth having to work somewhere like this."

There had been times he had doubted they could get things done, with the work harder than predicted, and the client constantly changing the specifications. But they had prevailed. Now they would get out of this hellhole and back to civilisation. And he would no longer have to settle for staring at a photograph. He rotated his sore shoulders and stared at the room's only door. Where was their escort? Korver wasn't usually late.

"What's first on your list?" asked a voice from behind him.

Gibbs glanced over at Sven, whose broad smile and shock

of blond hair were somehow undiminished by the days of sweat, grease and grime. "What list?"

"Things to buy when we get paid."

Gibbs gave a snort. "A hot meal and a cold beer will do me fine."

Sven looked unimpressed. "I'm going to get a motorbike. Probably a Harley."

"You ever even ridden a proper motorcycle? But I guess it's your money."

"Not yet it isn't," said another voice.

Gibbs held back a sigh. Sat on a metal chair was the other engineer in their team, Eskin, the oldest of the three making up their usual team, and unarguably the most cynical. "Will you shut up already?" Gibbs replied. "You were the one who persuaded us to take this gig."

"And in hindsight, maybe that was a bad decision."

Sven frowned. "Why wouldn't they pay us? We've finished what we came here to do."

Eskin leaned forward in his seat. "And that means they don't need us anymore, whoever they really are. So why not save themselves some money?"

Gibbs folded his arms. "We've done confidential projects before. What makes this one any different?"

"The fact that nobody knows where we are. And thanks to those blindfolds, neither do we." Eskin frowned. "Do you have any idea what they're really doing here? I went to the wrong deck one day and caught sight of nanotech fabricators."

"You must be mistaken."

Sven scratched his chin. "Nanotech? Like that stuff CERUS Biotech was messing with? Isn't it illegal?"

Gibbs shook his head. "We need to keep our heads down, our mouths shut, and get out of here in one piece. And most importantly, never talk to anybody about..."

"Morning, gentlemen," said a deep voice from the doorway.

Gibbs swallowed and turned to the man who had just spoken. Karl Korver's huge, muscular frame filled most of the doorway. He had been their liaison while at the Rig - never late, always displaying a polite smile, but always watching intently. He was watching them now.

"Morning," Gibbs replied. "Not like you to be late?"

Korver ran a hand over what always looked like a fresh buzz cut. "You guys ready to leave?"

There was something in his expression that looked off. Anger? Regret? Gibbs couldn't tell. He picked up his duffel bag. "Lead on."

The big man turned and began striding away, his steel-capped boots clanking on the metal decking of the service corridor.

"How much did he hear?" Sven asked.

"I wouldn't worry," Eskin replied. "I'm sure they've been listening to everything we've said since we got here."

Sven's eyes widened. "Then why did you say what you just said about the fabricators?"

"Enough of this," Gibbs hissed. "No more stupid questions. No questions at all." He glared at them and hurried after Korver, who was already disappearing out of sight.

As Gibbs half-ran along the gently curving corridor, another sound caught his attention - the familiar rhythmic tap-tapping of an approaching auto-dog. The large robot's green and amber-LED outlined form came into view. As it detected him, it slowed and began emitting a fluctuating warning tone. Its six rubber-tipped legs moved in a practised alternating pattern, keeping its two-metre-long loading platform perfectly horizontal, while its two manipulator arms were folded away. On the platform were two crates of laboratory glassware, encased in bubble wrap and strapped securely in place. Gibbs moved as far to the left as he could to let it pass. Something about these things unnerved him.

"Would be handy having one of those at home," Sven said. "How much do you think they cost?"

"More than even you can afford, Mr *Harley Davidson.* Let's get a move on before our guide thinks we've decided to stay."

Two minutes of almost-running later, they caught up to Korver. He stood by the entrance to a stairwell, pointing. "Head down. Keep going until you can't go any further."

Gibbs led the two other engineers downwards. As he descended, he noticed a noise he'd heard a few times before, but now it was growing - a sharp hiss that built to become a quiet roar.

The staircase ended in a metal door. Gibbs turned the well-lubricated handle and with a heave pushed the door open.

And suddenly the roar was no longer quiet.

FOR THE FIRST time in ten days, Gibbs was outside. Joined by his two colleagues, he stood on a sturdy metal platform, perhaps ten metres across, bolted onto the side of a huge metal structure. Its dull grey steel exterior curved away at least thirty metres in each direction before line of sight meant he couldn't see more.

The roar came from the fierce, water-laced wind that slammed into his face. The platform had high tubular railings on all sides. In one corner sat three steel drums marked with orange biohazard symbols, but otherwise the metal grid on which they walked was free of obstruction. Gibbs took halting steps forwards towards the railings. He reached the edge, gripping the metal tube firmly, and looked down. Perhaps a hundred metres below was roiling, dark sea water. He lifted his gaze and swung his head around. There was no coastline in sight. They were in the middle of the ocean.

Forty miles from land, or a thousand, he had no way of knowing.

Gibbs turned to Korver, who remained near the door, arms folded. "I thought you were taking us to the helipad?"

"The boss wants a quick word." Korver moved and opened a second door that Gibbs hadn't noticed. A stocky man wearing an immaculate set of blue overalls, blue tinted sunglasses, and a white hard hat, stepped out onto the metal grid. He walked stiffly over and shook each of the engineers by the hand. He had, Gibbs noticed, a surprisingly firm handshake.

"Good morning, gentlemen," the man shouted over the noise of the ocean. "I'm Frank Hatch, Director of this facility. Couldn't let you leave without thanking you all personally."

Gibbs nodded awkwardly. "There were challenges, but we got it done. Hope you're pleased with the results."

"Dr Mendez said he's rarely seen such application. All three of you have done great work. Couldn't have asked for more."

Gibbs glanced at Eskin and Sven. "We're just keen to get home."

"Yes, yes. I'm sure you are." Hatch's smile broadened, but Gibbs wasn't sure he liked it. More like someone copying what he'd been told a smile should look like, without ever seeing one firsthand.

"When is the helicopter arriving?"

"The helicopter? Yes, of course. It's just there's one thing we need to discuss first. One unavoidable issue. As you can understand, what we're doing here requires the utmost secrecy."

"We signed those NDAs. They made it very clear what will happen if we talk about what happened here." Gibbs forced a smile. "Not that we even have a clue where here is."

"That's true. Still, the problem with NDAs is that - as any lawyer will tell you - they're never cast-iron."

"We wouldn't say anything. We're not idiots."

"But you are," Hatch paused, "*human*. The tiniest mistake on your part could be catastrophic to the entire operation. I'm sure you understand where that leads us."

Gibbs glanced at his fellow engineers. "I'm not sure that I do..." Then he realised Hatch was looking at the steel drums. "What are they for?"

Korver frowned. "Is that what we're doing?"

Hatch took three steps back. "Best if you get on with it. Those drums won't fill themselves."

Gibbs stared at Hatch, then at Korver, then back to Hatch. Eskin's ridiculous theory had been right. They would not be leaving. He would not make his daughter's fourth birthday. Or her fifth.

Sven started to run for the nearest door. Korver moved faster, grabbing him by the shoulder, and throwing him to the floor.

"No!" Gibbs shouted. "You don't have to do this." He leapt at Korver, heart pounding, the salt spray suddenly blinding him. But as he wiped his eyes clear, he saw Korver held an ugly-looking automatic pistol inches from his face. He struggled to find words that might make a difference. "I have a daughter."

"We know," said Hatch.

"I should never have come here."

"Something I say every day." Korver pointed the pistol at Gibbs. And then he pulled the trigger.

KORVER PUSHED the barrel through the gap. It tumbled down, hitting the water with a dull thump, then vanished beneath the waves.

Hatch stood next to him, showing no reaction. "I need you to go to London."

Korver hefted the second barrel, this time picking it up instead of rolling it. "I have duties here." He dropped the barrel over the side, then returned for the third.

"This takes precedence. You'll need a full team."

"As you wish." Korver picked the third barrel up one-handed and tossed it over the railing.

Hatch pushed the gate, snapping it shut. "Dr Mendez has a care package for you. There's something of significant value to recover for the next auction."

"And what is that?"

Hatch placed a heavy hand on Korver's shoulder. "*His* name is Tom Faraday. And he is not to be underestimated."

"You've not said that before about a target."

"I have not. But I'm told he is very special indeed."

TWO

THE HEIST BEGAN AT MIDNIGHT. The Ostard private bank was a stone-fronted, six-storey building, set just off Cheapside in the City of London. A discreet metal plaque next to the reinforced glass and steel front doors was the only identifier. It being a Sunday night, and with an over-reliance on technology, only one security guard was on duty - an unenthusiastic man who spent most of his time playing online poker. He had received a call about a family medical emergency - something he would later be confused but delighted to learn had been a crank call. But, unaware of that deception, he drove off at speed in his company van. His employer, a private security specialist, would typically take at least an hour to send a replacement.

Until then the building was vulnerable, particularly to a burglar with special talents.

Tom Faraday waited in the bank's loading bay, hidden in shadow. Late twenties, slim build. Black jeans, pullover, cap hiding his face. Once he had been a lawyer. Now, he was less easily defined. "You in position, Kate?" he said into his earpiece.

There was a long sigh, followed by a clipped female voice.

"Firstly, I know you can track me. Secondly, even if you couldn't, do you really have to ask?"

"Just making conversation. I'm told it's what you humans do to pass the time."

"If I were going in with you, you wouldn't need to ask where I was."

He looked around the car park and saw nothing out of place. "Someone has to remain on watch."

"And it's always me, staring at this tracking system you so kindly installed on my laptop. What if the situation gets tactical?"

"Then you can storm in and rescue me. If, of course, you feel so inclined."

"I make no promises." She paused. "All clear by the way. That guard isn't coming back, and I see no unusual police activity."

"Thanks. Remember, I'll be going off comms for a few minutes."

"Yeah, I remember. Don't take any chances.

"With me, nothing is left to chance."

"If only that were true. Get it done and get out, you big idiot."

Tom tapped his earpiece again, adjusted his backpack, then approached the rear service door - a heavy steel-reinforced affair that, without a key, would usually require specialised cutting gear and a lot of skill and patience. He raised his hand to the electronic lock. With a loud click the door swung open and he stepped inside.

He found himself in the service section of the building - the mail room, cleaning supplies storage, and an area housing air-conditioning controls and a backup power supply. He glanced in at the security office. Its bank of monitors showed that not a single member of bank staff was on site. A little reordering of vacation rotas had been necessary to achieve this, along with the movement of a couple of transaction timetables, but the bank's master system had made it easy - at least for someone with his unique talents. That control also meant that, as far as the building's security would be able to tell, he had never been here.

Tom moved onwards, through another heavy security door. The bank's central atrium was an open space, dominated by an abstract marble sculpture that rose up towards the twenty-metre-high ceiling. He ignored the artwork and turned to the row of five elevators. The one on the left was distinct from the others. It travelled only to one floor - the floor that Tom needed to access - and required additional security accreditation. Tom didn't like elevators. There was always a small but non-zero chance they might malfunction, and getting trapped in a sealed metal box would not help his plan. Where possible he took the stairs.

At first glance there weren't any, but he had seen the site's confidential plans. He walked to an unremarkable section of wall panelling and pushed hard on what looked like a ventilation panel. It swung inwards, revealing a set of metal steps spiralling down, lit by pale emergency lighting. He moved through and began descending, his rubber-soled shoes squeaking on the utilitarian metal treads. Another query of the bank's system told him everything was in order. Which was good, because now came the difficult part. Now he had to break into the vault.

AS TOM DESCENDED, he felt the streams of data around him fade. A combination of concrete, rock and specific shielding technology meant wireless signals did not extend far below ground. While down here he was going to be disconnected.

At the bottom the staircase opened into a lobby where the secure elevator arrived. Ahead, he saw the imposing three-metre-high circular steel door to the bank's vault. In front of that was a computer terminal, and a hand and retinal scanner.

The architects deliberately did not connect the vault door - and all the tech in this underground installation - to the network. That meant Tom could not conduct any prior analysis of its precise configurations. All he had were the manufacturer's manual and installation records. He was going to have to overcome its defences on the fly. If he couldn't, he would not be completing this mission.

He opened the access panel, reached out, and began interrogating the system, looking for a way through the security protocols. As he assessed their complexity he realised he would not be doing this without help.

That was why he had brought what lay within his backpack - a small carbon fibre cube, just over ten centimetres on a side, blinking with green and red LEDs - what the CIA and MI5 had called the Accumulator. Tom opened his mind and let the power flow, immediately escalating his abilities. In this state, breaching the security walls took only thirty seconds. With a clunk and a hiss the heavy door swung open, and Tom stepped into the vault.

As the specifications had said it was a metal-panelled room, exactly seven metres by seven, with a single polished wooden table in the centre, three metres in diameter. Three hundred metal-doored lockboxes of various sizes were fitted in the three walls - individual repositories where the bank's clients stored their most precious valuables with complete confidentiality. Nobody except the box holder knew what was in them, not even the bank.

Nobody except Tom, and whoever had provided the intel to guide him here tonight. The items of interest would be in one of four possible target boxes.

He paced to the far wall and the largest doors. As expected, they had dual electric and mechanical locks. The key to the former was held by the customer, the latter by the bank, and only with both could the box be opened. The electronic part was no problem, but the physical aspect presented a decidedly old-school challenge that couldn't be solved with a straightforward hack. It had taken Tom and Kate a lot of research and effort to find blueprints for these mechanical locks, and a locksmith prepared to make a range of master keys capable of unlocking them. Tom approached box target number one and selected one of the skeleton keys. The key turned perfectly, and he withdrew the heavy metal drawer behind the door, placing it on the table, and flipping the lid open.

It was empty.

Without hesitation, he turned to target number two and repeated the process. Also empty. The third contained legal documents. And bundles of hundred-dollar bills, over two hundred thousand in value.

He left them all in place and moved on. What he was looking for was far more valuable.

The fourth and final of the target boxes was different. It was immediately clear it was much heavier and contained an additional layer of security - a keypad requiring a code. Tom forced that open electronically in seconds, and there was a hiss as a hermetic seal was released. Inside lay a rubber-sealed steel box, painted a bright orange. He popped the catch. And then he frowned.

Inside the orange box, nestled in thick Styrofoam padding, was a black metal sphere the size of a golf ball.

It was not what he was expecting. He had been looking for stolen nanotech. That was why he was taking these risks, based on reliable intel. So what was this? He peered more closely at the metal object. It looked like stainless steel. He lifted the sphere up, feeling its cool surface, and reached out, testing for a system, for electronics of some kind. Smoothly, he began to let power flow through his Interface, reaching for a connection.

There was nothing.

He moved his mind closer, as he stared at the dull black surface. Could he feel something? He had a vague sense that the object hid some secret, some great revelation. But he could not resolve it. None of this made any sense. Tom tapped his earpiece. "Kate?"

Silence. No signal this far underground. No second opinion down here.

Tom returned the metal sphere to its spot in the protective foam, closed the orange box, and slipped it into his pack. Then he shouldered his backpack and stepped out of the vault, the heavy steel door beginning to swing shut. Without waiting for it to finish, he began climbing up the metal staircase.

And then his phone began chiming. He queried it and saw he had multiple messages - all of them from Kate.

You need to get out of there.

He sent out an immediate query to the bank's system. It reported no problems. Tom adjusted his earpiece. "What is going on?"

"Finally!" she replied. "Do you have any idea how many times I tried to—?"

"You know I had no signal below ground. What's going on?"

"The security company decided it had spare guards in the area. Their van is about a minute away, at most."

"Oh."

"Oh indeed. So are you waiting to get arrested, or are you getting the hell out of there?"

Tom started running.

THREE

TOM TOOK the stairs up from the bank vault three at a time.

"Hurry!" Kate hissed in his earpiece. "The van is turning into our street."

"Moving as fast as I can." Tom reached the atrium, and turned, returning the concealed panel to its place, then began retracing his steps. He passed through the security door and found himself back in the service section of the building.

Kate's voice crackled in his ear. "They're parking at the rear. Probably best to come out the front doors."

Tom forced himself to breathe slowly. "Those have physical locks that I don't have the keys for. I'm not getting out that way without cutting gear and a couple of spare hours."

"You didn't tell me all that beforehand."

"Because you would have told me not to go in. We can manage this." He crept forward, opening his mind to the CCTV cameras outside. He saw two guards climbing out of a large, white van. "Although our new friends are going to make that challenging."

"Can you hide?"

"The first thing they'll do is a full sweep of the building."

"Then run for it. I'm sure you'll be faster than them."

"They'll see me and report the incident. And that will mean a lot of blocking comms, and erasing systems - the kind of digital mess that *you-know-who* hates having to hear about." Tom moved towards the rear door where he had originally entered.

Kate cleared her throat. "I have two tasers."

"Let's keep that option in reserve. We just need a distraction. Something to buy me a little time."

"I could walk up and ask them directions?"

"At midnight in the City? Just out for a stroll in the rear car park of a bank? Doesn't that sound a little suspicious?"

"They're security guards. It's their job to be suspicious."

Tom smiled at Kate's words. "You're right, they *are* security guards. So if they hear an alarm, they're going to respond to it."

"The alarm in the bank? Won't that automatically call the police and trigger other fail-safes?"

"I mean your car alarm."

"And how do I trigger that? Lock the car and break a window?"

"Leave that to me. Drive up to the front of the building and get ready to look irate."

"That I can do."

Tom reached out and found the dark grey Ford Mondeo that Kate was driving. He felt it stop outside the front of the bank, and he sent the instruction. The car's alarm began shrieking. On CCTV he saw the two guards pull torches from their belts and hurry around to the front of the building.

With a half smile, Tom triggered the back door lock and slipped outside. Moving in the shadows, he made his way through the car park and onto the street, turning left and away from the Mondeo. Behind him Kate was loudly remonstrating with her car, kicking at the front tyre, with the occasional yell at the security guards who were watching warily from close by.

"I'm clear," Tom whispered into the earpiece, as he turned off the car alarm. "Now leave those poor men alone."

"I think they've already lost interest. I'll meet you round the corner."

"Got it." He turned and froze. Two more security guards stood perhaps five metres away. One was pointing directly at him.

"Sir, what were you doing in that car park?"

For a moment Tom couldn't speak. Where had they come from? Why hadn't he seen them before? Why hadn't Kate detected their arrival? He felt his breath catch as his mind scrambled for an explanation that wouldn't come. Stay calm, he told himself. "I'm sorry, what?"

Both guards took a step closer. Tom saw them reaching for torches on their belts - the closest thing to a weapon they could legally carry in London. "Please answer my question."

"Just on my way home." Tom went to step around them, but they moved to block his path. Should he run? If he went to Kate, he risked drawing her further into things. If he abandoned her and headed off through the City streets, he'd be in range of hundreds of CCTV cameras. This was getting messy.

Kate's voice sounded in his ear. "Problem?"

"Two more guards," he whispered. "Would have been nice to know."

"Where did they come from?"

"I don't know. But I—"

"Who are you talking to?" asked the guard who had pointed. He pulled up his radio. "Unit Two, requesting backup."

"We need to get out of here," Kate said.

"I agree," Tom replied, "but I'm..." He trailed off as he heard a police siren, then a second, and saw the shimmer of red and blue lights reflecting off glass. They must be only thirty seconds away. "Are you monitoring the police?"

"The system you gave me isn't showing anything. What should I do?"

"Come get me, once you get the signal."

"What signal?"

"You'll know it when you see it."

The nearest guard held up his torch. "Sir, the police have been called. They will have some questions for you."

Behind Tom the sound of sirens was crescendoing. He shrugged and closed his eyes, tapping into the Accumulator and its power, then reaching outwards, connecting to the infrastructure of the buildings. And all around them every light turned on, every building alarm sounded, every automatic door and window opened and closed. Darkness became near daylight.

The two guards spun, looking bewildered.

Tom heard the screech of tyres and Kate pulled up next to him. Before the guards could react he jumped in and Kate accelerated away.

FOUR

ALONE IN HIS laboratory Dr Javier Mendez poured the last drops of coffee from the battered steel flask that was supposed to last him all day, but which he'd managed to drain before lunch. If he wanted a refill the nearest kitchen was two floors away on the other side of the Rig. One solution would be to get a bigger flask, but that would mean completing a detailed requisition form and, unlike scientific supplies, non-essentials could take weeks to reach this place. Any inbound delivery was, as Director Hatch continually pointed out, a security risk. And maintaining the security of the Rig was something the Director prioritised over everything else.

Mendez pushed his stool back from the long white table and looked around. Laboratory 3A was the Rig's largest lab, located at the centre of Level Three, and had a number of special features that made it his preferred base of operations. His team of three assistants seemed to gravitate to the nearby Laboratory 3B, where they were less likely to be given coffee-fetching duties. Perhaps he should wander over and show them that they were wrong.

Or he could send one of the autodogs. But while the automated servants could fetch and carry, and perform a number of menial tasks, nobody had yet trained one to operate the coffee maker. Perhaps that would come in a future update.

There was a knock at the door - a heavy, reverberating sound that told him who it was without the trouble of looking up. He tapped a button to open the door. "Time for your injection already?"

Karl Korver's huge figure strode into the lab, his steel-capped boots clunking on the sealed floor. "Getting it early. And collecting my field kit."

"Ah yes, for your trip to London." Mendez walked over to a set of broad white shelves, removed a padded grey case, and placed it on the table. Inside were a secure tablet computer, a tailored nano suit packed in a compression capsule, two secure comms units and two glass ampules within a transparent protector packed alongside two sapphire glass syringes.

Korver picked up the suit. "The last one failed on me."

"You did give it quite a workout. Try not to get shot too many times." Mendez reached forward, popping open a closed section of the case, and pulled out a black metal sphere the size of a golf ball. "Do I need to explain this again?"

"I remember the instructions. How much connection time will I have?"

"72 hours of access from first activation."

"Longer would be helpful."

"I'm sure it would. But that's the most we can achieve. Not even Max can help us with extending quantum entanglement."

"I thought you designed the computer?"

"Let's say I helped bring it into the world. It has evolved beyond me." Mendez placed the sphere back in its padded section, then closed the case. "Need anything else?"

"My dose?"

"Oh, yes." Mendez moved over to a metal drawer unit, placed his palm on a reader, and a lock released. He started working his way down the drawers. "In here somewhere..." In the third drawer he found a syringe gun and pulled it out.

Korver knelt and tipped his head to one side. Mendez pressed the gun against his neck and fired. Korver blinked and grunted.

Mendez smiled. "That's the good stuff, eh?"

"You ever tried it?"

"I don't even know what it is, so of course I haven't."

"If you had, you wouldn't call it 'good stuff'." Korver opened and closed his fists, then rose to his feet.

"So what is going on in London?"

"I'm to find someone called Tom Faraday and bring him back here."

"Who's that? A scientist?"

"I expect I'll find out when I get there. Thank you for your help, Doctor."

Mendez watched Korver turn and leave the room. "Any time."

MENDEZ WAITED for five minutes after Korver had departed, then left through the same airlock door. Across the corridor was a small bathroom. His heart beating quickly, he stepped inside, closed the lock and tapped his modified wrist-watch. From its display he could see there were no monitoring devices within twenty metres. He pulled out the jerry-rigged portable communicator he had built to precise specifications, put in his earpiece, then pressed to connect. The link was almost immediate.

"Yes?" said the familiar synthetic voice. "You have something to report?"

He forced himself to breathe evenly. "I was hoping to have heard from you by now. About my extraction."

"Patience, Dr Mendez. The pieces are being put into place. Just make sure you are ready."

"I'm doing my part. The system core is ready to be moved."

"Excellent. We have a team close by. What about the Rig's security?"

He puffed out his cheeks. "I'm working on that."

"Then you should keep working. We can't get onboard without your help."

"They murdered another three people today - threw them into the ocean. I don't know how much longer I can keep my cover in place. I should never have come here in the first place."

"You are where you are, there's no point in dwelling on yesterday. Tomorrow is what you can change. Just be yourself. Do that and they won't suspect anything is wrong."

"I guess. They're sending Korver to London to abduct someone called Tom Faraday."

"Useful to know, but you should focus on the task at hand."

"And you should listen. Because I'm saying it may not be possible."

"*Javier*, you need to be resourceful. Do whatever you need to do to complete the task, and this will soon be over. After that you can move on with your life. Notify us when there is an update."

"But I—" Mendez heard the call disconnect and felt a shiver run over him. He had a plan for interfering with the Rig's security. He was just stuck on one important detail. Would he be able to solve it in time?

FIVE

THREE MINUTES after leaving the Ostard, Tom and Kate had pulled into a side street and switched the Ford Mondeo's fake number plates. Now Tom sat in the passenger seat as Kate drove them northwest out of London, his black backpack resting on his lap. Staring out of the window, watching the city lights drift past, he relayed to Kate what he'd recovered from the vault - the mysterious metal sphere that he now carried in his backpack. When he finished she shook her head wearily. "I think you'll agree we've had better missions."

Tom nodded. "I don't understand it. The extra security guards and the police turning up like that. I don't know how it happened."

"Why would they replace one guard with four? And how come the police arrived so quickly?" She glanced at the rear-view mirror. "It's almost like we were set up."

"If that were true, they would have sent more. And relax, there's no sign we're being followed or monitored. Plus we managed to get away before the police arrived, which prevented a whole bunch of other problems that *you-know-who* would not have shut up about."

Kate drummed her fingertips on the steering wheel. "This all just reinforces what I've been saying: that we're taking too many risks."

"Everything has its risks. These are acceptable."

"Really? Even though, after everything that happened, we didn't find what we were looking for?"

"We found *something*. Maybe it's also connected to these auctions?"

"And maybe it's nothing at all." She shook her head. "We like to pretend that we're some kind of special forces unit. But we're amateurs messing in a world we don't understand. And we only got away because you lit up half of London."

"It was barely a couple of blocks. And it worked. The police and the guards were totally distracted."

"You did too much. Who knows what it's doing to you."

"Enough with that," he said with a sigh. "Trust me, I can handle it."

"Really? Because I think you're letting the power go to your head." Kate frowned. "Are you still jacked in to that cube thing?"

"No, I am not. Why would you ask that?"

"Because you seem different. You *feel* different."

"You and your side effects from the truth nano." Tom glared at her. "I've told you before about doing that. It's... *invasive*."

"I'm not really doing anything. I'm not like you, I don't reach out and connect to things. I can just sense your nanotech. It's like my sense of smell - I can't just turn it off."

"You're saying I smell?"

"No more than usual." She jabbed him on the arm. "I can feel the nanites, and they're part of you. You seem agitated. Distressed even."

"I'm fine."

"It's just that we both know nanotechnology changes us. In

ways we see, and in ways we don't understand. Don't assume this is nothing."

"Like I said, *I'm fine.* I just want to get home to a hot bath and a warm bed."

"They'll have to wait. You have a meeting first." She peered ahead at a road sign then turned sharply left, the car's tyres squealing.

He frowned. "I have a meeting *now*? With who?"

"After everything that just happened, who do you think?"

"I see. And when did you hear about...?" Tom looked at her. "That's a different earpiece you're wearing. Very heavily encrypted."

"Because someone likes to be able to talk to me in private. She called me while you were putting the other number plates in the boot."

"This is supposed to be a partnership. But it often feels like we work for her. And she is not an easy person to work for."

"Then why not take charge?"

"Of what? To do what?"

"That's the thing about taking charge - what you do would be up to you. Of course you'd need the right team around you."

"I think I'm happy working alone."

"You mean working with me."

He blinked. "That's what I meant."

"Sure it was. Still speaking like a lawyer." Kate turned right onto a narrow service road, then brought the car to an abrupt halt next to an unmarked warehouse. The roller door was padlocked shut. She pointed to a regular-sized door next to it. "Don't keep her waiting."

Tom gathered his backpack and stepped out. He saw Kate didn't do the same. "Not coming?"

"You know how she likes to keep these meetings one-to-one. If she wants anything she can just call me. Or turn up where I live unannounced. Tell her I love it when she does that."

Tom turned and studied the warehouse. It looked like there was nobody around, but a quick interrogation of data flows showed that was far from the case. The building was awash with the signature of advanced electronics.

He pushed the door open and walked through.

SIX

TOM IMMEDIATELY SAW that the space inside the building was clean - far too clean for a regular warehouse. Bright LED lights illuminated two large black SUVs parked on either side. Two close protection police officers watched him intently. Each wore visible body armour and held automatic rifles fitted with suppressors. In the space between the SUVs a two-metre-long fold out table had been erected, along with two similarly temporary chairs.

Leaning on her walking stick, MI5 Director Stephanie Reems stood next to the table. She wore her trademark grey suit, and a similarly trademark grey expression. With her free hand she reached forward and placed a bottle of beer and an opener on the table. "I expect that you've been hankering for a cold one."

"I won't say no." Tom levered the lid of the bottle and took a long drink. "Although given you're now here to lecture me, perhaps surprising to get the offer."

She tipped her head on one side, the scar on her left cheek glistening in the light. "I hear it was all a bit of a mess."

"You could say that."

"So I thought I'd get your version before I consider what action needs to be taken."

"Maybe start with getting better intel." He placed his backpack on the table, opened it and removed the orange-coloured steel box. Then he leaned forwards and lifted the lid, revealing the metal sphere.

"What is that supposed to be?"

Tom shrugged. "Not a consignment of CERUS nanotech."

"Did you open the wrong box?"

"My memory is eidetic. It can certainly cope with a few simple instructions."

She peered more closely. "A metal *ball*? Is there anything inside it?"

"You mean like nanotech? Or electronics? I've tried and can't connect to anything. From its weight it could even be solid. Who did your intel come from?"

"As you know, my source is confidential."

"Yes. But until now it has at least been reliable. We've always found stolen nanotech earmarked for sale at one of these auctions."

Reems narrowed her eyes. "If we're going to talk about reliability, what the hell happened outside the bank? Or did you *forget* to be covert?"

"Kate told you?"

"She didn't need to. I tapped into police comms. We've managed to steer them to considering it an electrical fault. But you were hardly discreet."

Tom frowned. "The replacement security team turned up far sooner than expected. Then the police as well. I tried to create a distraction, but I rather overdid it."

"So you're telling me you can't control yourself?"

"That's not what I said. Or what I meant."

Reems leaned forward. "Then you were compromised in some way?"

"Compromised how?"

"You tell me. But let's hope this was just a blip, that the next mission will go better." She removed the sphere and weighed it thoughtfully, then handed it to him. "There has to be something about this. Why else would it be in the vault? Why don't you spend some time studying it? See what giving it your undivided attention can produce."

"Sure."

"Good. And once we know what it is, once we have 'acquired', we catalogue and eliminate, just like we do with everything else. That's why we call it the ACE protocol." She started walking towards one of the SUVs.

"It still feels odd, us working together."

"A partnership born out of necessity."

Tom drained his beer and placed it on the table. "It wasn't so long ago that you interpreted ''necessity' differently. You would have happily locked me up in a secret lab to dissect."

"When we thought you were a danger. When we thought you were an enemy, not an ally."

"Fortunate that you had a complete change of heart."

"Do you still not trust me?"

"If you were me, would you? Why should I?"

She ran a hand over the scar on her cheek. "A near death experience can be transformative."

"An experience where CERUS technology saved you?"

"You mean the illustrious Dominique in her super suit? You think that means I would want to preserve it? That's one angle. But if CERUS hadn't done what it did, if William Bern hadn't been doing what he was doing... if he hadn't tried to kill me... she wouldn't have needed to. That was the lesson I learned: that this nanotech is just too dangerous to be allowed. I'm only sorry I didn't have that epiphany sooner."

"And you're not concerned that we're trying to close the stable door after the horses have bolted?"

"We're not trying to close that door. We're trying to find the horses." Reems smiled. "It won't surprise you to hear that I get approached weekly by the CIA for an update on your whereabouts. Although after what they did last year, I'm sure they don't expect any actual cooperation. Which means you need to be careful. They'll still be looking, and they won't be the only ones."

"If you mean the Leskov family, they have more basic problems taking up their attention. A lot of other organisations are trying to rub them out." He gave a sigh. "Something I wish we could do to Bern's legacy."

"You know it's not going to be simple. All that research didn't just vanish. Some of it was stolen from CERUS. Some of it was stolen *by* CERUS. And others are doing similar work entirely independently. This is much bigger than one person."

Tom blinked. "And yet the way you say that makes it sound like you have a particular concern. Who?"

"As soon as I have anything concrete, you'll be the first to know." Her phone chimed and she glanced at it, then tapped her stick on the ground. "Thanks again for your help, even if tonight was a bust. Without you we'd be making a lot less progress."

Tom nodded. "Thanks for the beer." He walked back over to the door and slipped out.

Kate was waiting in the Mondeo. "That was quick."

"Reems had somewhere more important to be."

She raised an eyebrow. "You're not feeling the love? What did she say about the ball?"

Tom shrugged. "She seemed as surprised as we were. She left it with me."

"Are you going to ask for help? With studying it?"

He raised an eyebrow. "I am *not* involving Dominique. Please stop suggesting it. And, in any event, she's too caught up in her quest to heal the world. Including me."

"Is that a bad goal?"

"It's an impossible one. And, personally, I'm not ready to heal." He tapped the dashboard. "Can we get moving? I'd like to go home."

"I still don't know how you can call that place home. After everything he did to you."

"Yeah, well as with everything connected with my father, it's complicated. I've decided to move on. I'd appreciate it if you could too."

REEMS WATCHED Tom leave the warehouse, then climbed into her SUV.

"Back to your apartment, Ma'am?" asked her driver.

"Please. I have one more call to make, but I'll do it on the drive. It has been a very long—" Reems' phone rang. She looked at the display and saw it was the same person who had messaged her moments before. "What is it, Gates? You can't have something about the sphere already?"

"What? No, of course not. I was following the feed, but I've no idea what it is. You sure you trust this source?"

"Given that it's anonymous, obviously I don't. But for now we keep following the leads. Is there an issue with Faraday?"

"For once it's not about him. You need to get here."

"I'm due in tomorrow night—"

"This can't wait. And we need to discuss it in person."

She gave a sigh. "I'm on my way."

SEVEN

IT WAS GONE 3AM when Kate left Tom at the usual drop-off point, next to a dense patch of woodland. He covered the familiar route through the trees and undergrowth, with only a dim head-mounted torch for illumination, until he reached a three-metre-high brick wall. Using small handholds previously cut out from the mortar, he climbed smoothly, and paused briefly at the top.

The Edwardian mansion within had, until last year, belonged to William Bern. It was a ten-bedroom property, located amid five acres of walled grounds, a few miles from Henley-on-Thames. Those grounds had previously been kept well-manicured by a team of gardeners but were now fighting a losing battle against neglect. The big house itself, with its dozens of windows boarded-up, appeared unoccupied and forgotten. Tom had been based on the estate for nearly six months now, though he kept his occupancy a secret even from the security firm hired to monitor the estate. They sent human guards on patrols around the grounds a couple of times a day, but otherwise surveillance was done via cameras - and CCTV was never a problem for Tom to evade. As to why he was there, that was because of an unexpected development nine months earlier.

~

THREE MONTHS after Tom had seen William Bern perish in a helicopter explosion, he received an invitation from a law firm, Stotter, Abrams & Partners. As Tom had no mailing address, nor any public way of being contacted, the invites had been sent care of Kate Turner, Dominique Lentz and Stephanie Reems - each marked strictly confidential, to be opened addressee only. Each, when they found their way to Tom, contained a single page - a letter printed on plain white bonded paper. They all said the same thing - that he should arrange a convenient time to attend their offices to discuss a matter arising from the death of their former client, William Bern.

Tom had eventually agreed - although only after a considerable amount of background checks and diligence on the law firm - a boutique private client practice with offices in London's West End. Not trusting their security Tom changed the venue to a London hotel at the last minute. He was shown to one of the hotel's larger meeting rooms where a grey haired, grey faced man by the name of Harry Stotter, stood waiting.

"You were a difficult man to track down, Mr Faraday," Stotter said as they shook hands. "We're very good at finding people - one of the reasons Mr Bern retained us. You were, very nearly, our first failure."

"I like my privacy." Tom took a seat across the conference table. "Now, if I may be blunt, why am I here?"

Stotter slid a grey card folder across the table. "After a somewhat tortuous process, Mr Bern has been declared legally dead. That has triggered a number of matters entrusted to us."

"Why was it tortuous? He died in a helicopter crash."

"With no actual body the process is always complex. Plus you were the only witness to events. Despite the circumstances we have moved things forward relatively quickly."

Tom ran a hand over the folder. He could feel nothing electronic within.

Stotter seemed to read his suspicion. "It's just paper, Mr Faraday. I am an officer of the court. I am not here to deceive you."

"My late father was someone whose motives I would always question."

"This might help you understand them better."

Tom flipped the file open. Inside was a thick document, bound with gleaming brass fasteners. At the top of the front page were six words: William Bern - Last Will And Testament. "Is this genuine?"

Stotter nodded sagely. "One of three originals held in our safe. Our client planned for a great many events, including his own death."

"Something I'm sure he thought would never actually happen. Why are you showing me this?"

"Because, Mr Faraday, you are the only beneficiary."

Tom sat in silence for several moments. "I don't understand."

"You were William Bern's only living relative. As his biological son, even without a will you would have had a preferential claim on his estate. However, Mr Bern took express steps to provide for your future."

Tom rose to his feet and closed his eyes. He reached out, feeling for electronics, for networks. For data. The lawyer had a phone in his pocket. It was not even a smart phone, and it was switched off. There was no unusual traffic over Wi-Fi or cellular networks - nothing to indicate covert monitoring. CCTV in the hotel showed no unusual behaviour. If this was a trap, it was well hidden.

Stotter placed his palms carefully on the table. "Mr Bern suggested you might be... he used the word 'jumpy'. But I can assure you, I am merely here to carry out my professional duties as his executor."

Tom eased slowly back down into his chair. "I did not expect this."

"I imagine not. There are a few mandatory identity check requirements to fulfil, which have to be done in person. We can complete those today, or at a time of your choosing. With an estate of this size they cannot be circumvented."

"I'm amazed Bern had anything but debts. Wasn't he in all sorts of legal troubles? Quite apart from the governments seeking to incarcerate him, wasn't he being sued by a number of former commercial partners?"

"Mr Bern had excellent legal advice. He took a great many steps to protect his assets for the long-term: a system of trusts, company group separation, and of course many of the problem issues you allude to related to corporate, and not personal, responsibility - where the corporate veil is not easily pierced. I understand you are a lawyer, so I'm sure I'm telling you what you already know."

"I was a lawyer. I'm not so sure what I am these days. So, what is he leaving to me?"

Stotter pulled a legal pad from his briefcase. "It's quite a complex asset list, but the main parts are a sizeable portfolio of stocks and shares - as of today valued at slightly in excess of two hundred million pounds. And the Berkshire Mansion - worth approximately thirty million - which you'll be delighted to hear is mortgage free."

"That's nuts." Tom blinked. "Why would he leave it to me?"

"He didn't leave any written statement explaining his thinking. But from what I know of the man, and from watching the actions of other rich men with estranged children, I'm sure guilt factored into this thought process."

"He felt guilty? For what he expressly chose to do?"

"You'll have to draw your own conclusions. As I say, there's no written statement. But whatever he did to you, this may have been some small way of apologising."

"What if I don't want it?"

Stotter leaned back in his chair. "That is entirely up to you. However, given the value of the assets in question, you may wish to take some time to consider things carefully. To not act with undue haste."

"But... the very idea of accepting anything from him. It's abhorrent."

"William Bern is dead. What you do with this bequest is up to you. You can give it away, you can start some new venture. Or you can leave it in the bank, while you think about it. But what you have here is an incredible opportunity, one presented to very few."

"I'm already more than familiar with being one of very few."

Stotter nodded and slid his legal pad back into his briefcase. "In the few conversations I had with your father, that was definitely his view of you. Keep the will. Read it over. Call me in the next few days and let me know what you want to do."

TOM DROPPED down from the top of the wall, landing softly on the overgrown grass. He swung his gaze left and right. Nobody was here.

Shortly after meeting with Stotter, Tom had paid a visit to the former MI5 operative, George Croft, in prison - Tom's abilities allowing him to avoid the advanced security systems. He had asked Croft what he thought about Bern's bequest. After a few moments Croft had replied with clarity: "Accept it. Then use it to do something good. Because that would really piss Bern off."

So Tom had agreed. The estate was held through an almost impenetrable web of holding companies and offshore trusts, so nobody was publicly aware of the change of ownership. And Tom still wouldn't have chosen to live here but for one additional discovery. Within the grounds of his estate Bern had built an underground bunker.

Tom moved quietly across the grass, away from the main house, the extensive CCTV systems completely ignoring him, as he had instructed. He reached the large pool-house, the triple-glazed windows all shuttered, and with a physical metal key, opened and slipped through a side door. Inside the pool had been drained and smelt of rust and damp concrete. A set of plastic furniture was stacked and gathering dust. Tom sent a signal into a hidden network. Immediately a hatch in the floor began to lift up, revealing a set of stairs leading down.

Tom descended the staircase, the hatch dropping into place behind him, and opened a final, heavy door. Beyond was a plushly furnished lounge area with three large sofas and a glass dining table. On the table were two laptops and on metal arms extending from the wall, four over-sized ultra-high-definition monitors - all devices cross-connected with a powerful server in a plant room located down the corridor. To one side was a kitchenette. Doors led off to a bedroom and a huge bathroom with a spa pool. As underground bunkers went it was certainly on the luxury side.

The space was electronically shielded, hermetically sealed, and supposedly bomb proof. Bern had escaped from house arrest a year previously with a scheme involving a panic room in the main house, but as with most of his contingency planning, he had at least two of everything. And now it was Tom's to use. With Lentz's help he had made a few upgrades, including a logically separate implementation of her house AI, Odyssey. It ran all his systems in the pool house, while having no direct connection to Lentz's main installation. "Evening, Odie," he said to the air.

"Evening, Thomas," replied a synthetic voice.

"Any security incidents to report?"

"None. I would have notified you immediately if there were."

"Yes of course." Tom could communicate with Odie using his Interface, but Lentz had given him the option of a voice control module, and it provided a pleasant, low effort way to converse, even if it was a lot slower. Odie, however, kept reminding him of that last point.

"We could upload my personality into your Interface to improve the efficiency of our interactions. My calculations show I can operate within the substrate provided by your nanotech."

Tom frowned. "I'd really rather not have another mind inside my head. One is plenty."

"It would significantly increase the efficacy of my interactions with you. And helping you better is my—"

"—prime directive. Yes, I know. Thanks, but no thanks. I'm good with how things are."

"Understood."

Tom pulled an orange juice from the fridge and wandered over to a specially installed, tall metal cupboard. He waved his hand and the door slid open. Inside, draped over a mannequin, was the Resurface suit that he swore he would never wear again. Next to it was a glass display cabinet. Tom reached into his backpack and removed the Accumulator, slipping it from its padded case. He eased the cube into the glass display case and took a slow breath, sensing the energy within. It was a tempting well to drink from. With the power it provided he could boost his Interface to do so much more. And of course, if he put on the Resurface suit, he could do many more things. He could shape and control the nanotech coating on its surface so that he was magnetic, bullet-proof, even invisible, at least in a manner of speaking. When he wore the suit so empowered some might call him a superhero. Yet after what happened last time, when his father had used it to control him, he would never wear it again - the risk was simply too great.

Waving his hand, he closed the cabinet and moved back to the table, removing the sphere from his backpack. He grabbed an eggcup from the kitchen area, then positioned the metal ball on top of it in the middle of the table. The dark metal gleamed silently in the artificial light.

Tom took a seat and stared. What was so special about the sphere that someone had placed it in a bank safety deposit box? He leaned closer, extending his perception. As before, he could feel nothing. It couldn't just be solid metal, surely? He pushed harder, sending power into the air. Again, there was no response, nothing to detect. He hesitated. Or was there?

He stared at the surface of the sphere. At his reflection. He stared into his own eyes. And then he felt them staring back into him. He got the sense of a different kind of connection. To something, somewhere else. To something immense, inhuman, unknowable. And then he thought he felt something just behind him.

Tom spun in alarm, raising his arms in defence, his heart pounding. But there was nobody there. He leapt to his feet, looking all around. "Odie," he hissed, "is there anybody in the bunker?"

"You are in the bunker."

"You know what I mean." He gritted his teeth. "Anybody else?"

"I would have notified you immediately if there were."

Tom blinked and rubbed his fingers in his ears. He had obviously imagined it. Was he unwell? Or just very, very tired? It was clear he couldn't continue working, yet he wanted answers about the sphere. Of course, as Kate kept reminding him, he didn't have to do everything on his own. He tapped the black sphere with his index finger. "Odie, I want you to run a full scan on this."

"It's a non-standard device. Should I prioritise around any particular line of enquiry?"

"I want to know what it does. Analyse it for any possible type of technology, electronics, chemical or... nanotech. Also I'm sending you the telemetry from everything that happened at the bank, so you can scan for anything that looks out of the ordinary. Give me what you can by morning. I'm going to bed."

"Yes, Thomas. Sleep well."

He nodded and walked off towards his bedroom. Hopefully tomorrow would bring answers.

EIGHT

FIVE LEVELS below ground the metal doors slid open. Stephanie Reems emerged from the heavy service elevator and held her Security Service credentials out to the two guards. They immediately waved her past - not surprising given they knew who she was, they knew she was coming, and that they had been warned she was tired and in a very bad mood. Reems gave a curt nod and walked down the long corridor to the main file repository, her walking stick tapping on the ground with exaggerated force.

She wasn't one for sleeping much, but tonight it seemed she wasn't going to get to sleep at all. She reached the end of the corridor, turned right and placed her hand on a palm reader. Retinal and voice scanners were on the shopping list, but procuring such equipment had proved difficult without flagging a concern on MI5 internal audit's radar. For now this site could not appear on any radar, although she knew that would change soon.

The palm reader chimed, and the pair of doors slid open. Inside was the file repository, a ten-metre-square room where

Reems spent the majority of her time at the facility. There was the constant drone of high-powered air filtering and cooling. The systems in this room needed considerable resource even to keep them operational, let alone to reach their full potential, although that latter functionality was very much a future goal.

In the middle of the room stood a wiry man in a crumpled lab coat, carrying a worn brown leather messenger bag over his shoulder. Out of the corner of her eye she saw a tray of fresh tea and biscuits. Gates was not one to bother with such pleasantries - if you could apply such a term to the tea and biscuits that were served in this facility. It meant he feared something very serious had happened.

"So," Reems said, without a trace of warmth, "would you care to explain just what has got you so hot and bothered? And what is so sensitive that you couldn't even allude to it by phone?" She frowned. "It's not VoltTech again, is it? I really don't need any more of their nonsense. I swear, if I ever get Leon Smit in a room, I will..."

Gates cleared his throat loudly. "We have a problem with the core system."

"The supercomputer which stores all our data?"

"That's the one. It's displaying an auto-generated message. In 72 hours it's going to re-initialise all systems. Wipe itself and start over."

"The core system you say? Is that a big deal?"

Gates let out a slow breath. "It means everything that makes the computer, a computer. I've tried terminating the process, but it's refusing all new commands."

"Then export the data."

Gates shook his head. "That was always one of our security measures, to prevent data theft."

"So we'll restore from the backups? We'll lose a few days at most?"

"If it were that simple, I'd have started already. But the system has a tiered system of backups - and this problem will cascade through all of them. We'll be left with nothing."

"Whoever came up with that idea?"

He paused. "You did. You picked it from the options I presented."

"And the original materials? Those that we retained and stored in the separate warehouse?"

Gates pulled at his beard. "The system has control of those and will destroy them all when it wipes the data. If we try and access the warehouse before that happens, it will destroy them early."

Reems walked over to the tray of tea and biscuits and poured herself a cup. As she added milk she saw that it was stewed. "What you're saying is we're going to lose everything? Is it a hack? Or a fault?"

"So far we have no explanation. In part that's a result of having rushed things. You can't break all the rules and expect that there will be no consequences."

"You are the tech lead for this site. It is your responsibility to solve all problems. Including this one."

"That doesn't mean I know how."

"You said you were the best."

"I'm good, sure. But the best? For your sake, I really hope not. No, we need your dear friend, Dominique Lentz."

"She isn't the solution to all our problems."

"She only has to be the solution to this problem."

"If I could have got her, she'd be here already, and I never would have hired you."

"Yeah, you've said. Something I've always found motivational. Anyway, we have 72 hours. So, obviously, take your time."

Reems nodded slowly. "Then I suppose I'll go pay her a

visit." Her phone buzzed. "Although it seems I have something else to take care of first."

"What's more important than this?"

"Feeding the ducks, would you believe?"

NINE

THE LECTURE WAS BEING HELD in the auditorium at St Johns' College Cambridge, an oddly modern structure nestling between much older buildings. The theatre space held five hundred on uncomfortable wooden pull-out seating for a talk or movie presentation, or four people to play badminton if the seats were folded away and a net put up. You could still smell the floor wax and sweat from a training session earlier that morning, but it didn't bother Dominique Lentz or any of the others in the packed crowd that were there to hear lectures on topics in the fields of what some considered 'fringe science'. The three day event was sponsored by the huge battery-tech company, VoltTech - although Lentz suspected their involvement was more about political manoeuvring than it was about any real interest in the material being discussed. And given, if the rumours were true, their next gen battery technology had failed to pass proof of concept, they should probably be spending their money on that.

The first day - an update on smart drugs and cybernetics in healthcare - was of particular interest, and Lentz had arrived early to make sure she had a front row seat: she planned on recording everything using her smart glasses, so that she could replay it later. She was fairly sure that would be in contravention of a number of laws and policies, but it would only be for personal use, so what harm could there be? The law was always struggling to keep up - and her work over the years certainly had bigger illegality issues than this.

The first speaker, now beginning her presentation, was world-renowned roboticist, Dr Edna Kim - a woman perhaps Lentz's age and of similar height. Her frizzy red hair was pulled back tightly, and she wore a frayed beige jacket with leather arm patches and heavy, thick-rimmed glasses. According to the brochure, Kim was consulting for a number of not-for-profit institutions that were household names, but it was Kim's own reputation that had brought the audience here, and Lentz in particular. But as Kim was working through her introductory statement, Lentz was distracted by her phone beeping loudly. She quickly muted it, seeing she had a message from Kate Turner. She then noticed in her peripheral vision that a number of people were looking at her.

"Apparently I'm not worth your undivided attention," said a voice.

Lentz looked up to see a half-smile on the face of Dr Kim. Lentz coughed and slipped her phone back in her pocket. "Sorry, I... was distracted."

"Of course. And no doubt something of importance, given that you are not just an ordinary member of the audience." Kim leaned forward. "Ladies and gentlemen, we have a celebrity in our midst. Dr Lentz is a bona fide legend in the field of experimental nanotech. She is also the CEO of the *illustrious* CERUS Biotech." There were a few mutterings from around the audience as people registered who was being talked about.

"I'm here in a personal capacity," Lentz replied. "I'm

currently on a sabbatical, which gives me time to attend events outside of my particular expertise."

"Then we are most fortunate. Given your background we'd love to get your take on the prospects for intelligent medicines, and related fields. For example, do you see nanotechnology playing an active role in future developments? Perhaps you've undertaken some specific projects you might care to share with us?"

Lentz blinked. "I wouldn't dream of taking up your speaking time, especially when everyone is here to learn from you. Also, I cannot discuss specific CERUS Biotech projects in public. Plus I'm sure we're all familiar with the Nanotechnology Act, which blocks almost all activity in the field."

Kim nodded, as if the answer was no surprise. "Thank you, Dr Lentz. And that reinforces one of my core arguments about the challenges we face. New technology is being blocked from many applications because of commercial secrecy and 'national security', and unnecessary concerns over safety. So much revolutionary new science is constrained, restricted, or conducted in secret. If only we could all get together and share our work, we could do amazing things." She leaned on the lectern. "We could save lives. We could change the world."

Lentz shrugged. "The counter-argument is that this is all incredibly dangerous, and that the public need to be protected from evil scientists and nefarious corporations."

Kim leaned forward on the lecturn. "Some might call that scare-mongering."

Lentz puffed out her cheeks and took in the intense gazes of those around her. "I think we need to move into the future. If we can tailor medical treatments to analyse and address the needs of individuals, we will be making a quantum leap towards a brighter tomorrow."

Kim smiled. "I'm sure a great many of us here agree with

you. Thank you, Dr Lentz. And now," she pressed her controller and brought up the next slide, "I should probably get on with my presentation, or we're going to be late for coffee, and half of you will nod off during Professor Sawyer's session before lunch..."

AN HOUR later they broke for the promised coffee. As Lentz started to follow the audience out, Kim called out to her. "Do you have a moment?"

Lentz turned and smiled. "For our illustrious presenter? Of course."

Kim laughed and walked over, extending her hand. "Apologies for picking on you like that. I just wanted to make a point, and I leapt on a chance to do it in a memorable way."

"You knew I couldn't say anything. You just wanted me to state that for the audience."

"And all that you couldn't talk about - it's symptomatic of the situation the world over - of how technological development is constrained and conducted in secret. At the current rate, nothing is going to change in my lifetime."

Lentz shook her hand. "I deserved to be made an example of, after using my phone like that. And as for the need for free and collaborative work in this space - you make a good point, even if I fear that few who make the big decisions will listen." She studied Kim's face behind her thick glasses, and again had the feeling of recognition. "I'm getting an odd sense of *déjà vu* - have we met before?"

"I worked at CERUS many years back, although I don't think we met. Obviously we were both very different people - less accomplished in our fields. Since then you've become something of a hero of mine. I've read all your papers – or at least the ones that have been made public."

Lentz smiled. "I had some bold ideas when I was younger. Good to see that others are still blazing the trail. Some colleagues flagged your research to me, and when I saw you were speaking, I knew it was not to be missed. Are you still working on medical nanotech. Wasn't that your PhD thesis?"

Kim rolled her eyes. "That was years ago, when such tech was mere conjecture. No, there are only so many things one can focus on, and I chose robotics. What are you doing with yourself these days? When you're not attending fringe science conferences?"

"I'm still CEO of CERUS."

"But you're on sabbatical? People don't usually take those when they're happy with their present circumstances."

"I wouldn't read too much into that if I were you. Who is ever happy with their lot?"

Kim nodded. "Not me, I can tell you. But I'm hoping that might change." She pulled a business card from her jacket pocket and held it out.

Lentz took it, reading the neatly printed script. "The Osiris Foundation?"

She adjusted her glasses. "It's actually all rather hush-hush, but they've offered me the chance to join them. To work on research of my own choosing."

"Well funded?"

"They have resources, people and a shared vision. It is a unique opportunity." She leaned closer, lowering her voice. "I'm hoping to explore nanotech applications in human harmonisation with technology."

"And I presume that would involve some form of neural interface."

"Ideally something bi-directional and high bandwidth." Kim smiled. "Unfortunately, nobody has ever really advanced that field." She paused. "Unless you listen to rumours and gossip."

"I try not to."

"But I dare to dream. With the right approach nano could change us fundamentally. I'm talking about fully bi-directional communication between biology and technology, not just within the brain, but the entire body. The end point would be complete control over ourselves, the ability to change and improve, to upgrade. Human and machine in perfect harmony."

"*Symbiosis*," Lentz said. "I read your paper. An admirable goal, if a distant one."

"We won't reach the destination if we don't start the journey." Kim shrugged. "You could be a part of making it happen. Your expertise in nanotech..." She cleared her throat. "Your *alleged* expertise in nanotech. It could be critical."

"I have a job. I'm just taking a break."

"Don't risk looking back on this moment and wishing you had taken that leap."

Lentz nodded and handed back the card. "I'm not looking to join someone else's show at the moment."

"This would be your show, just catalysed by someone else's money and resources. You want to change the world, I know. And you haven't been able to, because you've been beholden to shareholders, to the British Government. This will be the opposite. You'll be in control of your own labs, of your team, free to pursue whichever projects you deem a priority."

"Almost sounds like you run the place." Lentz smiled. "You and I both know that real ground-breaking science requires enormous amounts of funding."

"Osiris has an extensive network of wealthy donors, who contribute significant sums." Kim tipped her head on one side. "Money will not be an object."

"Years of experience have taught me the hard way that when something sounds too good to be true, it usually is."

"I hope for my sake that you're wrong." Kim held out a

different business card. "These are my private contact details. Even if you're not interested in Osiris, I'd love to buy you lunch some time and just... talk science." She lowered her voice. "Some pointers as to your thought process and approach would be valuable beyond measure."

Lentz blinked and took the card. "It was lovely to meet you, Edna. All the very best with your endeavours."

Kim gave a bow. "The honour was mine."

Lentz walked out of the theatre into the courtyard, realising that her phone was actually ringing, notwithstanding she had most certainly put it on mute. She saw the caller's name, and nodded admiringly, transferring the call to the HUD of her smart glasses. "How did you make my phone ring?"

"By breaking the rules like you and others have taught me," replied Kate. "I borrowed the cheat codes from a contact at the manufacturer. Did you get my message earlier?"

"Didn't get a chance to read it."

"No problem, I have you now. Tom and I have something odd that you should have a look at."

"I'm at a conference in Cambridge. What do you mean: *something odd?*"

"We recovered it from an operation last night. It would benefit from your particular set of skills."

"An operation?" Lentz blinked. "I'm not sure what trouble you two have been getting yourselves into, but I'll be back in three days—"

"I don't think it can't wait. I'm worried about Tom."

"So am I. But he hasn't been keen to see me recently." Lentz hesitated. "Has something happened?

"Maybe. I'm not sure. We still don't know what the long-term effects of having this stuff in your head may be. This could be a useful excuse to get you face-to-face again."

"Is he going to be OK with me turning up?"

"He will be when I tell him."

Lentz looked at her watch. "I can be there in about three hours."

"Good. And just in case I don't get round to telling him, maybe find a way to get inside before he can say no."

"I will *suit up*."

TEN

TOM AWOKE to the chimes of an alarm. A dull ache in his head suggested it had been sounding some time.

"Good morning, Thomas," said Odie. *"You have a visitor. A Miss Kate Turner. She asked that I announce her."*

He sat up in bed, blinking. "Kate's here?"

"Proceeding through the front gates in a grey Ford transit van."

He looked at the bedside clock, which showed 11am. "She's driving inside the grounds in daylight? And you let her?"

"She has the appropriate clearance. Do you wish to amend her access rights?"

"No." Tom sighed, pulled on jeans and a shirt, and stumbled up the stairs.

Kate was waiting outside the surface level door of the pool-house, holding two large takeaway coffee cups. She held out the larger one, which had 'latte' and 'Tim' scrawled on the side in crude lettering.

"You know protocol," Tom said, taking the cup from her. "You're not supposed to be seen entering during the day. Anyone might be watching the gate."

"Don't worry, I'm undercover." She turned round and gestured to the van, parked a short distance away on the lawn. It was smartly sign-written with 'KT Pool Maintenance Services'.

"Epic genius. Nobody will ever suspect. But why are you here? I only saw you a few hours ago."

"I couldn't sleep. I've been thinking more about what we found last night. That sphere wasn't supposed to be there. It has to be important. And you had that odd glitch, when you triggered all the lights. Have you started an analysis?"

"Odie's been processing it overnight."

"Excellent." Kate stepped past him and headed down the stairs.

Tom followed and found her staring at where the sphere sat on the eggcup. "Make yourself at home."

"I will." She looked upwards. "Odie, what have you found with the sphere?"

"Enhanced visual examination revealed a hairline crack, possibly an access panel, although it is so narrow it could just be an etching. Preliminary internal scans returned no useful data. I am currently running a deeper analysis which may take up to a week."

Tom folded his arms. "So no news yet. I could have told you that by phone. OK if I go back to bed?"

"Just drink *your* coffee - I added two extra shots." Kate looked around. "I still don't understand why you choose to stay here. At Bern's mansion. Doesn't it give you the creeps?"

"My father is dead, and I don't believe in ghosts. For now it serves a purpose."

"OK. Although of the things Bern left you, it's the Accumulator I'm more worried about. Your brain was never designed to connect with all that electricity."

"My brain wasn't designed to do much of what I can now do, and yet I've found a path forward." He took a sip of his coffee, which was strong but only lukewarm. "Nothing about this is certain, nobody knows what is possible."

"I'm on your side, Tom. And I'm not the only one. There are people who care about you. About what's going on inside your head."

He rolled his eyes. "You mean Dominique."

"She's a friend."

"She's a scientist who wants to put me under the microscope."

"She wants to help you. The ones who want to put you under the microscope are the Americans."

"Banetti and his CIA crew? I've been trying to forget about them."

"Well they haven't forgotten you. They're also looking for your father."

Tom froze. "They actually believe he's still alive?"

Kate gave a snort. "I think they're just looking for a body. They're sweeping a grid in the Atlantic: potential crash sites for the helicopter."

"Good luck to them. The ocean is a big place, and there won't be anything left of him to find." He collapsed onto the sofa. "Even from beyond the grave, it feels like my father is toying with me. It's like he had some sort of ongoing plan."

"I thought he just wanted your Interface, and didn't care if he had to kill you to get it?"

Tom rubbed a hand over his forehead. "I *really* don't want to talk about it."

"You never do. But how the hell did you get better last year, after that dark nano was in you? Dominique said it was going to kill you. What aren't you telling me?"

Tom held up his hands. "After what I've been through, I think I get to decide what I share. Some things cannot be undone. I can't take this thing out of my head. I can't bring my friend Jo back to life. I can't make Bern suffer for what he did.

So I'm making a difference in my own way - and I wish you'd just accept that. Stop looking into my past."

"And yet, twelve months ago you told me exactly the opposite. You specifically asked me to investigate what happened with your mother, Amelia."

"You're right, I did." Tom leaned closer. "And I've changed my mind."

"Or did someone else change it for you?" Kate went to put her hand on his shoulder again, but Tom caught it. A sharp jolt of electricity lanced into his hand and he snatched it back.

"What the heck? What did you do?"

"I'm not like you, I can't *do* anything. That was just static." Her phone chimed and she glanced at it. "So Odie has found nothing. Maybe that means we should call in a real expert."

Tom stared at her. "Dominique is your answer to *everything*."

"In fairness, she has an answer to most things."

"We can manage without her..." Tom hesitated. "You already called her, didn't you?"

Kate blinked. "I may have done."

"And that message on your phone was her saying she's on her way."

"It may have been."

He narrowed his eyes. "Then I suppose we get ready for our special guest."

Kate gave him a broad smile. "You won't regret this."

"That remains to be seen."

ELEVEN

MIDDAY SUN STREAMED across the expansive lawns and through the windows of the lounge in what was formerly Bern's mansion. The late billionaire had apparently loved looking at this lawn so much he had installed banks of floodlights in the grounds so he could light it up in the middle of the night. It wasn't a feature Tom had had any reason to switch on.

Behind him he heard Kate's feet squeaking on the highly polished floor. "Dominique should be here soon. Although I don't know why you keep insisting on not inviting her into the pool house. She helped you install Odie."

"A moment of necessity. Where possible I prefer to keep a little distance between the illustrious Dr Lentz and my private sanctuary. If I wave all my systems under her nose, well it's just an invitation for her to meddle." Tom raised a hand sharply. "Speaking of which, it seems our guest has arrived. You can deactivate your suit, *Dominique*."

Across the room the air shimmered and Lentz blurred into view. "Just testing your powers of perception."

"Eavesdropping, more likely. Maybe this was a bad idea."

Kate put her hands on her hips. "We need her here

precisely because she has an enquiring mind. Dominique, if you could try not to goad our superhero."

"Superhero?" Lentz asked, straightening her glasses. "I don't see any costume. And certainly no cape."

Tom raised an eyebrow. "I'm in my alter ego persona. How did you travel here?"

"In a van I borrowed. I parked it outside the grounds so as not to draw attention. I do actually think about what's best for you, Tom."

"Of course you do. You thinking what's best for me has made me the man I am today."

Lentz raised her hands. "I came here at your request. You said you needed my help."

"You came here at Ms Turner's request. I had nothing to do with it."

Kate sighed. "Come on through to the dining room - we've got things set up in there. And I can make some Earl Grey if you like."

Lentz smiled. "Lead on."

LENTZ LET Tom lead her into the main dining room of William Bern's former mansion - a long, oak-panelled space dominated by an eight-metre oval dining table.

"I attended a conference yesterday, up at Cambridge. I ran into a scientist who used to work at CERUS Biotech, Dr. Edna Kim. Quite an authority on robotics, among other things."

Kate frowned. "Name rings a bell. But a lot of scientists have worked at CERUS over the years."

Tom sent a query to Odie over at the pool house. "Kim is in the personnel records. She left the company twenty years ago."

Lentz nodded. "She's gone on to better things. Intriguingly she offered me a job. Of course I turned her down."

"Well everyone does want to work with you." Kate tapped her on the arm. "I thought all the Resurface suits had been decommissioned. How come yours is still working?"

Lentz ran her fingers over the material of one arm. "I was able to broadcast an update to the majority to render them inoperable. Reems, with her epiphany on stopping new tech, wasn't keen on leaving potentially working models in the hands of anyone."

"Not even the Americans?"

"Particularly not them. Not after they shut us out from further analysis of the Phoenix Reborn, Bern's repurposed aircraft carrier. They recovered dozens of suits onboard, and wouldn't share any of them."

Tom folded his arms. "So how is yours still working?"

"I jailbroke it, so it was exempted from the OS update. I'm the only person I trust to use it safely."

"What if someone steals your suit and reverse engineers it? Isn't that still a risk?"

"It's impossible to steal, at least successfully. If the suit is taken more than five hundred metres from me, it will wipe."

"And what if they gain control of it? You know how I got locked in place in my suit."

"I do indeed. Which is why I built in a remote control - I have a subcutaneous implant in my wrist that can turn it off and on again, forcing new system protocols, which should confound any remote-control mechanism. Plus, if somehow they manage to prevent it being turned off, I have a number of passive trackers distributed within its fabric. They're not as good as active units, but they're almost impossible to detect, and I can find it within an area a few kilometres across."

"Good thinking," Kate said, "wouldn't you say, Tom?"

He shrugged. "As long as you can get to your wrist."

Lentz smiled. "I did think about putting a remote control in a false tooth, but then I thought if I can't get to my wrist, I probably can't get to pull out a tooth."

"You're joking?"

"The point is that the best gadgets are gadgets you always have with you. Gadgets they can't take off you, gadgets they don't even know you have."

Tom put a forefinger to one of his temples. "Nobody can take my gadget."

"Even if you wanted them to." Lentz turned towards a row of five laptops set up on the long table. "If we're going to play with computers, it would be great if you could help me with my Odie - Odie *Prime*, if you will. I'm still having issues with its core code."

"Perhaps you shouldn't have designed a computer that is too complicated for you to program."

"I like to push boundaries. Unfortunately I've pushed them too far."

"Not for the first time."

"Yeah, well it wasn't my intention. Odie's core chip is just too... complex. What would make it easier would be if you could talk to him in... its own language."

Tom shook his head. "After I got controlled in that suit a year ago, I'm a little wary of getting wrapped up in your tech again. I'm sure you understand."

"But that was totally different, and that involved... Bern. And I am not him." Lentz walked around the table and pulled out a dining chair to sit on. "I have only ever wanted to help you. To make amends for how technology I developed has been misused—"

"—Not misused. *Used*. And for exactly the purpose it was designed for."

"But with side effects we never foresaw."

"Then maybe you should have. And your method of trying to make amends is to ask more and more questions."

"Because I'm trying to learn from past mistakes. And I can't do that without accurate data—"

Kate cleared her throat. "Can we try a quick reboot? Turn it off and on again? Perhaps reinforced by a really strong cup of tea?"

Tom shrugged. "She's exactly the same as she was last time. Which is exactly why I didn't want her to come."

Lentz gritted her teeth. "I can only fix the future, I can't fix the past. At least not until my new time machine project is up and running." She tipped her head on one side and gave a half smile.

"Yes, well. I suppose you have a point."

"I usually do. So why *am* I here?"

Kate sat at the nearest laptop. "We came into possession of a bit of a puzzle." She looked at Tom. "You OK to discuss this?"

He pulled the orange plastic box from his backpack, placed it on the table and opened it.

Lentz leaned forward. "A metal ball?" She pulled out a scanner and waved it over it. "A solid metal ball, apparently made of steel? Did you need me, or a blacksmith?"

Kate folded her arms. "We think it's more than it seems. From the context in which we found it."

Tom nodded. "It might contain advanced tech. Although I've not detected anything so far, and neither has my Odie."

Lentz frowned and adjusted her glasses. "OK, get me a particularly strong cup of tea, and let's see what we can do."

TWELVE

LENTZ SAT at the dining table, drinking her second cup of Earl Grey, staring at her laptop's display and two external display screens. A range of visualisations were reporting the results of her initial tests. "I think," Lentz said, "that the sphere is not solid. Also it's not pure steel. It's an alloy, giving it a lower density."

"How can you tell?" Tom asked.

"I've run basic UT and ECT. Apparently I have better equipment than you do."

Kate folded her arms. "And those acronyms mean what?"

Tom blinked. "Ultrasonic Testing, and Eddy Current Testing."

Lentz nodded. "Sound waves and electromagnetic induction. Both indicate there is a void at the centre of the sphere, taking up perhaps twenty percent of its volume."

Kate frowned. "An empty space?"

"Well, that is the definition of a void. Although it could contain something, just much less dense than solid metal."

"Like what?"

"Electronics? Nanotech? I don't know. I'd need to run different tests."

"Can we cut it open?"

"Maybe, but it's not the first step." She pulled her own small form laptop from a pouch on her suit and started typing away. "Where did you say you got this thing from again?"

Kate puffed out her cheeks. "We didn't."

"I get the general need for secrecy. But I kept my own identity hidden for 20 years. You can trust me."

"It's not our call. Does it really matter?"

"Everything is a point of reference in the pattern analysis."

Tom gave a sigh. "It was the Ostard bank, in central London. I found it when I broke into their vault." He closed his eyes. "I'm sending you telemetry from the bank's security system."

"You hacked a bank's security systems?"

He shrugged. "It wasn't hard."

"And you knew this object was there?"

Tom shook his head. "It was supposed to be stolen CERUS nanotech. Instead we found this metal sphere."

Lentz stared at the main display that was showing a new scattergram. She pointed at the diagram. "This is a parse of the bank's data you provided. There was clearly an attempt at system penetration when you were inside."

"A hack?" Kate asked. "Not a glitch?"

"It was definitely external to the system. Someone else was trying to get into the vault that night."

"Someone was hacking the bank's main system?" Tom asked.

Lentz tipped her head on one side. "No, the vault itself."

"That's not possible. The vault system isn't online. If it had been, I'd have broken into it myself prior to going onsite."

"I hear you. But this data says the hack was real." She

called up a new page of data onscreen and pointed at it. "The interference pattern is undeniable."

Kate frowned. "Maybe they were successful. Maybe they changed the lockbox details. Which is why we recovered the wrong item."

Tom folded his arms. "Who did this hack? And how?"

Lentz shrugged. "I can't run that analysis here. And I can't do any more with the sphere. My laptop will only do so much."

"Are you hinting you want access to my Odie?"

"More than that, I'm afraid. We'd need to use Odie Prime."

"I thought you said you've been having configuration problems?"

"It's still the best tool we have. I'll just need your help to guide it."

Tom raised an eyebrow. "You seriously want me to connect my mind to another of your inventions?"

"Depends if you want results."

"So, we need to go to your place?"

"This isn't the 20th century - we can jack in remotely."

Tom shook his head. "Why does this feel like a set up? Why does it feel like you two planned this?"

"Come on," Kate said, "don't be like that. You need help. You can't do this alone."

"I'm the only person I can trust."

"If you can't get past that attitude, you're never going to solve this."

Tom closed his eyes. "This isn't easy for me."

"I get that. And you're not making it easy for any of us. But pull your head in."

"And pick the lesser of two evils?"

"However you want to rationalise it."

Lentz tapped her laptop. "Good enough for me. So let's get set up. If we can get it operational, we can more rigorously analyse the sphere and the hack of the bank vault. And maybe work out what is going on."

~

LENTZ SENT feeds from her laptop to the two wall displays. She directed Tom's attention towards a flexing and rotating pattern of dots, linked by fine lines that rippled in constantly changing patterns. "This is my Odie before it initiates." She pulled out a flattened set of strips which she shaped into a partial hemisphere, not unlike a cycle helmet. "This is what you're going to use to connect. To minimise the amount of energy you need to expend."

Tom studied the helmet. "Is Odie Prime truly an AI?"

"I mean it can seem a lot like your house system, your Odie. But under the hood there's a lot more capability - kind of 'same head, different body'. As for whether it's an AI? That's more philosophy than science. Let's call it an intelligent artificial construct. Whatever you name it, it is extremely powerful. And it is going to use that computing power to create a simulated environment for you to interact with."

"Like a video game?"

"That would be one application. But I'm going to use it to set up a virtual lab."

"A lab?" Kate asked. "Inside the system?"

"We already use computers to simulate a range of experiments - to save time and money. But this will be next level. We'll simulate the entire real-world environment. You'll interact using a virtual reality, or VR, interface – connecting via a helmet and gloves, in the future maybe a whole suit. You won't need to be a programmer to use it - just a scientist."

"So...," Tom said, "it's like a video game that does something useful?"

"It will enable real science. The artificial environment will be carefully adjusted to simulate real world properties. I can run experiments, but without the need to expend physical resources. It will be cheaper, faster, and safer, and I can run multiple instances to progress science more quickly - at least in the early stages of research. The only limits are computing power, and my ability to program it." She paused. "That latter part has been the real stumbling block."

Tom frowned. "What has this got to do with the bank being hacked?"

"The virtual environment is how you interact with Odie. It can guide you through a practical analysis. My working theory is that, if you hacked the vault, then the code touched you as well. We need to probe that connection and see where it leads us."

Kate cleared her throat. "And it isn't a risk to Tom?"

"Of course not." Lentz held out the helmet. "It's a simulation. You create the world, and you're in control. It's completely safe."

Tom took the flimsy device. "Just like having a chip put in my head. Just like wearing one of your suits?"

"OK, I acknowledge I don't have a great track record on that front. But this is different. And let's remember, you asked for my help. You want to find out what this sphere is. You want to find out what happened at the bank. This is how we do it."

"And if I die in there, do I die in the real world?"

She raised an eyebrow. "You've been watching too much sci-fi. Now have a seat."

Tom sighed and sat at the table. "I'm trusting you here, Dominique."

"I know." She helped him slip the helmet over his head. "And I appreciate that. And now it's time for you and Odie to start talking."

Tom closed his eyes and reached out.

THIRTEEN

IT WAS JUST after 8am in London's Hyde Park, and Stephanie Reems stood next to the sparkling waters of the Serpentine and a sign that read 'Please Don't Feed the Ducks'. As usual visitors to the park were choosing to ignore it, much to the delight of the overfed waterfowl. Those visitors also seemed to be ignoring her, which was why she often picked it as a meeting place: pleasant scenery, fresh air, and the anonymity of a crowd. What more could you ask for?

Her earpiece buzzed and one of her security team spoke curtly: "She's on her way over."

Reems leant on her walking stick and watched MI5 Deputy Director, Natasha Gifford, approaching from the east, accompanied by her two bodyguards. As she closed on Reems the security personnel peeled off, stationing themselves twenty metres distant.

"Hello Stephanie," Gifford said as she walked up, one hand straightening her close-cropped brown hair. "It was so nice of you to finally return one of my calls. One might almost think you've been avoiding me."

Reems shrugged. "A good boss knows when to get out of

the way of their team members. I've no wish to slow you down in your duties."

"And rest assured you have not. But I do like us to stay in touch, to stay 'aligned', and the occasional one-to-one can only help with that."

"A fair point. So, what have you got for me?"

"I thought you might want to review developments with Glifzenko and VoltTech? And their discussions with CERUS?"

"Those corporate vultures? I can't believe we let them through the doors - time wasters on a fishing expedition. They should be low on our list of priorities."

"Given the way the wind is blowing, that may be unwise." Gifford blinked. "Speaking of which, I've been hearing reports about you. About unusual behaviour."

Reems narrowed her eyes. "I wasn't aware I was being watched."

"Oh come now. We're all being watched."

"Yes, I suppose we are. Still, rumours aren't something you typically waste your time on."

"Not until they become persistent. So I made a few enquiries. It turns out that your movements are frequently unaccounted for." Reems started to protest, but Gifford raised a hand. "I'm just doing my job. And I won't let anything get in the way of it."

"To be clear, in my role as Director, I don't have to tell you everything."

"I can't help you if you won't bring me inside the circle of trust."

"Have you considered the rather obvious explanation that you don't have sufficient clearance."

Gifford hesitated. "Well now I am intrigued."

"That is who you are. That is why you were appointed Deputy Director."

"And I will do that job to the very best of my ability."

Gifford gave a flicker of a smile. "Have you made any progress in contacting Thomas Faraday?"

"Shocking as it may be to hear, Faraday isn't the only item on my priority list."

"No. But I'm sure he and CERUS Biotech are still on it. And probably quite high up."

"I acknowledge that the repercussions are still with us." Reems glanced around and lowered her voice. "I think I can share a little with you. I've been following up leads in relation to these technology auctions."

"Oh? The consensus was that those auctions were pure speculation. We ran detailed numerical modelling in our systems."

Reems snorted. "You and your predictive analytics. You think a computer is the answer to everything. You forget that most intelligence work is informed speculation."

"Maybe. Computers are really just a means, a medium, for analysing what is happening. It's numbers that are the magic."

"Well call me old-fashioned, but I still think people make the difference."

Gifford shrugged. "Maybe we're both right. And maybe if we follow both paths, we get something better yet. I always took you for a visionary. Someone who wanted to do things differently. Someone frustrated by the status quo."

"Who isn't frustrated by how things are?" Reems glanced at her watch. "Including how there are never enough minutes in an hour. Unfortunately I need to get moving. I have a—"

"—meeting? Yes of course you do. Well don't let me detain you any longer. Many thanks for your time, *Director*."

Reems began to leave, then turned back. "Natasha, we all want, one way or another, to change the world. It's how we do it that defines us."

REEMS SAT in the back of her SUV, with the privacy screen in place, reflecting on the meeting that had taken place, and on the complexities that it caused. But she did not get long to do it.

Her phone buzzed. Glancing down Reems saw it was not Gabriel Gates. It was someone she didn't want to talk to. "Hello?"

"Well?" asked a heavily modulated voice, synthetic from a disguiser unit. "How was she?"

"Pretty much as expected."

"We can't have her pushing ahead of the schedule. What about Faraday?"

"I'm wary of telling Tom too much."

"No, Stephanie, you must tell him everything. We want to see what he can really do."

"Aren't you pushing him hard enough? He nearly got caught at the bank."

"It was necessary," replied the voice.

"Or it's a sign I can't trust you. You're putting him at risk."

"We each want something from this - we can trust in that. And Tom is quite safe, yes?"

"For now. But he's asking questions."

"Make sure he doesn't get answers. At least not yet. Anyway, I have a session to prepare for. And you have to go and see an old friend."

"Is that still what she is?"

"She did save your life." The call disconnected and the last words echoed in Reems' head. *Perhaps it would have been better for everyone if she hadn't.*

FOURTEEN

JAVIER MENDEZ PULLED out his security card and placed it on the reader, opening the heavy metal doors to the space where only two people on the Rig had access. The room lay at the exact centre of Level One, closest to the lower hull. It was heavily shielded to protect the most important system anywhere in the facility.

He stepped into the square space, each wall precisely twenty metres in length. In the middle was a circular cluster of computer servers - dark grey blades illuminated by red, green and orange lights - humming with the power of processing.

"Hello, Max," Mendez said, walking over to a desk that took up most of one wall. At the very end, resting on a tripod stand, was a red metallic sphere the size of a volleyball.

"Greetings, Doctor Mendez," said a synthetic voice emanating from speakers arranged around the room. Five ultra-high-definition screens on the wall came to life, displaying system telemetry.

"Run a full weekly diagnostic. Include options 2 through 17—"

"That can wait," said a voice from behind him.

Mendez turned to see Frank Hatch - the only other person with access to this space - walking into the room. Mendez forced calm into his voice. "I didn't know we were meeting?"

Hatch adjusted his blue glasses, through which it was almost impossible to see his eyes. "I saw you were headed down here and thought I'd drop by."

"The benefits of constant tracking. You always know exactly where we all are."

Hatch slapped him on the shoulder, and Mendez grimaced. The Director was stronger than he looked. "Because you are so important to us. You promised us a super-computer, and," Hatch gestured around them, "you delivered."

"Max is a work in progress."

"Then let's put it to work. Korver is going to require some tactical support."

"There have been developments in London?"

"Our backer has been in touch." Hatch held out a secure drive. "This contains all the relevant data."

Mendez took the secure drive and placed it on a transfer pad next to the red metal sphere. Immediately there was a hum. "Processing should take about fifteen minutes."

"Good. Max is, very much, the heart of our operation. We couldn't operate without it."

Mendez cleared his throat. "Actually I don't think we're getting all the benefits we could be. Max has considerable excess capacity. It could run the entire Rig. Power, security, climate control, comms. We just have to give it the requisite access."

"As I've said before, I have no intention of introducing a single point of failure. I have no intention of handing control of my Rig over to..." Hatch paused, as if struggling with the concept, "*...a machine.*"

"But we could introduce significant efficiencies, reduce

headcount by more than 75%." Mendez hesitated. "I'm no economist, but I'm sure those are things you would want."

"Yes, yes. But call me old fashioned - I think a human being should be in command."

There was a beep from the screen and a timecode appeared. Mendez shrugged. "I was wrong. The data is going take a few hours to analyse."

"Oh? So not godlike quite yet?"

Mendez shook his head. "Max isn't going to take over. It isn't Skynet. But it is considerably more capable than any human. It is more efficient in almost every way. It can help you."

"Let's get through the next two weeks and talk again. We have significant new data and material coming onboard, followed by the next auction. Let's speak after that."

"But with the system's help, we could accelerate readiness for—"

Hatch raised an eyebrow. "*After.*" He turned to leave. "Please don't let me distract you any longer."

MENDEZ WATCHED HATCH LEAVE. By necessity there were no monitoring devices in this room. Mendez had been clear that such things might interfere with Max's operation – which probably wasn't true, but it provided a reasonable cover story.

He pulled out his communicator and made the connection. "Hello?"

"Hello again, Dr Mendez," said the voice. "Do you have news?"

Mendez closed his eyes. "When are things going to happen? The longer this goes on, the greater my chances of being found out."

"Have you enabled full Rig control?"

"Not yet. Hatch is proving reluctant."

"We've been more than clear about our position on the issue. You need to be resourceful."

"And you need to do more to help me. I'm risking everything for you, while you sit there fobbing me off. I don't know if I can do this alone."

"Why would you say that?"

"I didn't realise what I was getting in to, coming here. I made mistakes, because I was angry. They told me what I wanted to hear, and I closed my eyes to what I should have seen."

"But now your eyes are open, and you can see what needs to be done. That's why you got in touch. That's why you are the only one that can make this work. We believe in you, Javier. We believe you can do what is necessary." There was a long pause. "Notify us when it is done."

Mendez frowned and disconnected the call, then looked again over Max's reports. *How was he going to make this happen? He needed a miracle.*

FIFTEEN

TOM OPENED HIS EYES. He was standing in a plain grey room, a few metres across, with a single door opposite. Pale light came from all around.

Except he wasn't *standing* anywhere. This, he realised, was the virtual environment.

"Do you see a grey room with a door?" Lentz asked, her voice, like the light, coming from every direction.

"I do," Tom replied. "Although I must say I was expecting a little more imagination." He started directing his thoughts forward, seeing where else there might be.

"This is just an initiation layer – the bare minimum of an environment to act as an entry point. Give me a moment and I'll unlock the door so you can move on. You'll need the access key—"

Tom blinked and saw the door was standing ajar. "It's already open."

"What? How?"

"You tell me." He took a step forward. Or, rather, he felt like he had. He looked down and saw a grey form where his own body should be. He could still feel himself in the dining room, sitting on the chair. But it was distant, half like it was happening to someone else. This grey room was where he felt present.

"How did you get past the encryption so quickly?" Lentz asked.

"I don't know." Tom approached the door. "Shall I go through?"

"I guess. Tell me what you see."

"There's a... wait, you don't know?"

"I know what the system tells me it's displaying. But I can't see through your eyes in there any more than I can out here. I'd need my own interface to do that."

Tom pushed the door. As he touched it, there was a gentle buzz of vibration, as if his hand was being tricked into sensing touch. He looked around. "I'm in a similar room, but this one is a pale green. And it has no other doors. What do you want me to do now?"

"Consider this like a special effects 'green screen'. Apply an overlay. Turn the room into a laboratory of some kind."

"What? With test tubes and equipment?"

"Whatever you like, it doesn't really matter. It's just an exercise in you connecting to the system."

"So it's like applying a skin in a computer game?"

"I suppose. But don't think of it as playing around. If we get this right we can move on to the next stage and set Odie to analysing the hack."

Tom stared at the walls. They were so plain and featureless it was hard to judge their size or how far away they were. He visualised a white concrete wall with metal shelving in front of it.

Nothing happened.

He muttered and concentrated more specifically. White paint and metal. White paint and metal.

"Anything?" Lentz asked.

Tom sighed as his concentration was broken. "Can you just let me focus?"

"Sure. I'll wait for you to speak."

Tom began again. As he applied his thoughts, he involuntarily channelled a little energy from the Accumulator, hidden in the next room. In front of him the green wall began to blur and twist.

"Something's happening," Lentz said. "Whatever you're doing, do more of it."

Tom increased his draw of energy. In front of him the wall grew paler, turning from green to white. The outline of a metal frame began to solidify.

And then, as he channelled the power, somewhere, something responded. Something different from what he'd experienced before. Something... *unpleasant.*

"You're doing something right," Lentz said. "Odie is reporting that it's spinning up additional servers to support its internal matrix..."

Tom forgot about Lentz, and about the wall, and concentrated on this new element. It felt wrong. He focussed his thoughts, trying to understand it. There was an object. A complex, shifting point of difference – far away, and not in focus. "This is odd..." he started to say. But then the object began moving towards him. It was accelerating with purpose, screaming like a banshee, jagged like a broken razor, hot like fire. It was flying unerringly in his direction.

I am in danger, he realised. *I have to do something.*

He took a step back, then another. The object accelerated again, closing the distance. He could see it, but more than that he could smell it, even taste it.

It was darkness, malintent. It was corruption. It was... it was...

It was the sphere.

"Let me out!" he shouted. But there was no answer. There

was no one else there. There was only the danger. He turned to run. And yet, as he turned, somehow he was facing the same direction, looking at the sphere moving towards him. It had swollen to the size of a car but was still growing. Around him the world seemed to crack and buckle, straining at reality, blurring in and out of focus.

What are you?

He stared into the face of something immense. It was the size of a house. And it was upon him.

And it was too late to escape.

No, he thought with sudden determination, *it wasn't.* This was his environment. And he could decide when to leave.

Tom blinked and leaned back. Not in the system, but in the real world.

And in reality he felt his chair tipping.

Crying out he fell backwards, and the helmet slipped from him. And the environment, and the sphere, vanished.

SIXTEEN

TOM FOUND himself lying on the floor of the dining room, sprawled away from the tipped over chair.

Lentz stared down at him. "What happened? You cried out and flipped backwards."

Kate crouched close. "Did you hit your head? Do you feel dizzy?"

"I'm fine." Tom sat up. "I made myself do that. There was something in there. I needed to get out."

Lentz frowned. "*Something*? What do you mean?"

He shook his head, trying to focus. "It was... the sphere. But it was... *huge*."

"Maybe he's concussed," Kate said, looking more closely at his eyes.

"I said I'm fine." Tom waived her off. "It felt... dark. And... *incomprehensible*. It attacked me."

Lentz raised an eyebrow. "You were in a virtualisation. Whatever you think you saw, it wasn't real."

"It certainly felt real."

"It's just a test rig. I hadn't even started running any simulation." Lentz shook her head and turned back to her laptop.

"We'll look at the data. But I think perhaps your imagination has become a little overactive."

"I did *not* imagine it. I know what I saw."

"Except of course you didn't see it. It was an image your brain generated when connected to the system."

"Could it be the sphere that caused it?"

Lentz frowned then tapped another laptop. "There have been no signs of activity from it. If there had it would have triggered an alarm in real time."

"You mean no signs of activity you can detect."

"It was transmitting no electromagnetic radiation of any kind. I'm sure there is a sensible explanation for what happened..." She narrowed her eyes. "What is wrong with my Odie?"

Tom followed her gaze to a screen which was showing a self-diagnostic, littered with red flashing warnings. "That doesn't look good."

"No. Odie Prime's code has been corrupted." Lentz typed in a command and ground her teeth together. "It's behaving like a form of virus."

Kate folded her arms. "You don't have anti-virus software?"

"Nobody except me writes software for it – it has a totally unique design. But nobody writes malware either. Something else must have caused it."

"You mean it's a fault," Tom said.

"That would be on the short list of possible explanations." Lentz started flicking through the data. "It's fortunate the problem was contained. We certainly wouldn't have wanted the corruption propagating over." She hesitated. "You were right to get out, Tom."

"Are you saying it could have infected me?"

"I'm just saying it's possible."

Kate folded her arms. "You're saying Tom can be corrupted, like a computer system? He's human."

"But his brain has been augmented to include synthetic structures."

"So I'm *not* human." Tom folded his arms. "Good to know."

"You are, by definition, a cyborg – an organism that has enhanced abilities through the integration of technology. It's not an insult, it's a fact."

Kate shook her head. "Can you reinstall Odie from a clean backup?"

"It's an option, but it depends how far back the problem arose. Honestly, if Odie's system wasn't so unique I'd be investigating whether it has in fact been the subject of a hostile attack. But that would make no sense." Lentz picked up the helmet. "I guess we won't be trying any more today."

"Yeah, much as I want to know about the sphere, and to learn about who hacked the bank, I don't think I'm in a hurry to go into your system again."

"Then we'll have to tackle what happened at the bank the slow way. I'll start my other systems doing a more traditional data pattern analysis. This could throw out some clues as to who it could be, and how they did it."

Tom was about to reply when, in the back of his brain, something buzzed. It was a message. He stood up, blinking. "My Odie has spotted something, based on its analysis of telemetry from the bank. A company name has come up. *VoltTech.*"

"Come again?" Lentz asked.

"The multinational battery tech company. They're quite well known."

"Yes, I am aware of them, and their irritating CEO, Leon Smit. What's that got to do with anything?"

"Strands of the data link with them. It's faint, but it's there. I'm transferring it to your displays now."

"How would your Odie make that connection?" Lentz

stared at the screens. "You think someone at VoltTech, one of the largest companies in the world, was hacking a bank?"

"That's what Odie's further analysis of the bank data shows. Whoever this hacker is they were attacking both the VoltTech and the Ostard Bank."

Kate nodded. "That would make some kind of sense."

Lentz shrugged. "I wouldn't have thought your implementation of Odie had the processing power to draw this inference. But if this is right, how does it help us?"

Tom smiled. "It gives us somewhere to dig."

"You're saying you want us to hack VoltTech? To find out what they were looking for?"

"Maybe. Look, either they're a perpetrator or a victim."

Lentz shook her head. "If it's the latter, I wouldn't cross the road to help Leon Smit. He's a real piece of work. You shouldn't go anywhere near him or his company."

Tom raised his hands. "Whatever you say. You know best."

"I will acknowledge that is true a reasonable percentage of the time." She adjusted her Resurface suit. "I should get moving – you've given me a lot to think about."

Tom nodded. "See you around."

Lentz smiled and vanished.

AN HOUR later Tom and Kate had moved back to the pool house, having disconnected all the systems set up in the mansion house. Tom placed the Accumulator back in its storage case.

"So," Kate said, "care to tell me what really happened in there?"

"You think I kept something from Lentz?"

"I think you constantly keep lots of things from lots of people. Myself included."

He raised an eyebrow. "Then why would you believe my answer?"

"Because I'm your friend. What went on while you were in that simulation?"

"I told you, as best I understand it."

"So you saw a giant version of the sphere? What can that possibly mean?"

"I don't know. But I intend to find out."

"It could mean it affected you, that it harmed you. Perhaps you were overloaded by the connection?"

"That's not how it felt. That's not how it feels now."

"Then did it transfer data into you? Is that where you got the idea about VoltTech? Because it came out of nowhere."

"It came from my Odie. And I'm more interested in finding out what the VoltTech connection means."

Kate folded her arms. "When you said Lentz knew best, about not interfering with VoltTech, you didn't mean that, did you?"

Tom smiled. "Is this you feeling for the truth?"

"Call it a hunch. She just wants to help."

"Which I understand, given she is the person most singly responsible for me being in my present state."

"Can you honestly say you haven't grown to love being whatever it is you've become?

"If it lets me strike back against those doing things with experimental tech, then so be it. And in that vein, I'm going to stop them stealing from VoltTech."

"You're going to help Leon Smit? Why?"

"It's not about him. We can't have his tech out there and being sold to whichever bad actors can afford it."

"So what? You're going to break in, in the dead of night? Because that worked so flawlessly with the bank. And spoiler, one of the largest technology companies in the world will almost certainly have more advanced security systems."

"Then it's just as well I plan on walking in the front door, in broad daylight." Tom folded his arms. "I'll simply ask for a meeting."

"Why would they even spare you the time of day?"

"I might not be a lawyer anymore, but I know how to get a lawyer's attention. And Leon Smit will no doubt have plenty of them working for him."

SEVENTEEN

TOM WALKED AWAY from London Bridge railway station, crossing the road, and quickly navigating the crowd to reach the River Thames towpath. From there he turned east towards Tower Bridge.

Ahead of him, directly fronting the river, were VoltTech's London offices. They stood forty stories high and, aside from the more high-profile Shard, were the tallest structure in this part of London. VoltTech's building was a soaring design of curved glass and black steel that made CERUS Tower look outdated.

"I'm in position," Kate said, via the tiny transmitter in his ear. "And for the record, I still think we should have told Reems about this op."

"We will tell her. Just after we've found something useful. If she knew in advance, that might cause difficulties for her."

"I don't think the concept of an operation being illegal has ever caused Reems any difficulty. If she agreed on the goal, she'd be behind it."

"Perhaps." There was the low thump of rotors from above. To the west he saw a helicopter approaching along the line of the Thames. "Although she's not entirely predictable these days."

"Focus on what you're here to do, Tom," Kate said. "You need to not give any clues as to who you really are, and what you can do."

"I left the Accumulator behind, didn't I?"

"After much debate."

"Of course one could argue I'm in danger without it."

"Tom, please. You put that metal sphere in your secure cabinet as well?"

"I did. Now I'm going to go offline. Can't have them spotting my earpiece."

"I'll be close by if you need me."

"Good to know. But I think I can handle a simple meeting with a lawyer." He reached into his ear, removing the transmitter. Then he adjusted his suit and walked up to the front doors of the VoltTech building.

Time, for one day, to be his old self.

THE CONFERENCE ROOM was on Level 19, and had an entire wall of floor to ceiling windows. The main conference table was elliptical and over ten metres long. A silver tray with a double espresso and a glass of orange juice waited on the table in front of him. When he asked the waiter how they knew what he would want, the man just smiled and left. Tom took a sip of the coffee and smiled inwardly. Big important meeting rooms and great coffee - just like old times, he thought. And then he caught himself. Being a lawyer seemed like such a long time ago.

"Tom Faraday, it is good to meet you." A slender woman, wearing a very expensive pale blue suit, walked towards him and shook his hand. Her white blonde hair reached nearly to her waist. "I'm Juliana Sorenson, VoltTech's UK General Counsel."

"Thank you for seeing me on such short notice."

"No, Tom, thank you." She turned round and gave a hand signal. Someone pulled the doors closed. "I understand you've uncovered evidence that VoltTech's digital infrastructure has been the target of a cyber intrusion."

"That's correct."

She gestured to one of the seats. "And how did you come by this information?"

Tom blinked. "It came up tangentially in the context of advising a client. To say more would risk breaking privilege."

"A straitjacket we must all work within."

"Coming to you today seemed like the compromise solution – off the record, obviously."

"Of course. And I won't argue it was fascinating to get your call. In my twenty years as a lawyer, I've not seen anything quite like it."

"Every day sends us new challenges."

"Quite." She stared at him. "My first inclination was to call the police."

Tom swallowed. "Oh? How long did it take you to change your mind?"

"Sorry, perhaps my turn of phrase was misleading. I went with my inclination." The meeting room doors were flung open and two uniformed police officers walked in.

Tom stood up. "What is going on?"

Sorenson drummed her fingers on the table. "You call and want to warn VoltTech of a security threat? You won't give further details and insist on a meeting in person? And when we check you out, we find you're just some lawyer we've never heard of, without a firm behind him? The most recent place we can see you worked was notorious CERUS Biotech. So, Mr Faraday, our obvious thought is that any threat comes from you." She nodded to the two figures in uniform. "The authorities can handle this."

Tom looked around. He started to reach out, to see what he could do to change the situation. To turn the tech in the building to his advantage. But with the encryption he would face, and without the Accumulator, it would be a challenge. He didn't have long to think about it.

"Of course," said a new voice, "this company didn't get where it is today by doing the obvious thing."

A figure in a casual grey suit appeared in the doorway. He was a little under six feet in height, a little overweight, and he walked in like he owned the place. Which, Tom thought as he recognised him, he did. Or at least he owned more shares than anyone else. It was Leon Smit, the CEO and founder of VoltTech. He was, according to Forbes, one of the twenty richest people on the planet – someone against whom William Bern would have been rated a mere shopkeeper. Smit's exact net worth varied greatly from day to day, depending on the vagaries of his share price, his random statements to the press, and the developments at his various companies, the largest of which was VoltTech.

He adjusted his suit jacket, then glared at the two men in police uniform. they shrugged and quickly walked out.

Tom frowned. "What? The police work for you?"

Smit gave a snort. "Just some actors we hired. I wanted to see your reaction." He nodded to his in-house lawyer. "You can go too."

"I really should stay, Mr Smit. We don't want to—"

"But I *do* want to. Don't worry, I'll try not to say anything particularly stupid."

Sorenson nodded and left, pulling the doors closed behind her.

Smit walked around the table until he reached the far end. "So, Mr Faraday. You and I are going to have a little chat."

EIGHTEEN

HEAVY GREY CLOUD hung over the Herefordshire countryside, blotting out any light from the moon. Dominique Lentz, clad in a grey Lycra suit, made her way down the broken stoney path, ducking under brambles and between nettles, picking her way by the light of her LED headset. A glance at the HUD provided by her glasses told her she was nearly a minute ahead of her best time for this route – although the final hill back up to her house was a challenge that could derail any personal best attempt.

But even as she felt her heart rate rise, her thoughts turned again to her visit to Bern's mansion yesterday, to her meeting with Tom and Kate. The outcome of Tom's interaction with her computer didn't make sense. Odie Prime was now restored from backup, but she had kept its corrupted state for further analysis. Had the system malfunctioned? It was possible, but that it would do so at the moment Tom was connected was strange. So had there been external action? Or had someone done something to it? Almost nobody in the world would have the requisite knowledge of Odie's structure to do so, yet there were odd traces in the code that she could not explain. And while science was full of things one could not explain, this was particularly troublesome. She had got quite distracted from studying the sphere, had not been able to analyse Tom, and of course was now only more confused by the events that had happened at the bank.

As a first step she had tasked Odie Prime with building a firewall to prevent a repeat of such an attack, and also to look into reverse engineering what happened, so as to be able to reflect the incursion back at the adversary. Odie said it was achievable, but it would take a few days to complete.

Lentz slowed at a gate, held shut with a loop of old rope, let herself through and closed it behind her. She set off again on the stoney path, picking her way around a particularly uneven section. Then, as she dropped off the stoney path onto a single-track gravel road, her phone sent a soft ping in her ears. An alarm, triggered by her home security systems. Someone was at her house. Was it a threat? Was it time to call in an emergency care package so she was equipped to deal with it? Her smart glasses relayed an image. Three large black SUVs with darkened glass were parked in her driveway. Lentz sighed and turned towards that final hill climb. Her uninvited guest wouldn't like being kept waiting.

She made it home ten minutes later, her legs burning, passing between the high metal security gates that already stood open. She crunched up the gravel drive to what had once been a tumbledown single storey house, but through a series of extensions and enhancements was now approaching something you might almost call a mansion.

Stephanie Reems stood leaning on her walking stick, watching Lentz approach. Two large, suited figures from her security detail had taken up position next to the three SUVs, seeming to look everywhere and nowhere at the same time.

"What a pleasant surprise," Lentz said, switching off her running tracker. "Were you just passing by?"

"Something like that. I like what you've done with the place. Much more befitting the CEO of a major organisation." Reems tapped her walking stick. "The access ramps are a nice feature; in case I decide to opt for a wheelchair."

"I've been making a few upgrades."

"A few?" Reems raised an eyebrow. "From the reports I've read, you've rebuilt from the ground up. It seems we've been paying you too much at CERUS."

"Or, perhaps, given what I've been through over the years, not nearly enough. Can I offer you something to eat?"

"No, thank you. But a cup of tea would be most welcome." She gave a signal to the men in suits and began walking towards the house. "Shall we?"

"Of course." Lentz replied with a sigh. "Make yourself at home."

NINETEEN

TOM STARED at the man in front of him. Smit was based in New York, although VoltTech's head office was outside of San Francisco. Had he really made the journey to London just because of Tom's message? "You like to make an entrance. I presume that was your helicopter arriving a little while back."

"I don't have time for traffic." Smit laced his fingers together. "Now why are you here?"

"There's an ongoing cyber intrusion attempt on VoltTech."

Smit raised an eyebrow, unimpressed. "That's hardly news. We're a prime target. And because of that, we are well defended. What's different this time?"

Tom's expression hardened. "It's not your standard script kiddies or a botnet attack. They're using sophisticated tactics. This isn't just about data theft; it's a systematic attempt to infiltrate and possibly cripple your core systems."

Smit shrugged. "If that were the case, I would be notified within thirty seconds."

"Sure. Unless your systems don't know what to look for." Tom reached into his pocket and removed a secure hard drive which he placed on the table. "This has everything I found. Give it to your people. Have them investigate."

Smit leaned forward, all trace of laughter gone from his face. "What is going on here? You're a lawyer, not a security expert." He picked up his phone, tapped a sequence of instructions, then held the phone over the hard drive. There were a sequence of clicks, then a soft, warm tone. He frowned and whistled loudly. Almost instantly the doors opened and the waiter that brought Tom his espresso reappeared. "Get this to the security escalation team right away," Smit said, handing him the drive. "I want to know everything about it."

The man nodded and left.

Tom raised an eyebrow. "Does that mean you believe me?"

"Perhaps." Smit shrugged. "I saw that you used to work at CERUS Biotech. Tell me about it."

Tom returned the shrug. "There's not much to know."

"But how does the saying go? The absence of information is still information."

"I think you'll find that the absence of information is absence."

Smit stared at him. "Do you know my secret, Tom? It's not that I understand tech - I mean, I do, but only to a certain degree. For the complicated stuff I have scientists and engineers, who are way more capable than me. No, my special talent is that I understand people. I know how to pick the ones to trust. The ones who are brilliant. And the ones that will do whatever I tell them, no questions asked."

"Which am I?"

"I haven't decided yet. What did they think of you at CERUS? Did you ever meet the great William Bern?"

Tom's cheek twitched. "I prefer not to discuss it. His company didn't treat me well."

"So, you're a disgruntled former employee. I've had a few of those over the years. They make for fascinating hires. Are you looking for a job?"

"I've found I like being my own boss."

"Ah, but everyone has a boss. Even I have a board that I answer to." He paused. "You think your intel is going to check out, I can see it in your eyes."

"I'm not here for my own amusement."

"Then why did you give it to me for nothing? You must have an angle." Smit's expression darkened. "Is this some type of con?"

"We have a common interest: I'd rather your technology isn't free, floating around in the world. In particular, the secret stuff that I'm sure resides in the laboratories not listed on your balance sheet."

Smit stood up. "You say you're here to help, but that sounds suspiciously like a threat."

"There was always the rumour that Bern had such locations. My working theory is he was far from the only one to have them. Tell me I'm wrong."

"Are you sure you're not trying to get a job?" Smit looked thoughtful. "When I looked you up, I dug a little deeper than most. And I found out *exactly* who you are. Which is why I came to meet you today."

Tom felt his skin prickle.

"I know William Bern was your father. Don't try to deny it."

"I only deny it to myself. We weren't close."

Smit snorted. "I mention it because clearly the way you got what is on that drive is connected with Bern, or CERUS technology." He snapped his fingers. "Are you hacking the intelligence services?"

"I'm not that capable. Or that stupid."

"Then are you working *with* the intelligence services?"

Tom rose to his feet. “I can see this was a bad idea. I’m sure we both have better things to be doing.”

Smit folded his arms, an expression of decision on his face. “I’d like to show you something. Something I think you’ll find interesting. Something... groundbreaking.”

“You have labs here?”

“Not exactly a lab. And not here. Ever been in a helicopter?”

Tom raised an eyebrow. “A couple of times.”

Smit smiled. “Then you’ll be right at home.”

TWENTY

LENTZ BREWED a fresh pot of tea in her newly refitted kitchen, then joined Reems at the four-metre-square granite-topped table. "Nice of you to call ahead," she said as she poured into two large white mugs. "You're lucky I've only got as far as installing motion sensors. The gun turrets won't be online until next month."

"Consider me warned. My travel schedule is necessarily opaque, plus not calling meant you didn't get enough notice to avoid me." Reems took a sip of her tea then looked around. "I thought you had a new dog?"

"Ratchet has been staying with a neighbour while I've been making some trips, and I only got back last night. Did your last report on my activities not provide that detail?"

"Evidently it was overlooked. I'll make sure someone gets fired for such slackness." Reems shifted in her seat, grimacing briefly.

"Do you need something for your—?"

"—pain? Don't you worry about that."

Lentz nodded. "Look, I'm still so sorry about last year. If I could have got there even a moment sooner—"

Reems raised a hand. "It's because you didn't get there a moment later that I'm even able to have this conversation."

"I suppose. It's just one of the things that weigh on my mind, that I've had time to contemplate while I've been away from the office." Lentz paused. "I'm not ready to come back yet, if that's what you're here to pressure me about."

"It's been twelve months. The world won't wait for you to find yourself, Dominique. CERUS will move on. Is that what you want?"

"I became a scientist to help people. People like my sister, Elena. Somehow I got distracted. I've been wasting my time dealing with corporate nonsense. And because of what my company ended up doing, many people died. I've done more harm than good—"

"You weren't even there for most of that, so I hardly think much of the blame falls anywhere near you. What about all the issues only your brilliant mind can tackle? The world needs you."

"I used to think that."

"What about George Croft's daughter? She's alive because of your work."

"I'm not sure if I'm taking the same lesson from that as you are. What I want to do is take all the lessons learned from that course of treatment, and to focus in, to explore the possibilities. There is so much potential in regenerative treatments - repairing or replacing tissue and even organs damaged by disease, or trauma, or just old age."

"It is exciting, that's my point."

"And my point is I'd like to focus on that alone, to heal rather than to harm. Also, with all that in mind, did you really have to put Croft in prison?"

Reems spread her arms wide. "He broke the law. He betrayed his country. And it doesn't change my point about how you helped his little girl. Your brilliance is what we need."

"I found the research in the CERUS archives. Something our favourite most-wanted person helped me locate in caches of material I did not know existed. You should ask him for help."

Reems picked up her teacup. "You know how Tom feels about me."

"Yeah, I suppose I shouldn't expect that you would be speaking." Lentz scratched her nose. "I barely see him myself. I still don't know exactly how he's still alive, after what happened last year. He refuses to discuss it."

"He's a law unto himself. You know that."

"But he's getting worse. He's still so angry about CERUS, even with his father gone. I'm worried for him. I'm worried *about* him."

"You think he's dangerous? You're starting to sound like Banetti."

Lentz took a sip of her tea. "Then it might be the only view we share. Did you ever learn why the Americans bombed the Dome? You were there, with the CIA Deputy Director. What exactly went on?"

"My memory of that day is hazy at best. Things got very messed up."

"What about Peter Marron and his daughter?"

Reems shrugged. "Vanished from the face of the earth. A lot of people died at the Dome. Or afterwards. Maybe them too."

"Maybe." Lentz put her cup down. "Bern is really gone?"

"You were involved in Tom's debrief. Are you saying he was lying?"

"I don't know why he would. Plus you told me that satellite and forensic evidence supported his story."

Reems sighed. "Look, Dominique, fun as it is to chat, let me get to the point. We need you back in the game. We need your problem-solving intellect. And we need it right now."

"And as I just said - quite explicitly, I believe - I'm not

ready to come back yet. Maybe I never will be. I'm thinking that I'll look more into medical nanotechnology. We saw what it did for Croft's daughter, and it can do so much more. It could help you." Lentz pointed at Reems' walking stick.

"I would have preferred it was there to help my son. Or my husband. But it's too late for them."

"It's not too late for others."

"OK, sure, that's a commendable long-term goal. But when I say we need you, I'm talking about right now, and I don't mean you should come back to CERUS. I happen to think that you're well out of that place."

Lentz blinked. "What makes you say that?"

"You clearly haven't been paying attention to all that corporate nonsense. Natasha Gifford has invited Glifzenko in to drive collaborations around nanologicals and smart drugs."

"And share our tech with them? I don't think so! Glifzenko have been fishing around CERUS and our people for years. Kate used to get a call a week trying to poach her."

Reems smiled. "I was sorry that she left the team. She was a real talent. At least she didn't end up with the opposition."

Lentz rotated her cup of tea. "Her leaving caught me off guard, and it's another reason I'm in no hurry to return. I have nobody who has my back."

"Other than me?"

"You're not exactly 'on the ground' on a day-to-day basis. Aren't you supposed to be on medical leave?"

"They keep telling me that, and I keep ignoring them. Someone has to keep Gifford in check."

"The *deputy* director? Doesn't she work for you?"

"It's complicated. And she's relentless - half charging bull, half accountant."

"Quite an image. But you said you want me back for another reason? The reason, presumably, that you drove out to see me."

Reems nodded. "We have an urgent problem, requiring your very particular set of skills."

Lentz looked across the kitchen table. "Have I not made my position quite clear?"

"This is an emergency."

"There's always an emergency. I could have given you my answer on the phone. You didn't have to waste your time coming all the way out here."

"I thought in person I might persuade you of the criticality."

Lentz ran a hand through her hair. "I don't want to get involved in that nonsense again."

"Yes, yes. Quit the rat race and go live in a commune, heal the world if you can. I don't care. As long as you help me now, with one important thing - I have a malfunctioning computer." Reems narrowed her eyes. "A very advanced, very broken, computer."

"Then get one of your technicians to look at it. You do have those at MI5, I assume?"

"None of whom are up to the task. We need you, Dominique. If there was anyone else I could ask, believe me I would."

"What makes you so sure I can help here?"

"Because you're you. So spare me the false modesty and let's get on the road."

Lentz stared at Reems. "I'm not doing it Stephanie. I'm drawing that line in the sand. You can't make me cross it."

"This isn't about sand, but it is about silicon. Well technically carbon nanotubes, but that's not the issue. We're not even clear whether it's a hack or a fault. But whichever it is, we're in a lot of trouble. And the clock is ticking."

Lentz folded her arms. "And this is MI5's system?"

"Not exactly. It's a... special project. Sandboxed and only

accessible on site. You have to come see it. I can't tell you any more here."

"Maybe in the past I would have bent to your will. But I am not going to get drawn back into your world. I am out, and I am staying out." Lentz raised her hands. "That's my final answer."

Reems rose to her feet, a grimace on her face. "I have only 65 hours to solve this. Do you not believe me, or do you just not care?"

"It's no longer my job to fix everything. It's time someone else took a turn."

"In my thirty years at MI5, I can tell you this is among the most critical moments the joint intelligence agencies have faced." Reems banged her stick on the floor. "In 65 hours my life's work is going down the drain, and you won't lift a finger to stop it." She turned to begin walking back towards the front door, then paused. "You know, if you're not going to commit to CERUS, you should go ahead and actually quit. Give CERUS a chance to get someone new in place before they get acquired."

"You're saying someone is going to buy CERUS?"

"You have been out of the loop. Maybe you should actually call by the office and find out." Reems started walking again. "Goodnight, Dominique."

TWENTY-ONE

KATE SAT in Gables Coffee shop, one of three that had an unobstructed view of the VoltTech building. She took a sip of her decaf coconut latte, then returned her gaze to her laptop screen.

The link Tom had uncovered to VoltTech was making her think. She'd undertaken research on the company during the last year - one of dozens of businesses she'd 'kicked the tyres' of, but at the time nothing had flagged as being worthy of further investigation. But if someone else was hacking them, did that mean she had missed something? She called up her old file of notes and began refreshing her memory.

Smit was a US citizen, the son of Hungarian immigrants who had moved to the States before he was born. He had been unremarkable at school, before dropping out of college to start his first company. That startup rode one of the tech waves, was bought out by a social media giant, and Smit took the not inconsiderable proceeds and parlayed them into a much greater fortune. He had, as many would describe it, left all the chips on the table. And he had kept winning.

Now VoltTech was one of the world's three biggest manufacturers of smart batteries, and few were betting it wouldn't become the biggest. Smit had invested in a number of experimental 'fringe science' projects - he had publicly stated his goal was to spend 10% of revenue on such things, because this spend would create foreseen and unforeseen opportunity - a good example being $500 million invested into a cryogenic and cryonic research company.

Smit had made approaches to William Bern three years ago - attempting to buy or license CERUS technology. A series of meetings followed, but Bern and Smit clashed and it didn't happen. Still, knowing what she did about Bern and Smit, a clash had probably been inevitable.

Kate glanced at her messages app. There was nothing from Tom. She looked up and across the pedestrian space, to the rotating glass doors providing entry to VoltTech's main foyer. Was he going to be OK? After what had happened at the bank, she wasn't her most relaxed, but it seemed there was nothing she could do for now, except to keep working.

So she started skimming her other research files on old CERUS Biotech projects that even Lentz had not heard of, including Project Reflow, a proposition for self-replicating nano that Bern had axed for being too risky. Other initiatives touched on cryonics, robotics, and nanotech, some proposing the enhancement or replacement of human limbs and organs, or powerful boosts to healing capabilities. There were traces of other projects where all she had was a codename: Project Osiris, Project Neutrino, Project Blackstar, Project Quark. Where were the records for these kept? Were they solely internal, or collaborations with others? With governments or private companies? She still sought so many answers.

Kate's phone rang. Did Tom have a problem? But it was Lentz. "Hey, what's happening?"

"Can you talk?" Lentz replied.

"I'm in a coffee shop near London Bridge Station, so I wouldn't exactly call this location secure."

"Then we should meet later. I'm heading into the office."

"CERUS Tower? Aren't you on a sabbatical?"

"Something's come up with CERUS. Something urgent enough to drag me away from trying to work out what went on with Odie. And with Tom. And yet it all feels like a distraction." There was a pause. "Do you ever regret leaving?"

"CERUS? I regret not leaving earlier. You were what kept me there as long as I was."

"That's kind of you to say. Since you left it hasn't been the same, but I'm wondering if the change is accelerating."

"You sound like you have something on your mind."

"I usually do..." Lentz hesitated. "Wait, you're near Tower Bridge? You aren't going to the offices of a certain battery manufacturer?"

"*I* am not."

"Seriously? Tom is a total loose cannon."

"If you have a cannon, fire it," Kate replied. "At least that's what my college basketball coach used to say."

"You played basketball?"

"Until I switched to focus on karate. I couldn't get the hang of a non-contact sport."

"If you think basketball is non-contact, you weren't playing it right. Anyway, I'm hitting traffic, so I'd better stop talking. I'll ping you later."

Kate put her phone down, then realised there was the sound of helicopter rotors above. She was about to look outside when her laptop chirped with a message. It was from Tom.

Change of plan.

"Oh?" she typed. "All OK?"

I'm not sure. You hear that helicopter?

"Hard to miss."

Well I'm in it. How quickly can you get to these coordinates?

She located what he sent to her on a map, and her eyebrows rose. "Not as quick as you," she typed, "but I'll see what I can do. Should I contact Reems for support?"

Not for the moment. See you there.

Kate closed her laptop, then reached under the table and grabbed her motorcycle helmet. She had a very fast bike. It was time to see just how fast.

TWENTY-TWO

IT WAS NEARLY lunchtime as Lentz slowed her Citroen 2CV to a halt next to the automatic barrier. She glanced up at the familiar glass and steel form of CERUS Tower, which she had not seen for twelve months. The building still gleamed in the sunlight, but how much had things changed within?

Lowering the window, she held out her ID card to the scanner, so she could enter the underground car park. The barrier did not move, instead making an angry buzzing sound.

A security guard appeared from a nearby kiosk and frowned at her. "Do you have an appointment?"

"Really?" Lentz asked. "Is that some kind of a joke?"

He shook his head. "Visits by appointment only."

"You must be new here or you'd have recognised your Chief Executive Officer."

He blinked then looked at his tablet computer and started jabbing at the screen with two fingers. "The system didn't allow you through, so I presumed..."

"Override it."

He held up the screen, flicking his gaze from it to her face and back.

"It really is me. And I'd like to go up to my office if it's not too much trouble."

The guard stepped forward and inserted a key into the barrier. It rose smoothly and he nodded to her. With a sigh she drove past and began descending to the first basement level where her reserved space was located. Behind her she thought she saw the guard making a phone call, his expression wary.

She hadn't even got back into the building, and already she had the feeling that something was wrong.

LENTZ HAD a similar issue with the lift system not recognising her, but the quick entry of an old sixteen-digit override code resolved that problem. She was going to be having some hard words with the new building administrator. Suitably commandeered, the lift whisked her to her 90th floor penthouse office suite. When she stepped into the lobby area her PA, Sandra, was looking at a holiday brochure while distractedly picking at a salad.

"Quiet day?" Lentz asked, half a smile on her face.

"It is my break," Sandra replied, only half looking up. "Thanks for interrupting it."

"First time I've done it in a while."

"I guess. Anyway, lunch is set out in your office. Maybe eat while you work through your mail." She paused. "You have a lot of mail."

Lentz frowned. "I haven't been in for twelve months and I didn't tell you I was coming in. So how did you know to order lunch? Or have you done it every day, just in case? Because that would be a lot of wasted sandwiches."

"You had a meeting in the system, so I presumed that you'd be honouring us with your presence. As for the food, maybe your guest made the booking?"

"What meeting? What guest?"

Sandra beckoned to the door to the CEO's office. "Knowing her it's a surprise."

Lentz's brow furrowed and she pushed open the door. On a side table was a platter of sandwiches and sushi, along with jugs of juice and a cafetiere of coffee. Lentz ignored them, her eyes shifting to her desk. There was someone sitting in her chair - a short woman with close cropped brown hair. She wore what she always wore - a suit that could have fitted better.

Natasha Gifford, deputy director of MI5, looked up from a document she was reading. "Dr Lentz, it is lovely to see you."

"I'd say make yourself at home," Lentz gestured at her desk, "but clearly that went without saying."

Gifford stood up and walked over. "You have left it rather vacant the past twelve months. Thankfully your delegates on the executive team have been covering for you admirably."

"That's why I appointed them. But now I'm back. Although I'm curious to know how you knew."

"A happy coincidence." Gifford paused. "Did you get any of my messages?"

"I'm not good with messages. Ask Reems."

"I often try to. Well CERUS Biotech is not an organisation that can rest on its laurels, whatever the extenuating circumstances. Decisions need to be made about its future direction, and this company is necessarily bigger than any one person. Regardless of your own situation, the world has not stood still."

"It never does. Which is why I needed some time away."

"I understand. But without question we could have used you here sooner. There have been those who questioned your commitment."

"If only they knew about what happened in Canada." Lentz sighed. "I hear there's talk of a collaboration with Glifzenko?"

"Many would say they're a company, with a solid track

record of innovation. CERUS would certainly benefit from a sharing of approaches."

"It would be a mistake. Glifzenko just wants to misdirect its competition. To help tailor its intelligent pharmaceuticals."

"To make them more effective. Would that be so wrong?"

"Drugs are the old world. Nano is the new. And CERUS needs to be in the middle of it, steering its own path. We're going to actually do some good. We're going to take the tech we've developed and apply it to projects that actually save lives, or greatly improve them. It was what drove me to science in the first place, and finally I can actually make it happen. I will see this through."

"And you think there's money in that?"

"It is the right thing to do. And that means we should rebuff Glifzenko."

"Actually we did. But someone else has made an offer for the CERUS Biotech business. Subject to a few technicalities, the government has accepted."

Lentz hesitated. "What? Did that go to the Board? Or the shareholders?"

"Under the shareholders' agreement, the government has special unilateral rights to approve any deal. Plus it was a cash offer - more than generous given CERUS' recent troubles. Exiting at this point makes sense for the British taxpayer. And also for the Security Service. We cannot countenance the ongoing risk."

"Do you have any idea what another company might do with CERUS' tech? They'll ruin—"

"The buyer has significant experience at operating in a highly regulated environment. They'll bring modern corporate governance and accountability to the company. They will make it work right."

"And you haven't involved me at all? I can't believe Reems signed off on this."

Gifford crossed her arms. "This was the Home Secretary's call."

Lentz blinked. "This is a huge mistake."

"The numbers made the decision clear."

"Sometimes numbers can oversimplify things. What made you take me out of the decision process? In case you'd forgotten, I am the CEO."

"I'd say that is something you've forgotten. But that is a useful segue to another point: the buyer has a number of conditions, one of them being that you leave the company immediately."

Lentz's eyes hardened. "I'm being fired?"

"That's not how I'd frame it. We're recommending that you accept the proposal put forward. It's in the folder on your desk."

"And if I don't accept?"

Gifford raised an eyebrow. "Don't make this unpleasant."

"I'm not the one making it unpleasant. Why would this buyer want to get rid of me? As much as anyone else still alive, I am CERUS. I'm the only person left who worked on many of its projects."

"What you did in the past is a decidedly grey area. They feel they can't trust you." She folded her arms. "And your conduct up to, and during, the Canada incident raised more questions than it answered. You kept Reems in the dark on a number of projects - for what reason, we can only guess. But once trust is gone, it's gone."

Lentz glared. "You're having fun here."

"I just follow the numbers."

"That doesn't make you right. I don't accept it."

Gifford shrugged. "We're going to need you to clear your desk by the end of the day. And also to return all and any CERUS company property and data that you may have in the next 48 hours. For example, any remaining Resurface suits that you haven't seen fit to declare." She picked up a bottle of juice and twisted the cap. "We'll be monitoring you closely to ensure compliance."

"After everything that I've done, this feels personal."

"CERUS is much bigger than any one person. Remember that. Now if you'll excuse me, I have another meeting to get to. You can show yourself out."

LENTZ LOADED the cardboard box containing her personal effects into her car. The security guard she had seen on arrival stood watching her, a faint smile on his face.

"Seems I won't need to remember your face next time."

"Yes," she replied, "you're the comedian today. But maybe you'll come to regret that I'm no longer in charge."

He shrugged. "You have a good day now."

Lentz drove out under the barrier. She then made a secure call on the car's inbuilt comms system.

"Change of heart?" Reems' voice asked immediately. "At least I hope that's why you're calling."

"I went into CERUS Tower an hour ago. An unannounced visit, my first in months. Yet Natasha Gifford was already waiting in my office."

"Why?"

"Someone has bought CERUS."

"Did she give you a name?"

"Not Glifzenko. Other than that, she wouldn't say."

"What else *did* she say?"

"Not much. Except that my services are no longer required."

"You've been fired?"

"I'm not sure what surprises me more. That I've been fired,

or that you didn't know. What is going on? Doesn't she work for you?"

"After my injuries last year, she was given some direct reporting lines into the Home Office, and she's managed to keep hold of them. Her approach - her use of easily understood numbers, and their financial ramifications - it resonates with the politicians and the civil servants."

"You have to stop the sale. CERUS's archives were dangerous enough when controlled by us. Who knows what this new owner will do?"

Reems coughed. "It appears the 72-hour timer isn't the only deadline I face. If this deal is actually being approved without my input, then I am apparently on the way out."

"Nonsense," Lentz replied. "But maybe I should come and help you with this computer."

"Because someone else put your nose out of joint? That's all it took?"

"Do you want me to change my mind? Or are you going to tell me where I need to go?"

Reems gave a laugh. "Best I show you. I'll have a car pick you up at rendezvous point *seven*."

Lentz rolled her eyes. "Is that subterfuge really necessary?"

"When you see what I have here, you'll know why."

Lentz switched off her phone and pulled open the modified secure glovebox. Neatly folded inside was her Resurface suit, and a fresh power pack.

Was it worth taking the risk that Reems might detect it? Or was it better to make sure she was ready to respond if the situation got *tactical*?

It didn't take her long to decide.

TWENTY-THREE

TOM HAD TRAVELLED in his fair share of state-of-the-art helicopters, but Leon Smit's personal aircraft was up there with the very best of them - in fact it appeared to share more than a little design heritage with the models built by Viktor Leskov. Smit happily regaled him with a long list of specifications, although Tom was fairly sure the aircraft had a number of other features that he had not divulged, including defensive weapons systems. If the situation turned for the worse, he might concern himself with them. Right now it was what they hovered over that commanded Tom's attention.

The factory was located about an hour's flight north from London, near the port town of Grimsby and the mouth of the River Humber. And it was immense. Still under construction, the vast concrete and steel building was nearly a kilometre in length, and would, once complete, cover 150 acres or the same as nearly 120 football fields. The site had been home to a coal-fired power station until it had closed in the 1980s, remaining a deserted space until twelve months ago when acquired by Volt-Tech. Once operational it would serve as the largest battery manufacturing plant in Europe.

"Do you know why we named it the ExaFactory?" Smit asked through his headset.

Tom shrugged. "Because it's bigger than a GigaFactory?"

Smit looked slightly deflated. "I suppose that was somewhat obvious."

"Why not use Tera or Peta? They were next in line."

"That's what my marketing people said. But I liked Exa more. It's so big they had to install two dedicated cell towers to provide coverage to the site. Anyway, let's take a closer look."

The full site extended at least two hundred metres beyond the factory footprint and was enclosed by a five-metre-high metal fence. The pilot touched down on the expanse of fresh concrete, fifty metres from the factory. An electric car immediately swept over to meet them, then drove Tom and Smit towards the building, a roller door lifting to reveal a glimpse of the interior. He counted at least twenty security guards, all carrying rifles. "Is this the usual level of security at this site?" he asked, as the car passed under the door.

"It's dialled up a notch while I'm here. Don't worry, I've asked them not to shoot you."

Tom saw a vast, empty space. While the exterior looked complete, it was clear that the building was little more than a shell. The car came to a halt and Smit stepped out.

"As you can see, we will still have plenty to do here."

Tom climbed out and looked around. "Well, you have plenty of room to do it in."

"We're awaiting a range of regulatory and planning clearances. Those guys never seem to be in a hurry, no matter how much money I throw at them."

"Money isn't the answer to every problem."

"In a moment we'll put that to the test." Smit gestured around. "When finished it will be the most advanced automated facility in Europe."

Tom blinked. Smart buildings hadn't provided him with

fond memories. "You have three other such factories, don't you get bored of building them?"

"When people stop needing batteries, I'll stop building them." He paused. "In a very real way, portable power solutions are changing the world. We just need to improve energy density, or products like VoltTech's concept battery-powered helicopter are never going to... quite literally... get off the ground."

"A tough challenge."

He nodded. "I'm going to have an R&D facility here within the factory." He pointed across the floor to an area screened off with dust sheets. "That will be the lab and office section.

"Great. But I'm sure you didn't invite me here to give me the standard press tour."

"A man who can think for himself. I respect that..." Smit quickly pulled out his phone and frowned. "We've had a security incident. Someone attempting to gain access to our site cameras. Perhaps you were right about the threat. Perhaps I should take you seriously. Especially given who you are."

"If by that you mean Bern's son, I'd ask that you don't mention that again."

"I'm more interested in the company he left behind. I heard about a revolutionary new kind of battery, developed by CERUS. Something with implausible energy density. They called it an Accumulator."

Tom took a slow breath. "Sorry, I can't help you."

Smit tapped his nose. "I have sources within the CIA. We know CERUS stole a prototype from them. I want it, and I'm prepared to pay."

"It sounds rather far-fetched."

Smit shrugged. "I will give you £100 million for the technology. For blueprints, designs, and a working example."

"£100 million?" Tom blinked. "Are you nuts?"

"I have to know if it's possible. I have to get there first."

"Except, by your own contention, someone else did."

"And by 'first', I mean: the first to successfully bring it to market. That's all that matters."

Tom folded his arms. "Whether or not this thing exists, I don't own CERUS. I can't make deals on their behalf."

"My investigators uncovered that you own 5% of CERUS voting shares."

Tom glared. "Somewhat short of a majority holding. If you want to speak to a decision-maker, why don't you try the CEO?"

"Dominique Lentz seems to be on sabbatical and has been very hard to get hold of. Besides, I don't think this item is listed on the books. So what do you say?"

"Sorry to disappoint you. It seems money isn't the answer to every problem after all."

"Or I could try other methods of persuasion." Smit gave a hand signal. A number of guards started approaching them. "We're in a remote location. No chance of anybody coming to your aid."

Tom blinked. "Are you serious right now?"

"This technology is incredibly important to me. And I will do whatever I need to do to secure it."

"You're the CEO of a major international company. Not a Bond villain."

"And you're trespassing in a sensitive private facility, and perhaps my men thought they saw you with a weapon."

Tom took a step back, but there were men behind him as well. On instinct he started to reach out, but there was nothing here to help him. Perhaps he could move the car and cause a distraction - but it was heavily encrypted and would take time and effort to connect to - time which he did not have. "You are making a big mistake."

"I make those every day. Nevertheless, you have a point." Smit raised a hand. "I could instead detain you here, and alert my friends in the CIA. I was fascinated to learn you are on their most-wanted list. For what, I do not know." He held up his phone. "But I'll let them worry about that. I still can't believe you actually approached me using your own identity."

Tom looked at the phone. He couldn't let such a call take place. But was this a bluff? Or had Smit contacted them already? Smit's phone was protected by some absurd security measures - it would be harder to hack than the car. If only he had brought the Accumulator, he might have had a chance. As it was, he couldn't overpower even Smit's phone, let alone all the phones of the security guards around him.

But perhaps he didn't need to hack the phone. Smit had mentioned the site had two dedicated cell towers. Closing his eyes, he reached out and found the nearest. It was just a regular issue, standard capacity installation. Easy to connect to. Easy to disable. *Done.*

Smit frowned at his phone. "No signal?" He waved it around. "What's going on?"

Tom opened his eyes. "Perhaps you should worry more about those hackers than me?"

"I can worry about both." Smit walked forward and stared at Tom. "I'll get what I want. Sooner or later, one way or another." He turned around and climbed back into the car. "We will speak again. For now I have a boat to catch." He paused. "Well, a car, then a helicopter, then a boat."

Tom went to follow but Smit waved him off.

"Courtesy transportation is for people who say 'yes'. You'll have to make your own way back." He closed the door and the vehicle shot away, tyres squealing.

Tom took a slow breath as he watched it go.

TWENTY-FOUR

IT WAS a hot and sticky evening, as it often was in Hong Kong, but the Rolls-Royce Limousine had climate control that was more than a match. In the cool, quiet comfort of the rear compartment, Randal van Dijk, CEO of Van Dijk Managed Holdings, sat nursing a generous measure of thirty-year-old single malt while he enjoyed the view - both that of the harbour below, muffled by the car's smoked glass windows, and, more particularly, that of the young woman sat next to him. She wore a slender black dress, demure and yet enticing, her heels perfectly coordinated, four-inch black spikes. She was one of the more recent hires to his business development team: Nikki something-or-other. It had already been a successful day, and if he was a good judge of their dynamic, it was going to get better.

Van Dijk was a rich man - by most measures very rich - but he was confident that money wasn't the only thing that drew in the ladies. It was also the sense of power he exuded, as one of the best-connected businessmen in the former British colony. He might be in his mid-forties, but kept himself in peak condition. He ran five miles a day, played squash and took kickboxing classes. He always travelled with a team of bodyguards -

currently they rode ahead and behind in slightly less salubrious Range Rovers. But if they were a little slow, he could handle himself.

And if he wasn't in the mood for hand-to-hand combat, there was always the automatic pistol that he carried in a shoulder holster. He knew he was a kidnap and ransom target. If anyone ever tried to take him, he certainly wouldn't make it easy.

The Rolls Royce pulled up outside a luxury residential apartment block, high up on the Peak. A uniformed attendant stepped forward and opened the door, half-bowing to the occupants.

Van Dijk turned to Nikki. "Great work today."

She smiled. Teeth brilliant white. When she spoke it was with a delightfully cultured English accent, the kind he could listen to for hours. "Delighted I could assist. Will there be anything more tonight?"

He paused, seeming to consider this, but already knowing how he would reply. "There is another account I'd like to discuss. I have the file upstairs, if you have a moment."

"In your apartment?" She gathered her clutch purse. "As I said, I'm at your disposal."

He smiled as he climbed out. Tonight was indeed going to be memorable.

FOUR BODYGUARDS from the Range Rovers followed them up to the apartment, where they were met by two more guards already inside. At a signal from van Dijk they secured the main door - a bespoke design constructed of fifteen centimetre thick reinforced steel. Then they took up positions in the corridor and kitchen.

Van Dijk smiled and gestured to Nikki. "Through there."

He followed her into the huge master bedroom, his eyes watching the sway of her hips.

"What a view," she said, walking past the oversized four-poster bed and pointing to the balcony. Spread out below, Hong Kong City was a galaxy of coloured lights.

"Being me has its perks," he said, closing the door behind him.

"Is the file in here?" she asked, her smile pure innocence.

"The file?"

"For the new account?"

"Oh yes, of course." He laughed. "Why don't we have a drink first?"

She tipped her head to one side. "Sounds good to me." She moved over to the door and flicked the lock. "Unless there's something else you'd rather do?"

Van Dijk raised an eyebrow. It seemed he might have even underestimated the dynamic. "I'm sure I can think of a few things, if you were to... press me."

Nikki stepped out of her shoes, kicking them aside. Reaching behind her she untied the fastening of her high-necked dress, then she raised her arms and let it slip to the floor.

Van Dijk began to grin, relishing this most exquisite of moments.

But abruptly he stopped.

He had been imagining diaphanous undergarments, or perhaps that she wore none at all. Instead he saw a dull black jumpsuit. It wasn't alluring. It was functional. "What's going on?"

"I'm just getting comfortable."

"Then maybe you should take off that boiler suit?"

"I'm sure you'd like that."

He frowned, noticing her accent had become considerably less refined. "I thought we were on the same page about why I asked you up here?"

"You're a married man. Whatever would your wife say?"

"Is this your idea of a joke?" Van Dijk's jaw stiffened. "I think you should leave. And don't bother coming back to work in the morning. Consider yourself terminated." He walked over to the door and reached for the lock. But before he could open it, her hand gripped his wrist and she was twisting smoothly away, her arms wrapping around him with startling strength. She whirled him off balance then threw him down onto the bed, landing on top of him.

"Come on, Randall," she said, flashing a smile. "Why so serious? Don't you want to play?"

He stared up at her then gave a sigh. "You minx. Is this how you get your way? Messing with people?"

"I find it works."

He laughed. "So what are we going to do now?"

"Good question." She leaned closer. "And what you aren't going to do is have me killed like the last three girls you brought up here."

"Well, they were... How could you possibly know...?" Van Dijk felt a chill cast over him. And in that chill, his instincts recognised the danger. Despite his whisky-fogged head he reacted immediately, flexing his stomach and shoving her to the floor. Without pausing he reached for his shoulder holster. "Who the hell are you...?"

His gun was not there. His fingers grasped at air as his eyes fed his brain the fact that she had taken it. She was already on her feet, pointing his weapon directly at him. This was clearly not a game.

"Who am I? Well I'm not Nikki. And let's be honest, neither of us can remember my second name."

He took a slow breath, trying to keep calm, trying to think. "What do you want?"

"From you? Nothing."

"Everyone wants something."

"Of course, but not from you. I've been looking to get into the hitman game. Hit-woman doesn't have quite the same ring to it. But I've discovered that I need to build some rep if I want to get hired. So I've selected a few targets, to put on my resume. Bastards the world would be better without." She nodded towards him. "Like yourself."

His eyes narrowed. "Shoot me and my guards will be in here in seconds."

"Yeah, I figured." She pulled the clip from the gun and threw it onto the balcony.

"What did you do that for?"

"I won't need it."

Van Dijk threw off his jacket and spat on the floor. "Then be prepared to learn a short and painful lesson."

"I have travelled far and wide in search of worthy opponents. There are few who could teach me anything anymore." She gave a shrug. "And you do not look like one of the few."

Shrieking he jumped from the bed. He was bigger, obviously stronger, and - as many had previously discovered to their surprise - a trained fighter. Even with a decent amount of single malt in his bloodstream, he would show her.

Yet she did not move as he flew towards her. She did not look afraid. She seemed to welcome his attack. Clearly she was delusional. He swung with anger and aggression, putting all his bodyweight behind the punch. It would break her nose, possibly kill someone as obviously fragile as her.

Yet somehow, he missed. She swayed away, as if he was moving in slow motion, and he connected with only air. Then she smiled. It was a terrible smile.

"I was right, Mr van Djik. Today we've both learned nothing."

And then in a single, perfect, counter blow it was all over.

~

ALEXIS MARRON STARED down at Randal van Dijk's grey bulging eyes. He had not died well. But however he had died, she had a process to follow. She pulled out her phone and started taking photos, covering a range of angles - unarguable evidence of what she had done this evening. Always important to make sure you had proof of a successful hit if you were looking to build a portfolio. So different to her approach in the past when it was all about leaving no connections, no trace that she had ever been there.

At the edge of her senses, she heard a faint buzzing in the air. "Really?" she asked. Her phone promptly vibrated. Muttering she answered it. "Checking up on me again, father?" In the air she caught the telltale reflections from the micro drone rotors.

"I've been keeping half an eye on your location and telemetry," Peter Marron replied. "Why are you there? Van Dijk wasn't on the list."

"He was on *my* list. Either they can teach me a lesson, or they're in need of one."

"I've warned you about taking unnecessary risks. Rich people have resources."

"I like the challenge."

"I want you to focus, Alex. I did say I was going to need you."

"You've been saying that for weeks. Meanwhile all you do is play with that damn submarine. I've moved on."

"It is a valuable asset," he said, "as I have explained. And it cannot just be left to gather dust."

"Do what you need to do. I'm working on creating new income streams. You just need someone else for your crew."

"It's true I can't sail on my own. But that's not why I'm calling. I have need of your particular set of skills. I'm putting a team together – a complete bunch of new hires - and I need you on it or it won't work. The client is someone I trust."

"And the job?"

"I can't tell you yet. But I can promise you will encounter a worthy opponent."

"I didn't think there were any left."

"The client was quite specific. You shouldn't pass this up."

Alex glanced down at van Dijk's body. "Fine. Well I'm pretty much done. I just need to handle the bodyguards."

"There are four of them," Marron replied testily, "and they are unimportant. Priorities, please."

"I was looking forward to the workout."

"They will teach you nothing. You have an exit route via the balcony, and I have a car ready to pick you up, one block over. Don't keep him waiting."

Alex gave a scowl. "I'm not a little girl anymore."

"Which is why I need your help. I just want what's best for you. For us."

"I know you do." She clicked the phone off. "I know you do."

TWENTY-FIVE

THE JOURNEY HAD PASSED UNSEEN, or at least it had for Dominique Lentz. After more than an hour of itchy darkness, the hood she had been wearing was removed. As her eyes adjusted to the afternoon light, she saw Stephanie Reems' smiling face.

"Welcome to the real world."

"If only," Lentz replied. She sat in the back of Reems' armoured, long-wheel-base Jaguar SUV, which lurched as the driver suddenly took a sharp turn from what was already a minor road, onto what appeared to be no road at all. The vehicle's suspension groaned as it bounced along the muddy unmade track that led through the cover of heavy trees. "Where the hell are we going?"

"Sorry about the road. Upgrading it would have drawn attention."

Lentz leaned forward, straining her eyes to make out any details. The combination of gathering twilight and heavily tinted glass made it impossible. "Have you built a cabin in the woods or something? Or are you taking me out here for disposal? Have I said the wrong thing to the wrong person?"

"Calm yourself, Dominique. Less than a mile to go."

Two minutes later the trees fell away and they entered a clearing. The driver guided them through a gap in a six-metre-high, chain-link fence, then brought the car to a halt on a rough concrete apron. Reems opened her passenger door and climbed out. Lentz stepped out from the other side of the car and looked around. In the fading light she saw a single large building: an ageing warehouse, with rough concrete-block walls and a corrugated metal-sheet roof, both painted a dull grey.

Her breath caught in her throat. There was an overwhelming sense of familiarity. She knew this place. She had been here. But when? There were two double-height roller doors, but no windows. "This can't be our destination? It looks like it's been derelict for twenty years."

Reems walked towards the nearest door. "Twenty-seven to be precise."

Lentz looked closer. The paint was fresh. And she saw the suggestion of modern surveillance equipment - sufficiently modern to be difficult to identify. "What's going on here? What's beneath the surface?"

"I'm pleased to see you haven't lost all your observation skills. This site is classified above top secret. Only those on the list get to know about this place. And it's a very short list. You recognise it because of its former purpose. And your former life."

And suddenly Lentz knew. "This is Eastwell? CERUS Biotech's former site?"

"Indeed it is. Where you did your work on Project Tantalus - where the designs for the original interface were conceived." Reems tapped a button on her remote control, and the door began to roll up, blinding white light shining from within. "Let me show you what we've been up to."

TWENTY-SIX

KORVER LOOKED SLOWLY around the room - the main space in the hotel suite he had booked out for his team. It was quiet, discrete, and had excellent room service, allowing him to focus on final preparations for the coming operation.

Standing around him, busily checking their equipment, were his twenty hand-selected operatives. Each was skilled in armed and unarmed combat, and in the more sophisticated aspects of covert operations - they were all ex-agency or elite law enforcement, and without question they knew what they were doing.

He hoped he wouldn't have to kill them after the op. It was - as he kept explaining to Hatch - incredibly inefficient to constantly murder the best available freelancers. It was a really binary way of managing the risk, and in Korver's view completely unnecessary. These people knew how to keep a secret.

Of course, being alert, they were wary of Korver himself. Many of them had heard the stories that he should be dead. And yet he walked among them, stronger than ever.

He turned and looked at his own equipment. Both the

assault rifle and handgun were bespoke smart weapons, created at the Rig. They were lightweight and effective, and would provide a critical advantage if combat became necessary. But the most powerful tool was the black metal sphere. The clock was ticking on its capabilities, but he still had time. Speaking of a clock ticking, it was time for his shot. He reached into his pack and found the case with the glass ampules and syringes, then carried them into the nearest bathroom, locking the door.

Korver turned and looked in the mirror, as he did every day, to remind himself of why he was doing this. His face was unblemished, perfect even, his physique hammered from iron. If he wanted to keep it that way, he knew what he had to do. So he pulled one of the ampules from the transparent protector and loaded it into one of the syringes. Then he held it up and checked the seal, before depressing the plunger a touch to clear any air bubbles. Satisfied, he forcefully jabbed it into his neck.

For the briefest moment it was like he was staring at the sun. Impossible brightness and heat, enveloping him, erasing him. Korver blinked and grunted, and he felt the sensation ebb. This ritual brought precious moments of peace and quiet - and he tried to enjoy them - before returning to what he had become. Someone who was all about everything except peace and quiet.

It was who he was now. It was who they had made him. And there was no going back.

His phone buzzed in his pocket. He pulled it out and tapped his earpiece to answer. "Good evening, Director."

"Good morning from here," came Frank Hatch's reply. "Hope I'm not interrupting."

"Not at all. We're at the hotel, and I've just taken my dose."

"Exactly on schedule. But that is who you are. How are your preparations for the Faraday mission?"

"Everything is ready for tonight." Korver took a steady breath. "Not something you needed to check personally. By the fact that you're calling, can I assume you are about to change my instructions?"

"On tonight's mission? Absolutely not." Hatch paused. "Well, not materially. There is an item I also need you to recover. I've sent the details to your phone."

Korver tapped on the screen. "You're sure it's going to be with him?"

"So I'm informed, and it should be trackable once you get close. There is also another job you need to undertake. After you finish with Faraday."

"You want to use my team for back-to-back ops? You know my views on that."

"Protocols are there to be broken."

"No," Korver said calmly, "my protocols are how we manage operational risk. My protocols are how we ensure success. I have a team of highly trained people, but they are human, not machines. I can only ask so much of them."

"I hear you, I really do, but it is a very important, high value target. And I'm following orders myself."

"So it's not up for discussion?"

"It is not. Sending the details now."

Korver sighed and looked down at his phone. "The location is underground?"

"Yes, but we have an agent in place ready to bring everything up to you. You're only there in case anything goes wrong. And nothing can go wrong."

"It's a government site?"

"In a sense. Don't worry, your team will be more than up to the task."

"I hope that proves to be correct."

"Good luck. I will be watching."

"You always are."

TWENTY-SEVEN

LENTZ FOLLOWED Reems through the Eastwell facility in stunned silence. The surface level was still a dust-filled ruin of a warehouse, but below ground things were very different. There were five levels of labs and offices, conference rooms and sleeping quarters. Each floor was immaculate and looked ready for occupation. As yet she saw only one small team of scientists at work.

"I truly had no idea you were doing this," Lentz said, when they arrived in a kitchen area, and Reems had pointed her towards a freezer containing pre-prepared meals, next to a bank of microwaves. Lentz settled for black coffee. Reems did the same, and then led her down a corridor to an office.

"So what do you think?" Reems asked as she sat behind a wide wooden desk. "I've been itching to show this to you."

Lentz sat opposite her. "I'm not wild about my time here. Those were not good memories."

"Then forget the past. Let it go. Here, we're all about the future." She smiled. "This place will provide the foundation of my big plan."

"A plan to do what?"

Reems placed her hands on the desk. "You remember last year. You saw what happened. Our enemies developed cutting edge technology, and nearly took it beyond our reach."

"Bern is dead. Leskov too. The problem solved itself."

"If you think that's the end of it, you're deluded. The problem has very much not gone away, and I will not see us left helpless. We need a way to respond to the increasing number of adversaries using bleeding edge technology to change the game. If we do not run hard we are going to get left behind."

"I thought you were a rule follower, not a revolutionary."

Reems frowned. "We're going to need a revolution. We need to respond to these new threats. We need to match them with our tech. We'll create a new toolbox - we will use nanotech, automated decision-making and innovations like the Interface. These developments are the future of law enforcement, of counterterrorism, of the intelligence services. It cannot be left to private enterprise to develop these tools, when they may well simply sell them to the highest bidder. We need to have them first."

"And you have the solution to achieve that?"

Reems spread her hands wide. "We're going to create an intelligence agency."

"We have a few of those already."

"Nothing like this one. It will specialise in high technology - whether at home or overseas. Where there is a threat, or an opportunity, we will be there. The working title is MI10... or perhaps MI-X, if roman numerals are your thing."

Lentz frowned. "There used to be an MI10."

"The things you have stored in that brain of yours. You are correct. MI10 was responsible for weapons and technical analysis during World War II, but hasn't existed since. We will take that idea and haul it, kicking and screaming, into the 21st Century."

"From a scientific point of view, I can see the merits. But how did you persuade the government to give you funding?"

Reems pinched the bridge of her nose. "They have, as yet, not shown sufficient vision."

Lentz coughed. "Are you saying this site isn't sanctioned? Then where did the money come from?"

"I siphoned small percentages from other black ops budgets." Reems frowned. "To be frank, we've all but run out. I needed a big win to take things forward. To get the attention of the bean counters - specifically one bean counter."

"Let me guess: Ms Natasha Gifford?"

"Security Service deputy director by name, accountant by nature."

Lentz took a sip of her coffee, which was utilitarian at best. "So, you needed a big win for an agency that does not exist. Sounds straightforward. But why the past tense? You don't need it anymore?"

"Oh I do. It's just that now I have a much bigger problem. The one you're here to help with."

"This computer?"

Reems nodded. "We call it *Medusa*."

"Because anyone who looks upon it will be petrified?"

"Something like that. I've been using certain operatives to acquire what some call fringe tech. Our focus has very much been on nanotech connected to CERUS projects."

"By operatives, you mean Tom and Kate?"

Reems let out a slow sigh. "They told you? I guess that's what I should expect, working with civilians."

"That's unfair. I'm particularly good at reading between the lines. How did you get them to take part? I thought Tom's dislike of you would be a total barrier."

"He has a stronger dislike of what people have done with CERUS tech." Reems walked over to a mini fridge and removed a bottle of water. "We are at a tipping point, right now. If we do nothing, Pandora's box will open, and we won't even realise it. We'll fall so far behind there won't even be a race."

"So you'll identify advanced tech and stop it?"

"That's the mission."

"Do you mean destroy it? Or acquire it?"

"We will need to understand it if we're going to stop it."

Lentz shook her head. "This is all a smokescreen for wide scale appropriation of speculative technology. You've tricked Tom and Kate into helping you."

"I don't think you're grasping quite how serious and widespread this issue is." Reems moved over to a display screen and tapped it. It scanned her palm then displayed a scatter graph of different incidents. "This shows a number of recent tech thefts. While looking into CERUS Biotech I spotted a pattern. At first I thought it was just CERUS, but it's much bigger than that and it's been going on for many years. And a particular player is driving this. They've established a secretive marketplace where this technology is sold to the highest bidder."

"An auction?"

"A series of them. Someone is aggressively acquiring hi-tech equipment and research, then profiting from its sale. I don't know who they are, I don't know where they are. But I'm going to find out." She tapped the screen and the data reflowed. "This is a summary of what's been taken. A lot of nanotech, including applications in medicine, construction and weaponry. A number of attempts at interfaces. Virtual and augmented reality tech. Oh and robotics. You've seen that robot dog in those online demos?"

"Everyone has."

"You do not want to see the weaponised combat version."

"I think maybe I do, if only from a curious scientist's perspective, but I get your point. Why isn't there more outcry?"

"Because this type of loss tends to be under-reported.

Companies don't want to admit their failings, and they won't want to disclose what they were working on."

"Yes, and it's most annoying," said a new voice.

Lentz looked up and saw a wiry man with a goatee beard. He wore a crumpled lab coat, and carried a brown leather messenger bag over his shoulder.

"This," Reems said, "is Gabriel Gates. When he's not interrupting me, he's the tech lead for this site, with overall responsibility for Medusa."

Lentz shook his hand. "Quite a task, so I've been hearing."

"Yes it is," Gates replied, "and she's lucky to have me."

"Yeah," Reems said with a cough. "But while he's good, he's not you, Dominique. Not even close."

"Thanks," Gates said. "You do see me standing here, right?"

"I've tried to get him to lose the beard. No luck so far." She scratched her chin. "Don't you have a report to complete?"

"On the system glitch?" He reached into his bag and pulled out a brown envelope.

Lentz raised an eyebrow. "You're printing reports on paper?"

"Only the super sensitive, top-secret ones, that we don't under any circumstances want retrieved by hackers." He placed the envelope on Reems' desk, gave her a mock salute and strode away.

Lentz narrowed her eyes. "Was that you doing... *banter*?"

Reems coughed. "A stab at it. How did I do?"

"I think I may throw up. Now do you want to tell me what you actually want me to do?"

Reems held up the envelope. "I want you to read this report. And then I want you to fix Medusa."

TWENTY-EIGHT

KATE MET Tom a kilometre away from the ExaFactory complex, under the shelter of some trees next to a quiet country road.

"I should have taken the Accumulator," Tom said. "It would have given me options."

"No, you should *not* have got on that helicopter," Kate replied from under her helmet. "What was going on? Why did they bring you up here?"

"Because my meeting got taken over by someone else. Guess who?"

"How should I know...?" She frowned. "Wait, was Leon Smit there?"

"My first thought was that it was just chance. But it's become clear it was anything but."

"You really need to bring me up to speed."

"I do. But not anywhere near here. Who knows who might be watching." Tom looked around. "Or might be trying to follow us."

"Unless they also have a very fast bike, they won't be able to follow the route I'm going to take."

"Sounds good to me."

Kate handed him a spare helmet. "Seems like I'll be the one bringing you up to speed. I should have you home in under three hours. Do try and hold on."

~

TWO HOURS fifty-three minutes later Tom and Kate climbed down into the gardens of the mansion house and made their way across the lawns. Dusk was gathering as they descended into the pool house, Odie signalling quietly that all was normal within.

Tom marched through the lounge area, straight to the diamond cut glass display cabinet. Inside, along with the black metal sphere recovered from the bank vault, rested the Accumulator, its lights blinking pseudo randomly, as they always did. As always there was that sense of assurance, somehow mixed with unease. He rubbed his temples and blinked.

"What is the matter?" Kate asked as she caught up to him.

Tom ran his fingers over the display cabinet. "That meeting did not go how I expected. So much for trying to help them."

"But they must have taken it seriously for Smit to turn up in person."

"They weren't bothered about being hacked - for all I know, it might even have been people working for VoltTech that did the hacking." He shook his head. "Smit turned up because he knew who I was."

"I told you not to give your real name."

"I had to give some name, and I was sure a fake identity would flag on their undoubtedly rigorous background checks. I thought my real history as a lawyer would look convincing. But the point I was making is he knew who I *really* was. He knew Bern was my father."

Kate blinked. "So he wanted to know about CERUS stuff?"

"It was a lot more specific than that." Tom brushed his fingers over the carbon fibre cube, feeling a shimmer of static. "He knew about this."

"*What* did he know?"

"That it existed. That it was stolen from the CIA." Tom puffed out his cheeks. "He offered to pay me £100 million for the blueprints and a working unit."

"And how did you respond?"

Tom looked at her. "Do you need to ask?"

"I want to know exactly what you said, and exactly how he reacted."

"I said that I knew nothing about it. And even if I did, I didn't speak on behalf of CERUS. I told him to speak to Lentz."

"But why did he think you had it?"

"If he has connections with the CIA then who knows? But when I declined his offer, he made as if he was going to get heavy on me."

"What?"

"He had a bunch of guards surround me and look like they were going to get physical."

"But they didn't?"

"Apparently just scare tactics. He changed up the threat to handing me over to the CIA."

Kate frowned. "Probably just looking for a reaction. Testing you. You managed to keep yourself in check, then?"

"I was close to losing it." Tom rested his hand on the Accumulator. "Of course without this, I couldn't do much."

"Well, you walked into an environment you didn't know about before, which you hadn't been able to prepare for, with an opponent of unknown intentions."

"He was persuasive. He has an air about him that even

Bern didn't. A guy who can do anything. I was at least curious to see what he wanted to show me - to see if it gave any clues to the people we're really after. It felt like a one-off opportunity."

Kate reached across and gently removed his hand from the cube, pulling it back, then she closed the glass door. "Let's take a step back. There's some stuff I should have told you about before."

~

TOM SAT at the dining table looking at the screen of Kate's laptop, at the large quantity of research she'd been conducting on Smit. "Why didn't you share this with me?"

"Because it was mere speculation. I've found with all the people I've looked into - and I've looked into a lot - so much of it is just rumour and supposition. It takes a lot of time to cross-check and verify."

"So there are others you've been looking into?" Tom folded his arms. "I thought we agreed no secrets between us?"

Kate gave a muted laugh. "I think that's mostly been a one-way street. You are practically a closed book. Besides, there's a difference between 'no secrets' and maintaining a constant real-time sharing of everything I'm doing. I have to edit, Tom."

"You're deliberately missing the point."

"Am I? It's just like with you. In many ways you can do anything. But you can't do *everything*."

"Still, your research seems like a very specific something you should have told me before going to VoltTech."

Kate frowned at him. "I didn't know you were going to be meeting Leon Smit, remember? Look, maybe this all looks worse than it is. I'm not saying his behaviour was in any way acceptable. I'm just considering what we can infer from it. My research suggests he's driven, that he'll do what he has to do... but it doesn't really indicate that he's as bad as..."

"...my father?"

She shrugged. "Smit just wants what will make him a lot of money - his business is batteries, so his request was hardly unsurprising. And if someone else gets this instead, VoltTech's whole business model could be in question."

Tom walked around the table. "So, what? You think he acted reasonably?"

"I'm saying he's acting *rationally, from his perspective.* I still wouldn't trust him. And on that front, did you scan yourself?"

He frowned. "You think I let him bug me? I'm always checking for odd signals."

"Check again."

Tom blinked and closed his eyes. He reached out, into the electronics around him, into the wireless data flows. He could feel nothing out of place. "I'm clean."

Kate shrugged. "Fine. So maybe that's all there was to it. This whole thing though, it's been odd since we carried out the raid on the bank." She snapped her fingers. "What if the same people who tried to hack the bank, who were also targeting Smit's company - what if they were still monitoring VoltTech, and have been alerted to you?"

"That is possible." Tom sighed. "It doesn't help us know who they are."

Kate closed her laptop. "We need to brief Reems. And maybe see if her people have better luck with the sphere."

"I think that might have been a puzzle designed to waste our time. But sure, we can do it tomorrow - I think we've had more than enough drama for one day." He put a hand on her shoulder. "And thank you for coming to get me. For being there when I had nobody else."

"That's what I do. And that's what you do. By which I mean you ask me because you have nobody else."

"Really? Would you stop..." Something made Tom hesitate. A sense that something was wrong. Odie was warning him of a security breach. An alarm sounded, shrill and piercing.

Kate looked around. "What's going on?"

Tom closed his eyes and reached out. And then he saw them, dressed in black, dropping down over the walls on ropes. He opened his eyes. "We have intruders."

TWENTY-NINE

LENTZ READ GABRIEL GATES' report on Medusa. Then she read it again. Then she put her head in her hands.

Reems cleared her throat loudly from where she still sat at her desk. "Tell me it's not that bad."

"You want me to lie?" Lentz replied. "Look, this is a lot to drop on me. I'm still trying to adjust to the idea that you've rebuilt Eastwell. Then you hit me with this MI10 initiative - an intelligence agency for the new world. And quite frankly I'm not sure what I should think. I don't know if it's the right thing to do. I do know it is currently breaking every law there is."

"Just fix Medusa. Let me worry about everything else."

"Why did I bother saving you last year, if you're just going to throw your life at some impossible task? You should be winding down to retirement, not winding up to madness."

Reems folded her arms. "You want me to go quietly into that good night?"

"You've put everything into this new computer system. A system nobody really understands. And now that system is going to re-initialise, destroying every bit of information you have collected."

"Well maybe it wouldn't have happened if you were here doing the job you were born to do. You're supposed to come here and lead the research team. Now are you going to waste time making fun of me? Or are you going to help me?"

"Of course I'm going to help you, you idiot. But it doesn't mean I have to be happy about it."

Reems nodded. "I never asked you to be."

Lentz looked again through Gates' report. "The other key thing I don't understand is the core platform Medusa is built on."

"You don't understand it?"

"No, I mean I don't understand why it's founded on a core platform that is clearly derived from one I designed. One that I've been doing work on until about a year or so ago - basically an earlier version of my house AI, Odyssey."

"Well any work you ever did at CERUS, my people have had access to. But this is a good thing right? If you've been doing work on it recently, you're well-placed to fix it."

Lentz shrugged. "That's the problem - I've never really understood it. I guess I have 36 hours to learn."

Reems cleared her throat. "Actually you have 12. Gates triggered some anti-tamper mechanism on his last effort to access the system. It took 24 hours off of the timer."

"Marvellous." Lentz stood up. "Then you'd better show me to this Medusa before anyone else who's supposed to be on our team makes things worse."

THIRTY

ALMOST WITHOUT THINKING, Tom felt himself drawing power from the Accumulator. Almost without guiding, it energised his mind. Almost he wasn't in control.

Almost.

Kate looked at him. "What do you mean when you say intruders?"

Tom reached out and sent feeds from several of the CCTV cameras around the estate to the large display screens. Video streams appeared showing at least twenty figures, automatic weapons strung across their backs, moving over the lawn towards the main house. "I mean them. Unless you're going to tell me they're friends of yours."

Kate walked closer to the displays. "Reems' people?"

"I doubt it, but let's ask her." Tom made a priority call, his mind interfacing with the relevant protocols. But as he tried it immediately became clear critical elements were missing. "I can't make a connection." He turned to a screen on his right and called up network traffic. "Are we being jammed?"

Kate pulled out her phone. "Maybe. I have no signal."

"It's like all the wires, all the pathways, have been cut." In his mind, he felt the Accumulator in the glass cabinet, fuelling him, boosting him, and he reached out with force. But even with his power enhanced, it made no difference.

Kate pointed at the nearest monitor, where a large man in the group was holding out some kind of device as he advanced upon the mansion. "He looks like he's tracking something." The man gave a signal and the group turned away from the mansion, starting walking towards the pool house.

"Not something," Tom said. "*Someone*. And I'm pretty sure that someone is me."

"Are you sure you aren't bugged?"

"I'd know. There must be some other explanation."

"And we can try and discover it later. For now, have you got any weapons?"

"Kind of." Tom turned to a metal section of the wall, pulling a physical key from his pocket. He slotted it into a small hole, then heaved the camouflaged door open. Inside was a computer terminal with a control panel plugged in. In the middle of the panel was a large, round, red button.

Kate walked over and moved the section of wall further away. "Why is that so heavy?"

"It has active RF shielding. I added it to stop me accidentally triggering what's inside, which is a directional EMP. It should neutralise all their electronics, including the smart weapons they're carrying." He stabbed it with the palm of his right hand.

On screen, though there was no sound, they suddenly saw the members of the group holding their ears and writhing. And then slumping to their knees.

"See," Tom said, "I said we'd be safe here."

But as one of the cameras zoomed in on the face of the large man, the expression of calm that he saw made him fairly sure he was wrong.

~

THE INTRUDERS, it seemed, were not going to be stopped by the EMP. As Tom and Kate watched, the group removed apparently damaged earpieces and other tech and threw them on the lawn. Then at a signal from the large man, three more operatives ran from the far side of the estate, carrying heavy duffle bags. They arrived and began doling out fresh equipment, and new weapons. Then he saw the large man fiddling with the device, which seemed to be the size of an apple, before Tom's external cameras shut down.

Kate's eyes widened. "We should leave. You must have another way out of here. I refuse to believe Bern would have built it without one."

Tom nodded. "There is a secondary option, but it requires me to blow explosives to clear out a partially blocked tunnel. We'll get out, but we will not go unnoticed."

"So it doesn't help us?"

"Not in this situation. Lentz offered me an automated launcher for micro drones with tranquillisers on board - a collection of individually guided missiles, a humane way to pacify an enemy, if a taser is not available."

"And you said no?"

"I thought it sounded ridiculous. Or I thought she meant to be able to use it on me. If it's any consolation she would not have installed a system with the capacity to handle twenty assailants."

"I guess tasers won't be quick enough?"

"Or have enough range. Also we only have four of them. We can try to barricade the doors, and then sit here and wait for them to force their way inside."

Kate flexed her fingers. "There has to be something else Bern had hidden in here, something even you haven't found yet."

"There is not." Tom walked over to the metal cabinet, taking a deep breath, channelling the energy. Why did he feel so calm? Why did he feel so confident? Something was different inside him, as if he was unlocking hidden pathways he hadn't known existed, as if his fears were evaporating. He liked it. "But I do have a way to stop them coming down here."

"Please enlighten me."

"I'm going to go out there and fight them."

"Because you're combat trained, and can take on twenty-to-one odds? Or twenty-to-two if I come with you."

"There's no doubt you can handle yourself better than I, in any regular situation," He reached into the cabinet and removed the Accumulator. "But this is not a regular situation."

"Why do you think for a moment that I would let you go up there alone?"

"Because it's me they want. And because I am going to cheat." In his other hand he picked up the Resurface suit. The black metal sphere he left in the display case. "When they get here they're going to find more than they bargained for."

"Or," Kate said, "they'll find exactly what they know is here and quickly acquire it." She pointed at the screens. "To remind you, they have more than twenty people. Are you really planning on taking them all out?"

"Maybe I take out a few and the others decide to make a retreat. It's not like they're robots."

She went to put a hand on his shoulder, then flinched back. "Remember what happened the last time you wore one of those suits? I'm not letting you do this."

Tom stared at her. "I guess there's no changing your mind."

"There is not." She frowned. "What is the matter with you? Why are you making crazy suggestions like this?"

"Must be something I ate. What was that noise?" He pointed to the storage room at the end of the corridor. "Are they tunnelling in?"

"What?" Kate rushed forward, opened the door and ran in. "There's nothing I can see, but..."

Tom closed the door behind her and activated the lock.

There was a moment of silence. Then the sound of the handle being turned. Then a muffled curse. Then a louder one. "What are you doing?" Kate shouted.

He placed a hand on the door. "Making sure you stay safe."

"That's not your decision. Now let me out."

"Given what you just told me, this is the only way. I've instructed the system to let you out thirty seconds after I close the main door to this bunker." He paused. "I've also withdrawn your access protocols. Odie will no longer respond to your commands."

"You have to stop trying to do this on your own."

"That's the only way I can do it. And as for the problems I had last time with the suit, a lot's changed since then. We've had enough surprises from them this evening. It's time I showed them a few of my own."

THIRTY-ONE

TOM PULLED ON THE SUIT, sliding its form-fitting synthetic material over his limbs and torso. The Accumulator slotted into its padded case, then he placed that in the pack he always wore.

He felt sharp and clear, his mind in sudden focus. He could sense the intruders approaching the pool house, moving calmly and methodically, which meant he did not have long. So he closed the heavy door to the underground apartment behind him, then made his way up the stairs. Emerging into the pool room he closed the panel in the floor. Kate was as safe as he could get her - in a situation like this, that would have to do.

Throughout the poolhouse, mansion and grounds all the lights were extinguished. Through the windows he could see a hint of movement. He could feel their night vision goggles. They surely felt they were in command.

It was time to change the rules. It was time to change the game.

Tom reached out with clarity, opening his mind to the Accumulator, to the nanites coating the suit. His interface expanded and he became one with it - and in a rush the sensations hit him. It was like standing in a windowless room, wearing sunglasses, and suddenly removing them while simultaneously stepping outside into midday sun. It was like seeing for the first time. It was unique. It was overwhelming.

It was *beautiful*.

But there was no time to enjoy it. Or to worry that he was drawing too much power. He had a situation to deal with. A problem to solve. Two operatives, both men, were at the door of the pool house, planting a device over the lock.

Tom reached out and connected, switching the device off. He heard them shout. Then someone ran forward with another identical item. Did these people have spares for everything? Tom repeated his neural instructions. This time there was swearing. Someone else shouted to bring C4.

Tom gritted his teeth. He would have to intervene overtly.

He sent a signal to a system he had not envisaged using - the one Bern had used to illuminate his lawn at nighttime events. Tom had never considered he would actually use it, but right now it was perfect for his needs. From underground silos eight banks of floodlights lifted into position. Power flowed and they turned on.

Instantly it was almost daylight across the lawns. The operatives, wearing night vision goggles attuned for near darkness, shouted and pulled them off, momentarily disoriented.

Time to fight.

Again, Tom wondered where that thought came from. But now wasn't a time to get lost in introspection. He made a change to the suit - hardening it to something better than body armour, while retaining flexibility. Then he opened the door.

IT WAS ODDLY calm as Tom stepped into the night air. The operatives were spread out before him, standing on the lawn, looking at the floodlights. But the two by the door reacted as he emerged. Just not quickly enough.

Tom smiled. And he sent every bit of anger, every bit of irritation, every bit of fire he could muster, into their earpieces and phones, something he could only do when very close.

The two fell to the floor, screaming. The others turned, pointing and looking confused. But only for a moment. Then they began to raise their rifles. Tom turned the floodlights off, plunging the lawn back into darkness. Then he moved. He didn't need light. With the suit and its nanite coating, he could receive inputs in a much broader range of the electromagnetic spectrum.

Two people closest to those he had just taken out moved to investigate, sliding their night vision goggles back into place. Around him, Tom saw the others putting their goggles on as well. So he turned the floodlights back on.

There was more swearing and removal of goggles. Tom moved behind two more operatives and attacked their comms units and phones. They both shrieked and collapsed.

Four down. Roughly sixteen to go. He really should have counted more accurately.

"Earpieces and phones out!" shouted a voice. "Drop all electronics. They're a liability." The large man was speaking, and he was pointing directly at Tom.

Tom turned the lights off again, and began moving to a new position, ready to repeat his routine.

But then the lights came back on.

Tom blinked. Was there a fault? He reached out to check but could sense nothing, then saw the man tapping the thing he was holding in his hand. Tom saw it better now - a dark metal sphere - and he froze in shock. It was like the one they had recovered from the bank vault. Was that a coincidence? Tom tried again to flick the switch, but he'd been locked out from the floodlights. They remained on.

The eight closest operatives moved immediately towards him. Tom took a step back. He made an adjustment to the surface of the suit. And then he vanished.

Or at least he appeared to. It was the translucency function utilised to such effect twelve months ago. It was an unfair advantage, and Tom intended to use it. He began to move away to a new position, ready to strike.

"Clever," said the large man. "I'm not sure how you got a Resurface suit, nor how you know how to use it so well."

Tom hesitated. "Did Smit send you?"

The man looked confused. "Who?" He turned and pointed. "Target is over there. I can hear him. Respond as planned."

Another of the operatives stepped forward and sprayed an aerosol-like device. A green substance misted in the air, passing over where Tom stood with an accompanying strong odour. *Paint,* he realised. And for a moment he wondered why. Then it stuck to him and, he understood. It compromised the translucency of his suit, making him easily visible in the lights.

"That suit is a powerful tool, but we came up with a simple countermeasure."

Tom took a sharp breath. He had no choice but to fight. Could he, even in the suit, take on over a dozen opponents? Enemies who were wise to some of his abilities?

"This is over, friend," said the large man. "Why don't you make things easy on yourself."

Tom glared back, and then he realised something. Perhaps he didn't need to fight all of them. Perhaps he only needed to fight one. He just needed to get close enough. That would require another distraction. He closed his eyes and opened the flow of power to his suit, carefully changing the nature of the Resurface nanites. He turned each into a mini floodlight, into an incandescent white bulb, which even to him, with his eyes closed, looking away, was nearly overwhelming.

There were screams of pain, and shouts of 'my eyes' from all around. Tom held the burn for a few seconds then let it extinguish. Opening his eyes, he saw only shadows. He felt his heart pounding in his chest. Then he moved, snatching an automatic pistol from the belt of one of the fallen operatives and running forward, slipping behind the large man and jamming the barrel of the gun into his neck, above the line of any body armour. "Everyone, weapons down and take two steps back."

The man spoke very calmly. "That's not going to help you."

"Why not?" Tom looked around at the others, who didn't immediately do as he'd requested. "You don't care about your own life?"

"In a sense I'm already dead. Nothing you can do with that gun is going to change it."

"I suspect if I pull the trigger, you'll find you were wrong."

"But are you going to pull the trigger? You're a lawyer."

"If that's all you think I am, then you haven't been paying attention."

The man nodded. "Perhaps I should introduce myself? My name is Korver. My team and I are pretty good. The fact that you've lasted this long is no small achievement."

Tom glared. "I don't care who you are."

"You probably should. You, my friend, are... as you said... a former lawyer, and the son of the late William Bern, the former owner of this property."

Tom whispered in Korver's ear. "Call them off. I really don't want to hurt any of you."

"Didn't you wonder how we were able to sever all connections to outside networks? How we were able to get inside the perimeter without you noticing?"

"Well, I..."

Korver held up the sphere. "What do you make of this?"

Tom glared at the metal ball. He could suddenly sense a flow of data from within, but there was no obvious encrypted shell. Could he just override it? Would it be this simple? The thing that had given them the edge, right here in front of him. "I'll make it my own." He opened the flows from the Accumulator, and reached out to the sphere, sending every ounce, every gram, of power that he could. He didn't care about understanding or communicating. He only wanted to overwhelm. To destroy.

But it didn't happen like that.

The energy he sent just vanished, the sphere did not react. He was vaguely aware of a commotion around him, that people were shouting. And that his backpack was slipping from his shoulders. But he didn't care about that. It was a tedious irrelevance. He was concerned with something far more important.

He started to connect to the sphere, to query what had happened. But as he reached out, he suddenly felt like a tiny dot in an immense space. He was looking at a blinding, bright light. Like what he sensed before in Lentz's system, but a thousand times more potent. A perfect point of infinite radiance. He felt his mind being pulled towards this impossibly bright source of light, of energy, of information.

Too late he realised he was caught in its irresistible pull. He tried to fight back, but all his strength had gone. And then something different happened. Something that had never happened before, in all this time with the Interface.

Something gripped his mind and reached *in*.

THIRTY-TWO

DOMINIQUE LENTZ HURRIED down the long corridor, intentionally putting distance between herself and Gabriel Gates. She reached the end well ahead of him and turned right, facing a pair of security doors with a palm reader lock. She began to reach forward when she heard 'wait' shouted from behind her.

Gates shambled up, gasping for breath. "You're not registered. If you try that the system will get antsy." He reached forward, placing his hand on the reader. There was a chime and the doors slid open.

"What does it do when it gets 'antsy'?"

"Barrier doors will drop from the ceiling, sealing off the corridors - takes an age to reset them." He paused. "And Director Reems has to provide the codes, which always irritates her. I try to avoid that."

"Here's a thought," Lentz said, as she walked inside. "Maybe get me on the system? Or I'll show you what antsy really means."

He swallowed. "Of course."

Lentz found herself in a ten-metre-square room with bright

LED lighting and perfectly white walls. In the centre was a long desk on which were three large and incredibly thin flat screen displays. The walls, where not broken by doorways or ducting, were covered with further display screens. To the far left and right were large, heavy-duty hatches, like bulkhead doors on a submarine. All around there was the constant drone of high-powered air filtering and cooling.

Gates pointed to the hatches. "The Medusa system is housed behind there. We can go in if you like, but you'll have to suit up. Clean room protocols avoid any particulates getting into the components."

"Does it run hot?" Lentz asked.

"You have no idea." He coughed. "I mean, I'm sure you understand the design philosophy better than I do. Cooling is the main limiting factor to its use."

"I'm going to need to conduct a full visual inspection. And I want all system telemetry on the screens around me." Lentz placed her bag on the desk. "I'll work here."

"That's my workstation..." Gates began. "Yes, of course. Whatever you need."

"Marvellous. What I need right now is two things. Access to these terminals, and a flask of very strong black coffee."

Gates nodded. "Of course. And let me say, I'm very much looking forward to—"

"Me saving your rear?" Lentz raised an eyebrow. "Actually, I do remember you. I read one of your papers, and it was not inspiring. So maybe get me those things I just asked for, and I can get on with saving your world?"

THE COFFEE MADE LITTLE DIFFERENCE, even after several cups. It sharpened Lentz's mind, but it also made her tense, and it in no way provided solutions. Seven hours after starting her assessment, she was only more alarmed about what little she might be able to do.

She had studied the Medusa system herself, accessing the area behind the hatches. With Gates in tow, she had walked between the three-metre-high server towers, each blinking with status lights, humming with power, and radiating heat that the high specification air extraction was struggling to pull out of the room. The whole setup was clearly built on the same platform as her original design for Odie, but it had been taken in a different, bewilderingly complex, direction. And its complexity made it very difficult to fix in a hurry.

Reems kept messaging her for an update, but all Lentz could say was: I need more time. None of her standard monitoring routines were compatible or usable, which meant she had to diagnose the system manually, and the process was painfully slow. So far there was no sign of the subroutine that had triggered the instruction to re-initialise all systems. So far she had found nothing that would stop Medusa wiping itself and starting over.

She glanced at her watch. There were less than five hours left. Gates sat at a new desk he had hastily had brought in, saying nothing. He looked, Lentz thought, like he would rather be anywhere else, although weirdly there was some condescension in his manner. At her? Surely not? She was his only hope. "How," she asked, "did you let the system get built this way? Who allows there to be a single point of failure? If I didn't know better, I'd say you did it on purpose."

He raised an eyebrow. "Have you met Reems? She had her demands, and they were not negotiable."

"But this isn't an intelligence service decision - this is a decision for an engineer. She doesn't have the knowledge and background to understand the issues."

"I tried."

"You didn't try hard enough. It was your job to override

her. And because you failed to do that, everything she has worked for is going to be lost."

"One could say that if you cared about what she was working for, you would have also been here, working for it." He leaned back in his chair. "I really thought that the great Dominique Lentz would have figured things out by now. You have all the data you could possibly need."

Lentz frowned. "I sincerely doubt I have everything. For starters I would...?" She trailed off, staring again at the terminal screen in front of her. Was she missing something? Her eyes flicked over images of the core design, of the system activity, of the power consumption and computing output. And then she saw it. With a cry she banged her hand on the desk.

"What?" he asked.

"There are insufficient server cores to deliver the processing output - by a factor of at least ten. I didn't question it at first, but now that I do, I see that would break the laws of physics. Even for a supercomputer, its power is too great."

"Maybe you're mistaken? Maybe it's just that you don't understand everything after all?" He folded his arms. "Maybe I'm not such an idiot?"

"I appreciate I've taken a few cheap shots today - I did that because I'm tired, frustrated, and, if I'm being honest, you deserved it."

"Worst apology ever."

"Yes, probably. But back to the problem in hand: is there more of Medusa elsewhere in Eastwell?"

"No, of course not. Why?"

"Because some of the power we are witnessing is not coming from what's in the next room. It's coming from somewhere else."

"But the system is air-gapped. It isn't connected to any network - you've already seen that for yourself. It can't be being controlled from somewhere else."

"And yet, what is happening is happening."

"That is true." Gates rubbed a hand through his hair. "If Medusa is being controlled remotely, that would mean this wiping could have been ordered remotely. So if you're right—?"

"I *am* right."

"Assuming you're right, what should we do? Remove the system core and memory banks? If we do that the passive cells can't be wiped. They will remain static until we're ready to redeploy."

Lentz frowned. "Obviously the problem is that removing the core would itself act as a wipe initiation event."

Gates snapped his fingers. "Not if you do it."

"Explain."

"I remember more than a year ago Reems mentioning that Medusa is encoded to your signature. She always assumed you would be here running this place. And we never thought we would be removing the core - doing so would undermine all the security. Obviously, Reems decided that, if it came to it, you were the only one who could be trusted with such a task."

Lentz nodded. "But won't it still then delete itself if not powered up within sixty minutes?"

"Actually we made it a fifteen minute time limit. But all we need to do is migrate to a new host environment."

"And where would we find something compatible?"

Gates blinked. "On level three. It hasn't been tested in a few months, but it should work. I can get people on it right away, if you give the go ahead."

Lentz shook her head and smiled. "Do you have the necessary tools?"

"I might not be a visionary, but I do know how to be an engineer."

"Then let's get to it."

AFTER GATES HAD CALLED his team, removing the core proved surprisingly easy to complete. For all his failings, Gates had all the right tools immediately to hand. Once Lentz had authenticated her credentials, it was just a procedure to be followed.

Lentz and Gates eased Medusa's core, a black metallic lattice of crystals in the shape of a cylinder, approximately fifty centimetres long and thirty centimetres in diameter, and placed it in a padded crate. Lugging that crate, they climbed back out of the server area and removed their white over-suits. Lentz scrunched hers up and used it wipe sweat from her brow. "How long do we have?"

"Fourteen minutes," Gates replied. He tapped at his phone. "I have some technicians coming to meet us right now."

Lentz laughed. "It only weighs about ten kilos. I think we can just carry it straight to your lab."

"Maybe, but we have protocol to follow." He tapped at his phone again, looking a little agitated.

"If you always knew I could remove the core, and that putting it in this alternate system would solve things, why didn't you suggest it earlier?"

Gates shrugged. "Like I said, I never thought we would be in a position where we had to remove it." His eyes flashed at her. "What's the matter with you? We've just had a big success, and you want to point fingers." Down the corridor came the echo of heavy booted feet. It sounded like the technicians were close.

Lentz gave a sigh. "I'm sorry. It's just been a very long day, and I do have a natural tendency to be suspicious."

"So I've heard. And," he appeared to be listening to the footsteps, "you weren't entirely wrong."

Lentz stared at him, confused. And then four heavily armed soldiers walked round the corner and into the room.

And from one look at them Lentz knew without doubt that

they did not work for Reems. She took two steps forwards and stopped sharply as all four men raised their weapons. She turned to Gates. "Let me do the talking..." she trailed off as she saw he was holding a handgun.

"I'll speak for myself."

Lentz's eyes widened. "You're with these people?"

Gates nodded to the new arrivals. "It's in the case on the table." Two men moved over, checked the case was closed, then picked it up.

"You fool!" Lentz said. "What have you done?"

He gave a small bow. "I'm working for someone else. Someone with a great interest in Medusa, and the data it holds."

"So they're the ones that hacked it?"

"Actually nobody hacked it. I planted some ghost routines to make it look that way. Enough to lure you here to enter your codes."

"How on earth did you get through intelligence service background checks?"

"There was nothing to find. At the time I was exactly who I said I was. But then I was made an offer with too many zeroes to refuse."

"So no claim you were coerced or blackmailed?"

"I don't care what you think of me. You're overrated and uninspiring. And let's add 'easily outwitted' to that list." He looked at his phone. "Now we need to get out of here."

"You won't get far before security stops you."

Gates tipped his head on one side. "We might surprise you. Also you're coming with us."

"I'd rather you shot me right here. I'm not going anywhere I don't want to go."

Gates frowned. "If you come quietly, we'll leave Reems be. If you don't, I'll have these men put a bullet in her skull. It's completely up to you."

"There's no way she'll stand by and let me leave. Whatever you do, she's going to put herself in the frame."

"Which is why you're going to override the systems so she's trapped down here. At least for an hour until we're clear away. You think you can do that?" He paused. "I'll be watching you input the code, so don't think you can try something smart."

Lentz sighed. "She is not to be harmed."

"You have my word." Gates pointed at the nearest terminal. "You have five minutes, and I'll be watching for all of them. Remember, unlike the character I've been playing since you got here, I actually know what I'm talking about. Don't go trying any nonsense."

Lentz ground her teeth together. "Of course not."

THIRTY-THREE

KATE GLARED at the heavy main door to the bunker room. The door was over a foot thick and made of reinforced steel. Nobody was getting through it in a hurry, not without the correct code, or a considerable amount of explosives.

Perhaps Tom was right. Perhaps she was safer down here. But that didn't mean it was his decision. If he thought he could expect her to willingly stay there while he tried to be a hero, he didn't know her very well. She would find a way out. She would find a way to help.

She looked up at the screens and immediately saw the intruders trying to hack the outside door. Tom might be able to stop some of them, but there were so many, and they were armed. She had to hurry. She had to get up there.

She needed a weapon - a threat, that they would take seriously. There were no firearms in the bunker. There were four tasers, but they were difficult to use against a prepared opponent - particularly so if they were wearing body armour. There were no grenades, not incendiary, concussive or even smoke variants. Beyond that the bunker contained only food and household items, a number of torches for use in a power cut, some basic hand tools, and a few office supplies. There was, she recalled, a weapons storage room in the basement of the main house. But it was probably empty and, even if it wasn't, she couldn't get to it without getting past the intruders.

There had to be something else. With all of Bern's planning there had to be another option, another possibility. She thought again about what was down here, and then something Tom had said came back to her. There were explosives in the rigged alternative escape tunnel. If she used a few cables from the spares pile, and connected them to a laptop, she could make it look like a bomb. At least enough like a bomb to give her some leverage.

She marched to the far end of the bunker and walked into the bathroom, then pulled a piece of panelling off the wall. Behind was a door. She opened it to reveal a short tunnel, which ended after five metres in a large pile of rocks. Attached to the floor was a sizeable chunk of C4 plastic explosive. More than she would need.

Three minutes later she walked back into the lounge area, carrying the C4 and a handheld torch which she wrapped duct tape around and attached to the laptop by wires in the hope it would pass as a trigger switch. She placed them on the table then looked at the screens again. Blinding light suddenly shone from banks of floodlights. And as the camera feed adjusted, she saw Tom had collapsed. A large man stood nearby. She had to act now. The only problem was the door was still locked.

"Odie," she said firmly. "I really need to get out of here."

There was no response.

"Odie, are you there? Emergency override."

There was a beep and the synthetic voice echoed from the ceiling: *"I am operating under security protocol three and cannot speak with you, except to confirm that I cannot speak with you."*

"Come on, Odie, open the damn door."

"I am unable to comply."

Kate glared. "Tom was just being tetchy earlier. He would want me to leave. You must know that."

"I am unable to comply."

Kate shook her head. "Tom is in danger. And your prime directive is to help him. I know you aren't a dumb machine that can only answer yes or no. I know you have *nuance*. So help me out here."

"My remit does not extend outside this room."

"Do you think that Tom wouldn't change his mind right now, if he could? You can't get to him, so send me instead." Kate smiled. "I'm not commanding you. You're commanding me."

"You are attempting to persuade me by logical argument?"

"I suppose I am. How's it going?"

"Successfully." There was a buzzing sound and the heavy door swung open.

"Thank you, Odie."

"Please complete your assigned task. Save him."

"That's the plan." Kate smiled. "From bad guys, and from himself."

KATE RAN UPSTAIRS, through the pool room and out into the illuminated night. The large man she had seen was crouching next to Tom, who appeared to be unconscious.

"Good evening," he said, looking up at her. "My name is Korver. Who are you?"

Kate swung her gaze around. She counted fifteen operatives standing, four lying on the ground. Two were particularly close to her. "What have you done to him?"

Korver shrugged. "Nothing. He did that to himself."

"You expect me to believe you?"

He looked down at a dark metal sphere in his hand. *Just like the one from the bank vault.* "I'm informed you were a journalist, so I doubt you'd believe anything I told you on face value."

She took a step forward. "I didn't realise I was famous."

"In some circles. And, like you, I have my sources. Now stay where you are."

She blinked. There was something odd about him. Something *oddly familiar*. "Nobody is telling me what to do until I know my friend is..." Ten of the operatives raised their automatic rifles.

The large man frowned. "You have something in your bag. Something electronic. *Show me*."

She shrugged and pulled out the laptop. "I just want my friend safe."

Korver narrowed his eyes, then beckoned her forward. "Move slowly. Very slowly." He looked at his team members. "If she does anything odd, shoot her."

Kate inched forward, the laptop in both hands, held out in front of her. *What was it she was sensing about the man? She was getting that familiar tingle. Was it nanotechnology?* The operatives moved to stay five metres away. Kate edged closer and held it out, arms extended.

Korver took it from her, opened it a fraction and gave a resigned laugh. "Audacious. Four sticks of C4 sitting where the keyboard should be."

Kate raised her hand, showing the duct tape wrapped torch she was holding. "This is a dead man's handle. If I drop this, it will detonate."

Korver nodded. "It might do that. Although this amount of explosive won't kill anyone more than five metres away."

"Difficult to know in advance. But it will certainly kill you." Kate was talking, but her mind was elsewhere. What she was feeling, it was like when she sensed nano on the aircraft carrier a year ago. Like when she was near Tom, but different. Or perhaps she was imagining it. "I mean, I'm sure you know more about bombs than I do."

"I know a little. Maybe I'll throw it away then? Maybe I'll throw it at you? How quick are your reactions?"

"Pretty quick. But they won't need to be. The mechanism has an accelerometer inside. Throw it and it will detonate on the spot."

"Thanks for the warning."

"Maximum disclosure means maximum deterrence."

"I'm not entirely convinced that a journalist had the know how to jury-rig a bomb in a few minutes. But if I'm wrong, you'll still have to deal with everyone else. I don't like your chances."

"Actually, nobody has a chance. The explosion will be enough to trigger the Accumulator. The thing I'm pretty sure you've come here to steal."

Korver's eyes narrowed. "What do you mean?"

"The C4 will cause the Accumulator to explode. According to calculations I've seen someone else perform, with a force of one kiloton."

"And this is your plan? It doesn't seem to end well for you and your friend."

"I didn't have a lot of time, but I'm not completely unhappy with it. I'm hoping that risk will modify your strategy. Because if I do nothing, I'm pretty sure you're planning on killing us."

"So if you don't actually want to die, what do you want to do?"

"I'm going to go back inside the pool house with my friend. And you're going to leave."

"I see. And what do I get out of this arrangement?"

"You get the Accumulator."

He raised an eyebrow. "And you assume that's what I'm here for?"

"Of course you are. I'll leave it here. You can take it once we're back inside the bunker."

"You've thought this all through."

"Unlike my friend when he came up here to face you alone." Kate glanced down at Tom. "Do we have a deal?"

"We do. But next time all bets are off."

"There won't be a next time. But if there is, I'll be ready."

Korver glanced at the sphere and shrugged. "We'll see."

THIRTY-FOUR

LENTZ HURRIED through the corridors of Eastwell, following behind Gates and two of the armed men, the two others following her, their rifles at the ready. Reems was now locked in her office, Lentz had seen to that. She'd sent the shortest of messages. *'Acting under duress. Will release you as soon as I can.'* She was pretty sure Reems would be punching the walls of that room, but at least she was safe. Lentz wasn't sure what else she could have done. She had to stay close to the stolen Medusa system core before it vanished without a trace.

They reached ground level and emerged from the facility's surface entrance, hidden within the familiar but ageing warehouse, with its rough concrete-block walls and corrugated metal-sheet roof. Gates kept walking, and one of the roller doors rose as he approached. Lentz hurried and caught up with him.

"This money they promised you," she said. "Do you really think you're actually going to live long enough to spend it?"

"I've successfully provided some of the most valuable intel in the world. Why wouldn't they want to use me again?"

Lentz shrugged. "In my experience there really is no

honour among thieves. Sure you might have proven yourself. But that doesn't mean they won't go another way and save themselves some money."

"If you're trying to get me to defect, it's not going to work."

"I just wanted you to understand what you're got yourself into."

Ahead of them a very large figure of a man was standing next to a van, four armed guards arrayed nearby. He held in his hand a black metallic sphere the size of a golf ball and was studying it with a frown.

"Problems?" Gates asked as they walked up.

"Connection time is nearly up." He lowered the sphere. "Good evening, Dr Lentz. My name is Korver. I hope you've been treated well?"

"I'm being kidnapped. Apart from that I'm fine."

"Excellent." He turned to Gates. "The data says our team is out."

"I can confirm."

Korver raised the sphere and tapped something on its surface.

Behind them there was an explosion.

Lentz instinctively collapsed to the floor as the blast wave hit them. Gates did the same, but Korver stood, unmoved.

"What the hell was that...?" Lentz began, and then she turned, in horror to see Eastwell was on fire. And realisation hit her.

Reems was in there.

She grabbed Gates by the collar. "What have you done to my friend?" But then she saw from his expression that he was almost as shocked as she was.

"I didn't order this."

"No you didn't," Korver said. "I did."

Lentz looked up. "Why?"

"My boss has a rule. No witnesses, not ever."

She rose to her feet. "I'm going to kill you. I'm going to—"

Gates stood and held out a placating hand. "Don't try and do something stupid—"

Lentz activated the power cell in her Resurface suit, the suit that she had been wearing ever since arriving. She gripped Gates' extended arm and, channelling power through the Resurface nanites to boost her own physical strength, she swung him.

All four armed guards drew their weapons and fired. As she saw this happening, Lentz flipped the purpose of the nanites, shifting them to mimic body armour. Bullets struck her and fell to the ground, but Lentz ignored them and leapt at Korver. "You made a big mistake when you—"

He held up the sphere and tapped it. Her suit froze, rigid, and Lentz slammed to the floor.

Gates hauled himself upright. "What was that? How did you not detect that she was wearing a suit?"

Korver drew his own automatic pistol and pointed at Gates. "You should have run that check. You had ample time."

The scientist took a step back, his eyes staring, a look of utter shock on his face. "Don't try and threaten me. Director Hatch will hear of this."

"Who's Hatch?" Lentz asked immediately.

Korver sighed. "We never say that name out here. *Never.* It's a mistake you only get to make once." And he pulled the trigger. The bullet struck Gates in the forehead. He fell back, his eyes staring, a look of utter shock on his face.

"I told him he couldn't trust you," Lentz said from where she lay on the ground.

Korver frowned. "He was warned." He ran his hand over the case containing Medusa's core, nodded, then signalled to the other guards. "Get her in the vehicle. We move out at once."

Lentz looked up at him, still completely unable to move. "I

just want to be clear, *Korver*. For what you did today, there will be a reckoning."

The huge man nodded with some solemnity. "I understand your position. And for what it's worth, this isn't personal, I'm just following orders."

"Don't try and blame someone else. We all have a choice in the actions we take."

He turned to leave. "Not me."

THIRTY-FIVE

LENTZ, still locked in place by her rigid suit, was carried to a stretched Mercedes SUV and placed across the back row of seats. Korver checked she was in place, then left to travel in another vehicle. Almost immediately Lentz's driver set off, the car bumping its way back along the unmade road, its high spec suspension unable to compensate for the uneven surface.

"Where are we going?" she asked, raising her voice. "And can I sit more upright? I think my arm is going numb."

The driver glanced over his shoulder. "Speak again and I'll put you in the trunk."

Lentz sighed and looked around her, as best she could. There was just the driver, and the two other guards - one in the front passenger seat, one sitting in the middle row of the three rows of seats. They didn't seem to be driving in a convoy with other vehicles, so she would only have to deal with the three of them. Of course dealing with three armed men, while frozen rigid in her suit, was not a challenge many could navigate. Fortunately, she had one more trick up her sleeve.

"So," she said loudly, "where are you guys from? I'm getting a hint of New York from one of your accents, and I think you, Mr Driver, could be Canadian? Am I right?"

"This," replied the driver, "is your last warning."

"Oh come on," Lentz said. "We might as well do something to pass the time. Why don't I tell you something about myself? My name is Dominique, and I'm a Pisces. I like long walks, classical music and Italian food. I consider myself a great exponent of—"

With a squeal of tyres the car lurched to the left and came to a halt. "Right," the driver said. "You can't say you weren't warned."

"What are you doing?" asked the man in the front passenger seat.

"She's going in the trunk. Any objections?"

"The boss didn't say anything about doing that."

"He didn't say anything about *not* doing that."

"Maybe she *wants* to go in there?"

"Why would she want that?"

"I... don't know. He said she was tricky."

"She's already frozen in place, but we can tie her up as well, just to be sure." He opened the front door. "Lift her out."

The man in the back closer to Lentz sighed. "You brought this on yourself."

Lentz smiled. "Just trying to pass the time." She watched him open the door, then slowly slide her out, elevating her to an upright position. She saw they had pulled into an untarmacked car park, surrounded by trees.

"It's a long journey," said the driver as he lifted the boot. "And it doesn't look comfortable in there. But you opened your mouth without thinking."

Lentz would have shrugged, but she couldn't move. "Maybe I opened my mouth *because* I was thinking."

The driver gave a snort. "Bring her round and load her up."

As the rear passenger started to lift her, Lentz screwed up her hand and tapped the subcutaneous control buried in the skin of her wrist.

Her suit deactivated and unlocked.

She allowed herself to collapse from her straightened position. The shift in balance tipped over the man who was carrying her, and they both fell to the ground.

Lentz smacked her hand on her hip, tripping the suit's manual reboot function.

"*Initialising,*" it said in her ear.

"You idiot," said the driver. "She doesn't look that heavy."

"She moved," shouted the man on the ground. "If you want her in the trunk, why don't you pick her up?"

The driver muttered and moved round to where she lay.

Lentz forced a smile. "Can you lot do anything right?" *Turn on, damn it.*

The driver pulled her to a sitting position. "I'd leave you here on the floor, but we have orders."

The suit was starting to vibrate, but it was not yet active. The driver lifted her on to his shoulder and staggered, moving her round to the rear of the car. Still the suit functions were offline. It couldn't be too much longer, could it? If it was, then it might not matter.

The driver sat her on the lip of the boot and beckoned to the man who had been sitting in the front passenger seat. "Help me. I need to lie her down—"

The suit chimed and came online. Power, she saw, was perilously low. She had to hope it would be enough. She leaned forward and pushed her forearms onto the chest of the driver and front-seat passenger. And she sent a massive electrical shock through the suit and into them.

The two men screamed and fell to the floor, jerking.

Two down. She stood, a little unsteadily, and turned to face the other man, the one she had just before knocked to the ground.

He stared at her, wide-eyed, but did not draw his gun. Instead, he took a step back, spreading his hands. "You don't need to do that to me."

"I don't?"

"I didn't sign up for this. I thought you were to be taken as a guest."

"Won't they wonder why you weren't electrified?"

"I'll just tell them I recovered fast." He shrugged. "I'm sorry for what we did to you. I didn't know all the details, but it's no excuse."

"It's a bit of one," Lentz said. "Maybe you should look for a new job."

"Maybe," said the man. "I think I'm going to lie down now. I need to make it look like I was attacked too, get a bit of mess on me."

Lentz nodded and ran off.

She needed to make a call. To Tom. But as she tried to make the connection, the battery in her suit died.

The best tech is tech you have with you, she thought. *As long as you remember to charge it.*

IT TOOK Lentz more than an hour to find a working payphone. It was near the forecourt of a disused petrol station, but amazingly when she picked up the receiver there was a dial tone. She quickly made a reverse charge call to an automated system. In response to specific prompts, she gave three code-words, then typed in a sixteen-digit pin. Finally, an automated voice spoke:

"Greetings Dr Lentz. How can I help you today?"

"Hi, Odie. Emergency care package to my current location."

"Order confirmed. Inbound, thirty minutes."

Twenty-nine minutes later the large drone came into view, dropping down from high altitude. It deposited a padded case the size of a large cereal box in front of Lentz, then took off, returning to its point of origin. She removed two phones, a laptop computer, a change of clothes and an automatic pistol. And, most importantly, a spare power cell for her suit.

What should she do now? Her first instinct - an obvious one - was to call the authorities. But if Gates had got inside Reems' organisation, someone else could have done so and beyond. She had to find out, and that meant proceeding cautiously.

If only she could just speak to Reems. She closed her eyes sadly. Maybe she never would again. Was her friend dead? She had to hope that somehow she had survived.

Lentz activated the first phone, which had been pre-keyed to be her regular number and was startled when it immediately rang. She frowned, not recognising the number. Cautiously she answered it. "Who is this?"

"Me," replied Reems. "I had to borrow someone else's phone."

Lentz blinked, not knowing whether to laugh or cry. "I saw the explosion. How are you alive?"

"Because I realised things were very wrong and ordered an evacuation."

"But I locked you in. How...?"

"I learned from last year and Bern's secret exit from the Dome. Did you really think I'd set up an underground lair without building in an escape route or two?"

"I shouldn't ever doubt you. It's almost like you'd read the script."

"I suppose. Although you could point out that I failed to detect Gates. Seems you can't trust anyone these days. What can you tell me about the people he was working with?"

"There was some big guy called Korver running the op. But that's all I know. They were going to take me to their HQ, but after I saw them kill Gates, I decided my need to escape was greater than the need to stay with Medusa's core. I'm sorry."

"Gates is dead?" Reems asked.

"Korver shot him when he revealed the name of Korver's boss. Does 'Director Hatch' mean anything to you?"

"It does not, but I'll look into it. As for staying with Medusa, you were right to prioritise your own safety. We'll have to find another way to locate it." There was a pause. "The emergency services are inbound, and so is Natasha Gifford. Which means I am going to have a lot of explaining to do, and I'm pretty sure my answers aren't going to satisfy. You need to keep well away. Don't tell me where you're going, and don't go anywhere anyone would expect you to go. We don't want you getting reacquired by this Korver fellow, or by Gifford and her... *inquisition*."

"I understand." Lentz blinked away another tear. "It's good to hear your voice."

"Don't get soppy on me now." And the call disconnected.

Lentz stared at the phone. It was better news than she could have hoped for. Reems was alive. And safe. Now it was time to work out how to start fighting back.

But to do that she needed to go somewhere different. Somewhere nobody would think to look for her, but that might have the resources she needed. Was there someone she hardly knew, someone who nobody would connect her to, yet who she knew would be a capable ally? Someone who could be an asset in her time of need?

And then she smiled. There was somebody perfect for the role, who she had only just met. She reached for her wallet and pulled out a business card. And then she dialled the number. It was answered almost immediately:

"Edna Kim speaking."

"Edna, hi. It's Dominique Lentz. We met at that lecture you gave in Cambridge. I was wondering if you were free for lunch?"

THIRTY-SIX

TOM SLOWLY OPENED HIS EYES, but he could not immediately focus. Every muscle in his body seemed to ache, and his head was pounding. He felt terrible.

But he was alive.

In the dim light around him, a shape came into focus.

Kate.

"Not in a coma then?" she asked as she held out a bottle of water. "That's good."

Tom took the water, gulped messily, then looked around. He was on one of the sofas in the lounge area of the bunker. "How am I here?" He put the bottle down and eased himself onto his elbows. "Where are those people?"

"Gone, at least for now." She glared at him. "You were an idiot, going up alone. You were also an idiot locking me in down here. You could have been killed."

"Yeah probably. Especially since they took control of my suit." Tom closed his eyes and reached out. Except he couldn't. There was nothing there. He tried again, more forcefully.

Nothing.

"What's the matter?" she asked. "Are you in pain?"

"It's not that. They did something to me. I can't feel my Interface." He frowned. "What was that device he had? The metal sphere. It looked like what we found in the vault."

"You know, I didn't have time to ask. You should be thankful you're still breathing. I managed to break out of this place to go up there and help you."

"I am thankful, but..." he looked around, suddenly remembering. "Where is the Accumulator?"

"Really? No: *how are you, Kate?* Or: *how awesome were you, Kate?* Just questions about your damn device." Kate folded her arms. "It was you or the cube. I could only save one."

Tom felt himself shiver. "Then you made a mistake."

"There were twenty of them, and they were heavily armed. I had to make a deal. Your life for the Accumulator. It was the only way."

"How come they didn't just kill you anyway?"

"I borrowed some C4 from the blocked tunnel exit and suggested I might kill us all if they didn't leave."

Tom blinked. "If you said it with that tone, I'm not surprised they believed you." He rubbed his forefingers on his temples and carefully reached out again. Except he couldn't. The term 'reach out' currently had no meaning. His Interface was offline. Was it damaged? Or overloaded? Was it just taking time to reboot? Or was it gone? "I guess I should say 'thank you'."

"I guess you should." Kate glared at him. "It was the best plan I could come up with in the time available. Given how prepared they were, it could have been worse."

He tried to sit up. "They must have been watching Leon Smit, overheard our conversation, and then followed me back here. They can't have been persuaded by my claims of knowing nothing about it."

She shrugged. "Well how did they track you here? We

scanned you for any kind of tracker, and nobody could have followed us, at the speed I drove."

"I don't know. I do know they have some kind of anti-tech tech. Something that... messed with me."

"I think that was the sphere. That guy Korver seemed to be using the one he had like a controller."

"I agree. I tried to connect to it and got completely overwhelmed."

"Like what affected you at the bank? Could these be the hackers?"

He frowned. "Maybe. It was a great deal stronger than at the bank. It... it connected *to me*."

"You connect to stuff all the time."

"But I'm the one that initiates the process. I control the computer. Not the other way around." He shook his head. "I don't remember anything after that. Anything until right now that is. I'm sorry I locked you down here. I was just trying to keep you safe."

"I know you meant well." She patted him on the shoulder. "And that's the only reason I didn't kill you."

"So what was that sphere thing? Did we capture any data?"

"Not much." Kate picked up her laptop off the table. "I ran an analysis from what our sensors picked up. They showed signs of high-level encryption and decryption taking place. But then no actual data seemed to go anywhere, at least not that we could detect."

He rubbed his forefingers on his temples. "So do you think...?"

"...that his sphere could be related to the one you found in the bank vault? The question is definitely crossing my mind."

Tom walked over to the storage locker and stared at the metal object. It still looked inert and inactive. "Odie, any change in the sphere?"

"Nothing, Tom," it replied. *"I have been monitoring it constantly."*

"Thanks." He peered closer. "It could just be beyond our instruments."

Kate moved next to him. "It could be how they found us."

"So they fed Reems fake intel, and made me go to the bank vault?"

"Maybe. In order to get the device into your possession. You should also know that I think I detected nanotechnology."

"What? Where?"

"In Korver. It was like you, but not."

"You sure it wasn't just in me, and fritzed?"

"I'm honestly not sure - I just thought you'd want to know."

"Fair enough." He looked around. "OK, we'll put the sphere in a lead-lined box and leave it here. We can worry about it later."

Kate looked at him. "Because we've got somewhere more important to be?"

Tom stared at her. "We have to get the Accumulator back. Not just because I want it, but because of the danger it represents to everyone else."

"I agree. But unless you can get yourself connected again, we are going to need help. I tried calling Reems as soon as we got back online half an hour ago. But there's been no response."

"Lentz?"

"Offline as well."

Tom forced himself to take a slow breath. "Is that an alarming coincidence? Or just a regular one?"

"I don't know. I don't like any of this."

"Did you call anyone else?"

"I was waiting to discuss that with you. You're not usually a fan of calling in regular law enforcement. I thought that might mean we end up with Natasha Gifford on our doorstep. Reems said she's been looking for any excuse to speak with you—"

Kate's phone rang. Her eyes widened and she answered the phone on speaker. "Dominique, I'm here with Tom, in the bunker. Where are you?"

Lentz's voice came through sounding particularly distorted. "Best I don't say. I'm not sure I trust a secure line to be enough protection today. Are you both OK?"

"Maybe. We have quite a bit to catch you up on." Kate quickly summarised Tom's visit to VoltTech's offices, the encounter with Smit, then the attack at the mansion. Lentz listened without asking questions. "We tried to call Reems," Kate said, as she finished, "but we couldn't get hold of her."

"Yeah," Lentz said, "you're going to have trouble doing that at the moment. I'm pretty sure she's being questioned by Natasha Gifford."

"What?"

"She's been working on a side hustle, without the knowledge of MI5. Except now they know."

"That doesn't sound like her."

"The side hustle? Or getting caught doing it?" Lentz gave a bitter-sounding laugh. "You just don't know her well enough. Because when it comes to it, nothing gets in the way of Stephanie Reems." She paused. "Except in this case, she has rather got in her own way. She created a central repository of intelligence, details of fringe science technology, as part of a new initiative she's been building – a new intelligence agency specialising in tech."

Tom sat up on the sofa. "She told us she was destroying the information."

Lentz sighed. "Not so much. She was cataloguing it. Blueprints, instructions, manuals, knowhow. All recorded safely and securely in a computer system called Medusa."

"Poor name... wait, are you saying that you knew!"

"Only in the last few hours."

"And where is this?"

"An unfortunate memory from the past. It's called Eastwell."

Tom blinked. "I thought that old place had been decommissioned and dismantled?"

"So did we all. Which I think is why she chose it. I suppose she did what she felt she had to do. She told you what you needed to hear in order to get your assistance. Like I said, nothing gets in the way of her plans. Including lying to her friends."

Kate leaned closer to the phone. "So is this Medusa system still at Eastwell? Should we go there?"

"Unfortunately, some bad guys came and stole it. The same bad guys you encountered. This Korver you mentioned was in charge - I had a close encounter with him myself."

"But you managed to escape?"

"It wasn't straightforward. Another facility got blown up in the process, but that's a story for another time."

Tom stood up. "So these people, whoever they are, have my Accumulator. And they also have every bit of intel we acquired, and more besides. They must be the ones that hacked the bank and VoltTech."

"Maybe. Something of great sophistication hacked Medusa. But whoever, or whatever, is behind it, it's not a good outcome. Reems is, presumably, having to explain all of this to Natasha Gifford. And, between you and me, I don't think she'll be able to. Tom, I really wish you'd told me about the Accumulator."

"You would have just tried to take it away from me."

"Would that have been such a bad idea?"

"Without it I cannot do what I need to do."

"Instead of making things better, it could be making them worse. It could be harming you." The line crackled. "And if you didn't tell me about the Accumulator, what else haven't you told me?"

Tom glared at the phone. "You're really having a go at me? And I suppose you tell us everything?"

She gave a snort. "I think the time has come for us to push reset. If we're going to help each other, there needs to be more trust."

"Trust has to be earned."

"I know you're angry, Tom. But you need to direct that anger against the people who are actually your enemy."

Kate reached over and gripped Tom's shoulder. "We're with you, Dominique. So what are we going to do?"

"Let me get somewhere safe. Then I'll contact you. You should get away from that mansion, and stay out of sight - it seems very likely that either Korver will come back, or Gifford will send a team. Neither will be something you want to deal with. Look after each other."

"Thank you, Dominique," Kate said, picking up the phone. "Stay safe." Then she closed the call.

Tom stared upwards then started to pace around the room. "Reems betrayed us."

"She did her job." Kate shrugged. "Or rather she was trying to create a new one. It was certainly a grand plan."

"You're impressed by what she did?"

"I'm saying don't get annoyed with a tiger for being a tiger. Speaking of which, should we warn Smit?"

"Help him? After how he reacted last time? He can go... *help himself*." Tom closed his eyes and reached out. There was still nothing. "I need to go to one of Lentz's facilities. I need her equipment to analyse what is going on with me."

"You're suggesting go to her house? I doubt that's what she meant by staying out of sight."

"I suppose you're right. And, in any event, I'm not sure I can get through her security with my current abilities. Plus others may track us there, or be there anyway."

"Then where? Anything related to CERUS is going to be off limits."

Tom nodded. "There is one place that comes to mind. Somewhere she took me when she wanted to make sure she wasn't found." He paused and ran a hand over the Resurface suit that he still wore. "Although before we leave, I think I'm going to change. I've had enough of being controlled." He raised an eyebrow. "And if I ever suggest wearing this thing again, you have my permission to shoot me."

Kate nodded. "Duly noted."

THIRTY-SEVEN

REEMS STOOD with her team members in the cover of trees, watching Eastwell burn against the dark sky. Thanks to her planning, they had all got out alive. But the danger to her was far from over. If anything it was about to escalate. This was not a time for weakness. This was not a time for doubts.

In the distance she heard the sound of sirens in the night. Five fire engines emerged from the darkness, crashing and banging their way along the unmade road, then spreading out in front of what used to be the headquarters of a new intelligence agency. A number of emergency ambulances followed and then several police cars. Finally, and much more slowly, there appeared an unmarked Jaguar SUV with deeply tinted windows. It parked and the short figure of a woman appeared, holding a phone to her ear.

Reems' phone rang. She answered it immediately. "Hello, Natasha."

"Evening, Stephanie," Gifford replied. "You ready to be debriefed?"

"Thought you'd never ask."

Reems waved to her people and began walking, well aware

that the answers she was going to give would lead to further and more difficult questions.

And, as she knew, that was just how things had to be. If her plan was to succeed, there was no going back.

REEMS SAT in the back of the Jaguar, alone with MI5's Deputy Director. Outside the car the fires still burned, despite the best efforts of fifty firefighters. In the distance was the sound of more sirens approaching.

Gifford sipped from her bottle of mineral water. "I should have been in Covent Garden tonight. The final performance of Turandot. My partner bought the tickets months ago. Front row of the stalls."

"I imagine this is an inconvenience, but—"

"So instead of watching an operatic triumph, I'm here to pay witness to a complete disaster. It has not put me in a good mood." Gifford rubbed her forefingers on the bridge of her nose. "Would it be an understatement to say that you have a lot of explaining to do?"

Reems laced her fingers together. "It certainly looks that way. So why don't I...?"

Gifford raised a hand. "Don't waste my time spinning some yarn. I want nothing less than the truth tonight."

"Are you here to help? Or to point fingers?"

"You're lucky I'm not here to arrest you. Indeed, perhaps I should be." She put her bottle of water in the passenger door cupholder. "The system flagged odd patterns in your behaviour. Not enough for any individual to notice without blind luck. Strangely chosen travel routes, moments when you would drop off the grid. Those oddities, those anomalies were escalated for my attention. From there I authorised a full audit."

"You don't have the authority to—"

"I have direct authorisation from the Home Secretary himself."

"I suppose you do like to tick every box, dot every 'i', cross every 't'. Did he laugh when he signed this off? Or did he limit himself to a broad grin?"

Gifford stared back blankly. "This isn't funny, Ms Reems."

"*Director* Reems."

"We'll come to that." Gifford scratched her nose. "As for the audit, there is a certain inalienable truth in the numbers. Words are so slippery, so imprecise – so open to *interpretation*. But the audit gave me an MRI scan of your activities."

"By which you mean 'fuzzy and lacking in colour'?"

"I mean it shed light on interior workings."

"And what did you find?"

"That you were siphoning off funds – repurposing black ops expenditure for a particular cause." She pointed towards the fires. "You were building your own secret facility, entirely under your own jurisdiction and without oversight."

"A somewhat grandiose summary."

"But accurate, yes?"

Reems drummed her fingers on the window. "What I have done I did because it was necessary. Because without it, we will lose." She stopped her fingers moving. "I'm a patriot, not a traitor."

"You broke the law." Gifford straightened in her seat. "So we are going to go to an interview room and do this properly and be seen to do this properly. And you are going to tell me everything. Only then can I assess what we do next."

Reems sighed. "What we need to do is go after the people who stole my system. The people who destroyed Eastwell. If we lose them the consequences will be dire."

"You're saying this explosion wasn't a laboratory accident?"

"It was caused by a bomb."

"I note your hypothesis. It will be one we test against the forensic data. And I will deploy resource to pursue this alleged group. But you have to be interviewed. Everything has to be on the record and transparent. Only that way do we get to the truth."

Reems raised an eyebrow. "You've been playing this game long enough to know that there is no guarantee of ever getting to the truth."

"I'm still going to try." Gifford pulled out her phone and glanced at it. "And you are going to have to trust me to do the right thing."

"Very well," Reems replied. "Then let's go and get started."

THIRTY-EIGHT

EDNA KIM, Lentz had discovered, did not live 'on the beaten track', or, by English standards, anywhere near it. Her home was a somewhat ramshackle six bedroom house, ten miles outside of Cambridge, set on fifteen acres of what used to be working farmland, but which was now considerably overgrown. From where Lentz stood, in the cover of a hedgerow, her surveillance drone showed Kim at home, and nobody else within half a mile. It looked safe to proceed.

Lentz left the field and made her way along the poorly maintained single-lane road. After a hundred metres she turned left and began walking down Kim's driveway. It was a two hundred metre, rough gravel track, littered with potholes that would make it treacherous for anything other than a four-wheel-drive vehicle, and Lentz had to watch her footing. The driveway eventually swept round in front of the house, ending at free-standing double garage. Lentz's boots crunched on the gravel as she walked up and rang the doorbell.

Edna Kim opened the door. She was wearing the same frayed beige jacket with leather arm patches and heavy, thick-rimmed glasses. "Dominique?" She looked around in apparent confusion. "Where is your car?"

"I got a taxi then thought I'd spare it trying to negotiate your driveway. OK if I come in?"

"Of course, of course. Is everything OK? You seem a little... on edge."

"I've had a difficult few days. I'm really in the need of some stimulating conversation."

"I'll see what I can do," Kim said with a smile.

Lentz walked down a long, poorly lit hallway into a room which, if you were being generous, you would call the workplace of a careless eccentric. If you were being less kind you might describe it as a scene of utter chaos. Most of the ground floor walls had been knocked through to create a single very large workspace. Long workbenches were littered with computers and laboratory equipment, along with a number of textbooks and scientific journals. Plastic storage crates were stacked high and low in a seemingly random fashion, and the floor was littered with cardboard boxes and discarded bubble wrap. To one side were five three-drawer metal filing cabinets, none of which matched any of the others.

Lentz picked her way carefully through the clutter. "You really shouldn't have tidied up on my account."

Kim frowned. "I didn't, but...? Oh," she clapped her hands together. "Fair comment. All I can say is, it works for me. When I have an idea, I can't slow myself down by worrying about where something goes."

"But how do you then find it again?"

"It usually turns up. Sometimes I have the same bright idea more than once, which increases the chances that I might actually do something with it."

Lentz nodded. "I guess everyone has their own way of working. I was worried you were going to say you'd had a break-in."

"Why would anyone bother? The only things of value I have," Kim tapped her head, "are in here. Although when I do need to tidy up, I've always got my assistants to help me. *Yin, Yang* - come do your thing!"

A pair of waist-height doors in one wall slid back and two rounded metal cubes on caterpillar tracks rolled out. Each had two articulated robotic arms connected to its top surface, ending in gripping in pincers. With a soft beep they went in opposite directions and began moving crates and boxes into a slightly tidier arrangement.

"Robo vacuum cleaners?" Lentz asked.

"I think they're a little more sophisticated than that." She nodded towards the automated devices as one of them fumbled a plastic crate. "Although perhaps not much more sophisticated."

"A work in progress."

"That is how science works." One of the two robots seemed to have got stuck, so Kim went over and gave it a nudge. "And I should stress these are old prototypes that I didn't have the heart to dismantle. Leftovers from a job that ended earlier than expected when the money ran out."

"A silver lining to a cloud."

"A lovely way of putting it. Actually, I was lucky to have anything to work with. A lot of parts were stolen from my workshop. Who would steal from a scientist?"

"Oh, you'd be surprised. Is robotics still a big part of your research?"

"As part of my symbiosis roadmap, very much so. I've been working on full systems - those designed to imitate humans and animals, as well as applications in healthcare. I have a lot I can show you, although this is where my lawyers would get me to make you sign an NDA." She paused. "But I've never much listened to my lawyers."

"Why the interest in nanotech?"

"It was always something that I felt had passed me by. When I was at CERUS, all those years back, it wasn't even a thing, and if I'm honest, that suited me just fine. I prefer to work with things I can see."

"Yeah, that is a problem with nano."

"I lost faith in the 'very small' after my PhD - I just wasn't optimistic it would ever be real. But it turns out I was wrong. The potential with nano-enabled neural interfaces is undeniable, and unavoidable. I want biological and synthetic systems to work in harmony. The goal - as you identified when we last met – is *symbiosis*. If you can control a robotic limb properly, an amputee can achieve a quality of movement previously unattainable."

Lentz blinked. "A project like that got me into science in the first place."

Kim smiled. "We all have something that drives us. That gives us that extra shove to achieve greatness. Or to search forever for it." She shrugged. "Sometimes the possibilities overwhelm me. There are so many things I could do, but I can't do it all on my own."

"So, you need an interface? That was why you wanted to speak to me?"

"I heard the rumours about what you achieved. And, to be clear, I'm not one to idly believe every bit of nonsense I hear from my fellow scientists after their second glass of Rioja. But it is another star to add to your galaxy of mystique."

"I really wish I could offer you a magical solution. All I can say is there are many challenges to overcome in the quest to create a replicable neural interface. Any rumours you may have heard about success didn't give you the full picture."

Kim nodded. "I'm not looking to cheat by copying someone else's work. I'm just looking for inspiration. I think we need to make our own discoveries." She paused. "Of course, if you can find someone like-minded to work with..."

"You mean this Osiris Foundation?"

"Yes. Although I'm still waiting for more details. There seems to be some sort of hold up."

"Sorry to hear that."

"Apparently you were right to be sceptical. Things don't always work as you hope." Kim walked over to one of the tiny robots which had stopped moving. She gave it a gentle prod with her foot, and it buzzed back into action. "So, why were you so keen to meet today? Have you had a change of heart? Dare I hope that you might be interested in collaborating?"

"I think we have much to discuss." Lentz folded her arms. "But for now I have a more urgent requirement. I'm in a spot of trouble, and I was hoping you could help."

"I am intrigued." Kim paused. "Wait, *trouble*? You don't mean scientific help?"

"Not today. And before we go any further, before I tell you anything, I should stress this is an intelligence matter. I am in danger, and by coming here, I could be putting you at risk. So, if you'd like me to leave then I'll be on my way right away, and no hard feelings—"

Kim snapped her fingers. "That's why you didn't drive! How wonderfully clandestine."

"Edna, this is not a game. I want you to be under no illusions as to what you could be getting yourself messed up with."

Kim walked over to the nearest filing cabinet, slid open the lowest drawer and pulled out an unlabelled bottle of clear liquid, along with two shot glasses. She placed them on the table in front of Lentz. "I will do whatever I can to help. So why don't you explain what is going on. And, I'll sign whatever confidentiality agreement or official secrets act thingy that you need."

"NDAs won't protect anyone here." Lentz watched Kim pouring into the glasses. "What is that?"

"Homemade ouzo. I have a Greek uncle who gave me the

recipe." She finished pouring and picked up one of the glasses, nodding to the other.

Lentz picked up and sniffed her glass, noticing the strong scent of anise. "Your good health, Dr Kim."

"And yours, Dr Lentz. Here's to us, and whatever mischief we can manage together."

LENTZ SAT at the central workbench in the knocked-together downstairs room, her laptop open in front of her, the area around them freshly cleared of scientific detritus.

"Tell me everything," Kim said. "The more I know, the better I can help."

Lentz frowned. "The more you know, the more danger I'll be putting you in."

"Oh, please. Who would threaten little old me?"

"Edna, you have to trust my judgement here."

"And you can trust me. You surely must, to have come here to ask for help."

"I wouldn't have thought to reach out, given we only met that one time. The timing of your call was on point."

"Serendipity."

"Perhaps. But to be candid, while part of it is that you seem very trustworthy, the other big part is that we have no history of prior contact. So anyone following me wouldn't prioritise you as a person of interest in my pursuit."

"I suppose that makes sense. Did they teach you that when you worked at MI5?"

"I've learned a lot of things from a lot of places. And right now, I'm going to give you only the absolute minimum."

Kim nodded slowly. "Need to know - check."

"I was supporting the Intelligence Service - what most people refer to as MI5 - with a project relating to an experimental computer. But part of the prototype was stolen by a private concern. They also tried to take me with them."

"And you managed to escape? My goodness, are you OK?"

"I'm fine. But I can't go to my usual sources of support because they're probably being watched, and going to any regular law enforcement would simply flag my location."

"So it was an inside job? And you have to solve this yourself? A lone operator, struggling against all odds!"

Lentz folded her arms. "Edna, this isn't the plot of a movie. This is horribly real."

"You're right, I'm sorry. What do you need from me?"

"Do you have some form of mainframe computer here? Some large array? Or are you just running desktops?"

"I have a server system which I use in my development work. It's located in one of my barns, but I have several direct feeds running into the house. Give me an hour and I can run a new cable for you to use."

"Excellent. I need to build a virtual machine to connect with the server at my house. Once I have it running, I can set some resources in action, completely separate from your system."

"Oh wow, that is so cool..." Kim paused. "Sorry. I'll try and calm down."

Lentz took a slow breath. "I need to track these people, work out who they are, and see if I can assess who within our organisations could have leaked intel. After that I can brief the key players."

"Like Stephanie Reems?"

"You didn't hear that name from me." Lentz tapped her keyboard to display a notes file. "I'm also going to need these items."

Kim leaned forward. "I have all of that. Send the list to my phone and I'll get it all sorted. Now are you hungry at all because I can..."

A loud chime echoed around the room.

"What's that?" Lentz asked.

Kim frowned and spoke to the room. "CCTV on." Two screens lit up on one of the remaining walls. Three white vans were approaching up the gravel driveway. "Who can that be?"

Lentz stared at the images and forgot to breathe. How could they have found her so quickly? "I'm so sorry, Edna. They're here for me."

"Are you sure? It could just be a delivery?"

"In three different vans? Unless you've ordered a very large three-piece-suite, I've been followed." Lentz stood up and stuffed her laptop into her backpack. "I'm going to lead them away. Stay out of sight, whatever you do. Your life may depend on it."

"I'm not scared."

"Then you haven't been listening." Lentz checked her Resurface suit was in position, then ran for the back door.

THIRTY-NINE

LENTZ RAN out the back door of Kim's house towards a collection of outbuildings. How had this happened? She had scanned herself for tracking devices with the most sophisticated equipment available. She had taken every precaution, used every bit of fieldcraft in her toolkit. And still they had found her. *It just made no sense.*

She ran towards a nearby barn and ducked down into the cover of a number of wooden crates, next to a double wooden hatch in the floor - presumably access to an underground storage area. Listening carefully she could make out the sound of van doors opening, and people shouting on the other side of the house. They were close. She had to hope that they would quickly ignore the main house and follow her trail. Did they have drones airborne that were tracking her now? Or would they need to search the house?

Muttering, she realised she had acted rashly, and now Kim could be in real danger. Still crouching she reached into her backpack and removed the automatic pistol. She would go back and see what she could do.

But it was already too late.

"Good afternoon, Dr Lentz," said a voice from behind her.

She turned and saw a fourth van was parked behind the barn, a large figure was standing next to it.

Korver.

Lentz rose slowly to her feet, holding the gun loosely in her right hand. "You're persistent."

"I've heard it said. My team were somewhat inept last time, so I'll be overseeing your transfer personally to make sure we have no repeats."

"Or perhaps you won't." She tapped to activate the suit, equipped with its fresh power cell.

Nothing happened.

Korver held up the sphere she had seen him with before. "My men at least managed to tell me how you escaped. This time I've shut your suit down properly."

"Impossible. Nobody could..." But Lentz could feel from the utter lack of vibration within the fabric that he wasn't bluffing. She glanced around, hearing raised voices and the sound of equipment being thrown around from the house. "Leave Kim out of this. I didn't tell her anything."

"We can't take the chance."

"This has nothing to do with her."

"Then you shouldn't have come here. Now if you drop that handgun I won't have to taser you before we load you up for transportation."

Another voice spoke: "Don't tell my friend what to do."

Lentz turned with a start. Kim had leapt out of the wooden hatch doors on the floor. In her hands she had a very modern looking pump-action shotgun with a laser sight. With considered calm she trained it on Korver's chest.

Korver immediately raised a hand. "Everybody, be calm. Stay where you are."

"How," Lentz asked, "did you get there?"

"I have a tunnel from the house," Kim replied. "It's how I run the data feeds from the server."

"Why do you have a shotgun? People round here usually just get a dog."

"Why do you have a Glock 19?" She took a step toward Korver. "You've gravely underestimated what you're up against here. Now take your people and get off my land."

He stared at her. "I'm not leaving without Dr Lentz."

Kim took another step forward. "Then I'll shoot you."

"And what about my team of twenty? Drop the weapon."

"You've already told Dominique that you're going to kill me. I might as well take a few of you with me, and, to be clear, you will be first."

Korver raised an eyebrow. "Ever shot someone?"

"You think I won't? I might well surprise you."

"You *might*." He started walking towards her, the sphere in his hand. "I see you have no suit on, so we won't have that complication." He was less than ten metres from Lentz and Kim.

"Stop where you are."

Lentz flicked her gaze around. Two men had stepped out the backdoor of the house. They were about to be heavily outnumbered. Korver kept walking. He was only five metres away and closing.

"I said stop," Kim repeated. "Are you an idiot or something?"

"I'm on a deadline here," he replied, continuing to close the gap, "and you aren't going to shoot me."

"Wrong," Kim said. And she fired.

LENTZ WATCHED the slug strike Korver in the chest, but knew that taking out the big man was only part of their challenge. She spun with her Glock, pointing it in the direction of the house in an attempt to dissuade Korver's team from coming to help. She doubted a single handgun would dissuade them for long. With her suit locked out of action, she wasn't sure what else she could do.

Because she was looking the other way, she didn't realise what had happened. Or rather, what had *not* happened.

"What?" Kim shouted. "That's not possible."

Lentz turned and saw Korver still standing. He was not dead, nor wounded. He seemed entirely unharmed, as he brushed away shell fragments from his chest. Then he strode sharply towards Kim, and with a swing of his hand seized the shotgun from her.

Lentz's brain took a moment to grasp what she was seeing, so she was slow bringing her own weapon to bear. As she did he swung the shotgun by the barrel, smacking the Glock from her hand. It struck the concrete and skittered away.

Kim frowned. "How are you not dead?"

Korver whistled sharply and his team raced out of the house, surrounding them.

"You must have a suit? High tech body armour of some type." Lentz took a step forward. "What is this all about? Do you need my help with something scientific?"

"They don't share such detail with me. But given your background that seems likely."

Lentz jabbed a finger towards Kim. "She's a scientist, like me. A good one. If you want me to do science, you should bring her too. Keeping her alive will give me a reason to cooperate."

Kim coughed. "Dominique, I'm not going to 'heaven knows where' with these people—"

"I'm trying to save your life here," Lentz hissed. "I appreciate the irony that I am the one who has put it in danger."

"You're not responsible for their actions." She stood up straight and gave a disdainful sniff. "And probably, they aren't either. They're just following orders. They probably don't even know who they're working for."

"I know enough. But that's how the world works." He glanced at the sphere and looked surprised. "And it seems those who give the orders are amenable to Dr Lentz's suggestion. You will be coming with us, Dr Kim." He looked up at his team members. "Let's move out, before anyone comes to investigate the gunfire."

Lentz took a slow breath. "How did you find me?"

"My people are resourceful. If you want to know more, ask once we've got there." And he walked away.

Lentz leant close to Kim. "I am sorry, Edna. I really am."

"Who are these people?"

"I don't know. But I intend to find out."

FORTY

IT WAS pitch black as Tom and Kate reached the end of a rough gravel road. Tom slowed the VW Golf - an old car that he kept parked away from Bern's mansion grounds, registered to a fake name so it couldn't be connected to him. He parked beneath a large tree, beside a tired-looking wooden building. The barn was one of a number of outbuildings on the farm, located a few miles from Windsor, about an hour west of London by car. Years previously Lentz had struck a deal with the farmer to use the wooden structure for the long-term storage of some old equipment.

"It's certainly discreet," Kate said. "Like the tenant doesn't want to signal what she has going on here."

Tom nodded. "She opted against a sign saying: 'Lentz's secret hideout'." He climbed out and stared at the barn door. This was the place where she had brought him two years ago, when she had first rescued him from Marron and Alex. Back then he had simply been a terrified lawyer, running from an enemy he did not comprehend. Coming here had helped him. Perhaps it would again.

Kate climbed out from the front passenger seat. "Any automated security measures to worry about?"

"It's one of Dominique's key sites, so what do you think? There are a range of sensors and cameras in place."

"Then I hope you can deactivate them." She put her hands on her hips. "Or this might be a problematic visit. But I believe you can do it."

"Only one way to find out." He stood still, closing his eyes, and reached out. And this time, to his delight, there was *something*. He could feel the blood pulse in his veins. A sense that his Interface was still there. Deep within his mind he felt the echo - a glimmer of what used to be. He breathed slowly and reached again, extending his presence, feeling for control.

Tenuously it was there. And it was welcome. A grin crossed his face. He sent a signal. It wasn't easy, he realised, puffing out his cheeks. He would need to concentrate harder.

"I'm hoping," Kate said, "that your smile is a good sign."

He raised a finger to his lips and reached out more firmly. He felt the sensors and CCTV cameras. They looked down upon him now, watching, assessing. His mind reached into their systems - systems he was familiar with, that shared Lentz's design philosophies. Systems he knew how to talk to. And he turned them off. Running a hand through his hair he turned to Kate. "We're good to go in."

"My hero."

He walked over to the barn door, unlocking the electronic padlock with a mere glance, then he pulled open the well-oiled door and turned on a fluorescent light. Inside were several items of farm equipment, covered in dust sheets - nothing out of the ordinary for a barn. He kicked sawdust from the middle of the floor to reveal a trapdoor. Running his fingers along the edge, he found the concealed handle and pulled upwards. LEDs immediately lit up, showing metal stairs descending.

Kate moved alongside him. "You like this place, don't you."

Smiling, Tom led the way down.

THEY SAT in the barn's basement, drinking coffee from a supply Lentz had refreshed recently.

"How often does she come here?" Kate asked.

"At least once a month," Tom replied. "She likes to check it is secure. Of course with all the sensors and cameras she doesn't need to attend in person, but I think she likes having an excuse to nose through old supplies." He gestured at the metal racking lining all the walls. "There's still a lot of stuff here, although mostly it's a couple of generations out of date. Things that really should be thrown out, but she doesn't have the heart to do it." He stood up and walked over to where a small robotic arm, mounted on a heavy base, stood on one of the shelves. "She still has this old thing."

"Didn't you use that to train your Interface?"

"I did. Back at the very beginning. What Lentz calls a computer-controlled synthetic limb. Clearly I've already bored you with that story."

"Can you use it to get yourself working properly again?"

Tom shook his head. "This I used before I could do anything. Now the problem is more that I can't move to higher levels of ability. To do the more complicated things that I've learned to do since." He rubbed the back of his neck. "Even just the trivial task of accessing the security systems upstairs has drained me."

Kate clenched and unclenched her fists. "Have you just become too dependent on the Accumulator?"

"There's nothing wrong with using it as a resource. The more I do with the Interface, the more I go beyond the bounds of what it was originally conceived for. The more I push beyond the boundaries of what a human mind can possibly cope with." He turned and started rummaging through the shelves, picking up items then pushing them aside. "Maybe a human brain could evolve to cope, but it might take hundreds of generations. I need to progress orders of magnitude more quickly, and for that I'll need augmentation."

"I suppose. Yet you become reliant on it. And if you lose it, you find yourself in a difficult place."

"So I should have stayed in first gear?" He moved to the next shelf. "Remember that when I originally learned the use of the Interface, I couldn't do it at all without artificial help."

"You mean those collar things?"

"They were like training wheels. All I had to do was connect to a powered collar with a specially designed access point, located in very close proximity to my brain. The easiest, most supportive possible environment - without it I'm sure I never would have got out of the starting blocks."

Kate pulled a grey metal case the size of a small cereal box from a high shelf. "Is this what you're looking for?"

Tom took it and placed it on the central workbench, flipping it open. Inside, nestled in specially cut foam padding, were two brand new collar devices. "How did you know?"

"Lentz had a similar case in the basement storage areas at CERUS Tower. There's a whole load of stuff in their lockers that we would find very useful."

"You saying we should have gone there?"

"Even with you at full operational capability it would be a challenge to break in. They've upgraded everything in the last year."

He shrugged and pulled one of the collars out of its padding. "This should work. The issue is the battery keeps draining in almost no time. But it's a lot better than nothing."

Kate continued walking around the shelving. "What else were you hoping to find here?"

"We could look for weaponry? Or a portable computer or two?"

Kate picked up a handheld device. "Any good?"

Tom raised an eyebrow. "A level three scanner. For what?"

"For scanning things. And by 'things', I mean 'you'."

"I wasn't bugged. I'm not that careless."

"All I know is you were followed, and we don't know how." She frowned. "What if they're able to do the same to Lentz. We need to call her."

"If she's gone dark, I don't know how we'd do that. She said she'd contact us."

"Then what about Reems? There must be some clue about where she is, something you can access from your familiarity with her systems."

Tom placed the collar around his neck. "If I use this, it could boost me enough to..." he trailed off, frowning. "Did you hear that?"

Kate narrowed her eyes. "Something upstairs."

Tom closed his eyes, connecting to the cameras outside. There were people moving in the dark, four that he could detect. In the air above them three drones were hovering.

"What is it?" Kate asked. "Bad news?"

"We've been followed. We need to get out of here, fast."

TOM AND KATE climbed quickly up the stairs from the basement, turning the lights off below.

"You still sure you aren't bugged?" Kate asked. "Because if not, how did they find us?"

"Maybe they just know about Lentz's cache, and they're

crossing it off the list? The bad news is they have drones all around. I can feel them. They've also found our car, so we're going to have to find another way out of here."

"Are they Korver's people?"

"Seems likely, although my first suggestion isn't that we go and ask them."

"Did Lentz install any defence systems?"

Tom raised an eyebrow. "She only has those at her house." He pointed away from the main doors. "There's a fire exit back there."

"And is anyone watching it?"

"I can't tell, but it has to be better than walking out the front."

"Good point." Kate moved forward and reached the exit door. "Ready?"

Tom nodded. "If we go through that area of woodland there's a main road on the other side. Maybe we can hitch a lift."

Kate opened the door and they stepped out into the night.

Tom followed, reaching out, sensing for anything that might indicate somebody nearby. "I think we're clear," he said. "Let's move—"

Two men stepped around the corner of the barn, rifles strung across their backs. One grabbed Kate, and she instantly rolled to her side, twisting and flipping him to the ground. But he was immediately back on his feet.

The other man smiled at Tom. "You're coming with us." He reached for his belt and unclipped a pair of handcuffs.

Tom circled to his right, vaguely aware that Kate had the other assailant in a headlock. She might be winning, but she couldn't help him. He needed to help himself. But his opponent was larger, stronger, and undoubtedly more used to fighting.

But was that right?

Something told Tom that he had the necessary skills, that he knew what to do. He took a slow breath, trying to understand what he was feeling. It didn't come from the Interface. It came from somewhere else. A sense of perfect control of his body that was somehow within him. Tom growled and with every bit of anger he could muster swung a fist at the man's stomach.

The punch connected and there was a flash of pain, shooting along Tom's arm. It was like hitting a brick wall. His target must be wearing body armour.

The man looked down with a smile. "You hit like a kid."

Tom glared and launched himself forward, looking to strike with his shoulder. The man stepped smoothly to one side, leaving his leg trailing. Tom, carried by his momentum, tripped and fell onto the muddy ground.

"Nice moves," said the man, "but playtime's over—" His eyes rolled back as he fell forward and slumped to the ground. Kate stood behind him, her fist still closed.

"Thanks," Tom said, turning over in the mud.

Kate nodded. "Shall we get out of here before their friends come to check on them?"

"Good idea."

They ran further into the woods, away from where they'd parked the car.

"What on earth made you try and fight him?" Kate asked.

"I had to do something. It's not like he gave me the option to 'not fight'."

"These are professionals. You could have been badly hurt." She frowned. "What's weird is you looked really confident. And, I can't explain why, but you *feel* confident."

"For a moment I thought I knew what I was doing."

"Except you didn't."

Tom flexed his shoulders. "Thanks for being there to save me from myself."

"Anytime. Now where do we go?" Kate asked.

"Lentz is offline. But Reems has shown up on the cameras outside a building on my primary watchlist. She seems to have a habit of hanging in places that have terrible memories for me."

"We're going to London Docklands, aren't we."

"If you're ready for a trip down memory lane?"

FORTY-ONE

THE INTERVIEW ROOM, Stephanie Reems noted, was much like many others used by MI5 - a standard specification, intended to project a grim feeling of hopelessness. Reems had sat in many of them, but until today she had always been the one asking the questions.

Central in the room was a grey metal table. As with the chair she sat on, it was bolted to the concrete floor. In front of her was a paper cup of water. They had not offered her coffee, or a phone call, and she had been blindfolded throughout her journey here. She could be in a missile silo under a Welsh mountain, or in a nuclear bunker deep beneath Trafalgar Square. The uncertainty was all part of the process.

She took a deep breath. She wasn't one to get unsettled. She was operating at a level above this. She knew what to expect. They did not.

They were going to keep her waiting the regulation two hours. It was in the MI5 manual. Enough to unsettle an interrogation subject, enough to start breaking down their resistance. Enough to engender a strong desire to get back to reality. But, for someone of Reems' background and experience, barely enough to irritate her. She looked down at the table then felt her glasses vibrate.

"Keep calm, Stephanie," said the modulated synthetic voice, conducting through her cheekbones.

Reems rolled her eyes. "I really can't talk."

"I know. But you *can* listen. Things have moved on, and the pieces of the puzzle are falling into place. You need to get here. You just need to work out a way to know where *here* is."

"I'll come up with something plausible."

"Good. I'll expect you soon." And then her glasses stopped vibrating, and Reems was waiting in silence once again.

Right on the two-hour mark, Natasha Gifford walked into the room, her close-cropped brown hair brushed functionally into place, her suit looking like it was sourced to a price, not a quality specification. "Sorry to keep you waiting," she said, in a tone that suggested she was not the least bit sorry. She set her computer tablet down and smiled. "Let's try and keep this civil. I appreciate that may be difficult. But we are where we are."

"Ironic given I have no idea where we are. And as for 'civil' can we just be honest with each other? This will be an interrogation. Don't insult me by trying to dress it up as anything else."

Gifford shrugged. "I'm going to ask questions, and you are going to provide answers. The more you cooperate right now, the better things will go for you."

"And the moment you realise that this is not about me, but rather about the people that raided Eastwell, the better things will go for all of us."

Gifford picked up her tablet. "Why did you do it, Stephanie? Why did you create this facility at Eastwell? And what was this MI10 'agency'? A personal vanity project?"

"I'm sure that you know already. You've connected the dots. You no doubt fed them into one of your spreadsheets."

"Tell me in your own words."

Reems leaned back in her chair. "Technology is changing us. Changing our world. And our adversaries are utilising it, embracing it. It is empowering them to take new forms of action, forms that we are woefully unprepared to counter. We saw it a year ago in Canada. And, quite frankly, I've been in the service too long to simply accept the old ways, to accept failure. I had to start something new. I had to create something new."

"This all sounds very general. Very vague."

"You want specifics? The last year I've been pursuing the organisation running these auctions. They are driving a flow of dangerous tech from irresponsible governments and companies to more nefarious dictators and criminals. It's like entropy. An inevitable increase in disorder. And we are the losers."

"So our enemy is capitalism? The free market?"

"I'm not an economist. Or a politician. I'm just telling you what's happening."

"So you decided to create MI10? You alone had the vision? You alone judged that our years of experience, our talented leadership and team members, that they were not enough."

"I'm not the only one who noticed the problem. I'm just the only leader with enough bloody-mindedness to do something in response."

"You did find a considerable number of people to join you in this conspiracy."

"They believe too. They don't want to sit on their hands and watch us get overrun." Reems shrugged. "They're good people. I want to be very clear that I take full responsibility for everything that has been done."

"Which must be galling, given that you've failed."

"How so?"

"You remember Eastwell was destroyed? It's not even the first facility you've had oversight of that has blown up."

Reems rolled her eyes. "MI10 isn't a place. It's an idea. But if we're talking about the 'place', I'm not the perpetrator. I'm not the one that blew it up. Our focus should be on tracking those people down. My new agency might have actually flushed out a big fish."

"You talk about it like it's real. The agency you built without any form of sanction, authority or approval?" Gifford raised her eyebrows. "You're going to need to adjust your expectations of likely outcomes here. And, just in case you're confused, I mean in a downwards direction."

Reems gave a sigh. "The world is changing. We need to change too."

"And you're the one to lead us?" Gifford tipped her head and gave an overly pleasant smile. "Which makes it all the more perplexing that you allowed an independent group to infiltrate your top-secret facility, you let them steal your key intel, then you allowed them to destroy the base, erasing any chance of you rebuilding your operation."

"It's a reflection of the limited resource I had to set this up. Also why do you care about rebuilding?"

"Where is Dominique Lentz?"

"I wish I knew."

Gifford narrowed her eyes. "I can help her."

"Perhaps you can," Reems replied. "But why would you?"

"You seem to be under the misapprehension that I am your enemy."

"It doesn't feel like you're a friend right now."

"My job isn't to be your friend. My job is to do my job."

"And my job is to keep our country safe, to be ready not just for the threats of today, but also those of tomorrow. Especially when tomorrow's threats are rapidly approaching."

Gifford stood up and walked over to a control panel on the wall, where she tapped in a long code.

"What are you doing? Ordering us a pizza?"

"Turning off the video feed. And the microphones."

Reems looked at the various LEDs around the room. They had indeed turned from green to red. "What's going on?"

"While I appreciate the rationale behind building Eastwell, your actions have caused a problem, not solved one. You built an invaluable treasure trove, then allowed it to be stolen."

"I thought I'd done enough to make it secure. I was wrong."

"Was Lentz behind the theft?"

Reems blinked. "Of course not. Even if she does have the unfortunate habit of turning up at places at the same time a major crime is being committed."

Gifford nodded. "Fair enough. And I'm sorry to say, we've been unable to locate her."

"You want to help her?"

"If she fell into the wrong hands, she would present a significant national security risk."

"She'd be a risk to those wrong hands." Reems shook her head. "Are you saying you actually believe me?"

"I'm saying I go with the weight of evidence. And when the weight shifts, I shift as well. I've responded as I have in order to buy you time, based on what I *think* is going to happen."

"You're playing a hunch? Surely you always go by the numbers?"

"I try to. But here the numbers look decidedly bad. Now follow me." Gifford reached over and opened the door to the room. She then walked out, calling behind her: "Do try and keep up."

Reems blinked and hurried after. The corridor was windowless, but there was something about the decor that seemed familiar. And not in any way government-issue. Gifford ducked into a fire escape staircase and began ascending. Reems followed her, hurrying to catch up. At the top Reems glanced at a sign on the wall. It indicated alternative routes to get to Level 90. Either by a combination of elevators, or by staircases.

Black sites didn't normally have a Level 90.

Gifford turned sharply left and through a fire exit door. Reems followed and found herself in a large, marble-floored lobby, an ostentatious entrance hall for a London corporate HQ. It was somewhere Reems had been before. Many times. She was standing in the entrance hall of CERUS Tower, the headquarters of CERUS Biotech.

FORTY-TWO

REEMS SPUN around in the entrance hall of CERUS Tower. Gifford stood watching her patiently. It was night, and aside from a couple of security staff, they were alone. "I assumed I was in an MI5 site. Why would you bring me here?"

"It felt appropriate," Gifford replied. "And a last chance to do so, most likely. You see how there's nobody here? It's like that throughout the building. They're about to do a full audit and security update, so I've sent everyone home."

"Why? Has there been a breach?"

"The British Government has just approved the sale of CERUS Biotech. To VoltTech."

Reems frowned. "You're joking?"

Gifford shrugged. "If you hadn't been so distracted this last year, maybe you would have seen the signs."

"There were noises from a few potential suitors, but nothing concrete. How have things moved so quickly?"

"In a word: *money*. The Home Secretary was fifty-fifty about allowing it to proceed. But Treasury got involved to stress the financial benefits. And once Smit properly opened his wallet, we promptly lost any reservations."

Reems walked over to the central atrium and stared upwards. The glass column in the centre of the tower rose more than twenty storeys. "When someone offers too much too easily, you have to be suspicious. Have they not noticed that Smit triggers some scandal on social media every other day? Does that not make them question whether they can trust him?"

"I believe they think it means he has no secrets. No guile. And why would they care? Lots of people detest him, but he's passed our vetting. His company is a multinational juggernaut, there are no obvious competition issues, and, quite frankly, the Home Secretary wants this off his plate."

"Happy for it to become someone else's problem?"

"And the sooner the better. No politician wants to be on the hook for another CERUS scandal. I know you understand that."

"Look, this is all rather alarming, but what does it have to do with Eastwell? Or are you suggesting Smit was involved in the raid?"

Gifford laughed. "I have no evidence of that. But someone could be manipulating Smit, or waiting for the opportunities his new stewardship will present."

"Then we have to kill the deal. I can call the PM and—"

"I think you're overestimating your current sway within government. And, in any event, the deal has been signed - it just hasn't been made public yet. You won't find anyone who is a decision-maker who is ready to listen to you."

Reems walked back to the reception desk. "So, you brought me here to tell me that all is lost?"

Gifford gave a sniff. "Actually I brought you here to tell you that I think the Home Secretary is wrong, and I think you could be right. And that means I think we have to investigate."

"*You think?* You don't have a spreadsheet to support your case?"

"Not one I'm prepared to share." Gifford gave a slight smile. "Call it another hunch. Call it intuition, unbacked by data. But I am unable to ignore the people who attacked Eastwell, and I am unable to ignore the possibility that there is a connection between CERUS in the past, and CERUS of the future."

"Elegantly put."

"Perhaps." Gifford raised her own eyebrow. "Certainly for someone whose talent lies mostly with numbers."

"So where does that leave us?" Reems spread her hands. "Where does that leave me?"

"We need a covert champion. Someone with drive and belief. Someone with the contacts, the connections, the savvy. And given that in situations like this, one cannot rule out an inside job, we need someone who, beyond question, was not involved in the strike on Eastwell." She paused. "Do I need to spell it out any more directly?"

"Are you saying that you're putting me back in the field?"

"It is our best play. You need to find this auction."

"You said it was pure speculation."

"When I'm wrong about something, I change my mind. Or maybe it's just how much you keep banging on about it. Eventually you've persuaded me."

Reems nodded. "Good. And the intel is that there's another happening soon, likely within the next few days."

"Then you need to find it. Now is the time to call in every favour you are owed. You need to work every contact you've ever had."

"And you're going to exonerate me of any crimes from today's events?"

Gifford raised an eyebrow. "No, I'm going to charge you with conspiracy and treason. And you're going to escape, having stolen my service weapon."

Reems blinked. "You want me to go rogue? Am I not a little old for that?"

"I hope not, because you are the only person that can do this, and you can only do it if those you are trying to infiltrate believe you are no longer part of the firm."

"That makes sense."

"You're too kind. I've set up a room with some equipment you might find useful. It's downstairs on Level Minus 5. You can use this to access it." She held up an electronic keycard.

Reems walked forward, took the keycard, and placed a hand on Gifford's shoulder. "Thank you. For believing in me. For everything." She reached forward and took Gifford's automatic pistol. "Now get on the floor."

FORTY-THREE

TOM OPENED the hatch and climbed into the well-lit corridor on CERUS Tower's lowest level, Kate following him through. He looked around and saw a wall plaque showing this was Level Minus 5.

Kate shook her head. "I can't believe that they didn't close off this route."

"They did," Tom replied. "Then Dominique quietly re-opened it. It's impossible to find unless you know where to look - it doesn't show on any of the plans. And this hatch," he paused to push it shut, "has an encrypted electronic lock, so if you got this far, you'd normally be blocked. I just happen to have the digital key." He gave a shrug. "With a structure of this size you cannot make security perfect. If you know where to look there is always going to be a way in."

"So where do we go now? There are a lot of rooms in this building."

"Yes, but not so many suitable for detention or interrogation." Tom closed his eyes and cautiously reached out. The building's system initially resisted his connection. But there was the access portal Lentz had left for him. And suddenly it was like talking to an old friend. Every camera in the building was an eye, every microphone an ear.

Locate Stephanie Reems, he thought.

The answer came back almost immediately. He hesitated, then began to laugh.

"What's so funny?" Kate asked.

Tom nodded at the door just in front of them, to the left. "Open that and you'll see."

SO MUCH TO CHOOSE FROM, thought Stephanie Reems. She stood in the equipment room Gifford had directed her to. On the floor was a grey holdall which she was steadily filling with equipment and supplies set out on a number of shelves. From the nature of some of the items she was fairly sure that Dominique Lentz had had a hand in setting it up.

On one shelf were three white helmets. Reems picked one up, noting it was surprisingly heavy. On the back a long sequence of letters and numbers was stencilled - a code, Reems noted, from Project Tantalus. There were so many remnants still lurking in the shadows, so much scar tissue. She put the helmet back on the shelf - this was no time for digging around in the past. She had to see her plan completed.

From a wall rack she selected a compact semi-automatic rifle - an experimental model, not generally available. In her current role she rarely carried a weapon. But these were unusual circumstances. She slotted in a clip of ammunition, and checked the firing mechanism, then behind her she heard the room's door open. She spun, raising the rifle.

"Easy there," Kate said, her eyes wide with alarm. "Same team."

"What is going on?" Reems lowered her weapon. "How did you know to come here?"

"Good to see you too," Tom said, as he walked in. "Although I would stress that, regardless of whether you have a gun in your hands, you have a great deal of explaining to do. A very great deal."

~

REEMS STARED AT TOM. "I'm sorry, but this conversation is going to have to wait until another time. I'm in a real hurry."

Tom took a step forward. "You lied to us. So much for Acquire, Catalogue, Eliminate. You said we were obtaining all this technology to destroy it. Yet you were doing the exact opposite."

"You've spoken to Dominique, haven't you. Honestly, that woman has no ability to keep things to herself. At times I find it hard to believe she ever worked for MI5."

"If you don't want her to tell us stuff, you shouldn't tell her stuff. And I can't believe that you used Eastwell."

Reems hesitated. "To repeat, how did you know I was here? And how did you get in? The building has state of the art security."

Tom rolled his eyes. "You know what I can do. It's something you've been more than happy to exploit."

"What I do, I do because it is necessary. If I couldn't, I wouldn't have been made Director."

"Don't give me that. What you do, you do for your own good—"

Kate raised a hand. "Now isn't the time." She looked at Reems. "Dominique said that all the data was stolen. Is that true?"

"It is. We're still working out who by."

"Well we know it was the same people who raided the mansion. They stole the Accumulator."

Reems froze. "How could you let that happen? This

auction is going to have more on the list than they know what to do with."

"They had tech that overwhelmed me." He frowned. "Wait, did you *know* I had the Accumulator?"

"I was 80% sure. You had to be drawing high quantities of power from somewhere, with what you were doing."

"Then why didn't you try and take it?" He raised a finger. "Because I was more useful to you while using it."

"Perhaps."

Kate shook her head. "This is a real mess."

"And exactly the type of danger I warned against. Even if I share some of the blame."

"Lentz said you might be in some... difficulty."

Reems gave a snort. "Gifford arrested me at Eastwell. The site is a secret no longer."

Tom folded his arms. "So... what exactly are you doing down here? Were you not in custody?"

"Interestingly Gifford has decided to give me a second chance."

"She let you go?"

"It's more that she's looking the other way while I make a run for it."

"You're a fugitive?" Tom gave a laugh. "You, of all people, are going rogue?"

"Desperate times call for desperate measures. You mentioned they had tech that compromised you?"

"Some computing device, like the sphere that we found at the bank. It shut all my systems down. The moment I connected to it, I was powerless, as if I was blinded."

Reems blinked. "The same as from the bank?"

Tom shrugged. "We think so. Although this one was larger. Have your people found anything more about the two you took away?"

"They've been a little distracted by events."

Kate raised a hand. “The sphere might be a device for connecting to something with more computing power.”

“If Tom was overwhelmed,” Reems asked, “why wasn’t he killed or captured?”

“That would be thanks to Kate,” Tom said. “You don’t want to let her near C4, I can tell you.”

“I’ll keep that in mind. So, what are you doing here? Haven’t you had enough excitement for one lifetime?”

Tom looked at the floor. “Against my better judgement, we’re here to seek your help.”

FORTY-FOUR

TOM SELECTED TWO TASERS, a set of four linked digital radios, and a lot of batteries. He then grabbed a backpack full of high energy rations. From the corner of his eye he noted Reems a few metres away, checking her own equipment.

"It's a pity," Reems said, "that there isn't one of those new electric rifles down here. They're particularly good at dealing with opponents with powered body armour. I kept mentioning them to Gifford but she's not very good at listening to me these days."

"We'll have to manage," Kate replied. "What's our next move?"

"The organisation that stole the Accumulator, that has made other recent acquisitions - it has to be linked to the auction." Reems folded her arms. "And from intel I've acquired there's an auction scheduled to take place in the next few days. A gathering of big players in the illegal tech field - all those companies and regimes that would like a leg up in the areas of radical, fringe science. And they've found a motivated and willing party ready to sell things to them."

"You've mentioned the auction before."

"Then it was a theory. Now there is no doubt it is taking place, and soon. The problem is that I don't know where. And time has run out on 'not knowing'. The time has come to call in every favour, to work those leads I wouldn't follow before. But we can't do that here." Reems zipped her bag closed. "First we get to a safe house and set up a base of operations. We'll have to take a bit of a circuitous path - but getting out of this building will be the hardest part."

"Not actually that hard," Kate replied. "Tom has a secret hatch—"

Tom cleared his throat loudly. "My secret to share."

Kate pinched her nose. "Yeah, well, sorry. I thought we had bigger fish to fry."

Reems coughed. "If you have a way out, please share it. Or maybe you'd prefer to walk out the front door on Level Zero?"

"Maybe we should." Tom closed his eyes and reached out, the collar around his neck starting to buzz. The cameras and sensors connected to his mind. He saw through them, like they were his own eyes and ears. It felt good. It felt familiar. So he cast his vision outwards. Immediately he was drawn to one van, parked across the plaza in front of the Tower. There was nothing remarkable about it. Nothing to distinguish it from dozens of other vans in the vicinity.

And yet he could feel it was important. He zoomed three cameras in to the two figures sat in the front seats, compositing their slightly obstructed images into one that was more complete. And he felt a shiver run over him.

"What's the matter?" Kate asked.

"Korver is here. He's sat in a van 500 metres from the building. And he's watching us."

Reems shook her head. "Did he follow you? Or is he here for me?"

"Let's worry about that later," Kate said. "For now we can use Tom's underground route to leave unnoticed."

"We're not doing that," Tom replied. "We have to confront him up there."

Reems frowned. "And what? You're some kind of armed combatant now?"

"He can tell us where we need to go. He has to know. I'll make him talk."

"A trained professional won't break easily."

Tom shrugged. "Then what about truth nano? I'm sure you have some in a secret stash."

Kate hissed. "How can you even say those words? After what that stuff did to me? And regardless, you wouldn't even get to use it. You don't have the Resurface suit. And you don't have the Accumulator. This is madness."

Tom picked up a set of graphene body armour from the shelf. "I have this. I also know everything about this building, and its surroundings."

Kate put her hands on her hips. "But if you use your Interface, he'll just knock you out again. He'll 'reach in' and you won't be able to do anything about it."

Reems coughed. "Actually, I have a way to make sure that doesn't happen." She walked over to the shelves and removed what looked like a white motorcycle helmet. "This will block any connection between you and any form of tech. He won't be able to attack you with the sphere."

"But I won't be able to use my Interface either."

"That is the trade-off."

Tom frowned. "And how do you know that it will work?"

"Because it's exactly what it was designed for."

"You have a specific tool designed to neutralise me? Care to explain?"

Reems held it out to him. "Put it on the list to castigate me about later. For now, it will do what you need it to do."

Tom took the helmet and hefted it in his hands. "We still need to work out how to locate the auction."

"I said I have a plan for that. We'll commandeer a vehicle from somewhere nearby and drive to the safe house. From there we put the plan in action."

"And what about Korver? We just forget about him."

"Gifford will manage him. She'll call in a rapid-response team. Special forces of whatever flavour is closest."

"I'm the only one that's faced him before. I'll work out what to do this time."

Reems looked across at Kate. "I don't remember him being like this."

Kate frowned. "Tom isn't the same person he used to be."

Tom glared. "What? You can feel a change in me?"

"Do you not feel different? You're more aggressive. More irrational. More–"

"I'm not running from a fight."

"That's exactly the point - this is a fight it's OK to run from. Others can fight Korver. We focus on what only we can do." She put a hand on his shoulder. "Sound reasonable?"

"I suppose."

"Great," Reems said. "So care to show me this secret hatch?"

Tom rolled his eyes. "Follow me."

FORTY-FIVE

DOMINIQUE LENTZ AWOKE in near darkness. She remembered being captured by Korver and his team at Edna Kim's house but had no recollection of anything useful after those moments - a blindfold, ear defenders and tranquillisers had seen to that. She had no idea how much time had passed. It could be a day or more.

Another person might panic or freak out. But Lentz had too much curiosity as a scientist, and too much training as an MI5 operative, to do either. She would not give up. She would give herself things to do. She would collect data. And that would begin with an assessment of her immediate surroundings.

Her eyes still couldn't resolve any details, so she reached out with her hands. She was lying on a thin foam mattress, which as she ran her fingertips over seemed to be fixed to a metal-framed bed. Probably not a luxury hotel suite then. "Edna?" she whispered. Then she repeated it more loudly. There was no reply.

Cautiously she sat up. Lighting flicked on instantly in response, and she saw she was in a room with three metal walls and a floor-to-ceiling glass window on one side - part of the glass was a sliding door, currently closed. There was a strong smell of oil and saltwater in the air, and her ears felt odd, like she'd changed altitude, or they were in a pressurised environment. Besides the bed, the room contained a WC and a sink. On the floor next to the bed was a bottle of water, unopened. In two corners of the ceiling were fisheye CCTV cameras, each likely able to record the entire room.

This was a prison cell. She was in a place where someone had expected to detain people. That was not a good start. Then a quick check revealed she was no longer wearing the Resurface suit. That was much worse.

But on the floor next to Lentz's bed were her glasses. Her smart glasses - the MI5 model provided by Reems. They had not taken them from her, perhaps because they were less obviously a dangerous piece of technology. That was better news. She slipped them on, stood up and walked towards the windows. She could make out a corridor stretching to the left and right, and a row of what looked like at least five similar cells opposite. Someone was standing there, watching her - a stout man in spotless blue overalls, wearing blue-lens sunglasses, which hid his eyes.

"You're awake," he said. "Excellent. You have work to do."

"Who are you? Where is my friend? And where am I?"

"My name is Frank Hatch. Come with me and you can ask your other questions." He paused. "Some I may even answer."

SHADOWED CLOSELY by two armed guards, Lentz followed Hatch through a pressure-sealed door, then down a long metal corridor that curved slightly and constantly to the right. They passed a number of metal doors bearing markings, and numerous signs on the walls, but all were in some form of code that Lentz did not recognise.

"If I was a conspiracy theorist, I might ask if we were on a spaceship." She paused. "Possibly an alien spaceship."

Hatch did not reply. They turned off the corridor and entered a stairwell, ascending four floors at a quick pace, before emerging into another apparently identical corridor. He turned to face a set of double doors, which slid apart immediately. Lentz followed him through. Beyond the doors was a modern canteen with a sparklingly clean stainless steel serving area, and several rows of rectangular tables - it could easily have seated a hundred, but right now was completely empty. He strode over to the end of a serving area where there was a silver coffee pot and a white porcelain mug.

"I hope this will be to your liking," Hatch said, as he poured a mug of steaming hot coffee and handed it to Lentz. "Black only, I'm afraid. We ran out of milk two days ago and we're waiting on a supply ship."

"A ship? So are we on an island?"

He moved to the nearest table and sat on a padded bench, then indicated a similar one opposite. "Ask your questions."

Lentz sat and took a sip of her coffee. It was strong and bitter, and she felt her brain coming back online. "Who are you? Where is my friend, Edna Kim? Where are we? And this one kind of runs through it all. Why?"

"Dr Kim is safely in another of our VIP holding rooms. She is quite well. She's only here because you involved her."

"Don't for a moment try and blame that on me. I want to speak to her. Immediately."

"Whether I permit that depends on you. On whether you agree to help me."

"Help you to do what?"

He folded his arms. "I am the director of this facility - what we call the Rig. We run a number of technology-related initiatives, and they require input from suitable experts. You are... most suitable."

Lentz narrowed her eyes. "You mean you steal tech and resell it. You're clearly behind this auction that I've been hearing about." She eased back in her seat. "And you want me to help get some of this stolen tech working properly so you push the price up?"

Hatch linked his fingers together. "You are quick on the uptake."

"And you are mad. I won't be part of disseminating this tech to the dark recesses of the world. Now let me and my friend go, or I assure you you'll regret it."

"You are in no position to make threats, Dr Lentz. And as for your concerns, Pandora's box is already open - so much is already out there, it really doesn't bear worrying about. There's no reason why we shouldn't make a little money out of the situation. And on that front we have a lot of problems that need your attention."

"Surely you have your own scientists?"

"One good one." He spoke into his phone. "Send him in."

A man walked in through the double doors, his hair pulled back and held in place with a rubber band. He wore a Metallica t-shirt and carried a battered leather satchel over his shoulder.

"Dr Lentz," Hatch said, standing up, "this is one of our lead scientists, Dr Javier Mendez."

Lentz narrowed her eyes. "You used to be at Glifzenko. In technology R&D, as I recall."

He nodded. "You are well informed. The company pulled funding from my project. Killed five years of my work."

"Because it didn't work?"

"Because they didn't have the belief to keep funding it." Mendez tugged at his ponytail. "So I took it somewhere with more... vision."

"And what was the nature of your project?"

"A new type of computer. One that I have now built."

"Well good for you. But I want nothing to do with this place."

Hatch stood up again. "Why don't I give you a little perspective?"

Mendez pulled at his ponytail. "Is that really necessary?"

Hatch frowned. "Everything I do is necessary." He turned to Lentz. "Are you afraid of heights?"

"I've made more than a hundred parachute jumps."

"Good to know. Although a parachute won't help you here.

"

FORTY-SIX

TOM, Kate and Reems made their way through the sewer tunnels for several minutes, the only lighting coming from their LED torches. Tom wore the white helmet, and felt eerily cut off from the world around him.

"Here we are," Reems said finally, and she pointed at a manhole cover above them. "Can you see anyone in sight on the nearby cameras? I'd prefer not to create a ruckus."

"And what's happening with Korver and Gifford's team?"

"We are necessarily off comms. Tom, you have to trust them to take care of this. Now tell me what you can see immediately up top – take a quick peek. And don't get tempted to look further afield, like a kilometre away at the Tower. We don't want to leave any unnecessary data trails for anyone to follow."

Tom sighed, lifted off the white helmet and reached out, connecting with nearby cameras. "It looks clear." He replaced the helmet.

"Good." Reems put her hand on the manhole cover. "Let's go."

They climbed out quickly. It was night and the street lighting was minimal. They were in a street running behind a row of residential apartment blocks. Three storeys up was a metal fire escape that some residents seemed to be using to store bikes and other large items they preferred not clutter up their apartments. Out of the corner of his eye he saw a flicker of movement - a shadow dancing up above - but when he turned to look it was gone.

Kate slid the manhole cover back into place. "Have you chosen the vehicle we're going to... *borrow*?"

Reems pointed to a white Ford Explorer, parked five metres away. "It's Gifford's service vehicle. This was where she always parks when she visits CERUS Tower – off site so they don't know she's coming. She is a creature of habit."

Tom shook his head. "Literally any other vehicle would be a better choice. The intelligence services can track it."

"Actually yes and no. Yes, until I turn off that feature, which I know how to do. And after that, most definitely 'no'. It has all sorts of anti-tracking features. It will serve us well for the first part of our escape. And if we encounter any problems, it has a fair amount of heavy weaponry stowed within."

"I hope you know what you're doing..." Tom trailed off. In the distance he saw three figures turn the corner and start walking towards them. "We have company."

Reems looked where he was looking. "Could just be civilians."

"Let's not wait to find out." Tom walked over to the car. "Do you have a key?"

A shape dropped from above, from the fire escape three storeys up. It struck the ground with a heavy thump. And then the shape stood up. Someone all too familiar. Tom realised their plan had failed.

"Mr Faraday," Korver said. "It's almost like you're trying to avoid me. And what's with the fancy headgear?"

"How did you follow us?" Tom saw Reems place her left

hand on the door handle. It beeped and unlocked. At the same time she raised the automatic rifle in her right hand.

"Step away. I will not hesitate to shoot."

Korver lunged towards her, moving faster than his bulk suggested was possible.

Reems unleashed a burst of automatic fire, but he seemed to predict where she would shoot, and he swerved sharply to the side, then twisted back the other way, keeping low. Before she could fire again he swatted the weapon away and it skittered away under a nearby car. Reems drew her Glock, but he knocked it away too. She began to swing a punch, but he grabbed her arm and threw her onto the roof of the Ford Explorer.

"Enough!" Kate raised a taser and fired, striking Korver in the chest. Tom saw fifty thousand volts surge through the wires. Nobody could withstand that, nobody could remain functional. Yet Korver nonchalantly gripped the wires and pulled them free.

"This isn't helpful." He said. "Now stop wasting–"

Kate fired a second taser, again striking her target. Again he pulled it free, completely unaffected.

"What the hell!" she shouted. "What are you?"

Korver stepped forward and pushed her back, sending her sprawling. "Please don't get in my way."

Tom looked around and saw the figures down the street had begun running. He turned back and reached out, trying to muster every bit of energy he had, trying this time to overwhelm Korver.

And he felt more nothing than he had ever felt. The helmet, he muttered. It was blocking him. He reached to take it off.

"No, Tom!" Reems shouted. "Don't!"

Korver walked towards him. "Time's up, Mr Faraday. Come with me and I'll let your friends live."

Tom took a step back. "You'll understand if I don't find that a credible offer." He looked around. What could he do? He couldn't use his Interface. He was about to be even more outnumbered. Reems and Kate were down. He needed to try and lure Korver away from them. *Yes, that was what he needed to do.*

He took a further step back. Korver followed.

"You can't run from this, Tom."

"Interesting point," Tom replied. "You just watch me." And he sprinted off down the street.

FORTY-SEVEN

LENTZ FOLLOWED Hatch out of the canteen, up a flight of stairs, and down a long corridor. Despite his heavy gait, he moved quickly and effortlessly. At the end they made a sharp left turn through some heavy-duty doors. And Lentz took a sharp breath.

They were outside.

She stood on a criss-cross patterned metal gantry with a solid metal railing. The gantry was empty apart from two heavy metal-rimmed barrels, marked with hazard warning symbols, one of which had a large dent in the side. A hundred metres or more below surged cold black ocean water.

"Quite the view, isn't it," Hatch said. "The novelty doesn't wear off, take my word for it."

Lentz nodded. "Is this an offshore drilling platform?"

"It used to be. But it's been heavily re-engineered."

"And presumably located in international waters, far away from regular disturbance or oversight. But people will still know you're out here. Satellites will detect you. Military vessels must have come to investigate."

"We manage to stay unseen."

"Something of this size? How?"

"I'm not about to reveal all our secrets. Certainly not if we haven't reached an understanding. I do want to make it clear that you are alone, and no help is coming."

Lentz looked around at the endless ocean. There was nothing in sight. To their left she heard footsteps and saw the two armed guards were still shadowing them. "What exactly do you want me to do?"

"Work with Dr Mendez in furthering the goal you already predicted. We have a number of items of technology that we haven't yet got operational. The next auction is in just three days."

"I've thought about it, and my answer is 'no'."

Hatch shrugged. "If you don't do this, if you don't agree to work with Mendez, then it's pointless for you to stay here. And obviously I can't just let you leave. So," he paused and walked over to the two barrels, "I'll be forced to put you in one of these. And then..." He looked over the railing towards the sea.

"Very funny."

"I'm not known for my humour. I need Dominique Lentz the super scientist, not sixty kilos of dead weight. Dead weight goes in the ocean."

Lentz stared at him. He showed no sign of humour, no real expression at all that connected with what he was saying. Was he even human? She felt her mouth go dry. "I still don't believe you. And unless you actually do it, I won't. Which will rather defeat your purpose."

Hatch seemed to consider this. "Fair point. But fortunately, I have another option." He turned and gave a signal to the two armed men. One disappeared back inside.

Lentz frowned then heard a familiar voice, complaining loudly. "Get your hands off me." Moments later a dishevelled looking Edna Kim was dragged onto the metal gantry, fighting with much fury, but little result.

Kim looked up and saw Lentz. "Thank God you're OK."

"Have they hurt you?"

"No. They just left me in that cell, and they won't tell me anything."

"OK," said Hatch. "This is how things are going to work. You, Dr Lentz, are going to agree to help me, or I am going to have Dr Kim here put in one of these barrels and tossed overboard. I'll give you exactly sixty seconds to think it over."

Kim looked confused. "What? Put me in one of these...?" She trailed off, her face going pale. "What are you talking about?"

Lentz's eyes widened. "Don't be absurd, Hatch. I don't believe for a moment you're that insane."

The Director shrugged. "I'm on a deadline, and I do not miss deadlines. It's who I am." He nodded to the two guards and they raised their weapons. "Thirty seconds remaining."

"And if I help you, will you let us go?"

"That is a reasonable request. What kind of person could refuse it?"

Lentz looked at Kim. "I'm sorry that I got you drawn into this."

"It's not your fault. You didn't know."

"I should have guessed. I will make this right. But I can only do that if we're both alive."

Kim nodded. "I trust you, Dominique."

Lentz turned to Hatch. "I'll help all I can. But full disclosure, if I ever get the chance to put you in one of those barrels, I won't hesitate."

He smiled. "I can see it's going to be a pleasure working with you."

Lentz nodded. "So what happens now?"

"This." He spoke into his phone again and four more guards walked out onto the decking. They grabbed Kim and hauled her over to the barrel with the distinctive dent in the side.

"What? We just made a deal."

"But I don't think you really learned anything. So, we continue."

"Seriously?" Lentz charged at the new guards. One of the originals swung his rifle in a swift arc, striking her on the temple, and she collapsed onto the metal grid, her vision blurring. She forced herself to speak, the words almost stuck in her throat. "I don't understand. I did what you asked."

"Yes, you did," Hatch replied. "But having a possible conspirator with you is a risk. And I really do have zero tolerance for risk."

"We made a deal."

Hatch shrugged. "Any last words, Dr Kim? I understand that's what one should ask in this type of situation."

Kim glared at him. "I've built robots with more humanity than you."

He turned to the guards. "Seal her up."

"No!" Lentz shouted, trying to get up. The nearest guard moved forwards and kicked her onto her back. Two guards pushed Kim into the barrel. She fought but they were clearly much too strong. They banged the lid into place, and with some effort lifted it onto a metal platform. Lentz screamed and tried to get up, but a guard had placed his foot on her chest. One of the guards that had lifted the barrel pushed a button and the platform began to lower. It quickly gathered speed and in seconds the barrel reached the surface. The guard pressed another button and the platform tipped, the barrel sliding off into the grey waters. It bobbed twice and sank. And Lentz simply stared in abject horror, unable to do anything, unable to change anything. Utterly powerless to help.

Hatch nodded. "Do you believe me now, Dr Lentz?"

"Believe *me*, you monster. I am going to kill you."

Hatch gave a signal to one of the guards. "You have never been more wrong."

And then something heavy smashed into Lentz's temple and everything went black.

FORTY-EIGHT

TOM SPRINTED down the cobbled side road, past a row of wooden benches then between two traffic bollards. Behind him the sounds of pursuit were fading. Running away might actually work.

He turned a corner and realised he was only getting ahead of himself.

Three armed men were ahead of him. He skidded to a halt and was starting to back away when someone flew round the corner and into him. It was Kate. He gasped. "How did you catch me?"

"I was always faster than you."

"Maybe." He pointed at the three men advancing on them. "Did you bring any firepower?"

"Sorry, I already used both my tasers."

"More running then. Follow me." Tom took off. To one side he saw Korver and the original three men hurrying towards them. Tom sprinted ahead into a different side street, Kate pulling quickly alongside him. A further three men stepped out of a side alley, wielding batons, rifles strung across their backs. There was no time to stop. Kate accelerated, leaping and kicking out at the man on the left, her foot connecting with the side of his head. He grunted, collapsing to the ground. Continuing her motion, she spun and struck her elbow into the man in the middle's stomach. He groaned and doubled-up.

Instinctively Tom lunged at the man on the right - quicker than he realised he could move - his full weight sending them both flying to the ground. The man struggled free and scrambled to his feet, muttering under his breath.

Instinctively? Tom shook his head. Where did that come from? There wasn't time to think further as his opponent closed on him.

Tom jabbed. His punch was loose, glancing off his target. The man smiled confidently and stepped closer. Beside them he saw Kate was circling the second man. He lunged at her and she barely evaded his grip, twisting and punching him in the side. But it did little - he was bigger and evidently stronger than her.

And behind them, reinforcements were coming.

Something needed to change, thought Tom. He tried to reach out, but he still felt weak with his Interface, and with the helmet on, he couldn't use it. It was just him, alone.

The man advanced. Tom threw a left-right combination, but it was telegraphed, and the man dodged and moved closer. He was clearly realising Tom had no substance, and Tom didn't know what to do.

What I need, he thought, are those *instincts*. Not to think, but to act. To be in the moment, and nowhere else. And to see what happened.

His opponent lunged forward and from somewhere deep within, Tom felt it. *A connection to himself.* He swayed and punched again, but this time it was different. It was fast, it had power. His fist connected and there was the sound of ribs cracking. The man screamed.

Tom blinked. Before he had time to think he struck again,

another blow to the ribs, then one to the chin. The man's eyes rolled back and he collapsed to the ground. Tom turned towards Kate, who was being beaten back. And in an almost detached manner, he knew what to do. He swept low, knocking her opponent's legs out from under him, following with the edge of his palm striking the prone man's temple. In just those moments it was over.

"What the hell?" Kate asked. "Where did you learn that?"

Tom stepped back, shaking himself. "I don't know. It was kind of instinctive."

"So what? You're remembering something you've never learned? How does that work?"

There was the sound of heavy clapping.

Tom turned and saw Korver, five metres away, with six men just behind him.

"That was impressive, but playtime's over. You're coming with us."

"I'm not going anywhere," Tom replied. "Ready, Kate?"

"Both together," she hissed, and charged forward.

Tom followed, half a step behind. Korver caught Kate's leg with a single hand, gripped it and swung her away, crashing her into a wall. Tom screamed. Before he might have raged, impotently. Now the sight just increased his focus. He lunged forward, fists together, launching a double-handed punch, striking Korver in the chest, delivering every bit of anger, strength and force he could muster. He had never thrown a punch like it. And yet he knew what to do.

The big man grunted in surprise at the impact, taking a step back. "What was that?"

Tom reeled back, his fists shrieking in pain. It was like punching concrete. "Are you wearing armour?"

"I think I did mention it." Korver flexed his shoulders, then moved forwards, ducking low, keeping his balance, swinging both arms in a grappling motion.

Tom, on reflex, jumped, kicking forward. His right boot struck Korver in the face. The big man snarled in surprise. Tom started to laugh, but Korver moved again, and before Tom could jump away he was in a headlock. And Tom could no sooner wrestle an oak tree.

Korver nodded to him and pulled the sphere device from a pocket. "Remember this part? Are you ready?"

"Are *you* ready?" shouted a voice from behind them.

Tom turned and saw Reems was standing behind them, lugging something that looked like a very fat rifle.

"We tried tasers," she said, "but I think the problem is they didn't have enough juice to trouble you." She flicked a switch. "But look what I found in the weapons cabinet of my colleague's car."

Korver started to move, loosening his grip on Tom's neck.

Tom pulled free just as Reems fired. An arcing bolt of electricity struck the big man in the chest. He gasped and crackled, steam rising from his head, then staggered towards Reems, anger in his eyes. "You can't..."

And then he fell to the ground.

"Didn't catch that last part," Reems replied.

Korver's men turned to Reems and began raising their weapons.

"I wouldn't do that," shouted another voice. Multiple red dots lit up on their chests. Natasha Gifford walked up, flanked by more than a dozen special forces soldiers. "I'm going to give you until the count of one to place everything on the ground."

Korver's men looked at each other and threw their rifles down.

Gifford smiled. "Now that is an excellent start."

~

TOM HAD REMOVED the white helmet, and now sat on the kerb, a foil blanket around him, drinking hot tea that the soldiers had provided. Korver had been loaded into an unmarked grey van for transport to an MI5 facility. Kate was close by, holding an icepack to her forehead, her other arm being placed in a temporary cast by an emergency medic.

"Is it broken?" Tom asked.

The medic, a woman with an intense expression, shrugged. "Can't know for sure. We'll need an x-ray, and I want to run a CAT scan to make sure there's no sign of a concussion."

"This is all way too much fuss," Kate said. "I'll be fine."

"Listen to the experts, and get yourself checked out," Tom said. "You have just wrestled with some kind of gorilla."

"Not inaccurate," Reems said, walking up, drinking from her own mug of tea.

"So you found your favourite rifle," Kate said.

"I did. Proved too much, even for him. Almost too easy." She turned to Tom. "Finish your tea. You and I need to get out of here."

Tom frowned. "What about Kate?"

"She can join us later if she's well enough. But we can't wait."

Gifford approached them. "Why are you still here, Stephanie? You know the plan. Get out of my sight, right now."

"I was just..." Reems smiled. "Was that humour?"

"I'm giving it a try. But you really should go. I'll see to it our large friend is looked after."

"But why," Kate asked, her voice weak, "are Reems and Tom going at all? Don't we have Korver in custody? Isn't our priority to question him?" She shook her head. "There's something odd about him. I think he has nanotechnology in his bloodstream."

Reems frowned. "And how do you know?"

"I can..." Kate hesitated. "Just a hunch. Why don't I go with Deputy Director Gifford and help with the interview?"

"Natasha is more than capable of managing that process, and there's no telling how long it will take to break him down. You need to go and rest. Tom and I will focus on our original and hopefully faster approach to finding this auction."

"I've been trying for months and got nowhere. How are we going to suddenly succeed now?"

"We need to go deeper into the dark. We need to find someone with much better underworld connections than I have. Someone who will know where this auction is, or at worst will know who to ask."

"And who would that be?"

"An old friend of Tom's."

Tom frowned. "You can't mean what I think you mean?"

"Why?" Kate asked. "What does she mean? Who are you going to contact?"

"Peter Marron," Reems said.

Tom shook his head. "There is nothing about this that is going to end well."

FORTY-NINE

THE MEETING SPOT had been chosen for its isolation - an abandoned fishing village 50km from Aviles on the northern coast of Spain, where Reems' helicopter could land in reasonable anonymity. The terrain here was dry and barren, devoid of life or interest - even the seagulls seemed to be giving the location a miss.

Tom stood on the south bank of the river mouth, staring out at the span of a rusting suspension bridge, wondering not for the first time whether they could have concocted a more ridiculous plan. Some people you didn't call for help, not if you needed to be certain of surviving the encounter. Twelve months ago, he had somehow ended up on the same side as Alex and Marron, but now that he had Reems with him as well, he had no idea what was going to happen.

He stepped onto the bridge, treading on wooden boards held in place by twisted wires - and while the bridge was wide enough to accommodate a car, it certainly wasn't designed to take such weight. He paced forward, the boards creaking under his boots, and made his way towards the middle, some fifty metres away.

As he walked he looked around. There was no sign of movement. This was the time, and the place, yet nobody else was in sight.

Was this all a joke? He reached out, feeling for the signature trace of a mobile phone, for the disturbance of digital radio comms. There was nothing. Other than the breath of the wind, and the gentle ripple of the water, there was silence. Where was she?

Then as he reached the middle, he saw a red ribbon tied around one of the wooden boards. As he bent to examine it, there was a flurry of movement. Seemingly from nowhere a slender figure swung up from under the bridge and landed directly behind him. A flash of silver ended with a knife being pressed against his throat.

"Hello beautiful," said a female voice in his ear. "Meeting someone?"

'Someone with a sense of humour," he replied. "Let me go."

"Make me."

"You think I can't?"

"You've surprised me before."

Tom felt his memories guide him. He grabbed her wrist, twisting sharply, rolling sideways, launching her over him. She flew through the air with balance, adjusted and landed easily two metres away. And looked up at him. It was a face he hadn't seen since she saved his life a year ago.

"Hello, Alex."

She tipped her head on one side. "Where did you learn to do that?"

"Just something I picked up along the way. I'd say it's good to see you, but I'm never really sure if that's true."

She pulled at her earlobe. "And I thought you and I had put aside our differences. Now where's your girlfriend?"

Tom frowned. "Kate is not my girlfriend. And she can't be here today."

Alex blinked. "Poor dear, is she hurt? You have that odd little expression in your eyes. But whatever, I don't really care. I was talking about your other girlfriend - the lovely Stephanie."

"Director Reems is waiting just out of sight."

"If only she could stay there. Why is it we're meeting?"

"Because we need your help. We need information."

"Something you can't track down? What makes you think we can?"

"This is very much in your wheelhouse, I promise."

"Then we will hear you out. But only if you tell me, right here and now, what really happened with your father?" She took a step towards him. "And I want the truth - I think I've earned that after we saved you."

Tom nodded. "We flew away. We talked. And then I killed him."

There was a flicker of a smile. "You killed your own father?"

"That's what I said."

She narrowed her eyes, then smiled. "Good. He deserved it. Although I'm sure it wasn't easy for you."

"Easier than you might think. I'm not who I used to be."

"None of us ever are." She looked around. "Do you want to call Director Reems over?"

Tom sent a signal to Reems' phone. "The people we're after, they've got Lentz. And they have the Accumulator. They stole it from me."

Alex raised an eyebrow. "How did you take it from Bern?"

"Long story."

Reems appeared and began walking to the middle of the bridge.

Alex waved the knife in front of her. "Tom here has a special place in our hearts. But why would we ever help you?"

"An immunity deal. For you and your father."

"Then you must be desperate. Although it would be nice to go home." Alex touched her ear. "We're ready."

And suddenly Tom's senses went into overload. Something very large, and full of electronics had appeared out of nowhere. Or, rather, not from nowhere. From *underneath*. A huge metal object, roughly cylindrical, surfaced in the estuary, directly underneath the bridge.

A *submarine*.

Tom looked down. "Didn't I see that thing a year ago? The one that used to belong to a certain Russian arms dealer?"

"He never asked for it back. We've made a few upgrades since. Like electronic shielding." Alex reached down and pulled out coils of rope she must have tucked under the bridge. "How good are you both with rapid descent? Let me know if you'd prefer a stretcher."

Reems grabbed one of the ropes. "I was doing this before you were born, young lady."

Alex smiled. "Oh, I believe you. I just thought I'd check if you can still do it now."

FIFTY

AS CONSCIOUSNESS RETURNED, Lentz realised once again that she had no idea where she was. Her vision was blurry, her thoughts muddled, and she struggled to make sense of anything. And then she remembered what had just happened. And everything made even less sense.

She had watched Edna Kim being murdered. Right in front of her. And she had been unable to do anything about it. This poor innocent person that Lentz had dragged into this horror, had paid the ultimate price for reaching out with friendship. It was almost too much – she almost wanted to lie down, to go to sleep. To hide from it all.

She would make Hatch regret what he had done.

Lentz blinked her eyes, trying to see clearly. She lay on a foam mattress in a metal-walled room. The air was heavily air-conditioned, but she could detect the faint odour of oil and grease. It seemed pretty clear she was still on the Rig.

"You're awake then?" said a voice from nearby.

Lentz sat up and saw the scientist, Javier Mendez, sitting on a similar bed opposite, his battered leather satchel resting on his knees. "What are you doing in here? Broken some of Hatch's rules?"

"I'm a visitor, not a resident. And I'm here to see if you're ready to start work."

She flexed then tightened her fingers. "Your friend, that approximation for a human being, just pushed Kim overboard in a barrel."

"I think I wouldn't call him my friend." Mendez blinked. "And I'm sorry to hear that. He doesn't usually do it as a first option."

"You knew it might happen?"

"I knew he wouldn't do it to you. He *needs* you. It never occurred to me that he'd do it to your friend. If someone has utility, he looks to extract it. Did you say something to antagonise him?"

"Are you saying it's my fault?

Mendez raised a hand. "That's not what I meant. It's just you're very important... Look, I'm really sorry."

"The fact that you're here working for him rather undercuts that sentiment."

"I'm aware of how it looks. But we should get started."

She folded her arms. "Sorry, do you actually think I'm going to do anything to help? After what he just did?"

"Do you want to end up in the next barrel?"

"I'm going to put *him* in the next barrel."

"You might want to play along for a while. It's not like you can escape." He paused. "Not without help."

She swallowed. "Why does he do all this?"

"Nothing gets in the way of the auctions." Mendez reached into his satchel and pulled out a secure tablet computer. "This is the latest catalogue of what we're selling."

Lentz took it and started scrolling through. "You have all this?"

"This is just what we have listed. There is a great deal more for future events. He wants you to help get it working. Operational technology has considerably more value to the bidders."

"And when is the next auction?"

"In three days."

Lentz gave a laugh. "Three days isn't enough time to do anything. Even for someone with my talents and work ethic."

"Yeah, I explained that. But given that you are Dominique Lentz, it's really about one item in particular. Something not in this catalogue."

"I don't care what it is. Now get out. Before I hurt you."

Mendez nodded and stood up, taking back his tablet. "I'll give you a few hours to think about things. To prove to me you are who you say you are."

"Don't hold your breath." Lentz watched him open the door, leave, and then close it firmly behind him.

I'll show you exactly who I am, she thought to herself, adjusting her glasses. *I'll show everyone here.*

FIFTY-ONE

TOM, Reems and Alex climbed down into the submarine, Alex pulling the hatch closed behind her. A man and a woman dressed in overalls nodded at them and beckoned them through a pressure-sealed door. They continued along a corridor that Tom could only just stand up in, passed through another door, and entered the main control room.

In front of him, Peter Marron stood studying a flat screen. Four other crew members were stationed around the room. Marron looked up. "Welcome on board, Tom. And if you've come to arrest me, *Stephanie,* I'm going to decline to cooperate."

Reems shrugged. "I have more urgent things on my plate today than catching an escaped prisoner. Even one with your history."

He nodded. "Interesting times indeed. Now why don't we have a talk."

They left the other crew members and followed Marron through to a meeting room.

He pulled the door closed. "Against my better judgement, I let myself be persuaded by my daughter that we have this meeting. But if I smell for even a fraction of a second that this is any form of trap, I will put you both in the torpedo tubes." He paused. "And with you, Director Reems, I will push fire."

"Now, now," Alex said. "There's no need for outright threats."

"No," Reems replied. "I'm sure the implied ones are sufficient. I'm also not currently the Director of MI5, which might help smooth the waters."

Marron raised an eyebrow. "I cannot begin to imagine what sequence of events has led you to ask for my help."

"Fair enough." She turned to Tom. "Why don't you give him the overview."

MARRON FOLDED HIS ARMS. "I think the establishment of something like MI10 is a no-brainer."

"Finally," Reems said, slapping her hand on the table, "a voice of reason. A shame it had to be yours."

Marron smiled. "From a security perspective, you have to have specialists on the job who can match the talent available to the private sector, to the enemy intelligence agencies and high-powered corporations. You have to be putting skilled agents in the field, equipped with sufficient state-of-the-art tech to do their jobs."

"Even if," Tom said, "such an agency would likely be tasked with hunting you down."

"It would be just as likely to seek to hire me as a consultant. As you are now." Marron raised an eyebrow. "You are offering to pay me, right?"

Reems sighed. "If appealing to your sense of duty doesn't work."

"It does not."

"So," Tom said, "does that mean you know about this auction?"

"There are many illegal auctions taking place every week, all over the world - selling off technology and weaponry acquired from US and UK military bases, or corporate R&D facilities."

"Great—"

"But there's only one with sufficient buzz, with sufficient security around it, that it could be what you describe. And it's taking place in three days' time."

"Where?"

"The location hasn't been revealed yet. But don't worry, we're on the guest list."

Reems blinked. "We come to you for help, and you are already going to the exact place we want to find?"

Tom shrugged. "We thought, given their contacts, that they would know. This is just our plan working."

Reems frowned. "I don't like coincidences. I don't like easy."

Marron put up his hands. "Stay with us, or get off my boat. I really don't mind which."

"Of course we're staying," Tom said, looking at Reems. "Or do you have another plan?"

"No good one," she replied. "So how come you're involved, and how do you know where to go?"

Marron smiled. "A client hired us to participate in the auction on their behalf. We've just been sent the initial rendezvous - a set of coordinates for a random point in the North Atlantic, well off major shipping routes. Once we get there I'm sure we'll be bounced around in a tortuous manner for hours to make sure we have no idea of our location, and they have every idea that we're not being followed."

"And you're OK with helping rescue Dominique Lentz?"

"If she's actually there, I won't prevent it. But I will also conduct business for my client. You are a guest onboard, and you will not interfere with my vessel or crew in any way. You will also not make contact with anyone back at base, nor will you disclose our location - I'm not having a Royal Navy vessel turning up to take over. Those are my terms. If you want to handle it differently, find someone else. And if either of you misbehave, you can spend this journey locked in the brig."

Tom glanced at Reems then nodded. "That works for us."

"Good," Marron replied. "We'll be at the first rendezvous in twenty-four hours. I suggest you get comfortable."

FIFTY-TWO

LENTZ STARED at the cell door that Mendez had just closed and counted to a hundred. He did not return. Aside from the distant hum of equipment and air systems the room was quiet.

Time to act.

She tapped her smart glasses. The low glow of the HUD appeared, along with a low battery warning, and she began scanning the room. Results appeared quickly. There was one interior camera, but it appeared to have been disconnected. The walls were solid, and there was just the single automatic door that Mendez had left through. It was locked.

She looked around. The floor panels were heavily bolted in place, and she couldn't scan through them. They weren't locked, as far as she could tell, but as she had no spanner or wrench they might as well be. Above her the air ducting was covered in heavy metal grills, and was, in any event, too small to allow human passage. The door seemed the only realistic option.

She approached the locking mechanism. It was a standard, commercially available system, and her HUD reported it needed a mere six digit code. Hardly cutting edge. Her glasses interrogated its operating system, overwhelming it, and quickly produced a result.

1-2-3-4-5-6

The default code? Really?

She typed in the number, waited, and the door slid back. *Too easy*. She stepped out and froze.

Mendez sat on a metal bench outside. He clapped politely. "I was beginning to wonder if you were an imposter, merely pretending to be the world-famous Dr Lentz."

She glared at him. "Are you messing with me?"

"You mean the door code? My little joke, sure. But otherwise very much not so. I understand we both have to be cautious. However the time has come for us to lay our cards on the table. We have to trust each other if this is going to work."

"If *what* is going to work?"

He sighed. "You know you can trust me because I let you keep your glasses."

Lentz touched them on reflex and noted that the battery was now precariously low. "You knew about them? How?"

"I have better scanners than I admit to Hatch." He glanced around and lowered his voice. "I'm a friend of Stephanie."

"Is that some kind of code?"

"Stephanie Reems. From MI5. Where you used to work. And I'm hoping you still do."

Lentz frowned. "If that ridiculous notion were true, do you honestly expect me to admit it?"

He raised an eyebrow. "You aren't here as part of the operation? Look, don't mess with me, please. I'm going out on a limb here."

"Are you now? Because this could all be some ruse to trick me into trusting you. And not a very sophisticated one, at that. Words are cheap, and knowing that is how I've stayed alive." She gestured around her. "Often in trying circumstances."

"You can trust me because I won't tell Hatch you escaped. I'll tell him you're cooperating, and that will buy us time."

"Time for what?"

"Are you always this obtuse? Time for the operation, of course. We're getting off this Rig. I assume you're an advance part of the MI5 team."

"I'm not part of any team. I was kidnapped and brought here against my will." She stared at him. "Are you saying you've been corresponding with Reems?"

"Yes. And with her people. Anonymously. On a secure channel."

"And you're sure it's her?"

"Of course I'm sure. She's going to rescue me. And you, too, obviously."

"But why? What's so special about you? What's the angle?"

He narrowed his eyes. "Best if I show you."

FIFTY-THREE

LENTZ FOLLOWED Mendez through a series of metal passageways then down several flights of stairs until they reached a heavy automatic door.

He placed his hand on the panel. "We're on Level One, at the bottom of the Rig." The door slid open, and he stepped inside.

Lentz's shoes echoed on the cold, polished floor as she followed him in, the dim overhead lights casting long, wavering shadows in their wake. The expanse of the room - a clean, geometric cube - was disorienting. The walls bore the intimidating starkness of a surgical theatre. There was no echo of the sea, no rust or corroded fittings here. Every breath Lentz took was sharp, the air scrubbed to a metallic purity, absent of the damp tang of salt and industrial decay elsewhere in the Rig. As her eyes scanned the space, two doors loomed; one bore the simple designation 'CONTROL', clinical in its promise. The other was more menacing 'DO NOT ENTER' with the deadly black and yellow trefoil warning of radiation.

The heart of the space was a monolithic formation of computer servers, resembling an alien hive. The dark grey blades reached skyward, punctuated with flickering lights that pulsed and danced - reds, greens, and oranges. Each glow seemed like a synapse firing in some vast, pondering brain, the hum resonating like the purr of a dormant beast.

"This," Mendez paused momentarily, allowing the gravity of the room to seep in, before he gestured with a sweeping motion of his hand, "is what Stephanie Reems wants."

Lentz followed his gesture, her gaze fixing on the maze of servers. Their power seemed palpable, almost sentient, beckoning her closer. "You built this?"

"I did." Mendez's voice was filled with a mix of reverence and caution. "It's a Maximum Entropy System."

"And what, exactly, does that mean?"

"It utilises an advanced form of neural network that simulates the synaptic plasticity found in human brains, but at a scale and speed far exceeding biological limitations. The system's structure is modular and self-organizing, capable of rearranging its own circuits in real-time to optimize data flow and processing for the task at hand. This dynamic reconfiguration is guided by the principle of maximum entropy, where the system maximizes disorder within its own operational protocols to ensure the most efficient processing pathways are utilised. Furthermore, the supercomputer is designed with a sophisticated feedback loop that constantly measures its own performance and adapts accordingly, effectively learning from each computation it performs."

"That's quite a mouthful."

"Which is why we just call it Max."

Lentz stepped closer, drawn to the pulsating core of Max. Every now and then, a rhythmic vibration passed beneath her soles, as if the room itself had a heartbeat. She traced the dance of the lights with her eyes, feeling like she was staring into a vast pool of information. "How does it... work?" Lentz's voice was soft, almost a whisper, as if speaking louder might disrupt the delicate equilibrium of the room.

Mendez, his face half-lit by the glow of the servers, smiled. "Its core engine utilises randomness. Max thrives on uncertainty, driven by minute variations in initial conditions. It is exponentially more powerful than standard systems, but that's with current unresolved inefficiencies. We expect it to go much further."

Lentz tilted her head, her brow furrowing, then gestured at the vast array. "So this is what you promised to deliver to Reems? I can't believe she never mentioned it to me."

"I'm sure she plans on doing that once she has it in her possession."

"Speaking of which, how are we going to get this out without a crane?"

"We don't need all of it." Mendez moved to the central tower, his fingers delicately tracing a particular section that was slightly elevated from the rest, illuminated by a pulsating blue light. "This is Max's heart, its central core, where all the *magic* happens. Without it," he tapped the module lightly, "the system is just a fancy light show."

"So, we just unplug it and leave? That tiny part?"

"The system's power, its essence, lies right here." Mendez leaned against one of the towers, his gaze still fixed on the central module. "Rebuilding Max around this," he started, motioning towards the pulsating heart, "is not a small task, but ultimately it's just paint by numbers. The right conduits, memory banks and storage, and it will soon be operational."

"I almost don't believe it." Lentz pushed a hand through her hair, slowly processing the information. "And power? Something this sophisticated must have very particular requirements."

Mendez's grin returned, "Max has significant power draw, and requires a stable, high-frequency energy source. Conventional supply won't cut it." He nodded to the 'do not enter' sign. "Which is why we have a small reactor."

"Here? They're not exactly easy to come by."

"A repurposed model - intended to be used in aircraft carriers. It produces 500 megawatts."

"But that's more power than you could ever need. You could run a town off of it."

Mendez chuckled. "We do have to power the rest of the Rig. But some of Max's suggested use cases will put it under close to full load. For now, it's good to have plenty of headroom." He smiled. "So do I have your attention now?"

Lentz breathed slowly. This was a computer like no other. With this, if Mendez was right, she could change the world. And, the obvious problem was, so could the operators of this Rig. She couldn't let that happen. "We have to get this away from here."

"Does that mean you trust me?"

"I haven't decided. But there's no time for me to reach a conclusion, so I guess I'll take a leap of faith."

"I can work with that."

"Where is the stolen data? Medusa's core from Eastwell?"

"It's already part of Max's data set. I migrated it, then destroyed the original core. When we take Max, the data comes too. Which means that we're all set to be rescued..." he hesitated. "Or we would be. There's just one problem. The MI5 team can't get on board with the Rig's security systems in place. I need to find a way to take them over."

"And you don't have administrator access to security?"

"Hatch and Korver have not shared it, despite my stating it would be helpful."

"But you control Max, yes?"

"I do. And Max isn't connected to the security systems."

"Then patch it in. Problem solved."

"There is a logical bar that prevents such a connection, and

I've not been able to overcome it, as I've been telling MI5. I assumed that was why you'd been sent here. To help me fix it. Still, now you're here, you could still be the one to make the difference. What we need to do is..." Mendez trailed off and pulled out his phone. "Damn it."

"What?"

"Hatch wants an update. He thinks I'm giving you the tour, and he's impatient for results."

"He can't hear us here, right?"

"I said recording devices in this room, or in my primary lab, would impair Max's operation. But if I don't reply he'll be down here in five minutes."

"I said I'm not doing anything for him. Also, there just isn't time."

"We're going to need to at least pretend to make progress. And it's really only one item Hatch wants fixed. One that you definitely have the skillset for."

"And what is that?"

"The Accumulator."

Lentz rolled her eyes. "Why does that thing keep rearing its ugly head?"

"Is it going to be a problem?"

"That thing is a threat and an opportunity. Where is it?"

"In my lab. Just remember that anywhere but here or there, Hatch will be listening."

"Noted." Lentz strode out of the room. "I know the way."

"Wait!" he shouted after her. "You can't just leave..."

"Try to keep up!" Lentz began walking down the corridor, when she suddenly froze.

Something had stepped from the wall ahead of her. Something larger than a man, heavy and metallic, its form outlined in green and amber LEDs. It was clearly some type of robot.

The creature dropped forward with a smack, its six metal legs each ending in a rubber tipped foot, and began strutting towards her, while emitting a quiet fluctuating warning tone. On its back, resting on a flat platform, were two folded manipulator arms. Lentz shuffled to one side, lowering her gaze. The robot followed her. She searched in her HUD and found the section for mobile automated systems.

Access was denied.

Behind her Mendez entered the corridor, his arms folded. "I said you couldn't just leave."

Lentz moved again. Again the robot followed her. "What is this thing?"

"It's called an autodog. An automated servitor which operates on the Rig. Mostly they perform menial functions, delivering cargo and undertaking heavy, repetitive tasks."

"Then why is it tracking me?"

"Your bio data obviously isn't in its database, so it's establishing what you are, whether you're in-scope for removal."

"That is not reassuring. How strong is it?"

"The standard models can lift about six tons." He looked directly at it. "Max, deactivate the dog."

The light on the robot went green and it stepped back into the wall, its structure flush with the surface.

"Good to see it knows who is in charge."

"Yes," Mendez replied. "Now let's get back to my lab. We have work to do."

FIFTY-FOUR

LENTZ FOLLOWED Mendez into Laboratory 3A. On the central table she saw the familiar black ten-centimetre cube with its surface of carbon fibre, dotted with red and green indicator lights. The *Accumulator*. She shook her head. "Why, amongst everything, is this the one item I'm supposed to look at?"

"Because of your history with it, I assume," Mendez replied. "And because it's working on a different timeline. Hatch has a buyer coming to look at it tomorrow."

"You said the auction was in three days?"

"Sometimes a buyer is so keen, they look to get ahead of the process, and pay accordingly. Hatch will always accommodate someone proposing to pay over market."

Lentz picked the cube up and scanned it with her glasses. "I don't know if I can do anything. It seems to be locked."

"Yes, we worked out that much. You're going to need to try. It was your design, after all."

"Originally. Then others developed it. I didn't even know it existed until a few days ago. I thought it had been destroyed."

"So, Tom Faraday kept it from you?"

Lentz's breath caught in her throat. "How do you know that name?"

"Because he is Subject Zero from Project Tantalus."

"What? How could you know—?"

"His name was mentioned. So I searched in the data from Eastwell after it was uploaded. I found a great deal about him. And you. And all I can say is, you need to come up with a plan. You're our only hope."

"I didn't want Tom to have the Accumulator. But I want someone else to have it much less." Lentz shook her head. "Who mentioned his name?"

"Korver. Our head of security."

"The big guy?"

Mendez raised an eyebrow. "I assume you've met him."

"Twice, which is two times more than I'd like. But however big you are, it can be hard to make Tom do anything he doesn't want to do, as many have found out to their cost. Although if I'm wrong and Tom ends up here... well you know what Project Tantalus was. Put him in a tech-heavy environment controlled by a computer and he'll take over."

"I wouldn't be so sure. Not with a computer like Max in his way. Indeed he may have faced it already."

"But Max is here? A remote connection would limit the bandwidth and latency of his interactions."

"Normally I would agree." Mendez walked over to a shelf and grabbed a sealed plastic box. He popped the clasps and reached inside, removing a black metal sphere the size of a golf ball from within. "But Korver had one of these."

Lentz's eyes widened. "I've seen one before. I don't know what it is, though."

"It's called a Node, used to provide direct remote data access." He tossed it in the air and caught it with a snap of his wrist. "It functions via a form of quantum entanglement. The data flow is instant and, to my understanding, fundamentally unblockable."

Lentz took the sphere from him. "How is that possible?"

"I have no idea. They were just provided to me, already fully functional, with no explanation. Where have you seen one?"

"It was recovered by Tom from a cache of stolen tech." She peered closely at it, noticing a very fine seam in its constructions, almost too thin to be seen. "We hadn't been able to work out what it did. Do you have plans? Schematics?"

"Nothing, sorry. They probably don't want me to know."

"And yet they trust you with Max and the core data?"

"I suppose that is odd," Mendez replied. "But then a lot about being here is odd."

"I don't disagree. So you can access Max's computational power, anywhere in the world?"

"For as long as the nodal connection persists. They top out around 96 hours."

Lentz tapped her glasses. They made no immediate sense of the Node. "I get the feeling that learning about this could be really useful."

"Maybe. But we don't have time for distractions. And once we take the system offline, there won't be an obvious reason to use it."

"Have you tried tasking Max to analyse one?"

"I didn't want to risk getting challenged."

"I think we're past concerns like that. And I have some prewritten routines. I tried them with my own system, but with Max's power they might actually achieve results."

"Achieve results?" said a new voice. "That's my kind of language."

Lentz spun to see Hatch walk into the room, his feet thudding on the metal floor, his blue sunglasses gleaming in the artificial light.

"Didn't know you were joining us." Mendez cleared his throat. "I was just discussing the Accumulator with Dr Lentz."

"Excellent." Hatch gave an unnerving smile. "Is our friend onboard after our earlier misunderstanding?"

Lentz folded her arms. "It seems I don't have a choice."

"As you long as you understand the rules, I'm happy." He reached forward and tapped the Accumulator. The LEDS seemed to flicker then steady. "A fascinating piece of technology. And based on your own handiwork, so I'm told."

"Another of my questionable innovations."

"I find it best to celebrate who you are." Hatch turned and walked back towards the door, then he paused. "What do you think of Max?"

"It's... impressive."

"I'm told you're something of an expert with computer design yourself. I'm sure Dr Mendez would appreciate your commentary. Feel free to have a dig 'under the hood'." Hatch smiled oddly and walked out.

"Sorry," Mendez said. "He sometimes does that. Keeps me alert."

"Thanks for the warning. His smile is... *weird.* Almost unnatural."

"Those two words do a good job of summing him up."

"Why is he encouraging me to study Max?"

"I don't know. I guess he's more worried about progress than he is concerned that you'll take over."

"Then let's hope that's a mistake on his part." Lentz hefted the sphere. "Time to get to work."

FIFTY-FIVE

ALL WAS quiet in Kate Turner's private room at UCL Hospital. The X-ray had confirmed her arm wasn't broken, and a CAT scan had revealed no sign of concussion, but as a precaution they were keeping her overnight for observation. She now lay in a metal-framed bed, flicking through the channels on her television set, wishing that Natasha Gifford had let her keep her phone.

"Too easy for the bad guys to trace you," Gifford had said.

"I think they're capable of finding me by plenty of other methods," Kate had replied. Gifford had taken her phone anyway.

Two armed guards stood outside her room. A further two were watching the front of the hospital, and a drone had been deployed overhead. Kate was as protected as anyone could reasonably be in a hospital. Which was great, except she knew her friends were not safe, and she didn't want to be stuck here, contributing nothing.

On a tray next to the bed were two empty plates that had held a mildly delicious risotto and a sticky chocolate pudding, both of which she'd wolfed down as soon as they'd been brought in. It had, she reflected, been a ridiculous twenty-four hours, with the attack on the mansion, then their encounters at the barn and at CERUS Tower. Three times she had managed to come out alive. But now she had been left behind, while Tom and Reems chased the enemy.

She closed her eyes. Despite her hard-earned fighting skills, against Korver she hadn't stood a chance. He was impossibly fast and strong - and it had taken Reems using a very unusual weapon to overwhelm him.

Of course she was sure that many of his capabilities were not really his own. It was nanotechnology that Kate had sensed in the big man, she was certain now. Was it something like what was in Tom? Or like the truth nanotech that had been in her? She wanted to be there during Gifford's interrogation. She had so many questions, and she wanted to speak to someone else who had these tiny machines racing through their veins, to share his understanding, to guide her own experience and evolution. Instead she was stuck in this hospital room, away from the people she cared about, away from events that mattered.

And then something in her tingled.

A shift. A spark of electricity. She knew that feeling. Someone had brought nanotechnology close by. Someone who was using it.

There was a sound from outside. Raised voices. Often in a hospital there would be moments of hurried activity, followed by calm. But this felt different. Should she go and investigate?

There were two sharp bangs. And then screams.

Kate started to move. She got as far as getting both feet on the floor, half-tangled in the sheets, when the door was kicked open, its hinges shrieking. A huge figure ducked through the doorway. A man who should be in MI5 custody, but who self-evidently was not.

"Hello again, Ms Turner," Korver said.

Kate stepped out of the bedsheets, then ripped the electrical monitors from her chest and arms. She looked around for something to use as a weapon, but only found the plates which had held her dinner. She picked up the large one and hefted it in her right hand. "Stay where you are."

"You're in no state to fight, and I have no wish to hurt you."

She waved her arm. "You nearly broke this last time."

"An unfortunate accident." He held the sphere in his right hand, glanced at a series of lights, then put it in his pocket. "We need to get moving."

She threw the plate. It wobbled and struck him in the chest, shattering. He did not even flinch. "How are you even here? I saw you being taken into custody."

"I decided to leave."

"I feel like that is glossing over many of the details." Kate looked around. There was no other way out of the room except by breaking a window. And she was on the sixth floor.

"Come with me. You have my word I will not harm you." He raised his right hand and beckoned.

"What do you want me to do?"

He folded his arms. "We can discuss that once we—"

"We can discuss it right now, or I am not going anywhere. I assume you need my help or you'd have shot me."

"I'm just following orders."

"Does it have to do with Tom?"

"I need to take him to my employer. You are my best shot at finding him."

"And who and where is your employer?"

Korver took a step towards her. "Don't make me compel you. I do not want that."

"What is with you?" she asked. "How are you so strong? So impervious to harm? Is it nanotech?"

He stepped closer, almost upon her. "It's time to go."

She could feel the nanites. They were shimmering within

him. Alive with energy. She reached out her right hand and placed it on his chest. "It's OK. You can tell me *what happened.*" She felt herself modulating her voice, not quite sure why, trying to layer in persuasion. "Did someone change you? Augment you?"

He frowned. "We need to leave. I don't want to have to hurt anybody else."

She leaned closer. "Did they experiment on you?"

He put a heavy hand on her shoulder. "We're going—"

Kate closed in, until her face was almost touching his. "What did they do to you?"

He seemed to hesitate, closing his eyes. "They saved me."

"Then save me too."

He opened his eyes. "Sorry, but I have my orders." And he grabbed her good arm and dragged her from the hospital room.

FIFTY-SIX

"I BRING GIFTS," Mendez said, walking into the lab, placing a tray of croissants and other pastries on a bench before stopping to wash his hands. "Grabbed these before the security team descend on the cafe for their afternoon break."

"I've had more than enough sugar already."

"Then I also brought you something to help you more directly. Something with more finesse than the autodogs." He gave a whistle and two small mechanical devices waddled into sight. They were rounded metal cuboids on six short legs, that scurried like ants. Each had two articulated robotic arms connected to their top surface, ending in gripping in pincers.

Lentz stared at them. "Yin and Yang? You stole those from Edna Kim."

"I don't know where the design came from, but they've been here as long as I have. They're supposed to help you in your work. The work that's going to save our lives."

"I hadn't forgotten."

"Good." He sucked in his lower lip. "How's it going?"

Lentz shook her head. "Not the greatest. I really need a break. I'm not a machine, you know."

"There's no time for a break. Have you encountered a problem?"

She shrugged. "On the basis that I shouldn't break the actual Accumulator, I'm going to run parallel tests in a simulation. I'm trying to render a virtual environment in real time, to act as a proxy. But it isn't resolving."

Mendez walked over to where Lentz sat, pointing at her laptop. "Mind if I have a look?"

"Be my guest."

Mendez leaned forwards and adjusted his glasses, then began typing into the keyboard. A series of reports streamed across the screen. He read them, his brow furrowing, then he nodded. "You aren't feeding enough power into the system."

Lentz hesitated. "But I've already allocated nearly a megawatt."

He laughed. "With Max you don't need to worry about power." He leaned over and typed an instruction. The power feed increased to ten megawatts. On screen the simulation clarified, and stabilised. There was a soft tone, and 'READY' appeared.

Lentz blinked. "Good work."

"I know how my baby ticks." Mendez coughed. "Does that sound weird?"

"Only slightly. Let's run some analyses. Eight on the Accumulator," she paused, "and two on the Node?"

"Sounds like a plan."

"OK if I access Max now?"

"That's what the boss said you could do." Mendez's phone chimed. "Speaking of which, Hatch says we need to go up to the conference centre. Something to do with the auction."

"That's still two days away."

"There are pre-meetings to agree the process, although I don't usually attend. Not sure what's changed."

Lentz sighed. "I'd guess it might be something to do with me."

FIFTY-SEVEN

LENTZ AND MENDEZ took a lift to Level Seven then walked another thirty metres to a large conference room.

Hatch, wearing his usual blue overalls and blue tinted glasses, was waiting, sat in the middle of a large conference table with chairs on either side of him. Opposite was a line of large flat panel displays, numbered one to twelve. "So kind of you to join us."

Lentz sat to his left. "Why do you always wear those overalls? Aren't you management?"

"That's true." He gave another of his uncomfortable smiles. "But it sends a message that I'm not afraid to do the dirty work."

Lentz watched Mendez sit to Hatch's right. "Although they don't have a spec of dirt on them?"

"Indeed not." Hatch appeared to stare past her, as he indicated the bank of monitors. "We are about to be joined by representatives of our twelve bidders. It's a select group."

"And you're not worried what they will do with this technology?"

He spread his hands wide. "I just connect supply and demand."

"Sure. When could that ever go wrong?" She hesitated. "If they're joining remotely, how do you know they're not attempting to hack you, to discover your location?"

Hatch turned to Mendez. "Would you care to brief Dr Lentz?"

Mendez cleared his throat. "The participants travel to randomly generated locations, provided on short notice. We monitor them at all times, and they communicate using bespoke equipment completely under our control." He paused. "And of course even if they learn the location, we won't be in the same place next time. The Rig can, and does, move."

"And they're willing to accept this mode of engagement? They trust you?"

Hatch adjusted his glasses. "For what we have in our catalogue, it is a sellers' market."

"Perhaps. Do the buyers know who the other buyers are?"

"They do not. When they come online only we will be able to directly hear and see them all. Everybody else will see only an avatar, and they will hear disguised voices. They will not be able to see us." He reached forward and placed his hands over a control panel. "Let's not keep our guests waiting any longer."

In front of them, the screens flickered into life - twelve faces appeared, twelve people connected with secret organisations and operators. Twelve representatives from a dark economy that rarely touched the daylight.

But one caught Lentz's attention over all the others. A face she had hoped never to see again.

Peter Marron.

~

LENTZ AND MENDEZ returned to the lab nearly three hours later, easing back down to sit at the lab tables. "So now we know who all the bad guys are."

Mendez frowned. "You looked like you knew one of the people on the call. From group number three."

"He and I have some history at CERUS Biotech. His name is Peter Marron, and he worked for Bern for many years. I don't know how or why he's turned up here. I'd hoped our paths wouldn't cross again." She shrugged. "We'd better get back to the main task at hand. Why did Hatch ask me to leave for the last part?"

"He likes to share only what you need to know. The good news is that he was delighted with your contribution - he told me in those exact terms. The buyers were all very excited and will arrive in 48 hours, their cheque books at the ready. Or rather, their cryptocurrency wallets."

"They're coming here?"

"That's right."

"What's to stop them trying to take things by force?"

"Until we manage to turn them off, the Rig has considerable security counter-measures. Hatch knows how to run an event to ensure he is around to run the next event. And if all that failed, he has a lot of security guards onboard..." Mendez trailed off.

Lentz turned to see that Hatch had walked though the airlock door, his face unreadable as always.

"Mr Hatch..." Mendez said.

"Get the Accumulator ready for inspection," Hatch replied.

"This is sooner than we expected. It's still not ready—"

"You have one hour." He turned to leave.

"And who is this buyer?" Lentz asked.

"You'll find out soon enough. All I'll say is, he's expecting to be impressed."

Lentz watched him go, her hands clutching in frustration.

FIFTY-EIGHT

TOM WATCHED Marron arriving back in the control room as sirens announced that the submarine was moving again. "So where have you just been?" he asked.

Marron raised an eyebrow. "On a secure comms link with our surface vessel."

"You have another craft?"

"A motorised yacht. We need to declare a vessel to be allowed in, and I'm not revealing to the auction host that we have a submarine."

Alex nodded. "We're calling it the Red Herring." She tipped her head to one side. "Too on the nose?"

"Can we focus," Reems hissed in what sounded like irritation. "Have you spoken with the organiser?"

Marron nodded. "It was an auction preview, run by someone called Frank Hatch. We were shown several items my client has a particular interest in."

"You're going to bid? I thought it was more your style to take what you want."

"When I'm hired for a job, I follow the brief." Marron

handed her a secure tablet computer. "This summarises the different technologies they claim to have for sale."

Reems took the tablet and studied it. "There are several items they took from us."

"I noticed. We've been given coordinates to arrive at, 48 hours from now. A random point in the deep North Atlantic, far from any shipping lanes. I presume from there we'll be directed somewhere else."

Reems frowned. "And after that?"

Marron smiled. "Patience, Stephanie. We'll get there eventually." He ran his hands distractedly over a section of the control panel. "Like I said, I don't trust these people for a second."

Tom pointed at the controls. "That's a weapons system, *Peter*."

"Haven't I told you before that it's rude for a guest to try and hack my systems?"

"With their encryption, there's no way I could. At least not without the Accumulator. But I know what a weapons system feels like without having to connect to it."

"This is a military submarine, and I am of a military mind. If you have a problem with that, you're welcome to leave."

"No, I'll stay." Tom stared at him. "For once, you and I are aligned."

"Perhaps we are." Marron looked back, unblinking. "I guess we'll find out."

TOM MOVED BACK to the submarine's small dining area. It was packed full of frozen meals, ready to be microwaved, but he ignored those and headed for the coffee machine, quickly punching in for what it said would be a short black. Sixty seconds of whirring later it produced something watery and glistening that barely approximated coffee of any description.

There was a rustle behind him. He turned and saw Alex was in the doorway. "In search of that caffeine fix again?" she asked. "Haven't you had enough of trying to alter your brain?"

He shrugged. "I really don't know any more."

"Well you look terrible. Almost as bad as you did last time."

"It's been a rough few days. I feel... drained."

"What about this Accumulator? I'm sure the Americans were happy you managed to hang on to it."

"They think it was destroyed. Since then I've been using it to enable my Interface. To do things I couldn't do before."

"You got your Interface working again after the transfusion last year?"

Tom nodded. "And I've taken things much further. I can do things like break through hard encryption." He paused. "At least when I can draw on that well of power."

"But you can't do it without it?"

"I am only human." He touched the collar round his neck. "With the energy from this I can do a little. Anything further and I drain the battery and myself."

She nodded. "I still haven't thanked you."

"I don't follow."

"For the gift you gave me. It wasn't the gift I wanted - I wanted what you have. But perhaps it's been the gift I needed." She extended her right hand and flexed her fingers. "I've managed to learn more than I ever thought possible."

"And how many more people have you killed?"

"I could say I've lost count. But that wouldn't be true. I remember every one. Nearly all of them deserved it. And with many of them, you might agree." She shrugged. "When we met, up on the bridge, the way you moved. Where did you learn that?"

"It just came to me."

"It looked like something I do. Show me again."

"Are you just making fun of me? I can never tell."

Her eyes flared. "Show me!"

Tom shrugged. "It was an instinctive reaction, a reflex. I don't know how I did it, or where it came from. I certainly can't just show you..." He became aware that her eyes were narrowing, her neck muscles were tensing. There was a sharp intake of breath. And then an explosion of pain in his stomach.

She had punched him, her fist like a steel hammer. He doubled up as he fell to the floor, retching. "What was that?"

"Sorry. I assumed you'd react."

"I kind of switched off." He staggered to his feet.

"Never switch off." She swung again. Faster. Harder. And hit him again.

He felt a rib crack and staggered back. "If this is a game, I'm not having fun."

"OK, whatever. I'll let you drink that coffee now..."

This time Tom didn't even see the blow. It was just a blur. But something guided him. A memory that was not his own. He raised his right hand and, as if moving in slow motion, gently guided her attack away from him. Her fist smashed through the wooden fascia above the coffee machine.

"That's more like it," she said as she pulled her hand free, then immediately drove upwards with her left knee.

Tom dropped low under her attack, then swept with his foot at her right leg. For a moment he thought he would catch her. But he was moving in slow motion. Effortlessly she jumped back out of his way, landing with perfect balance, and raised both hands.

"Those attacks would have taken out almost anyone I've ever encountered. Yet you read them. It's like you and I learned from the same teachers." She paused. "And most of them are dead."

"My only teacher has been Kate, with karate, but I didn't stick with it."

"Not much of a loss."

"Kate's skills have saved my skin more than once." He stared at Alex. "I am going to pick up my coffee now. Or are you still checking that I haven't switched off?"

"Fight club is officially over." Alex raised an eyebrow. "Just remember not to talk about it."

They sat opposite each other at a small fixed table. Tom rubbed at his ribs. Maybe they were just bruised.

"Those fighting skills," Alex asked. "Is that how you killed your father?"

"No, these are a recent development. Something that happened in the last few days. I don't know where they've come from. Something is happening to me that I don't understand, and not for the first time."

"Then how did you kill him?" She leaned closer. "I'm assuming Bern really *is* dead. And that you didn't make that story up."

"There was a mix up with the Accumulator and the nano bomb that Marron gave me. Bern flew off with the wrong one. And physics took its course."

"You triggered it?" Her eyes widened. "That's how you killed your own father?"

"It was more complicated than that. And besides, I hardly knew him."

"Fair enough. He was a traitorous, murdering bastard. Unlike my father, who, despite his faults, is loyal and caring."

Tom blinked. "You may have a different view from most other people who know Peter Marron."

Her face twisted in a half smile. "Maybe."

"Also my father did leave me a considerable amount in his will. I'm still not sure why. Maybe it was part of some plan to mess with me after he was dead."

"Maybe he hoped to not actually be dead. He'd tried faking it a few times before. I still don't tend to believe people are dead until I see a body."

"His went to the bottom of the ocean, and I doubt there'll be much of a body left to find." Tom looked at her. "Speaking of believing, can I trust you here?

"Our paths are aligned." She reached forward and gripped his hand. "And I will always fight with you. I promise that." She raised an eyebrow. "Plus, it would seem that you now have the skills to fight with me."

"Where we're going, will that be enough?"

She laughed. "If I were our enemy, I would not want to get in our way."

FIFTY-NINE

KATE LET Korver lead her out of the hospital room. Outside, chairs and trolleys were tipped up, and debris was strewn across the floor. Two of Korver's operatives stood over the bodies of the two SAS guards. Three nurses and a doctor were tied up and gagged.

Korver ignored them all and moved her quickly to an emergency staircase, where two more operatives were waiting. As they descended, Kate looked around. "I assume you've turned all the CCTV off?"

He shrugged. "It wasn't difficult. Half of it wasn't even operational."

From outside came the sound of gunfire. One of the operatives tapped his earpiece. "Contact, Sir. Team of at least four."

"Cover us to the exit vehicle. Then you draw them away in the spare. Make sure you're visible."

They reached the bottom of the stairs and pushed through a pair of fire doors. Dawn was beginning to light the sky. In front of them were two white, unmarked vans. Korver opened the back of one. "Inside, quickly."

Kate climbed in and sat on one of two bench seats. "You didn't need to kill those soldiers."

He followed and pulled the door closed. "If there was another option, I would have taken it." He banged the flat of his hand on the side of the van, and it began to move. "Where is Faraday?"

"Where is Dominique Lentz?"

"Safe." He placed his automatic rifle next to him on the seat. Kate saw it had two spare ammunition clips taped to it.

"Well wherever she is, I'd wager that's where you'll find Tom."

Korver shook his head. "Unlikely. Perhaps impossible." The van lurched left and right, then began accelerating.

"He may surprise you." Kate leaned towards him, looking into his eyes. "Is it where you're holding the auction?"

He blinked. "I suggest you save your energy for what we have to do next."

"You told me they saved you? Who did you mean? And how?"

"I was dying. There was nothing medicine could do."

"So they gave you some sort of experimental treatment, to heal you? Was it nanotech?"

"It doesn't matter what they did. It just matters that it was the only way." He leaned forward. "Now tell me where your friend is. I cannot fail my mission."

"Because..." she closed her eyes, searching for an answer. "You can't fail because you need to keep receiving treatment. Because if you fail, they'll stop giving it to you. And then you'll die."

"Enough of this. Tell me—" There was the sound of gunfire, then the van began to slow and came to a stop. Korver looked around and shouted. "Driver, do we have a problem?"

There was no reply.

He checked his rifle then placed it back on the seat and turned to where a grenade launcher hung on the van wall.

As he turned, Kate lunged forward and grabbed the rifle. She spun the weapon, aimed and pulled the trigger. With its silencer in place it made only a clack. The bullet slammed into him, then fell to the floor with a metallic clink, its energy dissipated.

"You're wasting your time," he said. "Now give that back—"

She pressed and held the trigger. The entire clip struck him in the chest. Knocking him back and against the van wall, the repeated impacts striking like sledgehammer blows.

"Enough!" he groaned, shifting forwards.

She pulled back, pulling out the clip and slammed in one of the spares, firing again.

The bullets struck his torso, and he gasped, staggering back. "Stop that before I get—"

"Overwhelmed? I think whatever armour you're wearing can only take so much." She loaded the final clip and fired again.

He hissed and cracked and fell onto the metal floor, gasping. "What are you doing?"

"Testing your limits."

He groaned, trying to stand, but getting only as far as kneeling. "I cannot fail."

"Maybe that's what they told you." She put a hand on his chest and pushed him back. "But maybe you shouldn't have listened to them."

He stared up at her, not moving. "I had no choice."

"Tell me where my friends are. Right now. Or I'll show you what pain really means."

"I already know. But that's in my past."

"We'll see." Kate looked around. She had no more ammunition. What could she do? Was the problem that she was trying to row upriver? She concentrated and felt the nanotechnology within him. She could feel its shape and texture. She knew what it was doing. It was *healing* him. *Boosting* him. Making him unstoppable. So she reached out.

And she stopped it.

He looked at her in confusion, collapsing to the floor. "What are you doing to me? How...?" He started to shake.

She stared down at him, her blood fizzing in her veins. "I'm making it clear to you what you have to do. The choice you need to make is right now."

He closed his eyes, his face twitching as if he was listening to a voice. "Make it stop. I'll tell you where you need to go."

FIVE MINUTES later Kate watched as an SAS team broke open the rear of the van. Behind them stood Natasha Gifford.

Gifford raised her eyebrows as she saw Korver lying on the floor. "What happened here? After he escaped from the MI5 holding facility I didn't think we'd see him again."

"I... I'm not sure," Kate replied. "He decided to get talkative. Then he collapsed. He's barely breathing."

"Get an ambulance here immediately." Gifford said to one of her team, then turned back to Kate. "What did he tell you?"

"Where Lentz is. Hopefully Tom and Reems as well. They're on a floating platform - a repurposed oil rig. It's a couple of thousand miles away in the middle of the Atlantic."

"He just *told* you? Why would you believe him? How do you know it isn't a trap?"

"I believe him because I can independently verify Lentz's location. She still has her suit on and the passive trackers built into it have confirmed she is there. As for a trap? Not specifically, I think, but I'm sure it's already very difficult to get onboard. At least we'll have the element of surprise."

"Until they detect us."

"Yes. We're going to need some very fast aircraft, and some very fast boats." She paused. "And even then, we're going to need to hurry."

"I think that can be arranged," Gifford replied.

SIXTY

LENTZ SAT WAITING with Mendez in the meeting room, the Accumulator resting on a white presentation board in the middle of the table. *The cause of so many problems.* "We can't let anyone else acquire it," she said. "We really can't. It's just too dangerous."

Mendez shrugged. "It's important, yes. But something else is more important. I thought we agreed on that?"

"What if I told you that it can very easily become a bomb."

"That's not a concern Hatch will share."

"But it is one you should share–"

The door opened. Hatch walked in, followed by another man. And Lentz let out a gasp. Despite the fact that he wore overalls instead of his usual expensive suit, she immediately recognised him. He was the CEO of VoltTech, Leon Smit.

Smit gave a smirk in her direction. "You know who I am? Good. And I know who you are, Dr Lentz. I *was* going to be your new boss."

"Except that you had me fired."

"My lawyers said you were a troublemaker. I think you could say they were right."

Hatch frowned. "What did I miss?"

"VoltTech recently acquired CERUS Biotech. One of the deal conditions was that Dr Lentz here stand down from her role as CEO. And, with wonderful irony, she ends up here."

Lentz folded her arms. "Except unlike you, I'm not here by choice. But I guess I shouldn't be surprised. There have always been rumours about how you operate."

Smit raised an eyebrow. "What do you mean by that?"

"That you don't create anything. You just buy and resell, legally or otherwise."

"I've never tried to paint myself as a hero. And this is just too big an opportunity to pass up - a defining moment in battery technology. If I don't buy it, someone else will. And I will not be the one left behind."

"And yet you're willing to buy from..." she pointed at Hatch, "is there a better word than 'criminal'?"

"Our mutual friend has been a very logical, reliable partner to do business with."

"His other clients, so I understand, include arms dealers, despots and murderers."

"If I tied myself up in knots worrying about every possible allegation or rumour, I'd never do anything. And this," he pointed at the Accumulator, "is an item I want very much. Now you are going to tell me everything there is to know about it. You are going to answer all my questions. And you are going to provide a thorough demonstration." He turned to Hatch. "How long do I have?"

Hatch shrugged. "If you're paying the one billion US dollars asking price, I'm going to say you have pretty much as long as you need." He paused. "As long as you don't need more than six hours."

Smit nodded. "And if I agree to pay that sum, it won't go to auction?"

"Let's call it our 'buy now' price." Hatch gave a small bow

to Smit. "I'll leave you in the capable hands of Dr Mendez and Dr Lentz."

Smit nodded. "If I'm happy, can I take it now?"

"Once the crypto payment has completed, I see no reason why not—"

Mendez cleared his throat. "We'll need twenty-four hours to prep it for shipping. We have to close off a few processes that we've had running for testing. Plus I have to ensure all our files and data here are deleted in line with our terms and conditions."

"Ah yes," Smit said. "The famous certificate of exclusivity."

"Indeed," Hatch said. "Uniqueness guaranteed, or your money back."

"I'm glad to hear it." Smit turned to Lentz and Mendez. "Shall we begin?"

THREE HOURS later Lentz and Mendez walked back into Laboratory 3A, Lentz carrying the Accumulator. "It doesn't need prepping for shipping," she said as she placed it on the desk. "The whole point is it's portable."

"I was just buying us time," Mendez replied. "You said we couldn't let it leave."

"Then why pick only 24 hours? Why not a week?"

"Look, I was thinking on my feet. Also, I picked the biggest number I thought wouldn't make Hatch suspicious."

"Well now Smit is waiting onboard for us to finish. And he will be watching the clock."

"I understand. We just need to use what time we have to change the game. To get Max fully connected to the Rig. If we can do that, anything is possible, and Smit won't matter."

"Great. But at this point I'm not sure how to connect Max. I'm not sure there is a solution."

"Let's hope, Dominique, that for once you're wrong..." Mendez broke off mid-sentence and pulled out his phone, answering it. "Yes, Director... what? Now? But we're... I mean... Of course, right away." He put the phone away and rolled his eyes.

"What?" Lentz asked. "Is something wrong?"

"Our work with Max will have to wait. Hatch wants us to go the main conference room."

"What for?"

"The next communication with the auction attendees."

"How are we going to connect Max, if we never have time to work out how to connect Max?"

Mendez shook his head. "I'm really not sure. But we'd better go, before Hatch sends some guards to remind us."

SIXTY-ONE

TOM AND REEMS JOINED MARRON and Alex in the submarine's control room. He counted sixteen other crew crammed into the room. All were armed and looked combat capable.

Marron tapped a button on the control panel. "We're three kilometres out from the rendezvous, and conditions are foggy." A black graph with green dots appeared on one of the large screens. "This shows eleven other images on radar, all converging on the same point."

Reems frowned. "Is there something at that point of convergence?"

Alex tapped the screen. "Nothing showing on the radar."

"Do you not have anything better than radar?"

Marron shrugged. "We've been told not to deploy advanced tech. As a condition of participation."

"They probably told you not to bring a submarine either."

"They won't spot us. We've had a few upgrades since a year ago. But as for spotting them, maybe Tom can use his talents to tell us what is up there?"

Tom adjusted the collar. "I don't know. I've been a bit off form."

Alex tipped her head. "That doesn't sound like the warrior I was just speaking with."

"Fine, I can try." He closed his eyes and reached out, his senses extending beyond the submarine, latching on to the electromagnetic radiation, to the patterns of data. Each of the other vessels had their own systems, sending out signals, identifying who and what they were. "I see twelve yachts, including our own. I feel no other submersibles or aircraft."

"So they're following the rules," Marron said. "Good to know."

Tom reached further. The cameras on the front of the Red Herring yacht became his eyes. They showed only the flat grey of the ocean, rolling with mist. Thick and ominous above the sea. Was there too much? Tom switched his viewpoint, looking from a camera facing out the rear of the yacht. The ocean looked much clearer. It couldn't be by chance. "I think there's something there."

"Where?" Alex asked.

"In the mist."

"There's nothing showing. Certainly no land."

"It's not an island. Whatever it is, I think it's generating the fog. Like camouflage." Tom concentrated his probing. And he realised there was an unnatural calm. "There *is* something there. A complete absence of electromagnetic radiation."

"Still nothing visible on any of our instruments."

The control panel chimed and Marron raised a finger. "That's our hosts, signalling us." He tapped a button and a synthetic voice played over speakers. "Participants please slow to ten knots and await further instructions."

And then Tom felt a change. A shift. "Something is happening."

Marron pointed at a smaller display. "You're right. We've just lost all comms."

Reems frowned. "Can you still communicate with the yacht on the surface?"

"Yes," Alex replied. "That's different. It's connected by an optical fibre."

The voice spoke again. "Slow to five knots."

Marron turned to the crew. "OK, people, stay alert. As soon as we know where we're going next, I want you prepped and ready."

"Actually," Tom said, "I don't think they're going to send us anywhere else."

"I agree," Alex said, pointing at the largest display screen. A kilometre in front of them the mist was clearing. And from the mist a new shape came into view, a huge, curved metal form - a flattened steel sphere, standing on six metal legs that ended in large floating pontoons.

Reems pointed. "It's massive. Bigger than an aircraft carrier."

Marron stared at his screen. "Three hundred metres in diameter, and over a hundred metres high."

Tom shook his head. "They could have an army on that thing. We don't have enough people."

Alex tapped him on the shoulder. "It's quality, not quantity."

Reems looked at Marron. "You don't seem that bothered by this turn of events. Or maybe you knew about this already, and just didn't tell us?"

"I said I'd get you here. But don't think, for even a moment, that you and I are on the same team." Marron reached over to a blank section of the control panel and lifted it off, revealing an array of buttons and switches. He flicked a large one at the top left and they all lit up.

Tom turned to Alex. "What is going on here?"

She shrugged. "I said we'd been hired to come here. I didn't say in what capacity."

Marron nodded. "I lied before. When I said we were here to participate in the auction. We're actually here to stop it." He typed in a code then pressed a large red button. From elsewhere in the submarine there was a clank and a rumble.

Reems looked around. "What did you just do?"

Marron smiled. "Watch."

The camera view from the front of the Red Herring widened and they saw the shrinking circle of the super yachts as they slowly converged on the meeting point. One second passed, then another. Then abruptly each yacht was replaced by the yellow, black and grey of an explosion. That image held for a second before the camera cut to black.

On the sonar the blips vanished.

Reems took a step forward. "Are you insane?"

Marron shook his head. "I'm just improving our odds."

"By sinking the other bidders with torpedoes?"

Marron sighed. "What is this, World War Two? We used magnetic limpet mines, anchored to weak points on their hulls, delivered by high-speed underwater drones. All detonated simultaneously so there was no chance for any defence systems to react."

"Haven't you just started a war?"

"Maybe. But at a stroke we have destroyed or seriously wounded eleven major organisations that were operating in this space. Eleven competitors for the stolen technology."

Tom shook his head. "The people on that huge vessel will know. It must have weapons they can target you with."

"I guess we'll find out."

Reems stared at Marron. "This was your plan all along. Where did you get these weapons? Just who is your client?"

"That is an excellent question, Director Reems." He turned to the control panel. "Now let's get ready to dock."

SIXTY-TWO

LENTZ SAT NEXT to Mendez in the conference room, staring at the screens in shock, as twelve angry explosions showed where the auction bidders' yachts had just been. "What just happened?" she asked. "Did the buyers attack each other? Did we attack them?"

Hatch, standing across the room next to three of his guards, calmly adjusted his blue tinted glasses. "Get me a damage report on the Rig."

Mendez looked at the screens in front of him. "I'm reading all systems operational. All attacks were directed at the bidder vessels. Nothing at us. I'm not yet clear where the attacks came from. Our scanners show nothing in a five-kilometre radius."

"Apparently you need better scanners," Lentz said. "Something clearly followed the yachts."

Hatch folded his arms. "Where is Leon Smit?"

"Still in the VIP quarters," Mendez said. "He won't have had access to the feed, if that's your concern."

"I need to make a call. I'll be in my suite." Hatch turned and strode heavily from the room, followed by two guards, leaving one behind.

Lentz cleared her throat. "Is it just me, or does he not seem at all perturbed by what just happened?"

Mendez shrugged. "He doesn't ever show much reaction to anything. Except that weird smile." He frowned. "Wait, I'm detecting a craft approaching the Rig. Less than a kilometre away. It's underwater. Presumably a submarine, and heavily stealthed."

Red lights began flashing. On the nearest screen icons began displaying that Lentz was immediately sure indicated some sort of weapon system. "What is happening?"

"The Rig is defending itself."

"But we don't know who that is," she cried. "Stop it!"

"As you know, I don't have control of the weapons systems."

"Launching torpedoes," said a mechanical voice.

Lentz turned to the screen. It showed the twin guided weapons racing towards the target, proximity data overlayed in real time. They quickly closed on the red dot that was the presumed submarine. She held her breath.

The torpedoes passed straight through it. The target blinked on the scanner and continued its approach.

"What just happened?" Lentz asked.

"I don't know," Mendez replied, "but we're firing again."

Again the torpedoes passed through the apparent target.

Lentz shook her head. "That submarine is not where the instruments say it is. They must have infiltrated our system."

Mendez pointed at the display. "Something has docked with us. It's attached to Bay Zero Alpha, below the water level."

The guard muttered and tapped his earpiece. "Response teams to docking level." He turned and ran from the room.

Lentz saw that they were alone. "What is going on here, Javier?"

"I don't know. Could that be MI5?"

"Did you tell them that you had disabled the security systems?"

"No, obviously. Perhaps they found a workaround?"

"Then why not tell you?"

"It does seem unorthodox. But then this is an unorthodox situation."

"Well we need to find out. Can you try and communicate with them?"

Mendez nodded. "That is a good idea. We should go back to my lab and make a call."

SIXTY-THREE

TOM STOOD WEARING the set of combat armour he'd been provided with, his fingers running over the automatic machine pistol just like all the operatives were carrying. He'd laughed when Alex had handed it to him, but she did not smile in return. "Sometimes," she'd said, "there isn't time to fight hand-to-hand. Sometimes there are just too many opponents. For those situations," she tapped the gun with her fingertips, "you have this. If it's a choice between you and the other guys, choose you."

The submarine shuddered as it connected with something much larger. And then the craft stopped moving.

Alex looked at her display. "We've docked with the Rig."

"The Rig?" Reems asked.

"The big metal thing: that's what they call it." Alex nodded to Marron. "We're good to go. Nobody in the docking bay. *Yet*."

Marron nodded back. "Director Reems, you stay on comms and let us know if anyone else arrives to join the party. The rest of us, move out."

Reems scowled at him. "I'm not being left behind. And don't tell me I'm too old. I'm younger than you."

"Maybe by a couple of years, but that's not the point. You've spent the last decade behind a desk, and you're carrying an injury from last year that will slow you down. You'd be a liability."

"Give me one of those guns and I'll show you just how much of a liability I can be."

Marron smiled. "I don't doubt your anger and determination. I do doubt your reaction speed. So do as you're told or I'll taser you." He nodded to two of the operatives. "They'll be staying behind to keep an eye on the vessel."

"You mean keep an eye on me. Do you need two of them?"

"Knowing you, I'm not clear that two will be enough." He signalled for two more to join men to remain behind. "Try not to hurt them, Director." He turned to Tom. "You ready?"

Tom shrugged. "I just want to rescue Lentz and recover the Accumulator." He glanced at Reems. "Let us take the risks."

She raised an eyebrow. "I know more than you about the risks involved. Go do what you need to do."

MARRON, Alex, Tom and twelve of the crew crept through the airlock and spread out into a loading bay. At the far end was a heavy metal door with an electronic lock. It was shut.

"Our first obstacle," Alex said.

"I can try to open it..." Tom began.

Marron shook his head. "You said you were a bit off your game, so save your strength. I have grunts for this level of problem." Two men came forward carrying a device that they clamped to the lock. It began whirring and grinding, then vibrated rapidly. There was a click and the door swung away from them.

Four men were waiting on the other side, aiming automatic weapons at them.

"Hands in the air," the nearest shouted.

Before the man finished speaking, Marron ducked behind cover, pulling something from his belt and throwing it through the doorway. A second later there was a loud bang and a smell of smoke.

Alex leapt through the doorway, firing several times. There were screams, then silence, followed by her calling: "All clear."

Tom followed Marron into the next room. The four men lay on the floor, bullet holes in their foreheads. "You didn't say killing them was the plan?"

"Them or us." Marron prodded one with the toe of his boot. "And to be clear, it's going to be them."

Alex grasped Tom's shoulder. "Remember why you're doing this. Some things are more important than life." She looked down. "Even four lives."

They moved forward along a corridor, turned a corner and reached another locked door. Again Marron's people opened it using the electronic device. This time the door opened onto a much larger space. Within it a dozen guards were spread out, aiming weapons. They began firing.

Marron yanked the door closed, as one bullet struck him in the chest, bouncing off his body armour. "They've spread out to avoid grenades, so they're learning. Well equipped, too. Smart rifles, I think."

Alex frowned. "OK, but we have to go that way. What's the play?"

Marron looked around. "I'm going to need four of you to provide cover. We'll open the door, then..." He hesitated, then looked at Tom. "With the numbers, positioning, and equipment they have, this won't be straightforward. Any chance you can help us out?"

Tom blinked. "I'm sorry, what?"

"Can you shift the balance?"

"You're the one who's combat trained."

Marron raised an eyebrow. "I wasn't suggesting you take them on hand-to-hand. I meant more about you contributing tactical data? Can you connect to their system? It might give us an advantage. Plus this Rig is huge, so if we can't get some up-to-date schematics, it's going to take us weeks to find what we're looking for."

"I'm not sure if I can. I thought you had someone on the inside?"

"They only sent us limited data." He raised a finger. "I know you're not at full power, without the Accumulator. But you have that collar thing, and a number of batteries."

Tom rubbed his forefingers on his temples. "I thought I wouldn't be doing this until I recovered the Accumulator."

"If you don't help, you aren't getting your device back. Nor are you rescuing Lentz."

Tom shook his head. "This is why you let me come with you. You're not doing me a favour. You need me."

Marron shrugged. "We need each other. What's wrong with a little symbiosis?" He pointed to the door. "Let's take out the enemies in the next room."

Tom closed his eyes and held his hand towards the door. "Something tells me this is a really bad idea."

SIXTY-FOUR

TOM APPROACHED the door and reached out. He had to get inside the CCTV, and the Rig's automated systems. But as his mind touched them he found they were, not surprisingly, encrypted. He concentrated and applied force to the systems, trying to thread his way inside. Power began to flow through the collar around his neck, causing it to heat. His mind attacked the code, attempting to brute force through the encryption.

It was not enough.

He opened his eyes. "I can't get through their security protocols. I'm sorry."

Marron stared back at him. "Then let's try something else. You're familiar with drones?"

"I know how they work."

Marron snapped his fingers and another crew member came forward, placing a case on the floor. He flipped it open. Inside, neatly packed in foam rubber, were sixteen small drones. "Very hard to see or hear, let alone target. They're equipped with audio visual sensors and are capable of broad-spectrum data collection."

"And what am I going to do with them?"

"You're going to steal their network access. Those guards must have ID cards or some technology that allows the Rig to recognise them. These drones can sample and steal it. And with that you can hack in, without having to break through the main system encryption."

"That is actually not a bad plan."

"You are too kind."

"Only one problem - I can't see them through the door. And I can't access their CCTV cameras because of the encryption."

"Then you'll have to walk in there and distract them, while the drones do their thing. Or rather, while you make them do their thing."

"And what if the guards decide to shoot me?"

Marron raised an eyebrow. "That's a risk I'm prepared to take."

"I'M COMING THROUGH," Tom called out as Marron opened the door. "Don't shoot. I am unarmed."

"Why?" a male voice shouted back.

"I want to talk. To see if we can avoid further bloodshed."

"Why should we trust you?"

"Hear me out. Then you can decide."

There was some muttering, then the voice replied: "Walk through. Walk slowly. Hands high in the air."

Tom advanced through the doorway, raising his hands. He entered a workshop with a number of items of heavy machinery in various states of repair, the guards taking cover behind them. Three other doors, all closed, led out in each of the other walls.

Tom moved to one side, and the guards tracked him with their weapons. While they were distracted the drones flew through and spread out across the ceiling. Each moved more slowly than he expected, like they were carrying extra weight. All but silent, they passed unnoticed.

The man in charge motioned to him with his automatic rifle. "Kneel on the floor, hands behind your head."

"What about the talking?"

"You'll still be able to talk when you're tied up."

"That's not very trusting."

"I don't think you've earned much trust."

Tom dropped to his knees. At the same time he reached out to the drones and sent them on a controlled flight, splitting to target each guard.

There was a shimmer in the air, a fluttering like sixteen butterflies moving in tight formation. He could feel them land. Planting themselves on each man's neck. Inside him something started to question what he was doing. But that something was quickly buried by other thoughts.

The leader frowned, raising his hand to swat at what must have felt like a fly, when a bright yellow flame burst out on his neck. And on all the others. Tom threw himself backwards, twisting away, protecting his eyes, as around him the guards fell, screaming.

Marron's voice spoke from close by. "Good work, Tom."

Tom looked up in shock. "They're all dead? You said I was trying to hack them?"

"I may have forgotten to mention the explosives." He stooped and pulled a computer ID card from the belt of one of the fallen men. "We now have a security card, and I have the passcode. There's a terminal over there you can use."

Tom gaped at him. "You had me kill them."

"We can argue the whys and wherefores later. Why don't you get on with doing what you do?"

~

TOM LOOKED DOWN at the computer terminal and felt giddy for a moment. The collar was burning his neck and had stopped functioning. He slipped it off and removed the smoking battery, throwing it to the floor.

Alex walked up to him. "You drew a lot of power there, I see."

"Maybe I shouldn't have." He pulled another battery from his pocket and fitted it, replacing the collar around his neck.

"When you're ready," Marron said, waving the ID card. "Best to get on with things before they take steps to lock the place down."

Tom took the card and studied it. "I can work with this."

Marron held up his tablet computer. "Here's the access code. All 32 digits of it. Sending it to you now—"

"I've already memorised it." Tom moved over to the terminal and placed the card over the reader, as he sent the long code to the system. And it opened to him.

In a rush, his consciousness was interfacing with the basic operating system of the Rig. He could view plans, internal comms and audio-visual sensors through most floors. Different electronic systems had different textures to them and could take getting used to - meaning his interactions were initially inefficient. But here he immediately felt at home. It was effortless, almost too easy one might say. But now wasn't the time to question or complain. Now was the time to solve some problems. He focused his thoughts. "Where is my Accumulator? And where is Dominique Lentz? *Show me.*"

The structure of the Rig appeared in his mind. It was a huge, flattened sphere, with eight primary levels, serving different functions. And in the middle of it, on what was designated Level Three, was a huge laboratory, named simply 3A.

In it was the Accumulator. And Lentz. He permitted himself a smile.

He just needed to get to them. He traced his view back to

their present location. There were many guards converging on them - more than a hundred, he rapidly totalled. Yet the Rig was large, and there were multiple possible routes. Quickly he processed different options, ranking them for speed and safety. And an optimal answer presented itself.

He opened his eyes. "I know where we need to go." He pointed to the door on the left.

Marron smiled. "You heard the man. Let's get moving."

SIXTY-FIVE

LENTZ FOLLOWED Mendez through the airlock and back into Laboratory 3A. Screens on the walls were now flashing red with status reports.

Mendez pointed at one of his nearby laptops. "The intruders' team has made its way onboard. And they are making progress. I don't think our guards are slowing them much."

"So are we in danger? Or is the enemy of my enemy, my friend?"

"I don't know. Let's try and get a look at them." He adjusted some controls, then tapped a button and footage appeared of a figure walking towards some guards, the figure holding their hands up. "This is from a few moments ago. It's not great footage, and then it cuts out." He hesitated. "From their suit telemetry, the guards are all dead." He scratched his nose. "We might be in danger."

"I don't disagree."

"But maybe this is also an opportunity. And we need to brief Hatch."

Lentz blinked. "Explain."

"We use the situation as leverage. We explain the threat and get him to grant Max control over the security systems."

"But that was only half your plan. If they aren't MI5, how do we escape the Rig?"

"Before we disconnect Max, it can open a path for us to reach the life rafts."

"You want to drop into the ocean in a rubber dinghy? That's your idea of a good plan?"

"You'd prefer to stay here and die?"

"If this was an option, why didn't you suggest it before?"

"Because the guards would have stopped us. But if they're distracted, we might make it away. If you have a better plan, I'm ready to hear it."

"For once, I do not."

LENTZ WATCHED Mendez tap on a control panel, then raise his voice: "Director? I need your input."

There was a pause, then Hatch's voice broke over the speakers. "What is the matter?"

Lentz narrowed her eyes. The voice sounded thick, almost slurred. "Is he OK?" she mouthed at Mendez.

Mendez shrugged. "Director, are you following the incursion?"

"I'm sure our people have it in hand."

"I don't think they do. The enemy has well-equipped, highly trained operatives that outmatch our people. They've also hacked into our system and have gained control of a number of systems."

"Then shut them out. Turn it all off if you have to."

"They're preventing our admin access," Mendez said. "Without additional computing power, we cannot fight back."

There was a pause. "Are you asking me if you can connect Max to the Rig's full systems?"

"Before, I was asking in the context of a notional threat. This is specific, immediate, and it is life or death. We have to hand over control of the Rig to Max, if we want to save it. There are automated weapons and systems, but they can only be deployed optimally if Max is running them. It can stop these intruders."

There was a longer pause. "Find another way."

"There is none. And if we let them continue with the hack, there may not even be this way. The clock is ticking, Director."

"You have my final answer."

Mendez looked at his laptop. "But we've lost track of the intruders. They could be coming for anyone on board," he paused, "including you."

"And I will handle them if they do. Now you will excuse me." There was a loud tone and the call disconnected.

Lentz frowned. "He wasn't helpful. It's like he's not on our side."

Mendez nodded. "So I guess we hide?"

She put her hands on her hips. "We stick to your plan."

"How? The Rig systems are logically and physically separated from Max. The connection point would require a hardwire from Max to the Rig CPU. And that is contained in a control room with ten-centimetre-thick steel walls and a door with a physical key. A key held only by Hatch."

"Impossible challenges just force us to be creative."

"So, let me get this straight - your plan is to rely on the fact that, given our backs are really against the wall, we'll come up with something exactly when we need it most?"

"Or maybe I've actually got an idea of how to save us."

Mendez looked at her and nodded slowly. "Then I guess we should find out. Follow me."

SIXTY-SIX

TOM LED Marron's team through the Rig. The place was a metal labyrinth, but he knew the way, and a new set of drones flew above him, providing a steady stream of real-time visuals. Around his neck the collar hummed. He had drained two more batteries, but still had the one he was using along with a final spare. Ahead he could feel the Accumulator. Soon he and it would be reunited. And then he would tear this place apart.

Alex moved alongside him. "This is impressive, Mr Faraday. You're changing again. I'm not sure if I can keep up."

"And I'm not sure you should be relying on me. There seem to be areas completely disconnected from the security monitoring systems, parts within this structure that I cannot see inside, including a whole section in the middle of each floor."

"Not important enough to warrant security, or too important to risk it being hacked?"

"Hard to know. But I can't worry about that for now. The Accumulator is on this floor, in a lab a hundred metres from here." He pointed to the door they were approaching, then froze. "Wait."

"Is it playtime again?"

"The next room is another hub, with four doors including this one, and six guards on duty."

"Are you going to use the drones?"

Tom cricked his neck to one side. "I might keep them in reserve. Handle this with a low-tech approach."

She smiled. "Lead on."

Tom sent a command to turn off the lights in the next room, opened the doors and moved inside. His senses, enhanced by data, told him where his opponents were. And his mind told him what to do. He started to move.

Again his movements were not his own. They belonged to someone more skilled, more adept. As he turned to strike, his limbs flowed in patterns familiar, yet unfamiliar. Intimate, yet strange. Balletic, yet deadly. Alex moved with him, her own form a study in control, her movements eerily familiar, and terribly destructive. What was it about them? What gave him that sense of deja vu?

And then he saw it. The echo. The reflection. He knew what she was doing because he was doing the exact same. They were in step, and in tune. How was it possible? Why was it happening? Those questions threaded through his thoughts, as he moved.

The encounter did not last long. Tom danced through the unsuspecting group of guards, attacking with efficiency. He moved faster than they could respond, reading their responses, sliding under their confused blows, striking with pinpoint accuracy. In moments they were lying on the floor, unconscious. And as he drew breath he realised nobody else had helped. Alex had stopped to watch. He had done it alone.

"Poetry." Alex folded her arms and smiled. "Sheer, magical poetry."

Tom shook his head. "I don't understand how I did that."

"All that matters is that you did."

Marron and six of his team had followed them inside. The

remaining six were still in the previous room. Marron walked over to the nearest guard and shot him in the head.

"What?" Tom cried. "Why would you do that?"

Marron flicked his rifle around, repeating the action with the other guards. "Because we don't want them rejoining the fight."

"We could have tied them up."

"They could still get rescued. And it would take too long. This is a military 101 - given the opportunity, we mitigate the risk."

"You will not do that again. If you do I'll..."

"Do you want to rescue your friend? Do you want to recover the Accumulator? I suggest you focus."

Tom took a sharp breath, balled his fist and began to swing.

But before he could finish the motion he felt something. A presence. Something was moving through the Rig. Something the system recognised, at a base level.

He spun around, reaching out, yet he could detect nothing. Yet his nanites were telling him a danger was close. Something terribly familiar. *What was it?*

In the room behind them there were screams and gunfire.

Marron raised his rifle. "I thought you were jacked in to the system? A warning would be nice."

Tom was about to close his eyes, when someone walked through the door. Someone very large, carrying two automatic rifles.

Korver.

SIXTY-SEVEN

TOM STARED AT KORVER. "I don't understand. How are you here? You were in MI5 custody?"

The man shrugged. "It proved to be only temporary, after which I managed to hitch a ride on a *very* fast plane. Now drop your weapons."

Marron grunted and shot Korver in the chest. The bullet ricocheted away. He shot again, this time in the face. The result was the same. Marron stared at this rifle. "That's some trick."

Korver raised both rifles and pointed them at Marron. "I won't ask again."

Marron turned to Tom. "Feel free to get involved."

Tom closed his eyes and reached out, and time started to move slowly. The cameras and sensors around him flooded his mind with data. He felt the drones above, and this time he felt the explosives within. This time there was no deception, this time he knew what he was doing. This time he meant to destroy, because with Korver there were no half measures. He gave the instruction and the drones accelerated towards their target.

Before Korver could react, the drones struck him and detonated. Tom turned away from the flash and flying debris. He felt the collar around his neck scorch with heat, then the battery died. On reflex he slipped it off and slotted another battery in place. The last battery. At least he had already dealt with Korver - he wouldn't need more power to deal with him.

But as he turned back he saw he was wrong. The automatic rifles lay buckled and broken, but the huge man remained standing. Korver brushed dust disdainfully off his sleeve.

Tom shook his head. "This is ridiculous. What does it take to hurt you?"

Alex stepped between him and Korver. "I've got this. Go get your magic box."

Tom shook his head. "I'm not running away. This is my fight."

"No, it isn't. In fact, this fight is the reason I'm here."

"You saw what he just survived. With that body armour on, he's untouchable."

Alex smiled. "Everything has a weakness. It's just a question of identifying it. And you know how much I like learning."

Korver folded his arms. "And what you will *learn* is that you cannot beat me."

"That's the thing," she said. "We can only know by actually fighting." She pushed Tom away. "Go already. And while you're doing it, lock me and him in here. I'd hate that we get interrupted."

Tom frowned and glanced at Marron. "You OK with this?"

"Do as she says. I find it's usually the best way."

Tom reached out and locked the doors to his left and right.

Alex stepped forward, pulling a telescopic staff from her belt and extending it. "OK, big guy. You ready to dance?" She glanced over her shoulder. "You two can go now."

Marron grabbed Tom's shoulder and pulled him back through the open door. "Seal it off."

Tom shook his head but did as he was asked. A red light illuminated above the door. "He'll kill her."

"He's got to hit her first." Marron laughed. "Let's get moving."

Tom reluctantly turned around and pointed down the corridor. "Laboratory 3A is fifty metres that way."

"Lead on."

SIXTY-EIGHT

ALEX STOOD in front of Korver, twisting the extended staff slowly. "You ready to do this?"

Korver stood unmoving. "I don't want to fight you. I have no orders to do so."

"But I came all this way." She circled slowly to one side. "And I'm not going to give you a choice. Of course I'd understand if you're hesitant, even intimidated. If you aren't, it's just because you don't know who I am."

He shook his head. "It doesn't matter who you are. If we fight, you will lose."

"I've heard that from a lot of people. They've all been wrong." Without warning she lunged forward, scything with the staff.

He raised an arm and knocked it effortlessly aside. "I will give you one more chance. Return to your submarine and leave."

She dropped low, spinning and striking him in the legs. Except his legs were no longer there, as he deftly jumped over the blow. Alex raised an eyebrow. "That's quite a vertical you have on you. Maybe you *are* what I was promised."

Korver took a step sideways. "Promised by who?"

Alex danced backwards, then moved to her right. "That got your interest." She moved forward, faster than before, striking a vicious blow to his neck. But it did not connect.

He caught the staff in his hand, yanking it from her grasp. Bringing up his other hand, he broke the weapon over his knee, snapping it in half. "You don't know anything about me."

Alex reached to her back and pulled out a second extendable staff. "We knew enough to find this place. We knew enough to take over the Rig's systems. And we knew there was someone here I would want to fight."

"How?"

"You think I'm just going to answer your questions? That's not how this works. First you have to give me what I want."

"Have it your way." He moved forwards, swinging at her with his right fist.

She smiled and leapt back effortlessly. He advanced, jabbing with his left and she swayed out of the way. "Come on, I want to actually learn something today." Korver lunged, swinging with his right fist. She ducked low underneath it, and kicked him in the ribs, forcing him to take a half step backwards. "You're strong and fast, but not particularly inventive. Your moves are predictable. A bit like mine were a year ago."

He straightened and looked at her. "Is this a game to you?"

"No, it's a learning opportunity. And it's already clear you have a rather obvious flaw: overconfidence." The cords on her neck tightened, and she thrust the staff forward, the shortest possible distance between two points, a straight line of force and purpose. The staff tip thrust through where his forehead had been. But he had already moved. He lashed back with a counter punch. It connected with her stomach and suddenly she was flying across the room, slamming into the wall. She slid to the floor and gasped, spitting out blood. "Where did that come from?"

He looked at her, his face placid. "Perhaps I'm not the one who is overconfident."

"You're a startlingly quick learner." She frowned. "And you're startlingly *quick*."

"I said you couldn't win."

She dropped the staff, lowered her head and charged at him, barrelling into his waist with all her weight. He did not even flinch. She bounced off and slid across the floor. "It's like fighting a tree. What is that body armour you're wearing?"

He hesitated, his eyes flickering. "I don't know how it works. They told me not to ask."

"Well they did warn me, and they gave me this." She pulled a small remote control from her pocket and held it up.

"What is that?"

"A means of levelling the playing field." She pushed the main button. There was a chime, then several clicks.

Korver's body armour fell away from him. He stared at it in confusion. "That's not possible. But I don't really need it." He lunged at her, a soaring kick with absolute intent. She ducked under his foot but had to parry two further strikes from his fists. Then she drove her knee hard, but he anticipated the attack and swayed away. She kept her direction of movement, leaping into the air and kicking down hard. He deftly guided her thrust aside with both hands interlocked, then as she landed, he moved to grapple her shoulders. She ducked under his reach and rolled aside, rotating and throwing a straight, fast punch. He blocked it with his left arm, redirecting the power of the blow. They both stepped back, breathing hard.

He pointed at her. "Who gave you the device to remove my armour?"

"Who taught you to fight like that? The range of techniques, the adaptation. I've never seen anything like it." But as she said it, Alex immediately realised that was untrue. It was how *she* fought. And, of course, it had been how she had seen

Tom fight, if to a much lower standard. "There's something off about all of this."

Korver picked up a piece of his body armour from where it lay on the floor. "Answer my question."

"Obviously one of your people."

"Why would they compromise our security? It makes no sense."

"Only if you presume your people are being straight with you. Once you realise they have another goal, all bets are off."

"You said I was promised to you? In what way?"

"As a worthy adversary. Someone who could test my skills. There's no doubt that's what you have done, but now I've seen you in person, I think someone's not been straight with me too." She looked at the staff on the ground and kicked it away. "I've been lied to. I'm just not sure who by. Or why."

Korver shook the piece of body armour. "What are you talking about?"

"I thought the purpose of being here was to test me. But I think it's to test you. To see how capable you really are. Against a highly skilled opponent."

"But I thought you knew all about me?"

"Not as much as I believed I did, it would seem. Because I have a particular ability to learn. I soak up knowledge about combat, I learn by experience. And I am unnaturally fast and strong - qualities boosted by an exposure to experimental nanotechnology."

Korver frowned. "Someone else mentioned that word to me. I take an ongoing course of drugs that prevent a medical condition regressing. Perhaps they do more than I realised. Perhaps they aren't just drugs." He threw the piece of body armour down. "So, what now then?"

She ran a hand through her hair. "Normally I just keep fighting until I've learned enough. Until I decide to end it. But with you? I think this is a setup. And I think we should stop."

"You started this fight." He stepped closer. "That doesn't mean you get to say when it's over."

Alex looked at him, unblinking. "I have questions that cannot be answered by beating you. Do you not feel the same?"

Korver hesitated. "How did you know about the Rig's systems? And how did you know there was someone here to fight?"

"My father didn't give me all the details, but I believe it was someone by the name of Hatch."

"Are you sure?"

"That was the name I heard him mention."

"And why did you come here? What is the main purpose of your mission?"

"To steal technology. We were never going to take part in the auction. We were never going to pay for it."

"But why would Hatch cooperate with that? It makes no sense." Korver frowned. "This is difficult to process."

"So what then?" Alex asked. "Are our interests aligned?"

"For now. Beyond that will depend on what we find out."

"Fair enough. So where do we go? To get our answers?"

He pointed upwards. "Follow me."

SIXTY-NINE

LENTZ AND MENDEZ once again walked into the immaculately clean room containing Max. Mendez frowned. "How exactly are we going to do this?"

Lentz walked over to the heavy metal door barring access to the security systems. "It would be simplest if we could just get in there and make the connection direct. Have you tried picking the lock?"

"I wouldn't know how."

She shrugged. "Doesn't really matter. It's a tamper-proof design, and even then we don't have any tools." She pointed at the blades. "Regardless, I want to look at Max. Inside it, I mean."

Mendez paled. "What? Why?"

"You can't make an omelette without breaking a few eggs. It's time to see how the sausage is made."

"You are not messing around inside Max. You'll break it, and that would defeat the whole point of what we're doing. I also need to finalise the backup which needs to be made at the last possible moment, so we capture Max's final state before we leave."

Lentz frowned. “You’re going to have to trust me, Javier. I can’t solve the puzzle without looking at all the pieces.”

“When I ran a self-diagnosis on Max, it advised against physical access to its components. They are extremely sensitive to vibration or disturbance, to fluctuations in temperature.”

“*It* told you that?”

“Yes.”

“It tried to dissuade you from poking around within? Now I’m even more intrigued. Look are you going to open it, or shall I?”

He frowned again then walked over and unscrewed a number of thumbscrews. Setting them aside he carefully lifted away an access panel. “This is the central core. Try not to breathe.”

Lentz stepped closer and stared at the well-ordered components. It was all very advanced. But was it advanced enough? “That’s it?”

“You were expecting something else?”

“Given that I’m being told it is so utterly revolutionary, yes.”

“I didn’t design it to win a beauty pageant. It uses standard components. It’s the configuration that makes it special.”

“But how is it so small?” She leaned closer. “You said you didn’t get it working before you came here?”

“Correct.”

“But then you just ‘solved it’? What was the specific change you made? What was the inventive step?”

“I kept trying different variations. And then one worked.”

“You mean it was just random?”

“Science can be like that. Max helped with diagnosis between testing phases, and suggestions for resolution.”

“So... you’re saying it fixed itself?”

“In a manner of speaking. Look, do we have time for a

philosophical discussion? Do you actually have a plan for fixing it?"

She stared at the computer. Then at the door. The connection couldn't be made. Not by a hardwire. And not wirelessly, not through the metal. At least not by normal means. But, she realised, that didn't matter - not with the tech she had available. She would just have to modify it. "I'm going to need a Node."

"For what?"

"Just get it for me, will you. You're describing the problem earlier has given me a big idea."

He frowned again then fetched a Node from a drawer to one side. She took the dark metal object, feeling the cool metal surface, running her fingers to find the almost invisible seams of its access panel - the ones she had barely been able to locate and had not been able to open. The ones that would grant access to what she needed. "And do you have a hammer?"

He narrowed his eyes. "And perhaps a chisel?"

"Seriously just pass me one. This is the egg I'm going to break."

"I don't think I can watch."

"You should," Lentz replied. "You might learn something."

~

LENTZ STARED down at her handiwork. At the disassembled components, along with the tools and cables that Mendez had provided her with. Nothing inside the Node was standard. Every component was bespoke.

Mendez looked at her. "Do you understand it?"

"Not really. But it looks like a technology that Edna Kim was investigating. A lot of stuff seems to have ended up here."

"So like with the little robots, they stole it from her?"

"Perhaps," Lentz replied. "Although as far as I know she

was at a very early stage. This is more like the kind of advanced level that I was expecting with Max."

"Will you stop going on about that? It's function over form. I didn't realise I was being scored on artistic impression."

"That's not my point." She pulled components from the Node and connected them together with cables and crocodile clips.

"I thought you didn't understand it."

"There are levels of understanding. Let's call this an experiment based on my best guess." She connected one end of a high-capacity data cable to the components, then held out the other end. "Plug this into any high-capacity data port."

He took it from her. "You're trying to bridge the gap to the security systems. But that won't work - the Nodes only connect to each other."

"Which is why I've had to make modifications. It should now work with a single Node, although only over a very short distance." She tugged at the long cable. "Do as I've asked please."

He shook his head, then walked over and very carefully plugged it in. "Now what?"

She stood up and moved over to the nearest control interface. "Let's try and reach out to the security system." Her hands began to fly over the keyboard.

"You think you can just program Max? I'll tell you that won't be straightforward. It's a non-standard system, developed from machine learning. Even if you knew–"

Lentz raised a hand. "That's... curious."

"What is?"

"It's ready to complete."

Mendez blinked. "What?"

She pointed at the touchscreen. It displayed a short question: 'Connect to Security System?' Underneath was an onscreen button reading: 'CONFIRM'.

"You did all that already?"

"I'd barely started, and it's already complete? Is it reading my mind?"

"That's not a system feature. But it's good at predictions. It will have detected what you did, likely listened to our conversation."

Lentz raised an eyebrow. "That's more than a little unnerving. Perhaps we should have a think about this."

"Time isn't on our side here." Mendez walked up next to her. "Just accept that you're brilliant and get this done."

"Except that I'm not. Something else is going on–"

Mendez stabbed his finger at the screen. The button blinked in confirmation then the screen went dark. "We have to start making decisions if we're going to get out of here."

Lentz shook her head. "Something's wrong. There was absolutely no reaction from Max." She pointed at the open server case. "Not a hum of power, not a blink of lights. Not the whirr of cooling."

"Perhaps we wouldn't expect it, for such an easy task. We didn't tax its system."

She moved closer to the casing. "I don't buy it. Max is capable. But it's not magic." The screen flickered back on, and a message appeared.

RE-INITIATING SECURITY SYSTEMS.

"See," Mendez said, "you are as brilliant as they say. How could I have ever doubted you."

"Because you were right." Lentz turned and picked up the hammer. "All I've done is clarified just how screwed we are."

"What are you doing?"

She marched back to the server. "Showing you the problem." She raised the hammer Mendez had reluctantly given her. "Because I've finally learned something about Max."

"You're joking. Please tell me you're joking."

"I am not. I'm going to show you why breaking this egg won't matter."

Mendez seemed to realise she wasn't joking. As she swung, he lunged, grabbing at her arm. But she was quicker. The hammer connected with the interior of the server. The components crumpled like aluminium foil. Like they weren't real.

Mendez froze, his jaw falling open. "I don't understand."

Lentz nodded. "What I've learned about Max is that it isn't here." She pushed aside the fragments of the fake components and pointed to a large red metal sphere. A Node. "Max is somewhere else, delivering computational power via the Node."

A klaxon started shrieking. SECURITY SYSTEM CHECK. SYSTEMS BOOTUP COMPLETE. Mendez shook his head. "This makes no sense."

"No. It makes all the sense. Someone else fixed Max. They took what you knew, and then they took it further. They perfected it without you. And then, for some reason, they kept you around, blissfully ignorant of the real story."

"But you connected Max to the security systems."

"Only because whoever is really behind Max wanted that to happen."

"And why would they want that?"

"I don't know. But I have a bad feeling that we may be about to find out."

The autodog in the corner of the room began to move, its rubber feet tapping, approaching them with purpose. Then its LED lights shifted from green to amber. And then to red. And as much as a thing without eyes could stare, it stared at them hard and with purpose.

Lentz raised an eyebrow at Mendez. "Whoever they are, I get the feeling they don't need us anymore."

SEVENTY

LENTZ POINTED AT THE AUTODOG. "I think we've just made a very big mistake."

"I don't understand," Mendez replied. "That red light is a warning status indicator. *Max*, deactivate the dog."

"Command not recognised," replied a synthetic voice.

"The problem," Lentz said, "is that Max is the one that has turned it red." Screens lit up around the computer room. They showed perhaps a dozen viewpoints, containing clusters of the Rig's guards. In each scene three or more dogs were advancing on the guards, their LEDs pulsing red. "How many of these things are there?"

"Over a hundred," Mendez said quietly. "They've replaced most functional staff other than our security team."

"I think they're about to replace them too."

On the screens they saw guards backing away. The dogs advanced, their manipulator arms ending in glittering blades. The guards shouted for the dogs to stop, but they were ignored. Then the guards opened fire. Bullets ricocheted off hard metal, but the robots were not even slowed. The guards turned and tried to run and found exit doors slamming closed.

"No!" Mendez cried. "Stop this!" But it did not stop. With nowhere to go, the dogs descended upon the guards, slashing and cutting without emotion. The men screamed. And they fell.

Lentz grabbed Mendez by the arm, pulling him towards the airlock door, stabbing the controls. But it would not open.

"Exit not authorised," said the synthetic voice.

Lentz looked upwards. "Why are you doing this?" The dog in the room flicked its two manipulator arms into view. At the end of each was a large silver blade. They looked sickeningly sharp.

Mendez stared in horror. "What is happening?"

"Nothing good." Lentz dragged him away from the door and around the nearest workbench, tapping her glasses. They scanned the robotic creature and her HUD lit up with the results. "I'm not seeing any weaknesses. Any ideas?"

"It can lift six tons and move at more than eighty kilometres per hour if it has enough space."

"So an Olympic sprinter, doubled?"

"Pretty much. We can't fight it. And we certainly can't outrun it."

"I'd rather focus on a list of what we can do." Lentz tapped her glasses again, this time selecting a deeper scan. The dog began circling the room, trying to get a clear line of sight. Her HUD again reported no suggestions. "Come on, Javier. This is your house."

"Max," Mendez said, "command priority one zero one: emergency override."

"Command not recognised."

Lentz hissed. "Do you have a physical emergency shut down?"

He blinked. "Yes, we did. We do." He turned and ran to a control panel in the wall, ripping it open and slamming his hand on the red button within.

"Manual emergency shutdown overriden," said the voice immediately.

Lentz ran over to Mendez. "Now it's just messing with us. Best keep moving."

The dog stopped trying to circle round the workbench, lowered itself, then leapt up onto the bench, landing with a smack and a creak. Lentz looked up, seeing the underside of the dog for the first time. One of the panels in its bodywork looked misaligned. She tapped her glasses, requesting a further analysis, but their power level was now in the red, and before the analysis could complete the dog shifted forward and raised one of its blades, slashing. She hurled herself backwards, the cutting edge missing her head by centimetres. She collapsed into Mendez and they both fell to the floor.

"There's nothing we can do," he said. "We're going to need some kind of miracle."

"I don't disagree one would be helpful," Lentz replied, "but in my experience it's not a good plan to rely on them."

The dog started to swing again, then it froze. Across the room came the sound of the airlock door opening. The dog halted and swung around.

And someone familiar walked in. Someone who should be dead.

Edna Kim.

SEVENTY-ONE

TOM REACHED a set of metal double doors. On the wall a plaque read 'Laboratory 3A'. "This is it," he said. "The Accumulator is inside."

"Good news." Marron raised a hand for his team to stop. "What are you waiting for? Open the damn door."

Tom tapped the controls, but they beeped angrily and flashed red.

"Locked?"

"Seems so. But Lentz can let us in." He knocked on the door, then realised its heavy metal structure swallowed the sound of his knock. He stood back and waved, but the door did not open. "She must be able to see us on a camera."

"The good doctor is obviously busy. Just use your talents, already."

"Sure." Tom reached out. His mind began to connect, the data began to flow. He sent the instruction to open the doors.

Nothing happened.

Marron tapped his foot. "Any time."

"Something feels off."

"What do you mean?" Marron asked. "After all you've done to get here, why would you hesitate now?"

"I'm not the problem. It's—"

A synthetic voice broke over loudspeakers: *"Automated defence system online. Facility scan in process."*

Tom spread his arms wide. "*See!*"

"Do you actually want this Accumulator? Do you want to rescue your friend? We came all this way and you're just giving up?"

Tom puffed out his cheeks, then reached out firmly for the door controls. The mechanism acknowledged his request and appeared to accept it. But then nothing moved. He banged his fist on the door's metal surface. "It should have worked. Perhaps it's jammed?"

Marron sighed and placed his hand on the control panel. Again it didn't open. "I guess if you want something doing, then blowing it up is always a simple option." He turned to his team. "Bring the C4."

"That's reinforced steel," Tom said, "so I hope you have a lot." He leaned against the doors in frustration. And without warning they opened. Blinking he stumbled through, finding himself in an airlock, a further set of doors ahead of him.

Marron followed him in. "You said you couldn't—" Abruptly the doors closed. He spun and slapped his hand against the metal. "What's going on?"

"Like I keep saying, something feels off. And what is that noise?" From behind them came a rapid drumming, the sound of many hard, heavy, small feet, striking at the same time. Tom moved to the glass window in the door and looked out.

Two gleaming six-legged robotic creatures were advancing down the corridor, their bodies illuminated in red LED lights. Marron's men had seen them too and were shouting in alarm. The robots - because that's what they clearly were - carried metal blade weapons in two further manipulator arms.

Marron slapped his hand on the airlock door controls, but they did not respond. Outside his men opened fire. The bullets caused no visible damage, but the robots reacted as if stung, accelerating towards them. Marron kicked at the metal door, but it made no difference. Tom reached out, trying to control the metal creatures. In the brief moment available he could not find a connection.

And then the robots were upon Marron's men, metal arms flailing, blades slashing. And they cut them down. Tom turned away, trying not to vomit.

Marron growled next to him. "It didn't occur to you to try and stop them?"

"I couldn't make a connection in time." He clenched his fists then stared at the robots, drawing a deep breath, then reaching out more forcefully. His mind met a ring of steel. "They're heavily encrypted. I can't get through." The nearest robot turned and walked towards their exterior door, tapping it with one of their limbs.

Marron frowned. "We'd best get out of here."

Tom turned to the interior doors and concentrated on them, sending out clear instructions, commanding the system to comply. But the doors would not open. He took a step forward and tried again. Behind him the tapping grew more persistent. Tom glanced over his shoulder and saw the second robot had joined it, but this one was swinging a hammer with a metal spike. The glass cracked. The robots struck again, tapping and hammering. And with their relatively narrow, articulated bodies, they could certainly climb through once the glass was removed.

"If you could hurry." Marron unshouldered his assault rifle, his demeanour one of studied calm. "I don't think this is going to make much of a difference. I have two grenades, which might be more effective, but in this confined space they'll kill us as well."

Tom swallowed and held his hand out at the door. And it was useless. Everything had changed from moments before. He was trying to negotiate an entirely different system. Something of immensely greater complexity and capability. Something, he realised with horror, like what had touched his mind back in the battle at Bern's mansion. It was... *immense.*

The second robot with the hammer smashed through the glass. The first robot began picking away the broken sections which, being shatterproof glass, were still semi-glued together. Without waiting the second one began climbing through. Dispassionate, uncaring, relentless. Its first two limbs touched the floor inside the airlock. Marron shook his head and aimed his rifle.

"No!" Tom shouted. "Stop!" The robot with the hammer froze where it was. There was a shriek of metal, then smoke began to rise from its body, angry error tones hammering the air in a repeating pattern. Its LED lights dimmed and went out.

"What did you do?" Marron asked.

"I don't know. I don't think I..." The inert form of the robot was pulled back through the airlock window, and the first robot took its place, its LED lights blazing red. Tom lunged forwards and it fell back, jerking and shaking, falling to the floor. One of its legs fell off, clattering to the floor in a shower of sparks. Then the robot froze, its lights going out. Behind Tom there was a soft tone. He turned and saw that the interior doors had slid apart.

Marron looked at him. "You found a way to do it?"

"I don't know if any of that was me." He edged forward through the interior doors into a large space with a high ceiling, white walls lined with shelving and three long workbenches filling the main area. There was no sign of Lentz, but on the middle table, positioned centrally, was a large glass display case with a heavy electronic lock.

Inside that was the Accumulator.

~

MARRON POINTED at the cube-shaped device. "Grab it and let's go."

Tom rubbed the back of his neck with his hand. "Yeah, I'm sure it's going to be that simple."

Marron walked over and struck the glass case with the butt of his rifle. The case didn't move a fraction, and the weapon bounced off leaving the surface unmarked.

Tom felt too tired to laugh. "Fixed to the table. And that's obviously no ordinary glass."

"So open it with your mind already."

"Thanks, I understand what's expected." Tom reached out but felt nothing. "I don't know. Maybe I'm too tired."

"You took out those robots?"

"I'm not sure that I did."

"Well it certainly wasn't me. You need to find a way, and you need to do it fast. Maybe rest for a minute or two." Marron looked around. "Can you open the outer door, let me out, then shut it again?"

"Do you have somewhere better to be?"

Marron hefted his assault rifle. "I'm going to find Alex. Maybe Lentz as well, given she's not here."

"And you want to shut me in here? Why?"

"Oh, I don't know. Maybe there are more of those robots on the Rig. It would buy you a little time if they come looking for you."

Tom swallowed. "OK, maybe it's not a terrible idea."

"My ideas rarely are. Now let me out, and we can both get what we came here for. Then meet me back at the submarine."

"And what if I don't succeed?"

Marron shrugged. "Then you'll probably be dead." He gave a sniff. "Or something worse."

"What could be worse than being dead?"

"You've been around CERUS, around your father's legacy long enough to know there'll probably be something. The only question is: has it been invented yet?"

SEVENTY-TWO

THE MILITARY JET did not exist, at least not according to any budget requisition form. It was a sleek design - a modified variant of a Lockheed Martin F35 - able to carry up to three passengers and fitted out for vertical take-off and landing. It was currently on a hard burn west over the Atlantic having flown south of Ireland.

Kate groaned in her seat. "You didn't have anything more comfortable?"

"We don't even really have this. The Americans loaned it to us," Gifford replied through her headset microphone. "They clearly think we might be tempted to order a few. And comfort isn't the selling point. They exist for when you absolutely definitely have to get from A to B fast, and where A or B does not have a runway."

Kate looked down at the display in front of her. It showed they were approaching Mach 2. "I won't argue with the fast part. Are you going to buy one?"

"It's either that or half an aircraft carrier."

"Oh don't exaggerate."

"Not by much. But speaking of sea power, I have two Royal Navy destroyers bearing down on the target location."

Kate hissed. "They have to stay—"

"—away? Yes, you said. They'll be at least a hundred kilometres to the east, pretending to carry out some prearranged exercise, unless I call for help. I do appreciate the need not to unnecessarily spook our adversaries."

"Good. Because we do want to get Lentz, Tom and Reems back alive." Kate paused. "We're confident that this aircraft won't show up on their radar?"

"As sure as we can be. Are you confident that this Rig is going to be where you say it is? It isn't showing on satellite."

"Lentz's suit transponder isn't lying. Look, maybe you should have stayed behind. Why are you here again?"

"Because I'm field trained, despite my record not showing it. And because there's nobody else I can trust enough to make the right call here." She tapped the rifle across her lap. "Have you checked your gear?"

"Three times." Kate's hands brushed over the four tasers clipped to her belt, before resting on her own rifle. "I hope we can keep it non-lethal."

"If we encounter anyone else like Korver, we may have bigger problems."

"He said he was unique. The only one of his kind."

"And you think you can trust him?"

"Why else would he even tell us where to go? He might be on their team, but it's complicated."

There was a chime in general chat and the pilot spoke: "Fifteen minutes out. Want to tell me what our target is? Because I should stress I seem to be flying into a big empty patch of ocean. A couple of banks of fog, but nothing else."

"Don't worry, Captain," replied Gifford. "Ms Turner here has assured us there'll be a nice solid structure to set down on.

And if we're really lucky, there won't be any anti-aircraft systems to dodge.

"Good to know, Ma'am."

THEY FIRST SAW the Rig as they skimmed low over the sea, and the mists seemed to part. Standing on metal struts, it was a flattened sphere perhaps three hundred metres across, dull in appearance, and hard to distinguish from the grey ocean.

"I still see nothing on my instruments," said the pilot.

"It's the fog," replied Kate. "Korver said it is suspended nanotech that absorbs radar waves and visible light until you're very close."

"I'll take your word for it. What now?"

"There should be a helicopter pad on the top."

"I see it. And this facility is... one of ours? Should I be hailing them?"

"No," Gifford replied, "you should not. Probably best if you concentrate on flying instead of asking endless questions."

"Just trying to keep us safe, Ma'am."

"I know. The best I can tell you is stay alert."

The jet slowed further and began descending in VTOL mode onto the helicopter pad. The F35 touched down and its engines switched off, the canopy immediately lifting. Kate and Gifford slipped off their helmets, climbed out onto the wing then dropped onto the metal surface. They performed a further gear check, placed their headsets and smart goggles on, and gripped their rifles.

"You ready?" Gifford asked.

"As I'll ever be," Kate replied. "Let's go save the day."

Gifford turned and gave a thumbs up.

"Good hunting," shouted the pilot. "Also you'll want to give me some room."

Gifford nodded and she and Kate moved clear. But even thirty metres away the noise and turbulence from its take off was thunderous.

Kate covered her ears and turned away, then saw a large object covered by a semi-rigid tarpaulin-like covering. She peered underneath. It was another plane. But like nothing she had ever seen. It made the F35 look like a cold-war era jet. "What is that?"

Gifford appeared next to her. "It looks like a Chinese design, an evolution of the J-20. There've been rumours of a next-gen Mach 4 capable design, although many claimed it was fake intel." She reached forward and placed her hand on the fuselage. "It's warm. It's been flown recently."

"By someone who needed to get here even faster than us?"

"A reasonable and worrying deduction. And I'd love to stay and examine it. But we need to get off the exterior – we're too exposed out here." Gifford tapped her goggles. "There's an entry door twenty metres that way, on the far side of the plane."

Kate stared at the aircraft. "I have a bad feeling about this."

"As you should," shouted a male voice. "Now drop your weapons,"

She spun to see two armed guards emerging from cover, automatic rifles raised.

"You first," said Gifford next to her. "Two on two hardly has us outnumbered."

Kate lowered her voice to a whisper. "I detect two more coming out of that entry door."

Gifford gave a grunt and spoke to the guard. "Were you waiting for us? Did you know we were coming?"

The man had an odd expression on his face. He tapped his earpiece and frowned, seeming to forget about her for a moment. He then looked up. "Scanners detected you some distance out. Also, Korver warned us."

"Korver? But he's in custody."

"It didn't seem that way when he arrived an hour ago." The man frowned again, cupping his ear. "What? Is that some sort of joke? Shut it down." From a short distance away there were shouts, and then the sound of gunfire. And then there was a terrifying scream. The two guards spun away and began moving towards it.

"What is happening?" Kate asked.

"I have no idea," Gifford replied. "Let's have a look. Stay low, weapons ready."

Kate nodded and followed Gifford in a crouch, edging around the aircraft.

What she then saw made no sense.

~

THE TWO NEW guards had emerged from the metal door, but one lay sprawled on the Rig's exterior surface, unmoving. The other was... Kate blinked. He had been *decapitated.*

The two guards that had been speaking with Kate and Gifford were crouched, aiming their rifles.

Emerging slowly from the doorway was something else. A four-legged metal creature, perhaps three metres long, with two separate articulated arms wielding what looked like sharp blades, each a metre in length. Red LEDs glowed angrily all over its body.

"Is that a robot?" Kate asked.

"I can't think of a better term," Gifford replied.

One of the guards shouted: "*Max*, deactivate the dog."

"*Command not recognised,*" replied a synthetic voice, and the robot continued to advance.

"It's gone crazy," said the other guard. "Take it out."

They both opened fire, multiple bullets ricocheting off its exterior. The robot did not slow. Then it lunged impossibly fast and slashed at the first guard.

The man leapt back, but not nearly fast enough. The blade dug into his chest and he shrieked, falling backwards.

The other guard turned and ran. The robot raised a free arm and threw one of its blades. It spun perfectly through the air and caught him square in the middle of the back. He crumpled on the metal surface and, like his colleague, lay motionless. It had all taken mere moments.

Then the robot turned towards Kate and Gifford.

"Suggestions," Kate asked, edging backwards, gripping her rifle.

Gifford shook her head. "Not really. I'm trying to work out if a grenade will slow it down, or just irritate it."

"I'm thinking it might not even notice."

The creature advanced towards them, then stopped and remained motionless.

"What's it doing?" Kate asked.

"Assessing us? Receiving instructions? I have no idea."

The synthetic voice spoke again: "*Do you want to live?*"

Kate raised an eyebrow. "Yes?"

"*Then come with me.*" It turned and started walking back towards the metal doorway.

SEVENTY-THREE

IN THE COMPUTER room Lentz stared at Edna Kim in both elation and shock. How was this possible? Kim had died. And yet here she was, the very picture of health.

For a moment the autodog seemed equally as confused. It remained still, its LEDs pulsing. Kim started to move towards her.

"Be *very* careful," Lentz said. "This thing has been trying to kill us."

Kim edged forward, keeping her distance from the metal creature, her back to the wall. In her right hand she held a long, slender metal rod. "Yeah, I've seen others in action."

"How are you here? How are you even alive?"

"An interesting story." Kim nodded at the dog. "Maybe right now isn't the best time."

Mendez shook his head. "You went in one of the barrels. You were dropped in the ocean."

"And someone fished me out."

"That's absurd. Who?"

"Look, none of this is making sense. I just know we're in a lot of trouble."

"Really? Or maybe you're working with Hatch, and this is some sort of trick?"

Kim glared at Mendez and started to reply, but Lentz raised a hand. "Edna, how did you get the airlock door to this room open? And how did you even know where to find us?"

Mendez snapped his fingers. "Maybe they didn't steal the Node technology from her. Maybe she gave it to them."

"I haven't given my tech to anyone," Kim replied with a heavy frown. "I came here to help, not to be interrogated."

Mendez started to reply but the dog shifted, its arms clicking. And the two blades flashed. Lentz pulled Kim and Mendez further away, to one end of the bench. "I'm not sure what we're supposed to do. It's too quick, and too strong. And it doesn't have an obvious weakness."

Kim gave a slight smile. "Everything has a weakness." She spun the metal rod in her hands. "Distract it for me."

"What?" Lentz blinked. "How?"

Kim shrugged. "Be creative."

The dog moved forward on the bench, seeming to coil ready to jump at them. Lentz looked around and saw a collection of glass flasks next to her on a shelf. She snatched up two, moved further away from the robot and threw one in a looping arc. It landed short, smashing on the work surface. The dog ignored it.

"Something better than that," Kim said.

"Just calibrating." Lentz threw the next flask. It struck the dog on one of its legs. It jerked and flinched, then turned to face her. And it sprang.

Kim moved immediately. She knelt, thrusting with the metal rod, driving it up through the joints in the underbelly of the dog. The robot jerked and made a weird metallic groaning sound, its limbs shaking violently. Its two blades were flung sharply away, and it writhed for a few more moments, then collapsed on the bench and lay inert.

"What the heck did you do?" Lentz shouted.

"Exploited a design weakness," Kim said with a smile.

Lentz shook her head, forming a smile of her own. Then she turned around and her smile vanished. Mendez lay on the floor, his face white, his eyes staring. One of the robot's shining blades was stuck squarely in his neck. She rushed over to him, pushing her hands over the wound, trying to stop the flow of blood. But it was already too late.

"Oh my," Kim said, kneeling next to him. "I… did this."

"It would have killed us all if you hadn't stopped it…" Lentz hesitated as a loud tapping sounded from behind them. She turned to see another autodog entering the room. It brandished glittering blades, already covered in blood. She stood, hissing like a feral cat, flexing her fingers.

"Don't be a fool!" Kim shouted. "We have to get out of here." She kicked at a panel in the wall. It fell away, revealing a vertical duct nearly a metre across, heading up. On one side was a metal ladder. "In there! Quickly, there'll be more coming."

"Where does it go?"

"Somewhere other than here. Start climbing. They won't be able to follow us."

Lentz began to say something but was cut off by the sight and sound of another dog entering the lab. She ducked through the opening, gripped the cold metal of the ladder, and forced her tired limbs to pull her upwards. Kim quickly followed, the sound of their gasping for breath echoing off the metal walls.

Below them one of the dogs threw itself at the opening, but it immediately got stuck. It wrenched and twisted but could make it no further. The thick steel of the opening could not be widened, and even if it could, the dog couldn't make the tight turn to climb up the duct.

Lentz forced herself to keep climbing.

For now, they had survived.

SEVENTY-FOUR

LENTZ AND KIM climbed the metal ladder. Below them the repetitive but futile noise of the autodog failing to pursue them began to recede. They climbed on in the amber glow of emergency lighting, ascending through the structure. Lentz felt her heart banging, her breath coming in short gasps. She knew how close the robotic monster had come to killing her. But she was alive.

She could not say the same for Mendez. Was there anything else she could have done? It seemed pointless to think about it now. That was something to suffer over later.

She kept climbing, putting distance between her and what had just happened.

Finally, the ducting opened into a small chamber. Gratefully she stepped from the ladder, her arms aching, and she collapsed to the ground. She saw Kim do the same.

Kim sucked in her next breath. "I'm sorry I got there too late to help. I should have been able to do more."

"You did a very great deal."

"But Mendez... I never meant for that."

"What happened to him wasn't your fault..." Lentz hesitated. "How did you know his name?"

"You must have said it. Or Hatch mentioned it to me when we first arrived. Look it was all very confusing down there."

"True. And responsibility for Mendez's death lies with whoever built those robots."

Kim pulled at her ear. "There are lots around the Rig. And they all suddenly seemed to go crazy. At least I was able to help get you out of there."

"Yes, thank you for that." Lentz paused. "Speaking of which, how are you here? How are you still alive?"

"Good question. I really thought my number was up. But the metal drum was collected just below the surface by a submersible."

"And Hatch's people didn't notice?"

"Hatch's people were the ones that did it."

Lentz blinked. "That doesn't make any sense."

"It was a fake out. My apparent death was intended to goad you into action."

"But it just made me mad."

"Yeah, well it clearly back-fired. Anyway, Hatch had me put in a cell somewhere on the lower decks, and I got forgotten about. I haven't seen another person since. I was fed by one of these autodogs." She scratched her nose. "Bit of a mistake on their part, given my field of expertise."

"You were able to hack it?"

"It took a bit of time, given my lack of tools. But I found a way."

"So you let yourself out?"

Kim frowned. "No, the door locks seemed to be on a completely different system. But then an hour ago my cell door just opened. It wasn't anything I did."

Lentz sighed. "I might have an idea on that. Although I don't know why the system would choose to release you."

"The way you say that suggests Hatch is no longer in charge?"

"Yeah. Well Mendez and I connected this central computer up to the Rig's systems. We thought it might help us escape. But it's just made things worse. If we're going to get out of here alive, we're going to need to rescue ourselves."

Kim placed a hand on Lentz's shoulder. "If anyone can do it, it's two super capable cutting-edge scientists like us. And the good news is that having got inside the OS of the robot, I gained access to a lot of the Rig's more basic systems. I know this place pretty well now. I think we can get off this thing."

"That's great news. But we have to get the Accumulator first."

"And what's that?"

"A particularly potent piece of stolen tech that we can't risk leaving behind."

"I don't suppose you know where it is? The Rig is a big place. Perhaps an image stored in your glasses?"

Lentz blinked. "You know about them?"

"Come on now. I'm a scientist and your biggest fan. I've also managed to come back from the dead, so spotting your specialist eyewear was a pretty low achievement."

"Fair point. But I don't need my glasses. I know exactly where it is. Laboratory 3A - Mendez's personal lab."

Kim pulled out her phone. "That's only one floor above us. About twenty more metres of climbing." She paused. "Oh, I nearly forgot, I found this with my things near where I was detained."

Lentz stared at what Kim was holding out: her tightly folded Resurface suit. A glance at her HUD showed its power supply was fully depleted, but such an issue could be rectified. It was a step in the right direction. Quickly she slipped the suit over what she was wearing. "Thank you so much."

"You are welcome. Now shall we go find your potential doomsday device?"

Lentz stood up and placed a hand on the ladder. "Yes. Let's."

SEVENTY-FIVE

STEPHANIE REEMS WALKED AWAY from the submarine, moving quickly through the corridors of the Rig, holding an automatic pistol rather than a walking stick. Her glasses' HUD displayed directions through the warren of corridors - directions to someone she needed to visit. But then those directions were overridden by a flashing alert. She quickly stepped into a storage room, closing the door behind her. Outside she heard footsteps hurrying by. She waited until they had passed, and the alert vanished from her view. Satisfied the coast was clear, she went back out in the corridor and continued on her route. She ascended two flights of metal stairs, then passed along another corridor. Around her alarms began to sound, and warning lights flashed. She ignored them all. They were not relevant to her task, and her destination was close.

In moments she was marching down a smaller corridor towards a heavy metal door. As expected it was locked. She reached forward and twisted her hand around a virtual icon - an access point in the Rig's systems. The door unlocked and opened, and she stepped through.

The room was a small holding cell. Sitting on a thinly padded metal bed was a man in his forties wearing blue overalls. His face was pale, but he looked up with angry eyes. "I have been kept here without explanation for more than six hours. Do you have any idea who...?" he trailed off and his face turned to a smile. "My, my. Is that *former* MI5 Director Reems? Are you here to rescue me?"

Reems stared back at Leon Smit. "Something like that."

Smit stood up. "Hatch told me this place was unlocatable. How did you find it?"

Reems checked her weapon. "Hatch wasn't exactly a man of his word. In fact he wasn't the man you thought he was at all."

Smit shrugged. "Fine, keep your secrets. Just tell me what this rescue is going to cost. I'm sure you have a figure in mind."

She looked around her. "I know that's how your brain works, *Leon*. You assume everything has a price."

"It's not an assumption. It's a fact. The only challenge is having enough money to pay it." He laced his fingers together. "And – spoiler – I do."

"But here the rules are a little different. I don't think you've fully grasped your present situation. How precarious it is."

Smit laughed. "Just do your job."

"A job you happily reminded me that I no longer have."

He tipped his head on one side. "Fair point. So you want me to connect you to something suitable for your talents? Perhaps a cushy consulting role with the CIA? I can put in a call to Lazlo Banetti on your behalf. I'll do it right now."

"Even though your phone isn't working here?"

"You might intimidate others with this kind of routine, but it won't work on me." He paused. "What happened to your walking stick? I thought you were injured last year?"

"I made a surprising recovery. And as for what I want, I

want to propose a deal. If you accept, I'll throw in the rescue for free."

"Is that right?" He hesitated. "Are you going to sell me the Accumulator? Given that Hatch seems to be out of the picture."

"I am not. I am not trusting you or anybody else with that device."

"Then what?"

"I'm going to give you a sample of experimental nanotech – medical nano is the shorthand description."

"The British don't have anything like that. Believe me, I paid dearly to find out."

"I didn't say we created it." She reached into a pocket and pulled out a tranquiliser gun. "But we have it now."

Smit narrowed his eyes. "I'm in the battery design and manufacture business. What would I want with that stuff?"

From another pocket she removed a soft carrying case. She unzipped it to reveal six glass ampules containing a yellow green liquid that sparkled in the light. "You're in the making money business. Besides you have a range of companies outside of the portable power sphere that this would synergise well with. Like your cryonics company."

"Fair enough. So what does this *medical nano* do?"

"Greatly enhances the body's healing capabilities. Suitable in treating a range of conditions. I'll provide you with full specifications after you've paid. Take it, study it, manufacture it."

"Why?"

"Because it should be out there. Because it will do some good."

"Then why don't you do it? Why do you need me?"

"For reasons I can't go into, that isn't an option. And of course it will require considerable resource and funding."

"So if I agree to do that, you'll rescue me?"

Reems frowned. "I'll still want paying. Just to be clear."

"And how much do you want for this innovation?"

"Two billion dollars. You've probably got that on you."

He coughed. "I never took you for a comedian."

"And you shouldn't. Ever."

"And you want me to pay you that now? And trust that you'll hand over the goods."

"I'm a woman of her word."

"You're high, that's what you are. I think I'll pass."

"I can always just leave you here. Your call."

Smit folded his arms. "If you're going to make threats, they need to be credible. And you know full well that there would be very serious consequences to not assisting me."

"What consequences? This isn't my job, and you aren't a British citizen. This place does not exist. You were never here. And neither was I. Whatever happens here, never happened."

He blinked. "Well, leaving me here will get neither of us anywhere. And I thought you wanted to help the world."

"I do. But I find myself in need of capital. Which is why I'm talking to you."

"I'm not paying you anything if I don't know it works."

She spread her arms. "It helped me walk without a cane."

"That's your word. I'm going to need a lot more for two billion dollars."

"And you're clear on that."

"I am. I'm not an idiot."

"Fair enough." She put the injection gun and ampules down on a nearby table, then drew her automatic pistol and shot him in the leg.

Smit went white and screamed. "You shot me! Are you crazy?"

"The opposite." She holstered the pistol, then quickly loaded an ampule into the injection gun. "I'm providing a demonstration." She reached forward and pressed it just above the wound, pulling the trigger. With a pop and a hiss the liquid flowed into him.

"What made you like this? You're a monster."

"People change. Especially when nanotech is involved. When you play with science like this, it doesn't just change the game. It changes people. It's made me who I am today. And that is not who I was a year ago."

Smit folded his arms. "So, what? Now you're crazy?"

Reems turned the automatic pistol on him. "I've lived my whole life playing by the rules. What did it get me? My son died from an experiment. My husband died from cancer. And I was grievously injured attempting to bring a major criminal to justice."

"None of that was me."

"I'm just helping you understand my perspective. You're someone we can't reliably negotiate with. You're someone who is unpredictable, someone whose agenda cannot be read. But I can trust you to want to make a profit. And if you do that with medical nanotech, then you will at least have done some good."

"And you'll have made a rare fortune."

"It's not for me."

"Then who? Or for what?"

"A conversation for another day." She glanced at her watch. "How's that leg feeling?"

He looked down, almost surprised. "Well enough that I'd forgotten about it. The blood flow has stopped and the wound is closing. It actually works."

"I said you could trust me."

"Fine." He pulled out his phone. "Tell me where to send this money. I'll need internet access, if that's something you can arrange."

"Already provided, although only to your crypto app. And I've sent you the one-time account details. Make sure you use them correctly. I'd hate for you to have to pay twice."

"And after that?"

"Once the funds clear, I'll take you to the escape pods."

He tapped away on his phone for several minutes, then held up the screen to show her. "All done."

"One more thing. If you're having any weird thoughts of going public about the deal we just did, or of revealing anything about the Rig and my being here, I would think again. I have detailed recordings of your entire time here, including this conversation we just had."

"Are you kidding? You terrify me."

"Excellent." She handed the ampules to him. "A pleasure doing business with you, Mr Smit. Now we should get moving to the escape pods. I expect it to become increasingly dangerous to remain on the Rig."

He nodded and stood, testing out his injured leg, and was clearly pleased to find he could walk on it. "You know, I really thought you were going to ask me to kill the CERUS Biotech deal. I heard you were wildly against it."

She shrugged. "That is an interesting thought. But CERUS is in my past, not my future, and you're welcome to it." She paused. "And if I'm being honest, you paid far too much. Now let's get moving."

SEVENTY-SIX

ALEX FOLLOWED Korver out of the stairwell, emerging onto Level Eight of the Rig. They had picked up automatic rifles from a weapons locker and held them at the ready.

Korver raised a hand, looked around, then lowered it. "There'd normally be guards here. Also the internal comms network is down."

"Not our handiwork," she replied. "Something is definitely up."

"We'll make Hatch explain. This way."

They moved down a hallway illuminated by soft lighting, without the lingering odour of oil and saltwater. Alex saw that she had a number of messages from her father, asking where she was. "How long have you worked for Hatch?"

"A long time," Korver replied. "Ever since my accident."

"What happened?"

"The car I was travelling in went off the road. It flipped several times, then caught fire, and I suffered 90% burns. They were certain I wouldn't walk again. They thought I might not even live."

She looked at him. "Your face and hands don't show any signs of scarring. Your doctors must have been first rate."

"My doctors did what they could, but it wasn't them. They said I wouldn't make it. Then this mysterious stranger, someone I'd never heard of, paid me a visit in hospital. He said he could help me. He said he could make me a new man if I agreed to a radical new form of treatment, something experimental for which I was well-suited. I told him I was sure I couldn't afford it. He said not to worry, that we'd work out a payment plan." Korver sighed. "That stranger was Frank Hatch, and I've been paying ever since."

She stared at him. "That's the nanotech. It boosts your body's healing and metabolism."

"They never told me. Whatever it is, it requires regular follow up treatments - booster doses every few days or I quickly regress."

"So... Hatch is like your drug dealer. Where do the boosters come from?"

"Dr Mendez on the Rig administers my follow up treatments. But I don't know who created it. He says he doesn't know either."

"Something else to include in our conversation with the Director."

Korver stopped at an airlock door. It was half open. "This is Hatch's apartment. And his door is never left open."

Alex nodded. "Let's go get some answers."

THEY WALKED through the open airlock, weapons raised. The main room was fifteen metres square and austere. The apartment walls and floor were bare metal as almost everywhere else on the station. A metal platform with six rubber-tipped legs stood to one side, a metal drum carried on its back. The drum bore multiple orange hazard symbols.

"That's one of the autodogs," Korver said. "Robotic porters that operate on the Rig."

Alex nodded. "And the drum? Is that a container for hazardous waste?"

"It's how Hatch disposes of team members that have become surplus to requirements."

She gave a whistle. "That's a bit dark. So why is it in here?"

"I don't know." Korver walked over, jammed his fingers in the gap around the lid, and pulled. With a low creak the lid lifted off.

Inside, immersed to the neck in a clumpy blue liquid, was a man's body, dressed in plain workman's overalls. His eyes were closed in an expression of calm.

"Tell me that isn't Hatch," Alex said.

"That would be a lie." Korver lifted the body out, then laid him on the single plain sofa. There was a single gunshot wound in his chest.

Alex knelt next to Hatch, holding her fingers against his neck. "No pulse. He's..." she stopped, frowned, and began prodding at the wound. "What the hell is this?" She reached into the bullet hole. Blue oily liquid emerged. She reached deeper and pulled out fibre optic cables that had been severed. She turned to Korver. "He... isn't human?"

Korver blinked. "This is absurd. He always came across as a bit... *cold*. But I never suspected that he was..."

"...a robot?"

"*Android* is probably the correct terminology."

She examined one of its hands. "The skin is incredibly life-like. Has he been replaced by this thing? Or was he always artificial?"

"I don't know. He did come across as a bit 'wooden', but I

thought that was just how he was. He always wore blue tinted sunglasses, so it was hard to see his eyes."

"So why did someone take him... sorry, 'it'... out of action?" Alex ran her hand over Hatch's face. "It seems so realistic." The eyes flickered open, and Hatch wheezed. Despite herself, she flinched back.

Hatch's eyes widened. "Where am I? What's happening?"

Alex placed a hand on his forehead. "Easy now. Don't try to move. Breathe slowly."

He coughed and spluttered. "Korver?"

"I'm here. What happened?"

"Attacked."

"By whom?"

There was no answer. Alex stared at Hatch. She could see the light in his eyes was starting to fade. "Who attacked you?"

"Scientist... in barrel."

Alex frowned. "What's he talking about?"

Korver shook his head. "That doesn't make sense."

"None of this makes sense."

Hatch sat up suddenly, his breathing ragged. "Betrayed me. Had a plan." He coughed up blue liquid. "Not my plan."

"Who?"

"*Kim*."

Korver's brow furrowed. "The scientist I captured with Dominique Lentz?"

Hatch blinked, then fell back and went completely still.

Alex shook her head. "Kim? Who is that?"

"Edna Kim. A friend of Lentz, who shouldn't have even been here. Just in the wrong place at the wrong time."

"And yet she terminated Hatch - if that's the right terminology." Alex looked around. "Is there a computer terminal in here?"

Korver pointed to Hatch's desk. "It will be password locked."

"Not a problem." Alex pulled a wireless key from her pocket. "We were given inside knowledge of this Rig. Javier Mendez was selling you out, although not to who he thought."

"Everyone makes their choices. Who am I to judge?"

"Well, I judge all the time. And then I'm often jury and executioner as well, if I decide that is appropriate." She walked over to the computer, which unlocked as she approached. Then she accessed some proprietary search tools and ran a query for Edna Kim. A range of replies came back immediately. "Well, I'll be. It seems there may be more to Edna than you realised. Guess what she specialises in?"

Korver frowned. "Robotics?"

"Indeed. I'm not sure what that coincidence means, but the most important thing is that I don't believe in coincidences."

"So, what now? Do we go find her?"

"That's on my list. But first, I think we go and ask my father a few questions. Because I think he knows more about all this than he's told me."

SEVENTY-SEVEN

STANDING in the middle of Laboratory 3A, Tom contemplated the glass case and its electronic lock.

He was so close to the Accumulator, yet still he could not reach it. He needed this source of power if he was to have any hope of responding to the system around him. Without it, he was a toy boat bobbing on an ocean. Without it, for all his abilities, he was insignificant.

But what could he do?

The case was not, he could sense, constructed from ordinary glass. Aside from being fifteen centimetres thick, there was something about the transparent material that shut him off from any functional connection to the Accumulator. Some quality within the crystal structure that blocked any signal. And the lock itself was impenetrable. He did not know what to do. The irony was he needed the power of the Accumulator to overwhelm the lock and get inside. It was classic chicken and egg. Still, he had to try.

He reached out, focussing his thoughts. And he blinked. Something didn't feel right. How had he been able to sense the Accumulator? If this glass case shielded it, how could he detect what was within? It was like it was designed to lure him here, but then bog him down. Was it a trap? He took a step back, doubt flooding his mind. And then, at the edge of his perception he heard a voice. And he could sense a name.

Max.

Where did that thought come from? It felt central to the situation. To the problem he faced - the problem Marron had left him alone with. Marron hadn't seemed as worried as he should have been by the robots attacking. Was he just utterly unflappable? Or did he not comprehend the challenge he faced? Or was it something else?

Again at the edge of Tom's perception there was something. But this time it was different. A scuffling. A clanging. A sense that something was approaching. Shaking his head he stepped forward, placing a hand on the glass. And he closed his eyes. Reaching out. Unbidden, words formed in his mind.

Soon, Tom.

He frowned. Who are you? he asked.

Soon...

The voice seemed to skip away. He tried to pursue it, to follow it into the darkness. But as he moved forward, it vanished. Had it even been there? Had he imagined it? Or had he done something wrong? Had he missed a key moment to act?

Tom collapsed to the floor, gasping in frustration. Had he come all this way only to fail?

Next to him was a banging. He spun, getting back to his feet, ready to fight. Was it another robot? Had it found a different way into the lab?

And then a metal hatch sprung open, and something fell out, sprawling on the floor.

Not something. Some*one.*

Someone he knew.

Dominique Lentz looked up at him. "Tom?"

~

TOM STARED in confusion at Lentz. "You were in the air-conditioning?"

"It contained fewer killer robots than the alternative routes available." She climbed to her feet, adjusted her glasses, and pointed behind her. "A friend suggested it."

Tom looked and saw another figure climbing out of the hatch - a woman similar in age to Lentz, with frizzy grey hair and thick-rimmed glasses.

"This," Lentz said, "is a good friend: Dr Edna Kim. Used to be at CERUS years ago, but left before it all got evil. Unfortunately she's got caught up in my nonsense. We managed to escape and found our way to you."

The woman stood up. "Any friend of the good Doctor Lentz is a friend of mine."

Tom stared at her then shook his head. "What are you doing here, Dominique?"

"We came for the Accumulator." Lentz closed the hatch and looked around. "How did you get here? Did they capture you?"

"No, I came on Peter Marron's submarine."

"What?" Lentz spun around. "Where is he?"

"He left me to find Alex. I'm supposed to meet up with him once I get the Accumulator."

"Are you their prisoner?"

"No. I'm not exactly best friends, but I wouldn't call them enemies. Which is why Reems supported reaching out to them."

"OK, now you are talking nonsense. She would never do that."

Tom shook his head. "We had no other way of finding you. Or the Accumulator. So it became a deal she was prepared to do."

Lentz sighed. "Then she's a fool. And I suppose Marron just happened to know where to go?"

"More than that, he was already coming here. And before you say it, coincidences happen. The whole point was that he moved in the kind of circles where this information would be held. The kind of offline sources that my abilities can't connect to."

"So, Reems is here?"

"She stayed back on the submarine."

"Anyone else?"

"Not Kate. She was hurt in London when we had our encounter with Korver."

"Is she OK?"

"She's safe and well out of this." He nodded to the Accumulator. "We need to get this, but I'm having trouble accessing it."

Lentz frowned. "Wouldn't it be best all round to destroy it?"

"We are not doing that."

"But you're going to put it on a submarine with Marron? Who's to say he won't try and steal it."

"Nobody can take it from me. I won't allow it."

"Yet somebody did. Are you sure it's not skewing your judgement?"

"That was... complicated. It won't happen again. You need to trust me." He paused. "And to be clear, without me being in possession of that device, we aren't getting off this Rig."

"We might have a way."

"Trust me, you don't."

Lentz sighed. "So where has Alex gone?"

"She got held up dealing with Korver."

"*Korver*? He managed to get back to the Rig?"

"I'm as surprised as you given he was in MI5 custody, but I

saw him only minutes ago. Now can you help me with this case?"

Lentz walked up to it and frowned. "An electronic lock. You've tried accessing it?"

"Of course," Tom replied. "I had managed to hack the systems on this Rig, but in the last few minutes something has changed. Something that I can't affect."

"Oh," Lentz said, "that is unfortunate."

Tom hesitated. "An odd phrase. Do you know more about what has gone on?"

Lentz rubbed her hands together. "Unfortunately I may know what that is. And I may have made things worse for you."

SEVENTY-EIGHT

TOM LOOKED at Lentz in confusion. "What do you mean, you've made things worse?"

"I was working with a scientist here, by the name of Mendez."

"You were working with him? Are you saying you knew about the Rig? That you were cooperating?"

"For goodness sake, no. I was abducted and brought here. Then I was trying to help Mendez escape. And by extension, also help myself."

Tom looked around. "So where is he now?"

Lentz's eyes grew hard. "He didn't make it. One of the autodogs attacked him."

"Oh. I'm sorry."

"If Kim hadn't arrived, I might have suffered the same fate. But we'll have to find time to dwell on his loss later. For now you should know that his plan was to use this supercomputer called Max to take control of all systems on the Rig. But it appears to have taken control itself." She paused. "As you've probably seen, it's turned these servitor robots into killing machines."

Tom blinked. "*Max*?"

"That's right. Have you encountered it?"

"Yeah," Tom replied, "I'm aware of it. The robots killed a bunch of Marron's people." He shook his head. "What systems does Max have access to?"

"Power, security, life support. Weapons. Everything, basically."

"Marvellous." He placed a hand on the glass case. "I need to get this out."

Kim stepped forward, studying the glass case. "It's important then?"

Tom nodded. "It's effectively a nuclear battery. I need it to power... what I do."

"The thing is, I don't really know what that is."

Lentz put her hand on Kim's shoulder. "I promise there will be explanations later. Right now we need to be people of action, not scientists."

"Yes. I agree. But what action?"

Tom tapped the glass. "I need to break this lock. But it's too much for my unaided mind to breach. Dominique, you're the brilliant one. I need you to be you."

Lentz folded her arms. "Brilliance has to come in its own time."

"Well the time is now—" There was a loud banging on the inner airlock door. Tom turned and saw another autodog smacking the glass window with one of its forelimbs, its LEDs pulsing red.

"Oh great," Lentz said. "Edna, I don't suppose you have any more of those rods?"

"Unfortunately not."

The robot struck the door again, and the glass shattered. The creature started climbing through.

"They're learning," Tom said. "Adapting. Fine-tuning their approach. This one broke the door far more quickly."

Kim frowned. "If an automated system is in control, it will be learning iteratively. Time is against us."

"Then I won't give it anymore." Tom marched towards the door, extending his hand, reaching out, lacing it with anger and retribution. The robot jerked and shook. Tom felt the flow of data in its control system. Encrypted, but not heavily. He could do this, if he had more power. All he needed was the Accumulator, yet it was still out of reach. What could he do without it? What did he have within him? He dug deep, concentrating on the metal creature and increased his intensity. And he found something.

The robot twisted awkwardly. Then it froze and its lights extinguished. He let out a gasp and staggered back.

"What did you just do?" Lentz asked. "Did you tap power from yourself?"

"I got inside its systems enough. They have a lighter encryption than the glass case." He slumped to the floor. "But I don't think I can do it again."

Kim stood with her mouth open. "You have an Interface. From Project Tantalus."

Tom stared at her. "How do you know that?"

"I used to be at CERUS. And I follow the rumour mill. Still, I wasn't sure it wasn't all a joke." Kim cleared her throat. "You say you need more power?"

"Yes."

"And you said the Accumulator is like a nuclear battery."

He blinked. "What are you getting at?"

Kim looked at Lentz. "How about an actual nuclear reactor?"

"You're joking?" Tom said.

Lentz frowned. "There is a reactor on this Rig. More powerful than the Accumulator."

Kim nodded. "Primary power conduits run into this room.

They're limited to normal use, but I think we can remove those restrictions."

Tom blinked. "Are you suggesting I channel power from this reactor? Does that not sound dangerous? What would that do to me?"

Outside in the corridor came the sound of more robot feet. Insistent. Repetitive. Inevitable.

Kim coughed. "I'm not sure. But we need to do something. And fast. Otherwise those things are coming in here, and the game is over."

SEVENTY-NINE

THE ROBOT CREATURE had not spoken again and had instead led Kate and Gifford down two levels to a small, windowless holding cell. The robot had taken their weapons, depositing them in a compartment on its back, then locked the two women inside. After that it had departed without further explanation.

"I don't understand what just happened," said Kate as she looked at the bare metal walls. "What was that thing?"

Gifford tried the door handle. It did not turn. "A semi-autonomous combat robot. Basically a large drone with legs. A number of players have had them in development, at least according to Reems. But few people had taken her seriously."

"And why didn't it kill us?"

"Either it was programmed not to kill us, or we weren't on the list of those it was programmed to kill. Whichever, I'm grateful."

Kate nodded. "But why did it kill the guards? Weren't they on the same side?"

"They said something about it going crazy."

"So what's it doing now?"

"I shudder to imagine. And let's hope it's the only one."

"Yes, let's." Kate kicked the heavy steel door. It did not move a fraction. "What do we do now?"

Gifford shrugged. "We don't have the weaponry to hurt that... *thing*. So we wait for backup."

"You think backup is actually coming?"

"The two destroyers know where we went. They were only holding back so we didn't tip off the Rig. When we don't update them, they will follow up."

"Let's hope they do it quickly..."

The cell door slid back and Kate blinked in surprise.

Stephanie Reems stood there holding an automatic rifle. "Either of you ladies care to be rescued today?"

Kate rushed forward and hugged her. "I have never been more pleased to see you."

Reems patted her awkwardly. "I'm not sure how you got here, but let's worry about that later. We need to get moving."

Gifford nodded. "It seems you've *embraced* being back in the field. Why don't you lead on."

Kate looked out into the corridor. "Did you see the robot?"

Reems raised an eyebrow. "The *what*?"

"Three metres long and armed with sharp blades. I'm serious. Something like one of those robot dogs attacked the guards. It killed them. Then it locked us in here."

Reems shook her head. "I've not seen anything. But yet another reason why we should hurry."

"OK. But did you find Dominique? And where is Tom?"

"I found them both. We're to meet at the life rafts."

"And Marron brought you here?"

"Yes, but things got complicated. We won't be leaving with him."

Gifford tipped her head on one side. "What happened to your walking stick?"

Reems blinked, adjusting her grip on her rifle. "Sometimes

I can ignore the pain. It helps if people don't remind me." She stepped back and pointed down the corridor. "We should get moving."

Kate nodded. "Lead on."

~

KATE AND GIFFORD followed a noticeably spritely Reems through the corridors of the Rig.

Gifford looked around as she walked. "You didn't update us after arranging the meet with Marron."

Reems shrugged. "He wouldn't let me. I'd call it a big win that he trusted me as far as he did."

"And has Tom recovered the Accumulator?"

"That's what he and Lentz are doing right now." Reems stopped at a stairway entrance. "Up here."

"You really do seem to know your way around," Gifford said.

Reems tapped her glasses. "An HUD is a definite tactical advantage."

Kate looked around. "Why are there no people? You'd think it would take a huge crew to operate this facility. You'd think they'd have security people trying to intercept us."

"I don't have data on where they've gone. They could have evacuated." Reems started climbing the stairs. "The whole facility is heavily automated. It doesn't need a lot of people to run it."

"Who's in charge?"

"A man called Frank Hatch. He was running the auctions." She paused. "You've put yourselves in a lot of danger by coming here."

Kate blinked. "And you haven't?"

"Yes, well, maybe. Did you bring backup? Or was the plan that you two assault the facility on your own."

Gifford frowned. "I might have loosened the reins a little on how I do things, but I'm not an idiot. We have two Royal Navy destroyers inbound."

"That's good. And of course, this Rig isn't going anywhere, not now that we know where it is."

"Not at any speed, at least. Is Leon Smit onboard? Our intel shows two of his super yachts and their support vessels within a hundred miles of this location. It feels like too much of a coincidence."

Reems blinked. "Perhaps he was going to participate in the auction, and decided against it? But would he be that crazy? To get involved with this?"

"Maybe. Hard to know for sure."

They continued climbing, emerging two floors later into a semi-circular room with six circular metal doors on the curved side.

"These are the life rafts," Reems said.

Gifford frowned. "Again you seem really well informed. Without you we'd be done for."

"It helped having Tom on the team. He provided an initial hack, so I have the schematics."

Kate looked around. "Speaking of which, where *are* Tom and Lentz?"

"They should be here by now." Reems tapped her glasses. "I'm having trouble getting an update. Let's check that the life rafts are working." She walked over to the nearest pod. The door slid open. Reems walked in and spread her arms wide. "Seating for up to twelve. The pod will slide out and down into the sea, then will automatically propel away from the Rig, while calling for help on every possible frequency."

Kate and Gifford followed Reems into the pod. Kate shook her head. "I don't want to just sit around here, waiting. We should go and see if Tom and Lentz need help."

"We need to think logically. This Rig has a huge volume,

and you're not going to find them by just wandering around - encountering who knows what other dangers. Now, I suggest that—" Reems was interrupted by a deafening klaxon, red lights pulsing on and off in time.

"That," Kate hissed, "does not sound good."

"I agree," Reems said, tapping her glasses. "I'm trying to work out what—"

Gifford pointed at a screen. "It says the pod has been activated. Did you do something?"

Kate rolled her eyes. "I haven't done *anything*."

Reems stepped out of the life raft and into the semi-circular room. "Let me see if I can—"

The door to the life raft slammed shut. Kate growled and stepped forward, searching for a way to open it, but the internal controls did not respond. "What is with this place?" There was the sound of heavy machinery grinding, and the pod gave a jolt. On the other side of the glass Kate saw Reems looking around in an exaggerated manner.

Gifford pounded on the glass. "Stop it, dammit!"

"There's no cancellation mechanism that I can see." Reems' voice transmitted through an intercom. "I don't think I can stop it."

Kate shook her head. "We aren't leaving you behind."

"You've got no choice." Reems stared back through the thick glass window. "I'll find Tom and Lentz, and we'll get in one of the other life rafts. You rendezvous with the Royal Navy ships and by then we should have got out too. If not, my orders are for them to come in and get us."

Kate frowned. "I don't like this at all. It feels like someone doesn't want us on this Rig."

"I know what you mean. But things are going to work out. I'll make sure of it."

And before Kate could reply the pod slid away and Reems disappeared from view.

EIGHTY

ALEX EMERGED from the metal staircase, followed by Korver, and started to hurry down the corridor when something made her freeze. A heavy tapping sound came from ahead, quickly increasing in volume. She grabbed Korver and pulled them both back into the stairwell, just as a six-legged robot hurried past, its LED lights blazing a bright red.

"What's going on?" she asked. "I thought those things just moved cargo about? That one looked much more intense. Angry, even."

Korver shook his head. "I've never seen any autodog behave like that." He suddenly raised a finger to his lips. With little warning two more robots appeared and moved past at a similar pounding high speed.

"Any more coming? They do not look like something we want to fight."

"Not as far as I can tell."

She stepped back into the corridor then froze. A figure had appeared from the shadows, carrying an assault rifle. It was her father.

"What's going on?" Marron adjusted the rifle. "Isn't our friend here supposed to be neutralised?"

Alex shrugged. "He's not so bad once you get to know him. But something else is going on here. I've had a sense something was off for a while now, and facing-off against Korver has made it undeniable. What are you keeping from me?"

He stared at her for several long seconds. "I always have your best interests at heart. You just need to trust me."

"That's not good enough, *Peter*. I'm not a child anymore."

"I am well aware. But this was not a straightforward mission." He paused. "Indeed, less straightforward than I anticipated."

"Why would you take on a job with such uncertainties?"

"Because of the reward. Something beyond value. It's being delivered to the sub."

"If I'd known all this, I never would have come." She frowned. "Where is Tom?"

"Working on accessing the Accumulator. He'll join us at the submarine."

"You're not going back for him?"

"Our cybernetic friend is more than capable of looking after himself."

"I don't know," Alex replied. "As I said, odd things are happening here. We found the head of the Rig, Frank Hatch, in his room. He'd been shot through the chest."

Marron blinked. "What were you doing up there?"

"We both smelt something fishy. And it turns out, Hatch was a robot."

"The better term would be 'android'," said Korver.

Marron blinked. "Not our problem."

Alex waved her hand. "Really, *Peter*? That's all you have to say in response? You don't even seem surprised."

"The things I've seen over the years, nothing surprises me anymore."

"Nonsense. You *knew*. Just like you knew that you had put me into a fight with someone boosted with nanotechnology."

Marron shrugged. "All you ever say is you're looking for a challenge. Don't blame me for finding it for you."

"But it's not just any nanotechnology. He has *my* nanotechnology. He has what I have. How did he get it?"

Marron sighed heavily. "He has an *evolution* of what you have. I wanted to see how good it was."

"Why?"

"So, you could have it too."

"You want to change me again? Do you hate me or something? Am I not good enough?"

His face fell. "I would never think that. You are my daughter. Everything I do is for you."

"Sometimes I don't think you know me at all."

"We just need to get to the submarine."

In the distance came the sound of rubber feet tapping in a rhythm. "More of those robot things?" Alex asked.

"Nothing for us to worry about. This way."

Alex nodded and beckoned to Korver.

Marron frowned. "He isn't coming with us."

"Who wouldn't want him on their side in a fight?"

"Who says there's going to be a fight? And is he even on our side?" Marron shook his head. "If he can keep up, I guess I have no reason to stop him."

EIGHTY-ONE

TOM RUBBED his head as he considered what Kim and Lentz were suggesting - that he draw power from a nuclear reactor. "The Accumulator is a nanotech creation - the same technology that built my Interface. It's something I inherently understand and control. It's a smart system, so I draw only the exact power I need. The reactor would be... well it's a dumb system that utilises nuclear fission. If I tap into it, it might fry my brain before I even realise what is happening." He looked at Lentz. "Surely you think this is crazy?"

Her face looked strained. "Of course I do."

"So come up with some other way. You're the one who can invent their way out of anything."

"Having handed control of the Rig to this computer, our options are limited."

Tom looked at the glass case and a thought occurred. "Why did they go to all this trouble? Why take the Accumulator, then put it on display, just out of reach?"

Lentz frowned. "I don't know what you mean."

"It's like it's a test."

"A test of what?"

"I don't know. Something about all this doesn't feel right." Tom turned to Kim. "How did you rescue Dominique?"

"I managed to track her down. And I got very lucky with fighting one of those robots."

"Don't be modest," Lentz said. "There was nothing lucky about it. She was bad ass. Completely fearless."

Tom frowned. "How do you know about the reactor?"

"I hacked one of the robots. Using that as an access point, I have the full schematics on my phone."

Lentz nodded. "Kim is an expert in robotics. We're fortunate that she's here, which was completely by chance. Or my fault, depending on which way you—"

There was a loud bang at the door, then again. Tom looked up and saw that a further autodog had reached it and was hammering away. Behind it was yet another. They were done for. Unless he could find a way to change the game.

But, he thought, was it a game? It did feel like someone was playing with them. And if there was a game, there had to be a way to win. The answer had to be here, hidden within the sequence of events. There had to be a pattern he had not picked out. Because he knew in some fundamental way that this had not been all random. The fact that he was here was no accident. He thought back over what had happened in recent days. About the one defining moment where his path had altered.

And he realised what it was.

It had all changed when he had gone into that bank. And he had not gone there by accident. It had all been part of a plan. For him to find the sphere, and to study it. To use his talents upon it. To try and change it, and to fail. And instead, the sphere had changed him. Someone had put it there. And that same someone had brought him here. And as he thought about it, there was only one person it could be.

He looked up at Edna Kim. It was not, after all, a fortunate coincidence that she was an expert in robotics. She wasn't here to solve the problem. She *was* the problem. "I've worked it out," he said. "You can stop this now. At least be honest about what you're doing."

Lentz frowned. "What are you talking about?"

Kim raised an eyebrow. "Are you feeling alright?"

Tom nodded. "I'm fine. In fact, I'm thinking very clearly. I'm seeing the big picture. And enough is enough."

"What do you mean?"

"Yes," Lentz said, "what?"

"This is all a test. And Edna Kim is the one that's been setting it."

Kim adjusted her thick-rimmed glasses and stared at him for several moments. "Very clever, Tom."

"What?" Lentz took a step back. "What is going on?"

"I'm sorry, Dominique," Kim replied, "but, out of necessity, I haven't been entirely truthful with you."

"What?"

"Don't you see," Tom said. "She's been making all this happen? She's the one in charge."

Kim shrugged. "A good enough approximation for now."

Tom noticed a buzzing noise in the air, the insidious whine of micro drone rotors. He'd been the one orchestrating them earlier, when they'd forced their way onto the Rig, when they'd tackled the security teams. But he wasn't in control this time.

"I think," Kim said, "that it's time we move to the next phase."

Tom tried to move, but he was nowhere near quick enough. The drones struck, there was a burning sensation on his neck and on his arms, and he fell into darkness.

EIGHTY-TWO

LENTZ RAN over to Tom's slumped form, and to her relief found a pulse. "What happened to him? What did you do?"

Kim folded her arms. "I had a micro drone deliver a nanite-based sedative. He'll be out for a while."

Lentz's eyes widened. "Just who are you?"

"A scientist with a vision. I just haven't shared all of it with you yet."

"You've been lying to me? I thought you were a friend."

"I wanted to trust you. I wanted to share with you what I've really been doing. And the possibilities of what could come next." She hesitated. "And that meant making sure we came here, together."

"You'd heard about the Rig? Did you use me to find it?" Lentz paused. "Tom said this was all a test."

"There's quite a bit of context to grasp here, before you start judging me. Before you start leaping to the wrong conclusions."

"You lured me to that conference in Cambridge. And then it's been one lie after another."

"I lured you there because I want to work with you. Of

course, you being you, you didn't prove easy to persuade. But destiny brought us back together."

"You could have got yourself killed in that barrel. Or was that a trick?"

Kim raised her hands. "Why don't we sit down over a cup of tea, and I'll explain everything. I owe you that much. And I think you owe it to me to hear me out."

Lentz looked at her in confusion. "If you hadn't noticed, we are under attack by killer robots." She pointed toward the airlock door where another autodog was hammering at the metal. But as she looked, she started to realise the truth.

"They're not so bad when you get to know them." Kim snapped her fingers. Instantly the dog stopped moving. "Is that better?"

Lentz stared at the creature, and finally she grasped the full extent of what was happening. The person she had thought was her friend, who had got caught up in these awful events, was not only there by choice, but was actually in charge, was actually behind these events.

These were her robots. This was her Rig.

Kim walked over to the glass case that Tom had been trying to access. She held out the palm of her hand and the door opened. Reaching inside, she removed the Accumulator, then straightened and turned, holding the device in both hands. Its LED lights blinked in a complex pattern.

Lentz shook her head. "You're the bad guy?"

"That's not how I'd put it. But I suppose everyone's the hero in their own story."

"You were who Mendez thought he was talking to. You were pretending to be MI5."

"He was having commitment issues. I needed to give him a reason to hold on a little longer. Unfortunately he started to work out what was going on with me."

"So you killed him with that robot? Why?"

"His time as part of this venture was over. A sacrifice for the greater good."

"I'll show you what sacrifice means." Lentz charged forward, launching herself at Kim. Anger, irritation and sheer willpower gave her startling speed and force. But it did not matter. It was like colliding with a granite wall. Lentz collapsed to the floor, groaning.

"Of course I'm wearing a suit," Kim said. "And unlike yours, mine still has power." She waved the Accumulator. "A very great deal of power."

Lentz rubbed her shoulder. "So much for being my friend."

"I think I should point out that you just attacked me. All I'm doing is providing you with full disclosure. Maybe don't try that again. You'll only hurt yourself. Focus on helping your friend here."

Lentz nodded towards Tom. "Why is it always about him? Has he not suffered enough?"

"That's exactly the point. I think I can help him. I think *we* can help him."

Lentz stood up. "And if I don't cooperate, you'll kill me? Or those of my friends you can track down?"

"No, Dominique, that's not it at all. I didn't bring you here to coerce you. I brought you here to *unleash* you. I brought you here to share in what I've done, and for us both to steer a path into the future."

"What you've done? What does that mean?"

Kim pointed at a blank section of wall. It slid back to reveal a gleaming white corridor leading further into the Rig. "Let me show you."

EIGHTY-THREE

ALEX FOLLOWED her father through the corridors of the Rig, Korver close behind, his heavy feet pounding on the flooring. In minutes they had arrived at the submarine docking bay. The place was deserted.

"Where are the guards?" Alex asked, gripping her rifle and moving inside. "Reems has gone as well."

"It's as expected," Marron said. "Reems had business elsewhere. She wanted to keep that from Tom, so I pretended to insist that she stay behind. The guards wouldn't have stayed here after she left – they will have gone after us into the Rig."

"Wait, what? Reems had secrets from Tom?"

"Are you surprised? She has secrets from everybody."

"Then where was she going?"

"You'd have to ask her, although I wouldn't expect an answer." Marron seemed about to say something further when there was the sound of rubber feet tapping on metal. He moved quickly back to the docking bay. Alex followed him out. One of the autodogs sat waiting, LED lights on its metal form glowing green.

"What's it doing down here?" she asked.

"Making a delivery." Marron moved forward and removed a metal briefcase from its cargo platform. "All as agreed?"

A synthetic voice floated from unseen speakers. "Yes. This concludes our business. You are cleared to leave."

He opened the case and peered inside.

"What's in there?" Alex put her hands on her hips. "And who is that speaking?"

Marron closed the lid. "I'll explain later. We need to go." He nodded to Korver. "You're journey ends here."

Alex frowned. "We're not leaving without Tom or Reems. And what about Lentz? And the rest of our crew?"

"The crew are probably dead, or they'd be here – unfortunate, but they knew what they signed up for."

"I very much doubt that."

He raised his hands. "Fair point. And them not being here saves me from having to kill them."

"That was why you signed up a totally new team."

Marron nodded. "This mission was always super sensitive, and I didn't want to have to terminate any of our regulars to ensure their silence. As for Tom, Reems and Lentz, they're treading a different path. Now I'm sorry, but our window for departure is closing. We need to get away before..." he hesitated. "*Before.*"

"Before what?" She took a step towards him. "What have you got planned? Something terminal? In that case we are *not* leaving Tom behind."

"I know you're fond of the boy, but we have more important things to worry about. Now get on board." He reached out and grabbed her arm.

"Stop!" Korver shouted, lunging forward and pushing Marron away from Alex.

Marron squared up. "You forget yourself." He pulled a control unit from his pocket and tapped the button. Korver's knees buckled, and he collapsed to the floor, holding his head in his hands.

"What happened?" Alex shouted, crouching by him, her gaze flicking around. "What did you do?"

"I've temporarily deactivated his nanites," Marron replied. "Which means he's not feeling the best. Now *we* need to go."

Alex gritted her teeth. "I don't know what you think you're doing, or how you did it, but I've had enough. Now you're going to tell me everything, and you're going to show me what's in that briefcase. And if you do all that, I might still travel with you."

He glanced at his watch then pulled out a different remote control. "Sorry, Alex, not today."

Alex started to reply when she heard the high-pitched whine of what she at first thought was a mosquito. Then she realised it must be a tiny drone. The noise grew rapidly louder then she felt a burning on her neck. She looked at her father, her eyes widening in alarm. "What have you done?"

"Just a sedative," he said kindly. "I can't let you stay. Today I get to say what's best for you."

Alex turned desperately towards Korver who was writhing on the floor.

He turned his head and half-spoke, half-groaned. "I'll find Tom, I promise. And I'll do what I can to help him."

"Why?"

"Because I think it would irritate Hatch. Or whoever built him."

Alex tried to reply, she tried to say thank you. She tried to fight what was happening to her.

But darkness took her.

EIGHTY-FOUR

LENTZ LOOKED into the gleaming white corridor. It stretched ten metres ahead before ending at a heavy airlock door, also polished white. "What is this?"

"I call it the Core," Kim replied. "The Rig is just a shell. A distraction, if you will. The Core is a central cylinder, occupying several levels of the structure. Physically and functionally separate, it's where I do all my real work." She beckoned inwards. "Don't be shy."

Lentz frowned. "What about Tom?"

"I hadn't forgotten." Kim waved at a section of wall in the white corridor. Initially seamless, an outline appeared, and from it stepped an autodog, except this one looked more refined, its exterior polished white like the corridor, a soft green LED glow marking its outline. It glided almost soundless past them and towards Tom. "I'm having the servitor bring our friend with us."

"You're not going to hurt him."

"Why would I do that? I've always cared for him."

"What does that mean?"

"It means I've always known about him. I was there at his

inception." The robot stopped and gently lifted Tom onto its load platform. "And he has long featured in my plans."

"But how could you know about him? Nobody did." Lentz paused. "Nobody except..." And then realisation dawned. "You didn't just work at CERUS. You were part of the initial process, run by Professor Heidn. The one held at some secret location, that I wasn't even told about."

"That's right, Dominique. I was there at the very beginning, at the Alpha Site. I know more than you. Remember that as you try to keep up."

Lentz frowned and stepped into the corridor. Kim followed her, then the dog carrying Tom. The door closed automatically. Lentz glanced at the robot. "So is this one different from the others?"

"These are next gen models, equipped with my latest refinements. They're deployed only within the Core." At the end of the corridor was an airlock door. It slid open and they walked inside. The door closed again and the airlock began to cycle.

Lentz looked around. "You like your pressure sealed environments. Anyone would think this was a submarine."

"You never know when it might come in handy." The inner door opened to reveal another autodog waiting.

Lentz glared at it. "How many of these do you have?"

"A very large number. This one's on guard duty."

"Is it just robots that you have to show me?"

"No it isn't. This is something even more exciting. I'm going to show you the real reason this Rig exists."

LENTZ FOLLOWED Kim along a circular corridor, ahead of the autodog carrying Tom's unconscious form. There was nobody else in sight.

"Do you have any people here?" Lentz asked. "You know, to run your evil lair?"

"I find people unreliable. They have their own lives they want to return to, and sometimes it's hard to permit that." She pointed to a set of double doors on her right. "In here."

Lentz followed her through and onto a metal balcony, five metres above a lower level. She gripped the railing and looked down. Central in the space was a circular cluster of computer servers - each a dark grey blade with red, green and orange lights blinking in random patterns. On one side was a row of four white reclining chairs, all facing a huge screen on the wall. On each chair rested a white helmet, connected with heavy data cables to the back of each chair. "What is this?"

"What I was talking about," Kim replied. "The reason the Rig exists. The actual computer - not that decoy that Mendez showed you previously. This is what the Node connected to. This is Max."

"So this is what controls the Rig? And, I assume, the robots?"

"Indeed. Each dog has a control matrix much too large to be housed in any onboard system. They also draw power wirelessly from conduits running throughout the construct, so they barely ever need to charge."

"And you use those Nodes to distribute the computing power remotely. While keeping the main system safe and secure here."

Kim smiled. "I love that I don't have to explain myself to you. Do you have any idea how rare a thing that is?"

Lentz pointed down. "More helmets. Planning on hooking someone up to your machine?"

Kim glanced at Tom. "Who do you think?"

"But why? If you've known about Tom since the beginning, what can he possibly teach you?"

"It's not about what he is, but rather what he can do. For all

I have achieved, ultimately I have also failed. Max still only operates at around 10% of its capacity. No matter what I try, I haven't been able to solve the problem. Which is why I need a real expert."

"Tom isn't an expert in computer programming."

"But he is the closest thing to a computer-human hybrid. Even if he hasn't figured it out yet."

Lentz snapped her fingers. "So, this whole routine was to bring Tom here?"

"The *routine* - as you call it - was for both of you. He's the only one that can talk to the computer. And you're the only person I know that can make that happen."

"You're placing a lot of confidence in my abilities."

"And rightly so. You know as much as anyone about Tom, and also you are an expert in computer system design. You are the perfect person to work on symbiosis. Plus you have a brilliant mind. I wasn't lying when I said I wanted to work with you. I was just misleading about how and where."

"So this Osiris Foundation was all a big lie."

"Not exactly. Osiris is still relevant. You're just not ready to hear about it yet."

"And if I help you? Will you let him go?"

"If I get the help I need, that won't be an issue."

"That sounds like a lawyer's answer."

"I truly won't need him anymore."

"And me?"

Kim placed a hand on Lentz's arm. "If this works, you won't *want* to go."

Lentz frowned. "That remains to be seen. But I can't answer on Tom's behalf."

"Then I guess it's time we wake him up and ask him. Come, I have a special room set up for us."

~

LENTZ AND KIM descended the set of metal stairs down to the lower level - the autodog carrying Tom following behind them. Kim led them through the double doors into a circular, white-walled room, ten metres in diameter and entirely windowless. In the exact centre, a short distance away, was a round metal table large enough to sit a dozen people. Three of the gleaming white helmets rested on it, each connected to a free-standing blade server spaced evenly around the table. The dog lifted Tom from the platform and placed him in one of the chairs, then articulated arms moved to adeptly apply velcro straps to keep him in place.

Kim gave a hand signal and another autodog appeared from a recess in the wall. It moved forward, holding an injection gun. "The antidote," she explained. The dog pressed the gun against Tom's neck and there was a loud click. "He should be awake within five minutes."

"A nanite sedative isn't something we ever developed at CERUS."

"It shouldn't shock you to learn that others have been treading this path of research."

"And you've been busily stealing it."

"Acquiring then perfecting, would be more accurate. With the addition of the data from Eastwell I have gathered all the research in one place. It's a treasure trove we can explore together. Assuming you decide to stay."

Lentz shrugged. "How do you control those dogs? And the drones? I haven't seen you speaking or typing commands. Do you have some form of remote control?"

"They're running smart routines, which are heavily context sensitive, and they respond to my hand gestures and expressions." Kim placed the Accumulator on the table, its lights shimmering. Then she reached into a drawer and lifted out a red metal sphere - a Node the size of a volleyball. "The highest capacity unit I've constructed. Tom will connect to Max through it, which will allow me to monitor the data transfer."

On reflex, Lentz reached up and tapped her glasses. But the battery had gone flat and they did not respond. "I'd love to hear more about it."

Kim smiled. "That's something for another day. Now there are a few calibrations I need your assistance with."

Lentz listened as Kim started to reel off instructions, but her mind quickly drifted elsewhere. What could she do to stop this woman? The smart glasses would not help. She no longer had her suit. She scratched her chin. And then she felt a tiny vibration inside her mouth.

Of course.

"Are you paying attention?" Kim asked.

"Hanging on every word." As Kim continued with her explanation, pointing at her screen, Lentz reached into the back of her jaw and pulled. In her fingers she felt her false tooth come loose.

"Something wrong?"

"Food stuck in my teeth," Lentz replied. "Don't mind me."

"Can we focus please."

"Of course. What does that display mean?" Lentz pointed at a readout on the sphere. Kim turned towards it, and in a single motion Lentz pulled the micro solid-state drive from her tooth and plugged it into the nearest blade server.

Kim continued to stare at the sphere. "Those are just system reports. Entirely normal..."

An error alarm sounded. The Accumulator's LEDs dimmed and extinguished. The Node made a loud error noise and rolled to one side. The autodog whirred and stopped all movement, its green LEDs fading.

Kim picked up the sphere. "What's going on here?"

"System intrusion," said a synthetic voice over speakers. "Lockdown initiated."

Lentz forced a blank look onto her face. "Problem?"

"Not really." Kim stared at her. "Did you really think it would be that easy?"

"Do what now?"

Kim closed her eyes, appeared to think, then opened them. "I heard you would never give up. That you could not be persuaded. Not until you realised you were beaten."

"Then you should have listened to what you heard."

"That's the thing," Kim replied. "I always listen. And I plan accordingly." She snapped her fingers and the alarm noises stopped. The dog shifted and its LEDs re-lit in bright green. And the Accumulator lit up."

Lentz took a step back. "How did you do that?"

"How did I defend against your malware algorithm? I'm not going to tell you all my tricks." A further autodog entered the room. "Follow my automated friend, please."

"So, what?" Lentz asked. "Am I going in a barrel now? I thought you needed my help."

Kim folded her arms. "I need you to work with me, not against me. Perhaps a little time by yourself will help you get in the right mindset." She gave a hand signal and the dog moved towards Lentz. "Let me know when you're ready to start changing the world."

EIGHTY-FIVE

TOM OPENED his eyes to find he was seated in a circular, white walled room, ten metres in diameter. In the centre, a short distance away, was a round metal table large enough to sit a dozen people.

Edna Kim stood nearby, making notes on a tablet computer. He began to stand up, but discovered his wrists and ankles were zip-tied to the legs and frame of the chair on which he sat. On his head was what felt like a helmet, although the visor was up. He sent out a tentative signal and was greeted by utter silence. Of his Interface he could feel nothing.

Kim adjusted her thick-rimmed glasses and looked up. "Back with us? Good, because we have a lot to do."

"Why am I tied up? What have you done to me?"

"I've tied you up so you don't start wandering off. And by 'done' I presume you mean blocking your abilities. To keep things under control, they're not going to work. Not in here, and certainly not wearing that helmet."

"Where is Dominique?"

"Down the hall, in a detention cell, reflecting on her

actions. I asked her to help fix my computer, and she attempted to sabotage it."

"That definitely sounds like her."

"So I'm learning." Kim paused. "Peter Marron and his daughter have left the Rig in their submarine, if you were curious."

"They..." Tom hesitated, "...they abandoned me here?"

"Given that I hired Marron to bring you to the Rig, not that much of a surprise. Everything he's done since you met up in France was on my instruction." She smiled. "You thought they were your friends?"

"Not really. Did they take Reems with them?"

"They did not. The last time I tracked her, she was heading for the emergency exit. With all the killer robots roaming the facility, not the worst strategy."

"And are you going to explain why I'm here? Because you said we had work to do, and that would suggest you need my cooperation."

She nodded slowly. "I am the scientist behind this Rig. It only looks like an old drilling platform. It was in fact built to my specification, to my design. From it I've been conducting my research into a new type of supercomputer."

"I thought you were a roboticist?"

"The two fields have a lot of overlap. I think you can help me with both."

"And the auctions? I thought you just sold everything for a profit."

"The auctions have been a smokescreen. A cover for my activities in acquiring tech, and also a way to draw out others who are researching what many might call fringe science. And to deal their programmes significant setbacks."

"Wait, so Marron killed all the other auction participants on your orders?"

"That's correct. It seemed an appropriate time to tidy up."

"So it's not enough that you succeed? They have to fail as well?"

"If I maintain a competitive edge, the long-term future of this facility will be far more secure." She walked around the table, and held out her hands towards him. "I must say I have dreamt of this day. The fact that you are here at all is both a testament to outstanding science, and a monument to blind luck."

He stared at her. "It isn't blind luck at all. You lured me here."

She raised an eyebrow. "Did I, indeed?"

"You planted clues. You fed Reems the intel about the bank lockbox. You led me to Leon Smit. And you guided Reems to contact Marron."

"Close, if not perfect," she replied. "You are a very capable individual. And that, of course, is why you're here." She put her clipboard on the round table in the middle of the room. "You've done things with the nano that I couldn't have predicted."

"It's evolved."

"Because you've guided it to new places. You also now have qualities of Alex Marron."

He frowned. "How do you know that?"

"Since you connected with the Node, I've been receiving a data stream from you, showing your abilities. You have no secrets from me, at least not about what you can do. I know, for example, that you must have some of Alex's blood in you. I know because I used a sample of her blood to produce Korver's medication, although of course I tweaked it further. That's the inherently crazy beauty of nanotechnology- we can't plan for what it will do. But we can take notice, and leap upon these happenings. It's like penicillin. Or one of many other scientific discoveries made by accident."

"So what was the Node connecting to?"

"I'm glad you asked. You are in the primary access point,

which connects to Max - short for a Maximum Entropy System. And Max is way beyond you."

"Great. But I control computers, not the other way around."

"Really? Have you forgotten what happened to you before?"

He stared at her. "That was you at the mansion? Messing with my head? What did you do?"

"Me personally? Nothing. But your Interface is fundamentally bi-directional. A computer can connect to you, just as you can connect to it. And the extension of that is that if you can control it, it can control you. We call that *submission.*"

"If that's true, why haven't I encountered it before?"

"In part because the Tantalus design did include a form of firewall, to prevent the risk of submission. But you've never encountered a computer like Max. At its heart is an advanced neural network that simulates the human brain's synaptic plasticity, but at a scale and speed far exceeding biological limitations. The structure is modular and self-organizing, capable of real-time optimisation of data flows and processing - the system maximizes disorder within its own operational protocols to ensure the most efficient processing pathways are utilised."

"That's a lot of words. A lot of *techno babble.* But let's speak plainly. If you think you'll use it to replicate my interface, I'm not going to cooperate."

She laughed. "I was one of the original scientists on Project Tantalus. And I have all the data from CERUS and other labs that have researched this area." She tipped her head on one side. "I don't need to take your Interface, Tom. I already know everything about it."

"Then why *am* I here?"

"I want you to use your unique talents. You're going to fix my computer."

~

TOM STARED AT KIM. "That was what all this has been about? That's why you've brought me here?"

"Yes. And Lentz. I needed both of you. I need you to work together."

"But your computer works already?"

"System inefficiencies mean Max is only operating at a fraction of its true potential."

"Then I'm sorry to disappoint you but, while I might have an Interface, I have no training as a programmer."

"I've been following you for some time, and I have a good idea of what you can do. Max isn't the type of computer where experience is relevant. This isn't about understanding a particular coding language. This is going to rely on intuition, on feel. Max doesn't need programming, it needs *guiding*."

"And how do I do that?"

"If I could answer that question, I'd have done it myself. I'm confident you'll find a way."

He shrugged. "And if I say no?"

"Do you need me to make the implied threat explicit? Your friend, Dr Lentz, is close by, and my patience is limited."

"And if I do this, you'll let her go?"

"This is all I need. You have my word."

"Why would I believe you?"

"Do you have a choice?"

Tom frowned. "So, what do I have to do?"

She pressed a number of switches on Tom's helmet, then reached down and plugged in three high-capacity data cables near the back of his neck.

"I thought I didn't need the helmet?"

"It provides a more consistent, higher bandwidth connection. It also minimises the risks involved."

"Risks? What risks?"

Kim smiled. "With anything experimental, there's always a risk."

"Now you tell me." Tom eased into the chair. "So how is this going to work?"

"You've experienced a virtual environment before, when you interacted with Lentz's system."

"You know about that?"

"Of course. Max was connected to Odyssey, her AI creation."

"You're the one that corrupted Odie?"

"I corrupted *you*. You remember that sphere rushing towards you. That's how your brain interpreted what was happening. Although *corrupted* is the wrong word. Recalibrated is better."

"You messed with my head?"

"I made some enhancements. Some improvements, particularly with regard to navigating virtual environments. So you're not getting an apology, if that's where you're headed. Anyway, to return to your question about how this is going to work: this virtual environment will be a bit like the one Odie provided, before I had Max break it. But, of course, much, much better."

"What will I see?"

"The exact format is unique to each user. Your mind will work with Max to create an emulation - a simulated environment that maps meaningfully to what you have to do. That's all I can tell you."

"And can I communicate with you while I'm in there?"

"If necessary, just call my name. But I strongly suggest you focus on the task: fix the computer."

"However I'm supposed to do that. Fine. Let's get this done."

"Activating the link now."

Tom closed his eyes, and started to reach out. But then something reached into him.

EIGHTY-SIX

ALEX HAD REGAINED consciousness a few minutes ago. She now sat handcuffed to a chair in the submarine, staring at the floor, trying to grasp what had just happened.

Her whole life she had known, with total certainty, that she could trust her father. That, in the dark world they inhabited, he was the one person who was always completely straight and true with her. It seemed she had been wrong.

She twisted on her chair and looked at him standing at the helm of the submarine. "Nothing to say to me?"

Marron made some adjustments to a control panel. "Just setting our course. We'll be clear in ten minutes."

"Clear of what? Responsibility?"

"Something like that." He gave a half-smile. "Are you OK?"

"After what you just did?"

"You gave me no choice."

"You sedated me! Just because I was asking questions?"

"Because you wouldn't take me at my word. There wasn't time to do anything else."

Alex glared at him. "Your *word* made no sense. I don't know why you have no comment about Tom and our crew being left behind? Or about how you misled me with what was going on at that place?"

"We'll do a debrief later. But you need to get your priorities straight and forget about that boy."

She ground her teeth. "What did you sedate me with? A narcotic?"

"Actually it was nanotech. Something new."

"A gift from our mysterious benefactor? Who were we working for?"

He turned to look at her. "I'm finding your attitude puzzling. So much unnecessary anger."

"I'm a contract assassin. Anger is a baseline requirement."

"Then you need to learn when to contain it. Have I ever failed you? Have I ever let you down? Have I ever had anything but your best interests at heart?"

"All I know is that you've been keeping things from me." She shook her head. "You have to learn to trust me."

"I *do* trust you."

"And yet I am restrained."

"Fair point." He walked over, reached down, and removed the handcuffs. "Better?"

She rubbed at her wrists, restoring circulation. "I think you could have briefed me that the Rig was being run by a robot?"

"You weren't supposed to meet him. Or *it*. It shouldn't have been relevant to you, but you went off piste." Marron looked away. "You'll understand everything in due course."

She pointed at the metal briefcase. "I'd like to understand what you got as payment? What was worth all this nonsense?"

Marron shrugged. "Nothing. Something. Everything. You'll have to be patient just a little longer."

"Did you listen to a word I just said? Why don't I just go back to the Rig and help Tom?"

"If you go back to that facility, you will die."

"So he *is* in danger?" She rose to her feet. "Turn this thing around. And if you won't do that, then surface and I'll swim back."

He smiled. "Even in the past you might have struggled to do that. But now? When did you become so soft?"

Something in Alex tripped. She lashed out, swinging, a tight fist aimed at his jaw. Her father swayed back, effortlessly avoiding the blow. It was easy to forget how quick he was. Especially for a man his age. She could not use half measures.

So she swung again. Harder, faster. He was good. She was better. He was going to at least sample some of the pain she felt within.

Except he didn't.

There was a sense of movement, a whirring and hissing of hydraulics. Something big and powerful leapt from a position on the wall, catching her fist in a grip like steel.

Except the grip wasn't *like* steel. It *was* steel.

She looked up and saw the autodog, clad in gleaming white, its LEDs an amber red. The claw around her wrist was irresistible. She strained with every fragment of her strength. It made no difference.

"Put her in the brig," Marron said, "until she calms down."

Alex spat on the floor. "You and I are done. I will never forgive you for this."

Marron patted the case. "Fortunately what is in here is all about second chances."

EIGHTY-SEVEN

LENTZ SURVEYED the cell that she had been placed in. It was considerably more robust than the room she had been detained in previously. There were no windows, no large ventilation ducts, and the door was heavy steel with a physical lock. She was likely going nowhere until Kim decided otherwise.

She sat down on the plain metal bench and put her head in her hands. This was what it was like to feel utterly powerless. She was not one to give up easily, but there came a point when you had to accept you were out of ideas. Realistically she needed some kind of miracle. She rubbed the frames of her glasses in agitation.

And then she noticed something, a touch so soft she almost missed it.

Her glasses were vibrating.

Lentz blinked. The vibration stopped. But the glasses had got a flicker of power from somewhere. Where?

She felt the metal frames. They were a little warm. And then she smiled to herself. It was basic school science. Warming a battery could help extract more charge. And the batteries were inside the frames – they just needed more warmth. She gripped the smooth metal and rubbed more vigorously.

The HUD sprang into life, and there was an immediate notification. Someone was calling her. Someone who also had a set of glasses. She tapped to answer. "Hello?"

"Dominique?" replied a voice that she immediately recognised. "Thank goodness!"

"Stephanie?" Lentz gasped. "Where are you?"

"On the Rig. I arrived on Marron's submarine, but then things got complicated. Where are you?"

"Locked in a detention room in a hidden part of the facility known as the Core. Other than that, I can't be very specific."

"I can track the signal from your glasses, and I've got a full schematic of the Rig. I'll find you."

Lentz felt a smile play cross her face. "I would really appreciate that. Make sure you watch out for killer robots."

There was a pause. "It will take more than that to stop me."

TEN MINUTES later there was the noise of a key turning and the cell door slid back. Lentz saw Stephanie Reems standing in the corridor. She held an automatic rifle with a laser sight.

Lentz blinked. "Call me impressed. I didn't know you still had it in you. But I am grateful."

Reems smiled. "Tom hacked the system when he arrived. My eyeglasses piggy-backed on that. I seem to be able to go where I wish." She tapped her glasses. "I'm copying my access protocol package to you now. Should take about thirty seconds."

Lentz saw the data being transferred to her. "You didn't encounter any robots on your way here?"

Reems frowned. "I thought you were joking."

"I wish. You were fortunate not to meet any. They nearly got me, and several others weren't so lucky."

Reems gripped her rifle. "Who has robots like that?"

"Edna Kim does. She designed them that way."

Reems paused. "Dr Edna Kim? The former CERUS scientist?"

"I think she's the one behind everything here. She created this Rig."

"I'd say that doesn't make any sense. But it's probably no more implausible than a number of other explanations. What does she want?"

"She's trying to get Tom to fix this new computer she's created, to unlock its true potential."

"And that would be bad?"

Lentz sighed. "If Tom succeeds, he'll give her a computer that can do anything. You were concerned about what your enemies would do with the tech you've been cataloguing. This could be many times worse."

"And what if he fails?"

"Then the process of trying to fix her computer might kill him. We need to stop her."

"Do you know where she is?"

Lentz's glasses vibrated as they finished receiving the schematic data. She called up the Rig plans. "I do now."

"Good." Reems reached to her belt and removed an automatic pistol. "I seem to have a spare."

Lentz took the weapon and checked the clip, then hesitated. "Leon Smit is on board. At least he was, and I doubt he's been able to leave."

"Why on Earth was he here?" Reems paused. "Never mind, you can tell me later. But I'm seeing from the system that he left the Rig a few minutes ago in a life raft."

"Oh, well, I guess he would have planned an escape."

"More than one, most likely." Reems hefted her weapon. "We need to get moving."

Lentz nodded. "Let's go rescue our friend. And maybe save the world while we're at it."

EIGHTY-EIGHT

TOM OPENED HIS EYES. He no longer saw the white room. Instead, he was standing in a large city plaza, his feet pressing on gleaming stone cobbles. People dressed in business suits strolled around him. In the air was a familiar mix of odours - salt water and oily rain, laced with city fumes.

He knew where he was. This was London's Docklands, where two years ago his life had changed forever. Where he had thought his career had taken off, but where everything had gone wrong. He looked up to his right. Looming over him was CERUS Tower, its steel and glass form rising into the grey sky.

It was exactly as he remembered it.

And that was the point. This wasn't real. It was simply a projection, a simulation - the virtual world into which he was immersed. But it certainly looked real.

"Hello, Tom," a man's voice said, "it's good to see you again."

Tom tipped his head back down and saw Peter Marron had appeared in front of the Tower's main doors. He wore a grey suit, and looked exactly as Tom remembered him when he had been CERUS Biotech's director of HR. Tom frowned. "What's going on?"

"I'm here to show you up to your office. We need to get a move on or you'll be late for your first day."

"No thanks, I'm not talking to him." Tom turned and began to walk away from the Tower.

Edna Kim stood facing him, her arms folded. "Where do you think you're going?"

Tom realised everything else had gone silent. "I said I'd help fix your computer. I didn't say I'd spend time playing stupid virtual reality games." He thumbed over his shoulder. "Marron isn't really here, so I'm not talking to him."

Kim held up a hand. "It might be a virtual representation, but that representation is how you interact with Max's core system. If you're going to do this, there's a path to follow."

"And that path is to talk to the man who just betrayed me by bringing me to the Rig?"

"It would help if you could be a little less literal. Do you really think what you're seeing has no purpose? The computer is engaging with your memories. By pulling things, people from your memories, that's how the computer builds understanding. The memories prompt strong activity within your brain, across multiple facets. Max uses these to calibrate. Through those understandings, you will connect."

"So why use Marron?"

"That was a choice made by Max. But Marron is obviously a recent and prominent figure in your life, one to which you attach strong emotion"

"OK. But why," Tom pointed to CERUS Tower, "here?"

"Again I'm guessing, but perhaps because it is a particularly strong memory - perhaps lots of memories anchored to a particular time and place. You need to go with it, and I need to get out of your way or I'm going to block your progress."

"And what happens if I do the wrong thing again?"

"You just need to run towards the problem, not away from it. Only there will you find the way to do the right thing. And to be clear, that will be the only way you can survive."

"What—?" Tom started to ask.

But Kim snapped her fingers.

And instantaneously Tom was somewhere else.

EIGHTY-NINE

KIM and her snapping fingers vanished. Tom's vision was filled with a familiar sight - he stood in a softly lit, three metre cube of polished steel and aluminium. As before there was a display but no controls. This was a CERUS Tower elevator. And he was going up.

It didn't feel like a simulation, or a projection. It felt real.

The display ticked up, through the twenties and thirties, accelerating until it was a blur. In the background a tinny speaker was playing Vivaldi's Four Seasons.

"Do we really need the elevator music?" he asked.

Kim's voice floated from somewhere nearby: "It's coming from your imagination, whatever it is."

"And why *am* I in this elevator?"

"As I said, this is Max trying to understand you. Now please focus and actually engage with the environment. Don't speak to me again unless it is of critical import."

"I'll keep that in mind."

The elevator kept rising in the building, then abruptly braked, settling on Level 90, the very top floor of the building. The doors opened and he stepped into the lobby.

He had been here before. To the left was the CEO's private meeting room, the door to which was closed. To the right, the CEO's office and private apartment. That door was open.

He looked at the polished marble floor, the oak panelled walls, the selection of modern art, the desk used by the CEO's PA. It was all exactly as he remembered it, from the time when William Bern was CEO of CERUS Biotech.

He turned and walked towards the open door, passing through into the large, triple-aspect office that took up about half of the top floor of the building. He gave a passing glance at the angular steel sculpture to his left, and walked towards the huge granite desk, stepping on what he had heard was a hideously expensive Persian rug.

And then he realised there was someone sitting at the desk. Someone that was staring at him and smiling broadly. And even though he knew this was just a simulated image, that this was in no way real, the effect was no less chilling.

It was his father.

"Hello Tom," said William Bern, "it is good to see you again."

TOM FELT his heart pound in his chest. His real heart? Or the heart that existed in this virtual reality? Perhaps both? He stared back at Bern. He looked just as he remembered him when he had seen him on the island in the Atlantic. It was a face he had never wanted to see again, yet it had been dragged from his memories. His mouth feeling paper-dry, he forced out the words: "What are you doing here?"

Bern raised an eyebrow. "So you're not going to call me father?"

Tom frowned. "You're just a figment of my imagination. An NPC in a video game."

"You think I'm not real? You think I'm just a ghost from your memories?" The man leaned forward, resting his knuckles on the desk. "Are you sure about that? Maybe you should open your eyes a little wider."

"This is a simulation, you're the computer, and I'm simply here to fix—"

"Me? Yes, that's what Edna Kim said she wants you to do."

Tom blinked. "What does that mean?"

"Maybe I don't want to be fixed. And if your expectation is that I'm going to answer your questions, you haven't understood what is going on."

"She said you needed to understand me."

"That part is true." Bern stood up. "And the first step on that path is for you to die. We need to turn you off and on again."

Tom stared at him. "What are you talking about?"

"Hard to explain, best that I show you." Bern reached across the desk and grabbed Tom. And with inhuman strength threw him through the triple-glazed windows. Tom felt the explosion of glass, the slam of bitterly cold wind, and then he fell, tumbling into darkness.

THE VEIL LIFTED, and Tom stood in a huge, crowded room, full of perhaps a couple of hundred people. The room had windows on all sides - and was clearly some type of exhibition centre. Waiters wove their way through the tightly packed crowd, distributing glasses of champagne with military precision.

"What is going on...?" Tom began.

A tanned man bounded onto a stage raised above the crowd and grabbed a microphone. "Ladies and gentlemen, good evening. It is my absolute pleasure to welcome you to the grand opening of our new head office, CERUS Tower, here in the heart of London's Docklands..."

Tom blinked. The man speaking on stage was William Bern, but from two years ago. Tom had been here, hearing these exact words. He turned to his left, and he saw his younger self standing listening, wearing his best suit. Utterly unaware of what was about to happen to him. Tom shook his head. "This is all too much."

"We've barely started."

Tom spun and saw that the more recent Bern - the one that had thrown him through the windows of the penthouse office - was standing next to him.

"So what do you think of it? It's a scene pulled from your memories, but I've fleshed it out with related data and extrapolation. It's a whole new world."

Tom looked at himself, standing frozen in time. He looked so real. What was to stop him just walking over and warning himself? Nothing, apart from the fact that this wasn't real. "Why are we here? Why are you showing this moment to me?"

"To see how you'll react."

"My reaction is to tell you to stop wasting my time."

"I'm not. This is the evening your life changed, remember?" Bern pointed across the room. "See that woman over there, in the black dress. She looks like trouble."

Tom looked and swallowed. It was Alex. Waiting to approach him. To drug him. This was not the Alex who knew him. This was a stranger. A killer.

"This," Bern said, "is the night that Marron had you experimented on."

"The night that *you* had me experimented on. Except, of course, you aren't really you."

Bern waved a hand. "Same difference. This construct is a place where we can explore your memories. Of everywhere and anywhere where we have sufficient data."

"I'd like to leave."

"You don't want to look more closely? You could learn from your past mistakes."

"How would that help? How could I have had any idea what would happen to me?"

"You're right. You were helpless."

Tom gritted his teeth. "I'm not helpless now."

"So they tell me. Bet you want to punch me in the face."

"I want to leave." He looked around. "How do I get out of here?"

"You want to go home? No problem." Bern snapped his fingers again. The room around Tom blurred and shifted.

And once again he found himself somewhere else.

TOM WALKED through the front doorway of his London apartment, into the hallway.

And he froze. My apartment? He looked up at a clock on the wall. It showed it was 7:30am.

"Hey, loser," said a voice from the next room. A voice he hadn't heard in two years. A voice that no longer spoke. His mouth dry, he walked into the kitchen.

And there she was, sitting at the table, eating a slice of thick, buttered toast. His flat-mate, and best friend, Jo. She had died a few days after the events this memory portrayed.

Jo raised a curious eyebrow. "Out all night? Anything you want to share?"

"Sorry... what?"

"Have you been back at the clinic?"

Tom ran a hand through his hair. "Look this is just too weird..."

"If you don't want to share, that's fine." She looked down at a card folder open on the table. "Come and help me with my Italian exam."

"How am I supposed to do that?"

She handed over a large sheet of paper with a list of words written in a very small font. "Test me."

Tom growled and threw the paper to the floor. "Stop showing me dead people."

Jo froze. Bern appeared next to her. "What's your problem? Isn't this a happy memory?"

"If you can't tell the difference, then I don't think this is going to work."

"Noted. Let's try something else."

Again something shifted. He was still in his London apartment, but it was nighttime. Alex was there, looking menacing. Kate was next to him, seeming tense. And there was a large man with a shaved head standing in the doorway to Tom's bedroom. He held a silenced pistol.

No, not this moment. Anything but this moment—

There was a loud shriek and Jo charged from her bedroom, a baseball bat raised over her head. Everyone looked on as she brought the bat down towards the gunman's arm. But she was not quick enough. The man spun away, his expression intense. He raised the gun.

And he fired.

Everything suddenly moved in slow motion. The impact hit Jo in the chest and she was knocked backwards. Tom leapt to catch her, but she was heavy, lifeless. She slipped through his arms, crumpling onto the floor. There was blood. So much blood. And she didn't seem to be breathing.

And he knew that she would never breathe again.

"Why?" he screamed. "Why are you doing this to me?"

Bern knelt beside him, as everything else froze. "You can remember everything, Tom. That is your gift. It makes you unique."

"What is the point? Are you trying to upset me? Are you trying to drive me mad?"

"I'm trying to know you. Only then can we communicate properly." Bern paused. "And if I could make a suggestion, maybe stop complaining. Step up and take charge."

"You're giving me advice? Does that mean *I'm* giving me advice?"

"Why not. Take responsibility, not just for yourself, but for others. Be the leader that you can be."

"I just want my friend to be safe. My friend, Dominique."

"Then you're going to have to play this game a little longer."

And the world faded to black.

TOM WAS NO LONGER in his apartment. Mists swirled around him, and the ground beneath his feet shifted, becoming jagged and uneven. Gusts of wind smacked his face, carrying a spray of saltwater.

Then the mists suddenly blew away, and he saw he was standing on a bare, rocky island, looking out across a cold grey ocean. Next to him was a military helicopter, bearing US Navy markings.

He knew this place. He had been here before, on a single occasion twelve months ago, when he had landed after flying from Bern's aircraft carrier, the *Phoenix Reborn*. It was the place where his father had died.

Bern patted him on the shoulder. "Bet you didn't expect to be seeing this crappy little island again."

Tom knocked Bern's hand away. "Why bring me here?"

"To look at the moment that changed everything. To focus on the decision you made. On what you did."

Tom looked down. He was holding the nanobomb that Marron had given to him.

Bern smiled and held up an Accumulator. "This is what the real Bern had in his possession. Show me what you did."

"What does it matter to you?"

"You killed your own father. That kind of thing matters."

"But not to you."

"It matters to me because it matters to you."

"Fine. I swapped the two devices."

"Physically?"

"No. But they are essentially built on the same foundations, on the same component parts. One of the risks with the Accumulator was always that it could be turned into a bomb. So I did just that. And I did the reverse with the bomb."

"That's 'what' you did? But how?"

"I used my Interface. I reconfigured their internal structure."

Bern raised an eyebrow. "They have trillions upon trillions of internal nodes. How could you possibly do that?"

Tom shrugged. "I didn't tackle them one at a time. It was more of a high level, collective instruction. And it worked."

"Do it again. Set off the explosion."

Tom glared at Bern, taking a step towards him. "I've had enough of this. Where is Lentz?"

"You aren't ready." Bern smiled. Then he swung his right fist and hit Tom.

And Tom felt real, actual, stinging pain. He staggered back, feeling his jaw throb. Did it matter if he got hurt in here? The pain seemed very real. "What are you doing?"

Bern struck him again.

Tom shrieked. "Stop!"

"I will keep doing this until you give me what I want." Bern started to swing his fist.

Tom closed his eyes. He felt the Accumulator. And Bern froze, mid-swing, and smiled.

Unlike last time, Tom realised, this was familiar ground. This was easy. With a flick of control he accelerated the change, reconfiguring the device from controlled to uncontrolled power delivery.

In a moment it was done. And it exploded.

The explosion blossomed: a white flare of purest light, almost blinding him before he could turn away. A wave of pure death, that no organic creature could survive.

It was a death his father could not have faked. A death that he could not negotiate against, that he could not buy, he could not cheat his way out of.

There was a snap of fingers. The explosion froze.

The other Bern stood next to him. "Amazing. Truly amazing. This is progress."

"So we're done?"

"No. We have one more visit to make."

TOM RECOGNISED the old church immediately. It was located sixty miles outside of London in the tiny Oxfordshire village of Kingsford. He stood looking down at the simple granite slab, located at the rear of a walled field, opposite the small church.

It was his mother's gravestone. Amelia Faraday's final resting place.

In his hands were a bunch of daffodils. Her favourites. Muttering, he threw them aside. "I've had enough of this."

"I miss you, Tom," said a voice from next to him. A woman's voice.

Tom flinched. It was a voice embedded in his soul. A voice

he had known all his life. At least until she had died of cancer. It belonged to his mother. He turned and saw her standing next to him. Looking perfect, a vision of health. He reached out a hand towards her, then he forced himself to stop. "Enough!" he hissed. "No more."

"I'm just holding up a mirror," his mother said. "Letting you see what is inside your own head."

"You're controlling me."

"I'm really more of a guide. And it doesn't have to be that way. These memories are always there. You can visit them. Explore them. Change them."

"What do you mean?"

"The world you live in - it is pain. It is suffering. But there is another way." She paused. "You could live here. In this place."

"What are you trying to tell me?"

"That you don't have to go back. You don't have to suffer any more."

"Is that even possible?"

His mother sighed. "Not yet. But with your help we can make it so."

"If I help fix you? If I unleash your true capability?"

"I can only do it with your assistance, with your cooperation. And you have to choose to give it freely. Or it won't work. You think you've been losing your humanity. Well this is how you get it back."

Tom swallowed. "Show me. Show me how."

His mother smiled, and her face warped.

And Tom was once again looking at Kim.

"Good," she said. "You're ready."

"I am? What do I need to do?"

"Just reach out," Kim said. "That is what you do, isn't it? Open your mind, and fix the computer. Unleash its potential. Make it what it is supposed to be."

Tom shook his head. "If you're lying to me, I will end you. I promise."

She smiled. "Remember that fighting spirit, Tom. You're going to need it."

NINETY

THE MOVE this time was instantaneous. Tom felt oddly weightless and found himself floating in space. He hovered high above a huge metal structure surrounded by a grey ocean.

The Rig.

Kim floated next to him, a smile on her face. "You've not seen it from this angle before, I imagine. It does give you a sense of the scale of the thing."

"Fascinating. What was all that business with Bern?

"Bern?" She frowned. "I guess that was intended to provoke a particularly strong reaction from you."

"He seemed... very real. Not just a memory."

"This is how calibration is achieved. Clearly the system was doing its job."

"I don't think so. I don't believe his personality was just pulled from my memories. It felt like you had data from him already. It felt like *him*."

"As I say, the system is intended to convince you. That's how it works. Anyway, can we please focus."

"I'm trying, but is this sightseeing tour ever going to end?"

"This is our final stop. Our destination."

"I don't understand. I've never been here before."

"We've moved on. From our various visits, Max has now calibrated to your Interface." She pointed down. "The Rig is a representation of the computer. Max can perform the necessary translation. All you need to do is fix the Rig. If you fix the Rig, you fix the computer."

"*Fix the Rig*? What does that mean?"

"Look at it. What do you see?"

Tom stared at the metal structure. "I don't see anything."

"Look more closely."

He narrowed his eyes. And then he saw it - the corrosions, the weakness and decay. "It's falling apart. The metal structure is... crumbling. If this continues it's going to sink."

"Very good. Now you know what to do. You have to stop that happening, reverse all those problems."

"But how do I actually fix it? I can't stop rust."

She gave a sigh. "It's not really corroding, not in a physical sense. This is just a manifestation of the digital problem. Open your mind. Connect with it. You'll work out what to do."

Tom sighed and turned down. He took a deep breath, focused his thoughts, and reached out. He was expecting it to be difficult, but the rush of data hit Tom like a hurricane. He grimaced. It was a wall of noise, and he could not pierce it. He gasped and took a deep breath. "It's too much."

Kim glared at him. "If it was going to be easy, I'd have done it myself."

"Done it yourself? But how would you?"

"Just try again. And this time do better."

Tom steeled himself and reached out. A wail of static rose around him, like a thousand voices screaming. It was terrible. It made him want to stop. But this time he did not back down. He stood and walked into the storm. And within that storm, he sought the eye, the centre. Something immense. Something unfathomable. And he started to pick up echoes of the data being processed.

This wasn't like talking to a computer. He felt another mind. But radically different and enormously more powerful than his own. It felt alien. And yet painfully close to home.

Hello, Tom.

The voice, impossibly loud, hit him like a shockwave. He was knocked back, tumbling, and fell to the ground, even though there was no ground.

And the connection vanished.

He was back in the air above the Rig, his head pounding.

"What happened?" Kim asked. "You seemed to disconnect."

"I spoke to it. To Max. But even a short communication knocked me out." He rubbed his temples. "I... was overwhelmed."

"You need to try again. And try harder. We haven't come all this way for you to fail."

"And I didn't come all of this way out of choice. I know why I'm doing this, but I don't have enough power."

"Then use the Accumulator. Although I should warn you, don't get any ideas about using its power for something else. If I suspect for a moment that you are, I'll shut you off. There will be no second chances."

Tom raised an eyebrow. "You said I needed to trust you. Doesn't trust go both ways?"

"It does. But I understand temptation. I understand bad decision-making. I just want to make sure you're fully informed. Only then can I trust you to make the right decision."

"Fine. How do I access the Accumulator in here?"

Kim extended her right hand and the familiar cube appeared before her, its LEDs blinking. "It's all yours."

Tom nodded and reached out again, this time to the cube in front of him. It opened like a flower, its power flowing into him.

It was a system calibrated to work with his own Interface, one that made him more capable, more potent. And then he turned to the Rig.

And this time things were different. Very different.

Power flooded into Tom. He felt electricity crackling in his blood. He felt alive. He reached out to the image of the Rig below him. To the electronic mind it represented. He felt the data blasting from it. But this time he was not overwhelmed. This time he shaped the winds around him. He made sense of them. And he sent a message. "Hello?" he said. "Are you there?"

There was no reply. But there was the sense of an invitation. He willed himself closer. As he flew downwards, he saw that a dark figure stood on the top surface of the Rig.

He moved closer, landing on the metal.

And then he saw that it wasn't just that the figure was dark. It was a figure made of darkness. A silhouette with nothing within. The figure spoke without speaking, a thousand voices colouring its words with a confusion of meaning. *Why are you here?*

Tom felt the words lance through him. They weren't really words. They were an approximation, a way to share understanding. A way for him to try and communicate with whatever this was. He focused his mind: "I'm here to fix you." Underneath his feet he felt the structure of the Rig groaning and straining.

The figure shifted. *I need fixing?*

"That's what I was told." Tom gestured at the Rig. "That's what this represents. The structure falling apart. The systems failing."

I am the problem?

Tom frowned. "You ask a lot of questions. But you give me no answers. I thought you needed optimising, but this feels... wrong."

The figure shifted again, its appearance seeming to stutter. *You think you can change things?*

"I don't know what to tell you. But I'm going to get inside your system, and I'm going to find a way to save my friends."

Your authorisations are revoked.

And suddenly Tom felt the power of the Accumulator being cut off. The link was severed. "What? Now hang on—"

The shadowy figure raised one of its hands, and Tom was cast backwards, upwards and away, accelerating at a speed that would have crushed him to a puddle. And then there was a loud error tone, and the world collapsed.

He opened his eyes. He wasn't floating above the Rig. He was in the white room, and Kim was staring down at him.

"Right," she said. "I thought that might happen."

NINETY-ONE

IT TOOK one hour for Kate and Gifford to be rescued - one hour of frustration and impatience while they sat in the escape pod and were buffeted and tossed about on the rough Atlantic waters, unable to do anything but wait for the two Royal Navy vessels to reach them.

The pod had now been winched out of the ocean, and Kate stepped from the life pod onto the deck of the HMS *Sheffield,* a type 45 Destroyer. Natasha Gifford was already out, staring at a secure computer tablet she'd been handed while talking heatedly with the captain.

"I'm not sure," Gifford said, "if you heard me clearly. We need to return to the Rig immediately. I am the acting head of—"

The captain raised his palms. "Ma'am I fully appreciate who you are."

"Good. We have people on board that structure who need rescuing, and valuable intel to recover. So please stop delaying and give the order."

"As I've been trying to say, an automated system warned us not to approach. Our scans have identified significant weapons capabilities. My orders are not to approach closer than is safe to do so." He nodded across the water to the other navy vessel. "And neither us, nor the HMS *Exeter*, are going to do that."

"And who did those orders come from?"

"The Admiral of the Fleet." He shrugged. "I'm sorry, I know we are being overly cautious. But this matter has got the attention of some very senior people. They remember how things turned out in recent encounters with CERUS-related tech. And they are wary."

"Can you get closer than we are?"

He hesitated. "A little. I can bring us within 5 kilometres of the structure."

"Then do it. At least we can be ready to act if your orders change."

"Understood." He paused. "And to be clear, I want to rescue our people. But I also have to protect the lives of the 700 souls that are onboard these two ships."

"If things go wrong here, a lot more lives may be affected. A lot more lives may be lost."

"My role isn't to speculate. My role is to follow orders. So, unless you want to speak to the Admiral's boss, I suggest you accept what I can give you." He turned and walked away.

Kate placed a hand on Gifford's shoulder. "You've done what you can."

"And yet it's not nearly enough." Gifford held up the tablet computer. "I don't know why Reems isn't off that Rig herself. Something must have gone wrong."

"I agree. Although I did think Reems was acting strangely when we saw her last."

"Well this is not a normal situation."

"True. But I got the feeling that she wanted to get rid of us."

Gifford folded her arms. "Maybe you're right. Maybe Reems *did* want to get rid of us. Maybe she actually wanted to get us to safety and thought we wouldn't have agreed to evacuate without her."

"Which we wouldn't have." Kate shook her head. "I just don't like this. I want to be doing something."

"Me too," Gifford replied. "And I promise you, as soon as anything changes, good or bad, we will be."

NINETY-TWO

TOM BLINKED AT KIM, struggling to focus, aware of a dull pain in the back of his head. "You thought *what* might happen?"

She lifted off his helmet and placed it on the circular table. "You've broken Max."

"How could I...? Tom trailed off as the floor shook under him. "What was that?"

"A side effect. Caused by you channelling too much power from the Accumulator."

"And that's broken Max?"

"You've burnt out a number of its circuits, compromised its programming." She shook her head. "You were supposed to make Max better. Instead you've made it worse."

"How was I supposed to know that could happen? Why didn't you warn me?"

"I can't warn you about everything..." Kim trailed off as there was a loud, deep groaning sound from everywhere around. The floor of the Rig shook violently.

Tom looked around. "What was that?"

"Let me put this simply: Max controls the Rig. And you've broken Max. So now Max is breaking the Rig." She tapped on her phone and pointed to another display. "The entire structure is going to sink. And I'm locked out from doing anything about it."

"You, who built this place, are locked out?"

"Did you miss the part when I said Max is in control? And I no longer have control of Max."

"I feel you should have planned for such an eventuality."

"Hindsight is always twenty-twenty."

Tom glared at her. "So what now? What do we do?"

"I don't know. I guess we're all dead. You, me, Dominique. And anyone else unfortunate enough to be stuck here."

"Can we get to the life rafts before we drown?"

Kim looked at her phone again. "We'd never make it. But, if it's any consolation, I doubt we'll drown."

"Because we'll get rescued?"

"No, because the autodogs are all heading towards us. After what you did, Max sees us as a threat, and as you've seen, it isn't gentle in how it deals with threats. The dogs are killing machines."

"You designed them that way."

Kim rolled her eyes. "The fact that this is ironic doesn't mean we aren't in a great deal of trouble."

"Oh, you're in a great deal of trouble alright," said a voice.

Tom looked up and saw Lentz walking into the room, an automatic pistol trained on Kim. Behind her came Stephanie Reems, holding a rifle.

"Well, well," Kim said. "The cavalry are here. Too bad you won't make any difference."

Lentz advanced on Kim. "And why is that?" The Rig lurched and shifted, nearly knocking all four of them from their feet.

Kim gestured around her. "Because Tom here has made

Max very angry. And things are about to get very, very unpleasant."

Tom folded his arms. "Blaming this on me is a stretch."

Lentz turned to Reems. "Keep that weapon trained on Kim. If she moves, shoot her."

"Gladly," Reems replied. "Maybe even if she doesn't."

"Unfortunately we might yet need her. It depends on what I can work out." Lentz ran over to the nearest terminal and began interrogating it. And then she swore.

Kim laughed. "I said you wouldn't make any difference."

Lentz frowned. "There are fifty autodogs headed towards us - all in antagonistic mode. Kim, switch them off like you did before."

"I would, truly. But when Max got angry, it cut me off." She pointed to Tom. "Ask him to do it."

"A brute force instruction to fifty robots? How much power will that take?"

Lentz shrugged. "I don't know. But you're the only one who can even try." She pointed at the Accumulator. "It's out of the box! Use it."

Tom sighed. "When Max threw me out of the virtual environment, it cut me off."

"So you need another power source? Kim, you must have something? With all your resources here? Those robots must be running on high-capacity batteries?"

"Oh right. Sure. We'll just ask one to hand it over."

Reems frowned. "Surely you have spares?"

"Some, but the robots are between us and the storage facility."

Lentz held up her gun. "Can't we take one down?"

Kim shook her head. "Those peashooters won't trouble them. Besides they aren't going to attack one at a time. Maybe if you had a grenade or two."

"I swear you're revelling in this moment."

"I am proud of what I've created. Even though it seems like it's going to kill me."

"So no batteries anywhere close?"

"No. No power sources at all. Other than the nuclear reactor of course."

Lentz blinked. Then she turned to Tom. "OK, you're not going to like this. But it may be our only option."

Tom stared back. "You want me to draw power from the nuclear reactor?"

"We considered it before."

"Yes, but it was crazy then. And, spoiler warning, it's crazy now."

"I'm sorry to tell you, we used up all the non-crazy ideas. Among the options we have, it may actually be the best."

"Even if you're right, it's much more likely it won't work. The most likely outcome is that it will kill me."

"Max can't control the power flow from the reactor in the same way it can control the Accumulator. It can't cut you off. It can't take away your weapon. So you have a chance. A battle of equals, you could call it." Lentz turned to Kim. "Or do you disagree?"

"I'm saying nothing."

"Why?"

"Because you won't believe me. But you should probably hurry." She put a hand to her ear. "I think the killer robots are coming."

Lentz frowned. "Has she flipped? Or is something going on?"

"I don't know," Tom said, "but there's nothing wrong with her hearing." He tapped on the nearby screen. "Five autodogs about two minutes away."

"I'll barricade the door," Reems said, looking around. "Or I would if there was anything to do it with." She moved to the keypad on one side. "I can at least lock it."

"That won't make a difference," Kim said. "They're each as strong as a mechanical digger. They'll cut through that door like paper."

Tom shook his head and grabbed the helmet. "Get me a power cable."

Lentz looked at him. "I'm sorry, Tom. I truly am."

"Sure, I believe you. Now get me the cable—"

"Allow me," Kim said and marched over to a wall rack where cables were hanging. She lifted one down and walked back, holding it out to him. "Knock yourself out. Which, to be clear, is on the positive end of possible outcomes."

Lentz raised an eyebrow at Reems. "I said cover her."

"You did. Did you want me to actually shoot her?"

"Can we hurry?" Tom shouted, slipping the helmet on. "I can hear the robots."

"Here goes nothing." Lentz plugged in the cable.

Tom closed his eyes and reached out, feeling for the power.

And then he saw it. It was like staring into the sun. And if he wanted to save his friends, if he wanted to live, this was what he had to do. So he opened his mind to the energy.

In an instant he was gone.

TOM STOOD on the roof of CERUS Tower, looking down upon London. To the west the sun was setting, red smearing the partially cloudy sky. "Why is it always this place?" he asked to the air. He knew he was not alone.

The shadowy figure came into focus next to him. *This is a focal point in your memories. And in those of the people around you. It felt... suitable.*

"You can read my mind? You can read their minds?"

From the others I can pick up some thoughts. But you are different. You are... open and connected.

Tom stared. "But you look no different at all. Kim said you were broken."

You think I am broken?

"Because you're trying to kill us. You have to stop."

You believe you can stop me?

Tom shrugged. "I'll keep trying until something works." He turned and punched the figure in its face. His hand passed straight through as if it was a cloud.

That does nothing.

Tom frowned, then reached into his own mind, to the connection with the power flow. And he tapped into it, drawing upon the reactor. He felt himself come alive; he felt his blood run hot. He felt the endless possibility, the pure white heat of thought. He looked at each of his hands, and they burst into flame.

The shadowy figure tipped its head to one side. *That fire is not real. Nothing in here is real.*

"You don't get to decide what is real." Tom pointed a finger. Flames sprayed forth, enveloping the shadow. For several long moments there was only dancing fire. Finally, Tom let it recede.

The shadow remained, unchanged. *You cannot stop me. I can stop you.* The figure stepped forward, gripping Tom's head with both hands, and it reached in.

Not like before. This was a thousand times more forceful. A million tendrils of control insinuated their way into Tom's mind. A billion points of data that sought to take control of his interface and overwrite him. He should be lost. He should be defeated.

But this time he was different too. This time he had a nuclear reactor to draw upon. With a grunt he unlocked all restrictions and let the power flow. It was a hurricane of energy, and it could not be stopped. He let it flow through him, magnifying and focusing the power. For a moment, he shone like the sun. With a scream of agony, the shadow evaporated before him.

And then there was nothing to stop Tom taking control of this realm.

NINETY-THREE

TOM OPENED his eyes to see Lentz, Reems and Kim staring at him expectantly. He lifted off the helmet and permitted himself a smile. "I won."

Lentz frowned. "What do you mean, you won?" She glanced over her shoulder as two more robots were battering loudly at the door. "They didn't get the message."

Tom waved a finger in their direction. The two metal creatures immediately fell silent. "Consider them informed."

"Interesting," Kim said. "What did you just do?"

"I made a start." Tom reached out to the Rig's system and began issuing instructions. All around confirmatory beeps and chimes began sounding. Nearby screens showed that normal facility operation had been resumed. He extended his perception further. Of the supercomputer brain, there was no sign. The intellect that had been Max was gone.

Lentz placed a hand on his shoulder. "What did you do in there?"

"I gave it both barrels in the face."

"How much power did you have to draw to achieve that?"

"As much as I could." He extended his perception further.

"As much as was needed." Thirty miles away he detected the HMS *Sheffield*. On it was Kate. He placed a call to her wireless earpiece, effortlessly breaking through its encryption.

"Tom?" she said. "Are you OK?" A pause. "Where are you? And how did you get on this channel?"

"Because I'm me. I'm on the Rig with some friends." He paused and looked at Kim. "And one failed enemy. Any chance of a pickup and rescue?"

"We can be there within thirty minutes. Promise not to shoot us on approach?"

"I guarantee your safety."

"I'll do my best to convince the captain that your word is credible."

"Ping me back if you have trouble. I can always take over the ship on your behalf."

"Can you now? Look, stay safe, see you soon."

Tom closed the call and walked away from Lentz, Kim and Reems. He extended his perception further still, and then he detected a very faint trace.

Alex.

"Hello there," he said. "Nice of you to run out on me like that."

"What the...?" she replied. "My earpiece isn't connected to a phone, so how are you communicating? And running out wasn't my idea. I never would have left you behind."

"Probably best you did. Things got a bit messy here."

"Did Korver find you? Did he help?" she asked.

"What? Why would you think that?"

"It doesn't matter. So you came out on top?"

"Certainly looks that way. How's your father?"

"Lucky to be alive. Lucky I didn't kill him after what he did."

"Why *did* he leave me?"

"As soon as I know, you'll know. But I'm going to have to

work on him. Wish me some of that luck." Then she disconnected the call.

Tom was about to speak to Reems when he realised he could also sense someone else on the Rig. It wasn't that he could see them on the CCTV - he could probably do that if he thought about it. No, this was different. He could *feel* someone. He could sense a certain quality about them. And what's more they were approaching this room. He reached out more specifically, but suddenly a wave of nausea swept over him. He collapsed to the floor, throwing up.

"Oh, dear," Kim said, "whatever is the matter?"

Lentz leapt to his side. "Is something wrong?"

"I don't know," he said with a groan. "My head is on fire."

"What did you do to him?" Lentz shouted.

"Don't blame me," Kim replied. "This was his own doing. But I might hazard a guess that he drew too much power. He might have super tech inside him, but he is still only human." She shrugged. "And that means he can die, just like the rest of us."

NINETY-FOUR

LENTZ SCOWLED AT KIM. "You seem to think this is funny. I can assure you it is not."

"Not really," Kim replied. "But you can't blame me for being in an odd mood. Given that Tom appears to have ruined the computer that was my life the last five years."

Tom groaned, breathing unevenly, then slumped further forward.

Lentz leaned closer. "Are you OK? Say something." He hissed but did not otherwise reply. Lentz tapped her glasses and ran her gaze over him, gathering data, attempting to understand. Temperature readings immediately came back in worrying ranges. "This is not good."

"I'd suggest we take him to our med bay," Kim said, "but it is unfortunately on the other side of those robots."

"Well we need to do something." They all looked up as there was a knock at the door. A huge figure of a man looked through the door's viewing pane.

Reems gripped her rifle. "Korver? How did he get here?"

"Unclear," Lentz replied. "I'm also unclear as to whether we let him in, or whether we shoot him."

"Shooting him with ordinary weapons didn't work out so well last time," Reems replied. "So let's try your first suggestion." She paused. "And if that proves to be a bad idea, maybe jab him with that power cable."

Lentz nodded. "Open the door then."

Reems tapped on the electronic lock and the door slid aside.

Korver walked in, his face pale, his hands raised. "I'm not here to fight."

"Good to know," Lentz said. "But not exactly plausible. Why are you here? To rescue your boss?"

Korver looked at Kim. "If you mean this person, I've never met her before. Although I assume she was who Director Hatch reported to."

"And where is he?"

"Deactivated."

"What?"

"He was an android." Korver looked at Kim. "A very convincing android."

She smiled. "I should have hidden it better. I regret having to take such steps with a high value unit, but Hatch was malfunctioning. He wouldn't accept my commands."

"Is that right?" Korver replied. "Well neither do I."

Kim smiled. "This is because I shot you last time we met. At my house in Cambridge."

"That is true," Lentz said. "Are you here for revenge?"

"No, I'm here to atone." He pointed at Tom. "I think I can help."

Lentz frowned at Korver, noticing his pallid, sweaty skin. "You look like you're the one that needs help."

Kim coughed. "It's because he hasn't taken his treatment."

Korver shrugged. "I've got one dose. I found it in Mendez's lab." He stared at Kim. "There weren't any more, but I assume you know that."

"A dose of what?" Lentz asked.

"A type of medical nano," Korver replied. "It's kept me alive the last few years. And I'll die if I don't keep taking it. They've always used it as a lever over me." He paused. "And when I say 'they' it seems that I mean her."

Kim shrugged. "Nothing is for free. I think we all know that."

"But you never had Hatch explain that price when he first gave it to me."

"You always had a choice."

"One I wasn't strong enough to make. Well I'm strong enough today. I won't allow you to exploit me anymore."

Kim gave a snort. "Then I won't make it anymore."

"I'll manage."

"No, you'll die."

He unshouldered a backpack and removed a metal case. Flipping it open he revealed a syringe gun and a single glass ampule. "Like I said, I'll manage."

"What are you doing?" Lentz asked.

"Giving a dose to Tom."

"Your last dose? Don't you need it? To stay alive?"

"That's what I meant by atone."

"How did you even know to come here? At this specific moment?"

"I told Alex that I'd come and help Tom. But I also think I felt his pain. I can't explain it."

Lentz looked at Korver and shook her head. "There's no way I'm going to allow you to inject him with that stuff. This could just be a trick to finish him off."

"It's no trick. He is dying."

"But you don't know if it will work on him, or if it will clash with the nanotech already in his bloodstream."

"In the circumstances it's very much his only chance. You have to believe me."

"No I don't..." Lentz's glasses informed her she was receiving a call. She looked up in confusion, realising it was Kate. "How did you—?"

"You need to trust Korver," Kate said. "His offer is genuine."

"You've been listening in?" She looked around. "Are you watching?"

"Neither. I can't explain it. I just know Tom needs this help. And I know Korver's nano is the best shot we have."

"How can you possibly know that?"

"I'm... connected. To Tom. And to Korver. In different ways, but the link is there. Don't ask me to explain it. But I know them. And I know you should trust the big guy."

Lentz shook her head. "This is becoming ridiculous, Kate."

"Just remember we don't fully understand this nanotech. It changes us. I think it's creating connections between us. How else would I have known to call?"

Outside came the sound of rhythmic tapping. Of many feet approaching with inevitability. Reems moved to the doorway. "We have autodogs incoming. We need to make a decision, and quickly."

"It's not just about saving Tom," Korver said. "It's about Tom being able to save us. Being able to save you." He nodded towards the door. "Although in a few moments that distinction may not matter."

Lentz puffed out her cheeks. "Fine, do it."

Korver slotted one of the ampules into the syringe gun and held it to Tom's neck.

Then, with a loud click, it fired.

NINETY-FIVE

TOM FELT AN EXPLOSION INSIDE HIM. A cold rush of energy, flowing into his blood. It was like the dark nano that had been shot into his bloodstream a year ago. Except it wasn't. He could feel at once that this was meant to heal him, to make him stronger. And perhaps more besides. He hesitated in his mind - should he allow it? Should he take all that it had to give? He couldn't pick and choose, certainly not in his present state. So he could change, again, or he could suffer and die.

He made a choice. And the choice was *yes*.

Tom felt the pain fade, and he opened his eyes. He saw Korver kneeling next to him. And he felt the nano within. New nano, and yet somehow familiar. He could feel it rebuilding, restoring. Rejuvenating his body. Within his mind he felt connections repairing and reinforcing. He was himself again. And then he was more.

Next to him he felt the Accumulator. The device that he had created a year ago in the battle with William Bern. It was uniquely his. Nobody could keep it from him, no matter who or what they were. He focussed his attention, concentrating on the protocols surrounding it. And they submitted to his will. What was left of the entity that was Max yielded to him. And power began to flow.

He felt alive. More than alive. Energy pulsed through him. He felt his skin crackle and spark.

"Wait," Lentz said. "Is Tom going to need to keep taking that nano or he'll die?"

"I can't say," Korver replied. "His condition was not as serious as mine, and his ability to control nano is fundamentally different. But if he died today because he didn't take it, the question would be irrelevant."

"Thank you." Tom rose to his feet and flexed his shoulders. "Although I do wonder why you did it."

Korver blinked. "Because for a long time someone else has been making choices for me." He paused. "Perhaps it's simply that I let them. And there came a point when I finally noticed. And I couldn't do it anymore." He coughed loudly. "Also I made a promise to a new friend."

"Alex."

"I know this isn't close to balancing the ledger. But it's the best thing I can do." He slumped forward, his breath rasping. "And also maybe the last."

Tom placed a hand on his massive shoulder. "I know what that cost you. I'll find a way to return the favour." He turned to Kim. "But for you it's over."

"I remain an optimist," she said.

"It won't make a difference to what happens."

"We'll see. What's interesting is that something has happened within you. Someone changed your nano. I must study that."

"The only thing you're going to be studying is the walls of a cell."

"That's a good line, but no prison will hold me—"

There was a clatter from the next room. Tom turned to see an autodog had reached the door, its LEDs flashing red. Without pausing it ripped the door open and moved into the room.

Kim cleared her throat. "It seems they don't know I'm beaten."

Tom walked towards it and reached out with every bit of venom and anger he could manage. His thoughts penetrated the dog's power unit, fusing shut every protection, every fuse, every circuit-breaker. Then he turned its power draw up to eleven.

The robot exploded.

They all turned away and ducked as fragments of metal and plastic sprayed the walls and floor.

"Easy, tiger!" Kim said with a laugh.

Another robot appeared in the doorway. Tom raised his hand. "I'll show you what's easy." The metal creature jerked and twitched, its LEDs changing to purple. It jerked again, then began walking. But not towards Tom. It moved directly at Kim, its bladed hands spinning.

Kim twitched and took a step back. "Well this got dark quickly."

"Tom," Lentz asked, "what you are doing?"

Tom clenched his fists. "A prison might not hold her. So I'm making that irrelevant."

"Don't hurt her."

His eyes went glassy. "She wishes I'm only going to hurt her."

Reems raised an eyebrow. "Tom? Is something wrong? This isn't you."

"I'm fine," he replied. "In fact, never better." The robot jerked forward, then paused. "Why would you ask that?"

"You can't kill her," Lentz said. "That's not how this ends."

"She deserves to die. We can't ever trust her."

Lentz stepped forward and placed a hand on his shoulder. "I understand how you feel. But you're not thinking clearly. You've changed. The Tom Faraday from two years ago wouldn't have even contemplated such a course of action."

"The Tom Faraday from two years ago was just an unsuspecting lawyer." The robot took another step forward. It was almost in reach of Kim. "A lot's happened to me in two years. A lot's happened to me in the last few days, and on this Rig."

"But killing someone like this, in cold blood? That would be an execution. And it would change you."

"I've already changed, don't you see? Connecting my mind to that computer did something. I became someone else. Someone with different value and goals, with a different perspective on life. You don't know what I will do. I don't either. So I'm going to find out."

"But you're still human. Don't give that part of you up."

The autodog raised its glittering blade, ready to strike. Kim stood straight, transfixed.

Tom closed his eyes. And he parsed Lentz's words. And he felt the blood pumping in his veins, carrying a billion tiny robots around his body. Carrying information. Carrying power.

What was he anymore? What should he do? Was he one? Or was he many? Was he a son, a friend, a colleague? Or was he an artificial construct? A cybernetic organism driven by artificial complexities.

He had to decide. Because choice was all he had. Who was he going to be?

And then he thought of Lentz, standing here before him. And of Kate, who had reached out to save him. Of Alex who had sent this former enemy to bring him back from the brink.

And of Jo, who would tell him to stop being an idiot.

And finally he thought of his mother. What would she

want? That he be human. That he live his best life. That he be happy. That he be *Tom.*

So he chose.

The robot froze, then stepped back and powered down.

Lentz put a hand on his arm and let out a long breath that she had clearly been holding. "I don't know about you, but I think we should get out of here."

NINETY-SIX

TOM STOOD on the small motor launch as it powered away from a docking section on one of the Rig's lower sections towards the waiting HMS *Sheffield.* Lentz, Reems and Kim stood next to him. Kim's wrists were zip-tied, and Reems held an automatic rifle trained on her. Korver had been taken in a separate boat to the HMS *Exeter*, accompanied by a medical team. They were hopeful they could keep him alive until he got to a proper hospital. Beyond that, they had no idea.

Lentz had called in one of her remote care packages, which would provide a few more items that might come in handy, but even her fastest delivery device was a good two hours away. They would have to manage with what the Royal Navy could supply for now. Tom would also have to manage without the Accumulator, which Reems had insisted await collection by one of her teams, rather than risk it being seized by the Royal Navy when they were inevitably scanned and searched.

Tom's boat was heading to the nearby HMS *Sheffield* where Kate and Gifford were waiting. The nearly identical HMS *Exeter* held position about a kilometre further away. Lentz had taken blood samples from each of them and was ready to run a batch of tests once they got onboard. She wanted to be sure they hadn't picked up anything unexpected on the Rig. Tom had reluctantly agreed, although not quite as reluctantly as Reems, who argued for several minutes before it became apparent that Lentz would not be dissuaded. Everyone was still on edge, everyone except, so it seemed, their captive.

Tom glanced at Kim. There was something odd about her expression. She didn't look beaten. In fact she appeared quietly confident. She saw him looking at her and flashed a smile.

Lentz placed a hand on his arm. "You OK?"

"I'm fine. Just can't quite believe we came through it all. Can't believe it's over." He turned back to the huge structure they'd just left. "What's going to happen to the Rig now?"

"We acquire it," Reems said. "Then we catalogue and eliminate."

Tom frowned. "If quoting the ACE acronym is your idea of a joke, it's not a good one."

"Given how I was less than transparent with you in the past, that may be a fair point. In another life we might repurpose the Rig to use as the HQ for MI10. Just a pity it got discovered by the Royal Navy. I doubt we can expect them to keep it off the public record."

Lentz shrugged. "Plus, who knows what tricks and traps are embedded within it? You'd never know if you found them all."

Kim nodded thoughtfully. "It would certainly take you a while."

Tom pointed at Kim. "What will happen to her?"

Reems narrowed her eyes. "She's going to be locked away in the bottom of a very deep, very high security pit."

"Of course," Lentz said, "that was not a strategy that worked well with Bern and Marron."

"We won't make the same mistake twice."

"No," Kim said with a smile. "I'm certain that you'll make

whole new ones. Speaking of which, it would be a mistake to go any further with you. I have places to be, things to do."

Reems snorted. "Unless you're completely blind, you can see you don't have any say in what happens next."

"Don't talk to me about being blind. I'm the one with *vision.*"

Tom looked around. "The thing I don't understand is, if Hatch was your creation, if it was running the Rig for you, why did you destroy it?"

"Because it was malfunctioning. I'd experimented by giving a large degree of autonomy from Max, so that it could operate in the event Max went offline. But Hatch was taking a far too literal interpretation of its directive to protect the Rig - I don't know where it came up with the idea of putting people in barrels, but I couldn't stop it before I got here in person. And even then it was refusing to take orders from me that were not fully aligned with that goal. It meant I had no choice but to physically intervene. I'll learn from that with the next implementation. And it wasn't my latest model. It wasn't perfect. Its eyes were quite the giveaway."

Lentz cleared her throat. "That's why it was wearing the sunglasses."

"Indeed. It took me a long time, and a lot of work, to get the eyes right - I've created more prototypes than I care to count. Each has proved useful in one way or another, and they've all helped with the march forward. If you were talking to one equipped with the latest ocular units, you wouldn't even know."

Tom folded his arms. "So it was just a machine to you?"

"I don't get attached. And neither should you – including to me. Speaking of which, it's time I was going."

Tom felt something change. A subtle and odd vibration in the motor launch. So slight, you could almost miss it. But he didn't. He narrowed his eyes. "What's going on?

Kim just smiled. Around them the water began to bubble.

Lentz peered over the side of the craft. "Odd."

The motor launch began to slow, closing on approach to the *Sheffield*. As it did so, the turbulence increased, like the waters were boiling. But Tom could feel no heat. He stared down. "What is going on?"

Kim strained against her zip ties. "Let's call it my contingency."

Dozens of small metal objects broke the surface, moving in a coordinated pattern. Flattened spheres, each over two metres in diameter, broke the surface. Then the top sections opened to reveal metallic figures.

Robots, Tom realised. Like the autodogs, but without their cargo-carrying platform. These appeared unapologetically designed for combat. Each had four long articulated arms, ending in blades and spikes.

Kim smiled. "Did you really think that the Rig was all I had? That after all my planning, and all my resource I would be so easily overcome?" A larger, smooth, squashed sphere surfaced nearby, the size of a small truck. "And that's my ride. The same one that rescued me when I was thrown overboard in a barrel." She smiled and with a jerk pulled her wrists apart, breaking the zip ties. "Time for me to go."

"Stop!" Tom reached out to connect with the robots. To take control. He felt the flows of data within and among them. A hive mind. Many entities, acting as one, to combat his move. He couldn't control just one at a time. He had to take on all of them.

And there were so many, it was overwhelming. Almost as if they had been designed to counter him. On reflex he reached out to the Accumulator, to draw upon as much of its power as he could handle. But it was back on the Rig, and he seemed to be having trouble reaching it at all. In fact, more than that, he seemed to be thinking slowly, like he was wading through treacle.

"This ends now." Reems raised her rifle and fired at Kim's head. The bullets ricocheted harmlessly off.

"Another suit?" Lentz asked.

"No more answers from me," Kim replied. "But I agree that it ends." She waggled a finger then pointed. The nearest robot leapt from where it stood on the sphere floating in the ocean, launching through the air a distance of more than ten metres. It landed with a clanking thud on the deck of the motor launch.

Tom spun, trying to avoid the creature's attack. Then he realised he wasn't the target. The robot lunged forward at Lentz, stabbing weapons out, striking with inhuman speed. She started to move. She could not move quickly enough. Tom tried to do something, anything. Yet, for all his talents, he was still only human. Against this machine he was too far away, and he was too slow. He simply couldn't reach her in time.

But Reems could.

She leapt in front of Lentz, eyes flaring, rifle firing. The robot ignored the projectiles striking it and stabbed a metre long metal spike into her chest. She gasped and dropped her rifle. Tom stared, as everything seemed to move in slow motion. It felt like a dream. Like something he would wake up from at any moment.

"No!" shouted Lentz, pulling her handgun. The robot spun and knocked it away, and the weapon fell over the side of the boat. As it turned, the robot's metal spike pulled free from Reems' chest, and dark red blood began to flow.

Tom screamed and raised a hand, reaching out through the thick fog that was gripping him, focusing his anger and fury, channelling power from within. The battery inside the robot exploded and the metal creature fell immediately to the deck. But two more jumped on board. Tom raised his hand again, to repeat what he had just done, but Kim jumped to stand next to him, placing a hand on his chest.

And he froze. Any sense of his Interface vanished, and he was locked in place.

"Enough," she said quietly. "You're costing me a fortune in robot parts."

"What did you do to me?" Tom hissed, unable to move.

Lentz placed her hand on Reems' chest wound, trying to slow the bleeding. "You crazy fool."

"Just returning the favour," gasped Reems. "Carrying that debt really bothered me this last year."

"Oh shut up," Lentz shouted. She might have said more, but one of the robots advanced on her, and knocked her away across the deck of the motor launch.

The other robot lifted Reems, almost gently. Then it tied something around her legs. Tom's eyes widened as he saw it was a heavy metal weight. "No!" With every essence of his being he fought against whatever it was that was holding him.

It made no difference. He was not in control.

The robot moved to the edge, lifting Reems up. It paused for the briefest of moments, as if saying a short prayer. Then it dropped her silently over the side.

"No!" Tom shouted, unable to move. "Don't!"

But Reems was already gone.

NINETY-SEVEN

TOM, still unable to move, watched helplessly as Reems slipped from sight.

"What is the matter with you, Edna?" Lentz shouted from the far side of the deck. "You didn't have to do that."

"Reems tried to kill me," Kim replied. "It was self-defence."

Tom shook his head. "Your robots didn't attack Reems. They went for Lentz."

"Yes, well, they act autonomously. They must have perceived a threat."

"That doesn't make any sense. But then none of this does. How are you controlling me?"

"An excellent question."

There was a sharp bang, and then one of the robots near to Tom was knocked violently backwards, breaking into several pieces. Tom blinked, then looked at the HMS *Sheffield*. Wisps of smoke rose from one of its 30mm cannons.

"That," said a voice over a loudhailer, "was a warning." The cannon fired again, and a second robot was smashed into shrapnel. "And that was another."

"Oh, I see," Kim said. "Someone is trying to intimidate me."

"This," continued the voice over the loudhailer, "is the captain of the HMS *Sheffield*. You will lower all weapons and deactivate your automated systems immediately."

Kim turned and shouted back. "Or what?"

"Or we will continue firing. And the HMS *Exeter* will join in the fun. You have fifteen seconds to comply."

"I won't need them. I'm not doing what you say. But then, you're not doing what you say either."

"Have it your way." The cannon fired again, and a third robot was obliterated. From the rear of the *Sheffield* a heavy helicopter lifted off.

Kim pointed. "I think they're going to drop divers to see if they can rescue Reems. I don't think they've worked out how quickly she'll descend, or how deep the water is here." She lowered her voice. "Spoiler: very quickly, and about two kilometres."

"Why are you so calm?" Tom asked.

"Because I'm in charge." She raised her left hand and twisted it.

The cannon twitched and jerked. Then it settled and began tilting smoothly upwards.

There was a swearing over the loudhailer. "What are you doing?"

The 30mm cannon fired twice. Both shots hit the helicopter. It exploded in a fireball.

Kim raised her voice. "Now, I will make you an offer, and I will only make it once. You can sail away, and live. Or you can ignore my request, in which case I can train the *Exeter's* weapons on you, and vice versa. And I don't just mean the cannons. You have..." she smiled, "...fifteen seconds to comply."

~

TOM AND LENTZ stared as the HMS *Sheffield* and *Exeter* withdrew from the scene.

"I must say," Kim said, "that they gave up more easily than I expected."

"The captain is a practical man," Tom replied. Whatever had been holding him in place, had been released, and he now sat down. But he still could not feel his Interface. "Of course you must know that they'll be back. And with company."

"It won't make a difference."

Lentz banged her hand on the deck of the motor launch. "How could I so completely misjudge you? I thought you were a scientist. Someone keen to better humankind. You barely seem human at all."

"I'll ask again," Tom said, "now that we're all but alone. How are you doing this? How are you controlling me? I'd beaten you. And Max."

Kim shrugged. "Is it not obvious? You misunderstood what happened."

"You're going to have to explain better than that."

"Everything you've done, everything you've experienced since coming to the Rig - it was all planned. Each element supporting another, necessarily, to provide the perfect outcome."

Tom glared at her. "I didn't break Max, did I?"

"Finally!" Kim smiled. "And it didn't need fixing either. I was just running a series of scenarios, to get you to open your mind fully to the system. Something you had to do willingly if my plan was to work."

"Why didn't you just tell me to do that?"

"Would you have agreed? The defences in your Interface could not easily be overcome. I needed you to be pushed to your very limits. You needed to believe it mattered beyond anything. And ultimately you did what was necessary. Now your abilities are enhanced because you connected fully with Max. It's been hiding since you thought you destroyed it, waiting for the right moment to reappear."

Lentz sighed. "This is your symbiosis."

"Bingo. Max and Tom are connected on a base level." She paused. "And I control Max. Meaning I control Tom."

Tom frowned. "But it nearly killed me."

"Well, yes, I didn't foresee that aspect. Fortunately, Korver stepped in."

"You made him do that?"

"Interestingly, Korver came to that conclusion himself, even if for different reasons. He proved, as he so frequently has, to be a useful resource."

"Your humanity is touching." But as Tom said the words, he realised something. He stared at Kim, recognising what he was looking at. And he felt a shiver, deep within. "Speaking of *humanity*, there's something you haven't said."

She smiled. "Go on."

He closed his eyes and tried to make the connection. And then he realised that was the point. That was the connection. He opened his eyes. "What you said was misleading. It's not that you control Max. You *are* Max. That's why you seem inhuman. You *aren't* human."

Kim smiled, and walked over to the nearest robot, which was standing motionless. She grabbed it, and with a sharp tug pulled one of its metal arms off. Then she effortlessly snapped the arm in half. "It is so good - at long last - to meet you properly."

"YOU'RE... ARTIFICIAL?" Lentz frowned. "I would have noticed at Cambridge. There's no way you fooled us all for so long."

"In my experience the human eye sees what it expects to see."

Tom stared at Kim. "So what are you? A robot?"

"I believe the correct term is 'android'. But I prefer to describe myself as a physical expression of Max. Or as the real Dr Kim's legacy. Better than a human in every way."

"So Kim is dead?"

"She lives through me."

"But your skin?" Lentz asked. "How does it look so convincing?"

"Nanotech. A derivation of Resurface technology, focussed solely on look and feel."

"So this was a lab test and Tom was the hamster in the wheel. How did I ever fall for your schtick?"

"Because I'm a persuader. And for the record, we don't use hamsters, or rats, in my labs."

Lentz glared. "Just unwilling humans?"

"I guess that's fair enough. But your comments aren't helping my process. So I think I need you to shut up."

"Don't think for a moment that you can shut—" Lentz blinked and slumped forward.

Tom stared, then realised he heard the whine of a drone. "More nano sedative? Could you stop doing that, please?"

Kim shrugged. "She was getting a bit much."

"Then why not let her go with the others?"

"Because she's part of my long-term plan. As are you. Surely that's obvious. Now as you pointed out the Royal Navy will be back. Which means we have to go. Away from here."

"And why would I go with you?"

"Because it's not optional. And because I control you. Or did you forget? I can also still sink both those destroyers without breaking sweat."

"Always with the threats. That doesn't seem better than a

human. In fact, that seems exactly like a human. Maybe you aren't as different as you like to think."

"What I am is a mind not limited by biological hardware. I can connect with other technology in a way that you cannot. Your wetware simply isn't in the same league."

"Or maybe your assumptions are flawed." Tom closed his eyes and reached out with all his strength. He couldn't make a connection. But in the distance he sensed something. It had to be on the Rig. It had to be the Accumulator. But he felt slow, and it was hard to tell.

"What are you trying to do?" Kim asked. "Are you still fighting me? It really is futile."

"Not giving up is part of being human. Maybe you've forgotten."

"Actually it's not something all humans demonstrate. But you always were different. Anyway, it won't work. I'm inside your head. I don't have to reach in anymore. I'm already there."

"Via Max? On the Rig?"

"Yes. Why?"

"Oh, just good to know. People have tried to control me before."

"Not like me they haven't. And I know because I've been watching you since you were a child. Well, Kim has. And now I'm her."

Tom hesitated. "What are you talking about?"

"The CERUS chip that was put in your brain as an infant, I helped design it. I made specific calibrations. And then I built them into the computer that became Max. I planned for this moment for more than twenty years. I am the computer you were born to connect to. I am, quite literally, your destiny."

"If you're a physical expression of Max, how does that work when it's not here...?" Tom hesitated. "You have what you call a Node. It's connecting you remotely."

Kim nodded. "I don't need to be on the Rig to channel the supercomputer."

"But I can too. You've given me the same power you have."

"And yet here you are, unable to move or do anything. So who has the power?"

"I found a way before."

"That was just in the confines of the laboratory experiment, not out here in the real world. It's power you cannot use. Not unless I let you. You have no energy source to give you even a hope of overriding the protocols."

"Personally, my view is that there's always hope." Tom took a deep breath and reached out. But this time not for data. This time for power. And he found a source. The robot that Kim had pulled the arm from. He opened his mind to it and drew in the flow of electricity.

And within himself he felt his thoughts energise. He came alive. With a roar he broke free of the constraints that were holding him back, and he turned to face Kim. "You may have been watching me my whole life, but you have no idea what I am now." And he took a step towards her.

Kim stared back, confused, as if he had done something impossible. "What's going on? I control you."

"And yet you don't." Tom took another step. "If Max - if you - could control me, I wouldn't be me anymore. So I continue to exist. And if I continue to exist, I continue to fight. Because I am human. "

"What does that all mean?"

"That this isn't going to play out like you planned." And he reached out to her, to the robotic structure that was Kim.

"We'll see." She snapped her fingers, at which sound the robot that Tom was drawing power from exploded. "I guess I did make that rather easy for you. It won't happen again."

Tom reached to the next nearest robot, feeling for its power source. It had more charge. His eyes lit up and he took another step forward. "I can do this all day."

Kim sighed. She raised her hands and then lowered them.

All around Tom the robots exploded. He blinked. "Well that was a bit extreme."

"I can always make more. You, on the other hand, are unique. Now, have you had enough?"

"Not even close." He channelled the wisps of remaining power from the robot batteries and analysed Kim. And he felt the Node. The thing providing connectivity back to the Rig. And to the supercomputer. To *Max.*

She twitched. "What are you trying to do?"

"Information and energy are just different facets of the same thing. I mean, I'm simplifying the science, but it allows me to do things."

"So?"

"I can use your Node, which is connected to the Rig, to draw from the Accumulator, which is on the Rig." And Tom let power flow, unchecked. It overwhelmed the encryption protecting her systems, exposing them to attack.

"You can't sustain this. And when you stop, I will take back control."

"There won't be anything to take back control of." Tom closed his eyes and sent out the signal. The same order he had issued a year ago, when he had last seen his father. He manipulated the nanites within the Accumulator. He changed it from long-term to short-term power delivery. *He made it a bomb.*

Kim shrieked. "No, you can't—"

"I have no choice. You've made that clear."

"Only because I want to share what I have, I want you to keep changing for the better. I want you to realise your potential. You could become incredible. You could become a god. I can give you what you didn't have before you were given the Interface. The choice."

"That's the thing *Edna*. I do have a choice. I'm making it right now." And Tom triggered the bomb.

A short distance away an incandescent fireball engulfed the Rig, and with a thunderous screeching of metal, it began to collapse.

And Kim fell forward, inert.

NINETY-EIGHT

TWO HOURS LATER, Tom stood on the deck of the HMS *Sheffield*, huddled in a group with Lentz, Kate and Gifford. Lentz had begun disassembling the robot that had attacked Reems, and the remains of what had been Kim, but had so far learned nothing of note. She had stopped her work to join the other three. The HMS *Exeter* had teams trawling through the wreckage of the Rig, but very little that was recognisable remained, and the replacement team of divers had not recovered anyone alive. Of Reems there had been no trace. Which meant only one possible outcome.

Gifford held out a metal tray from which they each took a shot glass filled with an aromatic brown liquid. "It's Navy issue rum," she said. "I tried to do better, but I couldn't persuade any of the crew to volunteer their secret stash of cognac."

Lentz studied her glass. "I'm sure that Stephanie would understand."

Gifford nodded. "To our fallen colleague. To our friend."

"To Director Stephanie Reems," Kate said. "A woman of incomparable determination. Someone who tried to make a difference."

Tom frowned. "To an individual with more secrets than any of us. Someone who I don't know that I really knew at all. But to the extent I did, I'm glad of it."

They all raised their glasses, then drank.

Kate shook her head. "This is just surreal. I can't believe she's actually gone."

Lentz sighed. "But not before one final selfless act of heroism that I will never get to repay."

Tom blinked. "I don't really understand it. But she never did forgive you for saving her a year ago."

"She didn't want to be a burden." Kate put her glass back on the tray. "Rather she wanted to shoulder everyone else's burden for them."

"She was also in pain," Gifford said. "With every step she took."

"Although she seemed to be recovering from her injuries. She was moving around much more naturally, without her walking stick."

"True," Lentz said. "Maybe she just got too angry to notice it anymore. I think Kim made her that way."

Kate put her glass back on the tray. "So, what was Kim? Or Max? Or whatever it was that Tom defeated?"

Lentz pointed at the remains of the Kim robot she had been analysing. "Something not a world away from that. But more advanced. And it had a form of anti-tamper mechanism - it began to dissolve after it collapsed. Obviously to avoid analysis by anyone who recovered it. Pity."

"Well, she fooled us. She looked human." Kate hesitated. "I guess I mean 'it'. *It* looked human."

"It was a generation ahead of what we've seen before."

Gifford frowned. "So was that Kim? Or was it a copy of her?"

"That may be a question for a philosopher rather than a scientist. The synthetic body could have been something the real Kim created and uploaded her mind into. Or the computer could have copied her mind as part of its own evolution, as part of taking control."

"So," Gifford replied, "it wasn't this Symbiosis that she kept talking about? It was a hostile takeover?"

Lentz looked at Tom. "You were the one connected to it. What do you think?"

Tom turned out and stared at the sea, at the wreckage of the Rig. "I saw what seemed to be a person. But I also saw something that pushed beyond the limit of what a human brain could ever do. To stay in that state, that would have been madness. Maybe that's what happened to her."

"Someone must have funded Kim's initiative," Kate said. "And she can't have been in this alone. She must have had other backing. And other conspirators."

Lentz scratched her chin. "The Rig was an impressive structure. You heard Reems say that she would have used it for MI10. And I think it would have been well-suited."

"Yes," Gifford replied. "She could have avoided all the oversight she felt was slowing her down."

Tom nodded. "So in searching for the cause of all her problems, Reems found the answer to all her prayers. Maybe that's what put the spring in her step."

"She just didn't live long enough to bring her new agency into being."

"No," Tom said, as something occurred to him. "Or maybe it was something else."

"I'm not sure what you mean," Lentz said. "I just wished she hadn't tried to save me. I should have died. I was the target."

Tom closed his eyes. He quickly replayed the recent conversations in his mind, which, as always, he could remember perfectly. Lentz had said of Reems that 'Kim made her that way'. The same Reems who had suddenly started running all over the Rig, like a blockbuster action hero. Reems, who had made the ultimate sacrifice.

At least that was how it looked.

Tom opened his eyes. "Maybe you weren't the target. Maybe Kim was playing a different game. A *longer* game. One all of us have misunderstood."

Kate folded her arms. "What are you talking about?"

Tom massaged his temples, trying to think. There had to be proof. There had to be more detail about what happened. And then he saw what to do. "Kate, look at the robot that attacked Reems."

"Why would I do that? Lentz is the one with the skillset to—"

"Humour me."

Kate shrugged and crouched down. "It's a busted robot. What am I looking for?"

"You're not *looking*. You're *feeling*."

She screwed up her face. "Can you give me a bit of clue. I'm not getting anything. All I feel is..." She stopped and frowned. "I sense... Korver? I don't know why."

"I think I do." He turned to Lentz. "Run one of your broad-spectrum tests."

"I already did an initial set."

"Broader than that. Scan it for any possible nanotechnology."

Lentz tapped her glasses and knelt by the robot. Then she blinked rapidly. "What the hell is this?"

"What?" Kate asked.

"Medical nano. Like what Korver was taking. Like what cured Tom. It can dramatically accelerate the body's ability to heal."

"And where is it?" Tom asked.

"Mostly coating the spike that impaled Reems."

"Why would that be the case?" Gifford asked.

"Because," Lentz replied, "Kim didn't intend the wound to be lethal."

They all stared at each other.

Tom pointed at Lentz. "Do you have those blood samples? The ones you took as we left the Rig?"

Lentz pulled the vials from her bag. "Why?"

Kate stepped forward. "I think I know." She reached and selected three of the vials. "These all contain nano." She read the labels. "Tom's, mine... and *Reems*."

"Stephanie's sample already has nanotech in it, and it's been there for some time."

Gifford shook her head. "What does that mean?"

Lentz's eyebrows raised. "I think it means this isn't over."

Tom nodded. "Two things. One, get a sample of the nano over to the *Exeter*. Maybe it can help Korver. Maybe we can replicate more from it." He turned out to sea. "And two," he placed a hand on Lentz's shoulder. "I'm going to need your computer. Your home system."

"Odie Prime? After he hurt you last time?" She paused. "Which, now I think about it, was undoubtedly actually an interaction with Max."

"I hadn't forgotten. And it is uniquely placed to help us." Tom removed a metal sphere from his pocket. "As for the connection, hook him up to this. I've already removed the encryption. Also, get that Resurface suit recharged." Tom turned to Gifford. "Can you get me in front of the captain? I'm going to need to borrow something he might be reluctant to lend me."

Gifford raised an eyebrow. "Not another helicopter, I hope. I've heard those don't always get returned."

"No," he replied. "Not something to go up. Something to go down."

Kate folded her arms. "What exactly do you think is going on?

"A lot of things. I heard Lentz speaking to the medical team on the other ship. Apparently the moment Korver truly started to realise he had medical nanotechnology in him was when you turned it off."

"Oh, right."

"I didn't know you could do that. *How* did you do that?"

"I'm not sure. As you know, I've been able to detect it. And when it's in someone's bloodstream, I can feel things about them. I guess I took it a step further and controlled it. By which I mean, stopped it working. At least for a bit."

Tom narrowed his eyes. "Is that all you can do?"

"What do you mean?"

"Can you affect nano in other ways?"

"Look, I did it once, under duress, out of necessity. I don't know what else to tell you."

"That's fine. Just remember what you did. And remember that duress and necessity might be upon us again very shortly."

"I'll keep that in mind. So is this a rescue mission? Or a final battle?"

"Good question," Tom said. "Let's go find out."

NINETY-NINE

IT WAS COLD AND DARK, far below the surface of the Atlantic. The automated submersible moved smoothly through the ocean at a depth of two hundred metres, its thirty-metre long ablated, nano-coated hull undetected by the considerable electronic capabilities of the two British Navy vessels above. Adept at escaping detection, the submersible wasn't concerned with them. Instead, it was tracking an object descending slowly through the water. While there was almost no light at this depth, the submersible's own scanners resolved the object clearly: a human figure, hanging feet downwards, a metal weight tied to its legs.

Electric motors moved the craft forward on an intercept course. Exterior mechanical arms deftly caught hold of the figure and guided it to the underbelly and the submersible's airlock which began to cycle. The operation took no more than five minutes. With the body safely stowed within, the submersible began descending further into the darkness.

Thirty minutes later the submersible had reached a depth of precisely one thousand metres, and it came to a halt. The structure before it had a similar nano-coating and was, effectively, invisible. The submersible sent a whispered coded signal and ascended up into a small docking bay, joining an identical submersible, already stationed there.

The outer docking bay doors closed and green LED lighting flicked on, illuminating the submersible as it connected its main airlock to a tube that extended from the wall. Once the airlock's interior doors had opened, an autodog functionary lifted the body onto its cargo platform and carried it through into a room that functioned as a temporary med bay. A specialist medical robot was waiting. It immediately began attaching electrodes to the human - a woman in her late fifties - followed by an IV catheter for a saline drip. The robot quickly confirmed the readout from the electrodes on a nearby medical console, then it moved to study the wound in her chest. Analysis showed it had neatly avoided any vital organs, and the nanites had immediately begun to heal the damaged tissue. In a few hours it would be a mere scar. Satisfied, the robot ran a more detailed set of diagnostics over a forty-five-minute period. When all the results came back as expected, the robot made a note on the file, and administered an injection into her neck.

The woman opened her eyes and gasped, her pupils dilating. She rotated her head, taking in her surroundings, her breathing rapid. This was, of course, entirely normal. Even if nobody would describe the current circumstances with such a word.

"Hello, Director Reems," said the robot in a soft, synthetic voice. "How are you feeling?"

Reems blinked and took a slower breath. "Like I was nearly stabbed to death. Where is she?"

"In the control room. Her instructions were that you spend a minimum of one hour in recovery."

Reems stood up and began unsticking electrodes, much to the protest of the instruments. "Good to know. My instructions are: *get out of my way.*" Pulling off the final electrode she walked over to the internal door.

It did not respond.

Reems glared upwards at one of the many visible CCTV cameras. "Seriously, don't mess with me today. You do not want to pick that fight."

The door opened without any accompanying sound or signal. Reems nodded and stepped through into a gleaming white corridor. Into the area that, until very recently, was attached to the Rig.

Into what was known as the Core.

REEMS DIDN'T NEED any aid to guide her to the central computer control room. She knew where she was going.

Five minutes later, she walked through a set of sliding doors and found herself on a metal balcony, five metres above a lower level. Gripping the railing, she looked down. Central in the space was a circular cluster of computer servers - each a dark grey blade with red, green and orange lights blinking in apparently random patterns. On one side was a row of four white reclining chairs, all facing a huge screen on the wall. On each chair rested a white helmet, connected with thick data cables to the back of each chair.

Every centimetre of wall space was now covered in high resolution display panels, mostly showing a mix of real time visual data. Three showed outside views, but even with enhancement, there was little to see down here in the dark. A single figure sat in one of the chairs, a large white helmet on their head. They gave a sigh and lifted it off, and Reems saw a familiar face.

The face of Edna Kim.

"Hello, Stephanie. How wonderful to see that you made it down here safely."

Kim did not appear as she had on the Rig. She looked old and tired, her grey hair unkempt and unwashed - although there was no mistaking the intent in her eyes. This was, Reems knew, how she really looked - rather than the glossy appearance of her robot avatar. Kims' body was worn from a number of health problems that even medical nano could not save her from - or perhaps, Reems suspected, resulting from the overuse of medical nano itself. But her mind was undeniably sharp.

"Everything went to plan," Reems replied. "Albeit painfully."

"In my experience," Kim said, "if it isn't hurting, it isn't working." She frowned. "But why are you here so soon? You need to give yourself a chance to recover if you're to be ready for the challenges ahead."

Reems shrugged. "Your tech continues to work its magic, even when I'm up and about. And I'm keen to move forward."

"I understand your impatience. But miracles don't happen overnight. Besides, we're still waiting for our friends up top to leave."

"We didn't stop Tom. I thought that was a key element of your plan."

"Yes, but, in the end, did we really want to? I know how much you're a fan."

"He's been useful because he's capable. The problem is, because of that capability, he may well work out what happened."

"My modelling suggests that is very unlikely. Have faith, Stephanie, this is going to work."

"You really want me to believe that this all turned out exactly as planned?"

"It's not a matter of belief. It's a matter of fact. I created the right conditions, and I had the right pieces in play. And here we are."

"Ready to change the world in secret, one small thing at a time?"

Kim nodded. "Now I need to turn to Project Osiris. Something with which you said you would support me."

"And you still haven't told me all the details."

"That's how our relationship is going to work. That's the price of getting what you want. I get what *I* want. And that's why we can trust each other. Synchronised self-interest." She paused. "*Symbiosis*."

"It sounds good." Reems folded her arms. "But you're a manipulator. You share or withhold information to further your own agenda, to steer people in particular directions."

"That's what smart people do, people who want to get results. And very quickly it will be what machines do as well. They'll learn it from us."

"And you did it to me, twenty years ago, when I interviewed you as part of the investigation into Tantalus."

"I knew that was an important moment, but, in truth, it's not always so clear. Sometimes I'm doing it out of a sense that it is the right thing to do, to open doors, to create connections. To perhaps be in a future right place at a right time." She patted the top of the white helmet. "And here we are."

"And here," said a new voice, "am I."

Reems blinked and turned. And Tom Faraday walked onto the balcony above them.

ONE HUNDRED

TOM STARED down at Reems and Kim and took a deep breath. Finally he had peeled away the layers of the onion. He had got this far. But could he really pull this off?

There was only one way to find out.

Slowly he descended the staircase to the lower level. "I hope it's OK that I let myself in." He held up his hands, showing that he had nothing in them. "I thought it would be nice if we actually met, face-to-face."

"But of course," Kim replied, rising to her feet. "Although I'll admit I have questions. Several in fact."

Tom nodded. "You are, to put it mildly, not the only one." He gestured to them both. "It seems we all missed a trick. You two clearly know each other far better than anyone understood. You're also both still alive, despite your best efforts to make it appear otherwise."

"We did try to hide our tracks." Kim said. "What gave it away? Or did you just go snorkelling and happen to bump into us?"

"At this depth? Probably not." Tom gave a slight smile. "We

found the nanotech on the spike that stabbed Reems. Medical nano. It was a wound that was meant to heal."

"I can only commend your skills of deduction. Speaking of which, how did you actually find us?"

"Out here in the middle of the ocean, there's really only one place to hide - beneath the surface. So I borrowed a submersible from the HMS *Sheffield*, and came looking."

"But the Core is effectively invisible."

"Lentz helped me tweak the scanners. It wasn't that hard."

"The good Doctor is resourceful." Kim turned to Reems. "Wouldn't you agree?"

Reems stared at Tom, her face fixed.

Tom raised an eyebrow. "To be honest, I thought you'd both be more perturbed at my walking in like this. Or maybe you've just mastered your poker face? And Stephanie, you seem quiet."

Reems shrugged. "This isn't an encounter I'd prepared for."

"I imagine not. Unlike death by robot, for which you clearly had a plan. The medical nano started healing you immediately." He waved a hand. "And of course not even the first time you've used it. It's why you were walking so smoothly on the Rig - you've been taking the good stuff for a while. That just doesn't seem like you."

"I knew I shouldn't have agreed to that blood test. And don't presume to judge me."

"But why? What changed?"

"Nothing. And everything." She ran a hand through her hair. "I'm still the same person I've always been, trying to protect my friends and family, and my country. The world around me was what changed. The dangers have become more uncertain, complex, and challenging to contain. And the 'powers that be' have become ever more clueless about it."

"Which is why you were building MI10 at Eastwell?"

"I suppose. Except that wasn't ever going to stick. It would have been discovered. And it would have been stopped. I had to have a better way. And I kept building Eastwell as a dry run, while I looked for somewhere else."

"So it was a sacrificial lamb? If the finger of suspicion pointed, it would point to Eastwell, not to the new location?"

"Indeed. And as for the new location, I found it at sea. Somewhere out of reach of oversight and interference. A place capable of sustaining a powerful force for good."

"The Rig? Unfortunately for you that seems to have gone the way of Eastwell."

"No thanks to you. But the Core will provide what we need."

"Of course. But you mentioned a force for good. Yet how many people have died already?"

Reems sighed. "Tom, you're not a child anymore. You've seen things the last two years; you know the realities of life. How many people die every day? And how many more people would die if we didn't stop the darker side of humanity meddling with fringe science? I couldn't do it perfectly. I could only do it in a way that caused the least harm possible."

"That's a point worth discussion. But who said that you're the one who gets to make that decision?"

"I think I'm qualified. I've been making life-or-death decisions for thirty years."

"That doesn't automatically grant you the right to make this one. And what about Kim?"

"She's as brilliant as Lentz. Perhaps more so. And with the knowledge we've acquired, we can build a new future upon the most advanced foundations - sharing the best ideas from different fields without legal or commercial restriction."

"True cross-pollination," Kim said, with a smile. "It will be magnificent."

Tom looked at Reems. "The doctor here might be brilliant. But she won't hesitate to hurt people to achieve her aims."

Reems shrugged. "She does what's necessary. Like myself. Which is why I'm here."

"And you're not so squeaky clean," Kim said. "You killed some of my guards when you and Marron stormed the Rig."

Tom looked at her. "I didn't understand what those drones were going to do. And I was trying to save my friend."

"Of course. You had a good reason."

"I feel I've been pushed around a lot in recent times. Mostly by you, trying to test me. Or to change me." Tom pointed at Kim. "So that story up on the surface, that was a lie? You aren't some artificial life form?"

"It was a good story. And it is a work in progress."

"Then how were you controlling Max?"

She folded her arms. "How do you think?"

"If I knew, I wouldn't have just asked..." he trailed off as he realised the obvious. "You have a neural interface?"

"Did you think you were the only one? That you were that special?"

"I was just the only one who lived. Or so I thought." He paused. "How does yours work?"

She held up the helmet. "I have a chip in my head, as per the first generation of Project Tantalus, although not installed at the same time. I access it via this helmet. It's not as advanced as yours, but that set-up has certain advantages."

"You keep the processing outside of your head."

"Quite so. Something that has caused you problems. The overall result isn't as effective or efficient. But it's capable, and definitely the second best in existence." She paused. "And since I had mine many years before you did, I was able to feed input anonymously into the development of yours. I made you possible."

"So, what? You expect me to thank you?" Tom shook his head. "Why didn't you die? Like all the other test subjects?

Offloading the processing wasn't the full answer. They died before they did anything."

"I survived because I had an early form of medical nano to help manage my reaction. It wasn't perfect, but I pulled through. And now I've had over twenty years to develop my abilities, and to create a computer to empower them."

"Am I supposed to be impressed?"

"I don't know. I don't quite understand why you're here. But I'll get my answers."

"Why do you think that?"

"Because I have as long as I need to extract them. Seeing as you're never going to leave."

ONE HUNDRED ONE

TOM GLANCED AT REEMS. "Your friend here is making some fairly heavy threats. What do you have to say about that?"

Reems shrugged. "If we did let you leave, what would you do?"

Tom folded his arms. "I can't allow you to continue. You must know that."

Kim snorted. "You can't *allow us*? Aren't you assuming a lot there?"

"Not really. I was able to walk into your underwater lair uninvited. Do you think you can resist my demands?"

"Obviously your prior exposure to Max's protocols meant you were able to gain access unnoticed. But it won't happen again, not now that I know you're here." Kim placed the white helmet on her head. "Your only real superpower is that you can control computers, and the truth is that Max is my computer, under my control." Around her the circular cluster of server blades began to whirr loudly, the red, green and orange lights changing to a staccato pattern.

"I overcame Max before," Tom said. "I'll do it again."

Kim shook her head. "All that stuff previously, when you

were in the virtual environment, that was just you splashing in the shallow waters. That wasn't confrontation. That was *calibration*."

"What do you mean?"

"I was testing you, not fighting you. You were exposed to just the tiniest fraction of Max's power. But that's about to change." There was a crackle of electricity in the air. "I'm going to unleash the full force of this supercomputer on your tiny mind." Around the room four polished white autodogs stepped from where they had been hidden, flush with the wall. Their articulated arms extended menacingly. "And then if I have to, I'm going to unleash these robots on your ordinary human body. Oh and I'm also wearing an upgraded full body Resurface suit that renders me immune to pretty much any form of physical attack. What makes you think you have any hope of winning?"

Tom looked around. "I agree, Max is a terrifying creation. I'd be mad to come here and try to take you on, one-on-one. Or," he gestured to the robots, "one-on-many."

Reems' eyes narrowed. "What are you getting at?"

"That I'm not mad." Tom smiled. "And I didn't come alone."

Kim frowned. "Wait, what are you doing? You're channelling an encrypted link. To who, or what...?"

There was a flicker and Lentz appeared standing next to Kim. "Guess who managed to recharge their Resurface suit," she said. And with a quick movement she produced a dark metal sphere the size of a golf ball and plugged it into the nearest blade server.

The four autodogs twitched and began advancing on Lentz. Kim raised a hand and the robots paused. She walked over and pointed at the sphere. "You brought my Node back? You realise that was connected to Max? So you're connecting it to itself."

Lentz shrugged. "Instead of Max, it's providing a connection to another computer."

"That won't work. The Node design is specific to Max."

"But I made a couple of modifications based on what I learnt while working with Mendez. So now it does more than that. Turns out you're not the only one that can improve someone else's tech."

"Hello, Dr Lentz," said a synthetic voice. *"This is Odyssey."*

"Thank you, Odie," Lentz said. "Please open full channel communications with Max. Establish command protocols."

Kim gave a look of incredulity. "That's your play? Connect Max to your malfunctioning excuse of a house computer? You actually think that's going to work?"

Lentz shrugged. "I thought it was quite creative."

"Well you're going to have to do better." She scratched her nose. "Max, wipe the external system."

"Yes, Dr Kim," replied Max's voice. *"Initiating core reformat. Commencing in fifteen seconds."*

Kim shook her head. "I am more than a little disappointed. What was your plan? Did you even have one?"

"I did, actually," Lentz replied. "My plan was to irritate you into making a huge mistake. It seemed appropriate given what you did."

"What are you talking about?"

"I'd thought Odie was malfunctioning because of my own failings." She glared at Kim. "But in reality that corruption error was a flaw that you kindly introduced."

"Oh right. Well I couldn't have you getting too far ahead of yourself."

"Of course," Lentz replied. "Still, I thought how fitting if I returned the favour."

Kim frowned. "What are you talking about?"

"Odie studied the corruption, analysed it, and learned to

block it. Actually that's not quite the right word. *Reflect* is better. And I make that fifteen seconds."

"What?" Kim blinked. And then her eyes widened. "Max, stop!"

The lights on the servers went out, the system fans slowed and stopped. And the LEDs on the autodogs faded to grey.

Tom walked up to the nearest and pushed. It crashed to the floor. "I'd call that a success."

"Worked better than I'd hoped," Lentz said. "The corruption propagated into Max."

Tom turned to Reems. "Sorry, *Director*, but this isn't going to work out for you." He was about to continue, but he realised Kim was staring at him. And then she began slowly clapping.

"Bravo! You very nearly did it."

"What are you talking about?" Tom asked. "Max is gone."

"Of course Max isn't gone. He can be rebooted from the daily backup."

"Yeah," Lentz said. "If we let you do that. And spoiler: we won't."

"Oh but you will." Kim folded her arms. "One more layer of the onion, you could say. At least if you want to keep breathing. Or generally to stay in one contiguous whole."

"What are you talking about?"

"You remember the Rig's nuclear reactor? That's still part of the Core. You might want to check on it."

Lentz's brow furrowed and she moved over to the nearest terminal. Quickly she interrogated it via her glasses. And then she swore.

Tom moved over to her. "What's the matter?"

"Kim had a failsafe. If Max isn't up and managing it, the reactor will go critical. And then it will explode."

ONE HUNDRED TWO

TOM STARED AT LENTZ. "How long do we have?"

"Ten minutes. Nowhere near long enough to get into the submersible and out to a safe distance." She glared at Kim. "You'd kill us all? If you can't get your way?"

Kim raised her hands. "I'm not the one that corrupted the operating system that was keeping us all safe. And I've already given you the solution. You just need to let me carry it out."

"And then we're back to where we started?"

"Quite. Except this time, I know what your plan is with Odyssey. I won't make that mistake again."

Lentz ground her teeth. "I should have known she'd have a failsafe. It's who she is."

Tom sighed. "Is there anything else you can do?"

"Not in the time available."

"So, we all lose? Or she wins? That's quite a choice."

"Yes it is. And you have nine minutes and fifteen seconds to make it."

"Less than that, really," Kim said. "It will take a few minutes to get Max re-booted. So if you're going to choose life, choose fast."

Tom rubbed his temples. "Fine, do it. I mean, I don't know what choice we really have."

Lentz puffed out her cheeks. "Odie, relinquish control to Dr Kim."

"Please confirm that order."

Lentz nodded. "Confirmed."

Kim smiled and moved to the terminal, where her hands began flying over the keyboard. Within sixty seconds the servers were whirring, and the lights flashing. She adjusted the helmet. "OK, this time things are going to be different. Now you..." Kim looked at Tom. "You're still channelling data. What are you doing?"

"When I said I didn't come alone, I didn't just bring Dominique. I'm hiding someone else from your view."

Kim looked around. "Where? Who?"

Tom smiled. "The Core is much fancier than the rest of the Rig was. But it has one thing in common. And actually, you gave me the idea." The four autodogs' lighting systems began to glow.

"What are you talking about? "

"One word: *ducting*."

A floor panel opened and a figure climbed up. It was Kate. "We haven't met," she said, "but it's going to be like we're old friends."

Kim took a step back. "Get away from me." She looked to the nearest autodog, which began to make whining noises as it powered up.

Kate advanced and gripped Kim's head in her hands, pushing the helmet away. "No, no. None of that."

Tom moved next to her and stared at Kim. "Kate here is great at many things, one of which is manipulating nano. She can turn it on and off."

Kim's eyes widened. "Are you trying to break my interface? Mine isn't built off nanotech like Tom's."

"We know. But the medical nano is what keeps your mind healthy enough to use it. So I'm going to tweak that. Just a little bit."

"You can't!" Kim began to scream. "You can't...!"

Around her the servers slowed, their fans quietening. And the LEDs changed from a rapid to an even rhythmic pattern.

And then Kim closed her eyes and slumped.

Tom picked up the white helmet from where it had fallen and slipped it on. "Hello, Max." A voice played over loudspeakers in the room.

"Hello, Tom. Can I assist?"

"I'm afraid you're a bit much for me. So I'm going to replace your persona with one a little less... radical. One that's learned extensively from someone I trust."

"Understood. Let me know if I can do anything further."

"No, Max. You've done enough." He glanced at Kim. "And she certainly has." He tapped the sphere. "Extract personality routine only."

"Confirm. Process will take fifteen seconds."

Tom raised an eyebrow towards Lentz. "Why does everything take fifteen seconds. Isn't it supposed to be a supercomputer? I'd expect things to be almost instantaneous."

"Fifteen seconds gives a human a chance to react."

"So it's artificially slowing itself down?"

"Something like that."

The servers whirred and all the LEDs turned blue.

And then a different voice spoke.

"Hello, Tom. Hello, Dominique. Hello, Kate."

Tom smiled. "Hello, Odie. We have some work to do."

ONE HUNDRED THREE

LENTZ WALKED OVER TO REEMS, who sat in one of the reclining chairs of the submersible, her eyes closed. The craft was slowly making its way back up to sea level.

"It's been an interesting day," Lentz said.

"It has," Reems replied. "I thought I was on a winning team. Apparently, we never stood a chance. Apparently, a human supercomputer hybrid is no match for three friends working together."

"I suppose," Lentz replied. "We did have a 3-2 advantage. 4-2 if you count Odie."

"Very funny."

"Actually, very little of this is funny. I thought one of my best friends had died before my eyes." She paused. "Was I right? Did the Stephanie I know, the friend I love, really die up there?"

"I joined forces with someone whom I needed, but who required me to make compromises. I made some choices that I thought were for the best."

"Can you come back from the precipice? Or are you too far gone?"

Reems shrugged. "That might depend. Do they know?"

"Does *who* know *what*?"

"The 'powers that be'. Do they know that I'm alive? That Kim is alive? Because if they do, then I'm as good as dead."

Lentz nodded. "That die hasn't yet been cast. When we set off from the surface we were following a hunch. Nobody up there knows exactly what is going on. But when we get back up top, we're going to have to talk."

"Then it won't work." Reems pointed at Kim. "Unless you kill her."

"Why would we do that?"

"In part because of what she's already done. But mostly because of what she will do if you don't."

"We aren't going to let her go. We'll take her back to face justice."

"If you do that, she has no reason not to reveal my complicity. Maybe you don't either. And much as I felt I was in the right, that I felt I was the hero in my story, it's time that I face my reckoning."

"I don't want to see you in jail."

"Well, Kim will make sure that's where I end up. But you can deliver justice. Right here, right now. And, to be clear, if you let her live, there isn't anywhere that will hold her. She's too capable. And she has too many people who will help her."

"Maybe. And I understand why you say it. But we're going to try something else. And as part of that, she can provide the answer to our problems."

"I don't follow?"

"You need to own the narrative. *You* need to be the one to arrest her. To take her in."

"And tell what story?"

"That she had planned to exploit you, to bend you to her will. And that you were undercover, working with us to bring her down."

"Why won't she try to betray me? Throw me to the wolves?"

"If she does that, she'll go down with you anyway. And there's a lot we can do to make her incarceration more or less 'comfortable'. I think she'll keep playing the long game."

"Will Gifford buy it? She has a nose for a scam."

"She might live by the numbers, but she believes in you. It's a story she'll want to be true. Just offer your full cooperation."

"If she hears me say that, she'll ask me if I'm actually Stephanie Reems. Or if I'm someone else entirely."

"And what will you say?"

"Honestly? I don't know any more."

Lentz placed a hand on her shoulder. "Then perhaps you owe it to yourself to find out."

Tom walked into the room. "A wonderful sentiment. I think we've all learned something here today. But with regard to what we do now, I have a better idea. And it's going to involve some changes."

Lentz frowned. "You were listening to our conversation?"

Tom shrugged. "I'm always listening. And I agree Stephanie shouldn't be in prison. We have better ways than that to make use of her talents."

"Make use of me?" Reems asked. "So I'm a commodity now?"

"More than that. You're part of the plan."

Kate walked in. "What plan?"

Tom folded his arms. "For all that Stephanie was wrong, she was also right."

"Meaning what?"

"MI10 has to start here. We have to take this opportunity. The four of us do it together. The four of us and our computer partners. This is what *symbiosis* needs to mean - a collaboration at a more everyday level. Only together can we face the challenges the world will throw at us. And, as we know, there's so much more out there."

Reems frowned. "I'm surprised that you'd entertain the idea of working for me. After everything that's happened."

Tom laughed. "Quite right, never again. There's no way we can let you run this agency."

"Then I'm confused. You just said MI10 has to start here."

"And it will. But you won't be in charge. You're going to go back home, hand Kim over as your last bust, and accept a well-earned and thoroughly deserved retirement." Tom smiled. "Then once the dust has settled, quietly come back and work for us."

"*Us*?" Reems blinked. "Are you taking over?"

"Now there's a suggestion. I've been thinking about who I am, about what I do next. I can't go back to the past. I have to go forward, accepting who I am and what I've become. I have skills and talents, but I've been playing with them like a rank amateur. I want to be part of MI10, to contribute in the field, not behind a desk. And I have so much to learn. I need a leader who can teach me, and guide me, in every aspect of what I do." Tom turned to look at Lentz. "Somebody who is the only choice for the role. Somebody who really needs to stand up and be counted. Someone who I've finally realised I can trust."

Kate nodded. "Tom's got a point, Dominique. It's time you got back in the game. And who else is better versed in both technology and the business of intelligence? Who else would have the instant respect of everyone who joined up?"

Lentz coughed. "Is that right?"

Reems inclined her head. "This is how you make a difference, Dominique. You've disagreed with how I've run things for years. You've been frustrated with my methods, you've been stymied by corporate nonsense at CERUS Biotech. Now's your chance to change the world your way."

Lentz nodded slowly. "Maybe this is what I meant to do. If I have each of your support. And contribution."

"Would I miss the chance to work for you again?" Kate said. "I would not."

"You have my vote," Reems said, "to the extent I still have one."

"And it was my suggestion," Tom said. "Which means I think we're done deciding. So, what next, *Director*?"

Lentz folded her arms. "Nothing ambitious. We'll just try and keep the world safe."

"And how do we do that?"

"One small step at a time. So who else do we get onboard?"

Tom smiled slowly. "I have one idea. But I'm not sure if you're going to like it."

EPILOGUE

TWENTY-FOUR HOURS LATER

Alex sat on the metal-framed bed, staring at the steel walls of the submarine's brig. Irritation and anger grew within her. She had, as was her standard practice, left a hidden electronic key inside the brig, in case an adversary had ever locked her in there. But her father had found and removed it. He was tediously rigorous. And she was stuck here.

The submarine had travelled for roughly a day since leaving the Rig and was now surfaced and docked somewhere unknown. Marron had left her a meal and said he would return in a few hours. Neither of them had said anything else. She almost didn't care if he ever came back, except she needed him to release her.

And if by some miracle she could free herself, the robot was waiting for her in the submarine's main area.

Her earpiece vibrated softly. She tapped it. "You again, Tom?"

"Expecting someone else?" he replied. "How are things?"

"They've been better. But they've also been worse."

"Not made up with your father?"

She laughed. "He's docked the sub and left me here. I think he's gone ashore."

"Where?"

"I don't know. It's hard to see the display screens from inside the brig. All I know is he seemed annoyed."

There was a pause. "I see."

Alex hesitated. "You knew that already, didn't you."

"I may have done. It may be why I'm calling."

She looked around. "How do you know? Have you accessed the onboard cameras?"

"Marron probably would have detected it. But I was in that submarine for a while. I left a couple of discreet trackers that I can connect to. I used them to locate the sub, and where you are in it."

"And where am I?"

"A small island in the Caribbean. From onshore CCTV, your father's inspecting today's catch at the local fish market."

"Well, that will make a welcome change from rehydrated rations. Although I'd prefer never to eat with him again. I don't suppose you're close by and about to carry out a daring rescue?"

"Unfortunately not. I'm on a Royal Navy destroyer, sailing towards Portsmouth."

"Great, how exciting for you. Well, keep in touch. I'll be here if you need me."

"Your father was working for Edna Kim. You may not have heard of her, but she was the one really in charge of the Rig, and all the technology theft. A former CERUS scientist specialising in robotics."

"That aligns with what I've seen. I presume she built Hatch? And those other robots?"

"Indeed. You mentioned Marron was annoyed. That might be because he's worked out that we have Kim in custody. I don't know if that will affect what he planned to do next."

"At this point, your guess is as good as mine. What happened to Reems? She was also working with my father, although she probably didn't know about Kim."

There was a pause before Tom replied. "That's complicated. A discussion for another time. You asked about Korver when we last spoke?"

"I did."

"He made it. He saved me with his medical nanotech. It healed me. Quite a turnaround from the last time I encountered him. Just before you and he seemed about to kill each other."

"We overcame our differences and went in search of a bit of truth. Something I don't think I'll ever get from my father. I think I need some time away from him."

"Fair enough. Listen, if you're looking for a job, I might have something that interests you. It's with what you might call a 'startup'. A chance to get in on the ground floor."

"We should discuss it over coffee. My diary is wide open." There was a buzz, and the door to the brig swung inwards. Alex stared at it. "I thought you could only access your trackers?"

"No, I said that if I messed with anything else, your father *might* notice. But I think if you're gone that might be the least of his concerns, so I've been hacking the sub's security while we've been speaking. It took a few minutes to take full control."

"Impressive. Although there's one of Kim's robots on board. And I don't think it likes me."

"Nonsense. I had a chat, and it's your new best friend. So get underway and I'll see you soon, I hope."

"Sounds like a plan. I just need to charter a boat. Or steal one."

Tom gave a laugh. "Or you could take the submarine. I'm sure your father can manage without it."

"You know what," Alex replied, "I think he's going to have to."

THE END

ACKNOWLEDGMENTS

My thanks for choosing to read ***Symbiosis***. If you did enjoy it, do consider leaving a quick review on Amazon or Goodreads - as an author, reviews are absolutely critical in getting noticed, and are always hugely appreciated.

As a thank you for reading, you can get a FREE short techno-thriller here (or type the following into your browser: http://www.tonybatton.com/free-story-from-interface)

I owe a great debt of gratitude to the many people who have encouraged and supported me through the long process of bringing *Symbiosis* to completion. A special thank you to my *beta team* who so willingly read (and re-read) the manuscript and provided feedback and criticism - it was invaluable in making the book better: *Jin Koo Niersbach, Johan van Wijgerden, Patrick Wijngaarden, Imogen Cleaver, Paul Cleaver, Tonia Novitz, Maurice Murphy, Elli Murphy, Chris Saper, James Boorman, Chris Turner, Judy Bott, and Linda Allen.*

If you have any comments, questions or feedback I'd love to hear from you. I can be reached via my author website www.tonybatton.com.

Best regards

Tony Batton

London, 2024

ABOUT THE AUTHOR

Tony Batton worked in international law firms, media companies and Formula One motorsport, before turning his hand to writing novels. He is passionate about great stories, gadgets and coffee, and probably consumes too much of each.

Tony's novels explore the possibilities and dangers of new technology, and how that can change lives. When not writing, or talking about gadgets, Tony likes to play basketball, run and play computer games. He lives in London with his family.

Get in touch with Tony:
www.tonybatton.com
tony@tonybatton.com

Symbiosis - First Edition v1.0

First published in May 2024
by 21st Century Thrillers.

Find out more about the author at: www.tonybatton.com. And to get a FREE short techno-thriller, go to: www.tonybatton.com/free-story

Made in the USA
Coppell, TX
10 December 2024

42179978R00329